Baba Yaga Laid an Egg

Dubravka Ugrešić was born in 1949 in Yugoslavia.She has published both novels and books of essays. Her books have been translated into more than twenty languages and she has received several major European literary awards. She is now based in Amsterdam.

Also by Dubravka Ugrešić in English translation

Fiction

The Ministry of Pain
Lend Me Your Character
The Museum of Unconditional Surrender
Fording the Stream of Consciousness
In the Jaws of Life

Essays

Nobody's Home
Thank You For Not Reading
The Culture of Lies
Have A Nice Day

Baba Yaga

Laid an Egg

Dubravka UGREŠIĆ

Translated from the Croatian by Ellen Elias-Bursać, Celia Hawkesworth and Mark Thompson

CANONGATE

Edinburgh · London · New York · Melbourne

This paperback edition first published in 2010 by Canongate Books

8

First published in 2007 by Geopoetika, Belgrade and Vuković & Runjić, Dudovec 32a, 10 090 Zagreb

First published in Great Britain in 2009 by Canongate Books Ltd, 14 High Street, Edinburgh EH1 1TE

www.meetatthegate.com

The publishers gratefully acknowledge subsidy from the Scottish Arts Council towards the publication of this volume

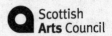

Scottish Arts Council

British Library Cataloguing-in-Publication Data
A catalogue record for this book is available on request from the British Library

ISBN 978 1 84767 306 0

Typeset by Palimpsest Book Production Ltd, Grangemouth, Stirlingshire

Printed and bound by CPI Group (UK) Ltd, Croydon, CR0 4YY

Myths are universal and timeless stories that reflect and shape our lives – they explore our desires, our fears, our longings and provide narratives that remind us what it means to be human. *The Myths* series brings together some of the world's finest writers, each of whom has retold a myth in a contemporary and memorable way. Authors in the series include: Alai, Karen Armstrong, Margaret Atwood, AS Byatt, Michel Faber, David Grossman, Milton Hatoum, Natsuo Kirino, Alexander McCall Smith, Tomás Eloy Martínez, Klas Östergren, Victor Pelevin, Ali Smith, Donna Tartt, Su Tong, Dubravka Ugrešić, Salley Vickers and Jeanette Winterson.

Contents

At First You Don't See Them . . .

You don't see them at first. Then suddenly a random detail snags your attention like a stray mouse: an old lady's handbag, a stocking slipping down a leg, bunching up on a bulging ankle, crocheted gloves on the hands, a little old-fashioned hat perched on the head, sparse grey hair with a blue sheen. The owner of the blued hair moves her head like a mechanical dog and smiles wanly . . .

Yes, at first they are invisible. They move past you, shadow-like, they peck at the air in front of them, tap, shuffle along the asphalt, mince in small mouse-like steps, pull a cart behind them, clutch at a walker, stand surrounded by a cluster of pointless sacks and bags, like a deserter from the army still decked out in full war gear. A few of them are still 'in shape', wearing a low-cut summer dress with a flirtatious feather boa flung across the shoulders, in an old half-motheaten Astrakhan, her make-up all smeary (who, after all, can apply make-up properly while peering through spectacles?!).

They roll by you like heaps of dried apples. They mumble something into their chins, conversing with invisible collocutors the way American Indians speak with the spirits. They ride buses, trams and the subway like abandoned luggage; they sleep with their heads drooping onto their chests; or they gawk around, wondering which stop to get off at, or whether they should get off at all. Sometimes you linger for a moment (for only a moment!) in front of an old people's home and watch them through the glass walls: they sit at tables, move their fingers over leftover crumbs as if moving across a page of Braille, sending someone unintelligible messages.

Sweet little old ladies. At first you don't see them. And then, there they are, on the tram, at the post office, in the shop, at the doctor's surgery, on the street, there is one, there is another, there is a fourth over there, a fifth, a sixth, how could there be so many of them all at once?! Your eyes inch from one detail to the next: the feet swelling like doughnuts in the tight shoes, the skin sagging from the inside of the elbows, the knobby fingernails, the capillaries that ridge the skin. You look closely at the complexion: cared for or neglected. You notice the grey skirt and white blouse with the embroidered collar (dirty!). The blouse is worn thin and greyed from washing. She has buttoned it up crookedly, she tries to unbutton it but cannot, her fingers are stiff, the bones are old, they are getting light and hollow like bird bones. Two others lend her a hand and with their collective efforts they do up the blouse. Buttoned up to her chin, she looks like a little girl. The other two smooth the patch of embroidery on the collar, cooing with admiration, how far back does the embroidery go, it used to be my mother's, oh, everything used to be so right and so pretty. One of them is stocky, with a noticeable bump on the back of her head; she looks like an old bulldog. The other is more elegant, but the skin on her neck hangs like a turkey's wattle. They move in a small formation, three little hens . . .

* * *

At first they're invisible. And then all at once you begin to spot them. They shuffle around the world like armies of elderly angels. One of them peers into your face. She glares at you, her eyes wide, her gaze a faded blue, and voices her request with a proud and condescending tone. She is asking for your help, she needs to cross the street but she cannot do it alone, or needs to clamber up into a tram but her knees have buckled, or needs to find a street and house number but she's forgotten her spectacles . . . You feel a pang of sympathy for the old lady, you are moved, you do a good deed, swept by the thrill of gallantry. It is precisely at this moment that you should dig in your heels, resist the siren call, make an effort to lower the temperature of your heart. Remember, their tears do not mean the same thing as yours do. Because if you relent, give in, exchange a few more words, you will be in their thrall. You will slide into a world that you had no intention of entering, because your time has not yet come, your hour, for God's sake, has not come.

PART ONE

Go There – I Know Not Where – and Bring Me Back a Thing I Lack

Birds in the Treetops Growing by My Mother's Window

The air in the New Zagreb neighbourhood where my mother lives smells of bird droppings in summer. In the leaves of the trees out in front of her apartment building jostle thousands and thousands of birds. Starlings, people say. The birds are especially raucous during humid afternoons, before it rains. Occasionally a neighbour takes up an airgun and chases them off with a volley of shots. The birds clamour skywards in dense flocks, they zigzag up and down, exactly as if they are combing the sky, and then with hysterical chirruping, like a summer hailstorm, they drop into the dense leaves. It is as noisy as a jungle. All day long a sound curtain is drawn, as if rain is drumming outside. Light feathers borne by air currents waft in through the open windows. Mum takes up her duster, and, muttering, she sweeps up the feathers and drops them into the bin.

'My turtledoves are gone,' she sighs. 'Remember my turtledoves?'

'I do,' I say.

I vaguely recall her fondness for two turtledoves that came to her windowsill. Pigeons she hated. Their muffled cooing in the morning infuriated her.

'Those repulsive, repulsive fat birds!' she said. 'Have you noticed that even they have gone?'

'Who?'

'The pigeons!'

I hadn't noticed, but sure enough, it seemed that the pigeons had fled.

The starlings irked her, especially their stink in the summer, but in time she reconciled herself to them. For, unlike other balconies, at least her balcony was clean. She showed me a messy little spot near the very end of the balcony railing.

'As far as my place is concerned, they are filthy only here. You should see Ljubica's balcony!'

'Why?'

'Hers is caked all over in bird shit!' says Mum and giggles like a little girl. A child's coprolalia, clearly she is amused by the word *shit*. Her ten-year-old grandson also grins at the word.

'Like the jungle,' I say.

'Just like the jungle,' she agrees.

'There are jungles everywhere these days,' I say.

Birds are apparently out of control; they have occupied whole cities, taken over parks, streets, bushes, benches, outdoor restaurants, subway stations, train stations. No one seems to have noticed the invasion. European cities are being occupied by magpies, from Russia, they say; the branches of trees in the city parks bow down under their weight. The pigeons, seagulls and starlings fly across the sky, and the heavy black crows, their beaks open like clothes pegs, limp along over the green city swards. Green parakeets are multiplying in the Amsterdam parks, having fled household birdcages: their flocks colour the sky in low flight like green paper dragons. The Amsterdam canals have been taken over by big white geese, which flew in from Egypt, lingered for a moment to rest and then stayed. The city sparrows have become so bold that they wrest the sandwiches from people's fingers and strut brazenly about on the tables in outdoor cafés. The windows of my short-term lease flat in Dahlem, one of the loveliest and greenest of the Berlin neighbourhoods, served the local birds as a favourite repository for their droppings. And you could do nothing about it, except lower the blinds, draw the curtains or toil daily, scrubbing the splattered window.

She nods, but it is as if she is paying no attention.

The invasion of starlings in her neighbourhood apparently began three years earlier, when my mother was taken ill. The words from the doctor's diagnosis were long, alarming and ugly (*That is an ugly diagnosis*), which is why she chose the verb 'to be taken ill' (*Everything changed when I was taken ill!*). Sometimes she would get bolder, and, touching a finger to her forehead, she'd say:

'It's all the fault of this cobweb of mine up here.'

By 'cobweb' she meant metastases to the brain, which had appeared seventeen years after a bout of breast cancer had been discovered in time and treated successfully. She spent some time in hospital, went through a series of radiation treatments and convalesced. Afterwards she went for regular check-ups, and everything else was more or less as it should be. Nothing dramatic happened after that. The cobweb lurked in a dark, elusive cranny of the brain, and stayed. In time she made her peace, got used to it and adopted it like an unwelcome tenant.

For the last three years her life story had been scaled back to a handful of hospital release forms, doctors' reports, radiological charts and her pile of the MRIs and CAT scans of her brain. The scans show her lovely, shapely skull planted on her spinal column, with a slight forward stoop, the clear contours of her face, eyelids lowered as if she is asleep, the membrane over the brain like a peculiar cap, and, hovering on her lips, the hint of a smile.

'The picture makes it look as if it is snowing in my head,' she says, pointing to the CAT scan.

The trees with their dense crowns growing under the window are tall, and reach all the way to my mother's sixth-floor flat. Thousands and thousands of little birds jostle for space. Close in the hot summer darkness we, the residents and the birds, evaporate our sighs. Hundreds of thousands of hearts, human and avian, beat in different rhythms in the dark. Whitish feathers are borne on gusts of air through the open windows. The feathers waft groundward like parachutes.

Some Of The Words Have Got Altered

'Bring me the . . .'

'What?'

'That stuff you spread on bread.'

'Margarine?'

'No.'

'Butter?'

'You know it's been years since I used butter!'

'Well, what then?'

She scowls, her rage mounting at her own helplessness. And then she slyly switches to attack mode.

'Some daughter if you can't remember the bread spread stuff!'

'Spread? Cheese spread?'

'That's right, the white stuff,' she says, offended, as if she had resolved never again to utter the words 'cheese spread'.

The words had got altered. This enraged her; she felt like stamping her foot, banging her fist on the table or shouting. As it was, she was left tense, fury foaming in her with a surprising buoyant freshness. She would stop, faced with a heap of words, as if before a puzzle she could not assemble.

'Bring me the biscuits, the congested ones.'

She knew precisely which biscuits she meant. Digestive biscuits. Her brain was still functioning: she was replacing the less familiar phrase *digestive* with the more familiar *congested*, and out of her mouth came this startling combination. This is how I pictured it working, perhaps the connection between language and brain followed some different route.

'Hand me the thermometer so I can give Javorka a call.'

'Do you mean the cell phone?'

'Yes.'

'Do you really mean Javorka?'

'No of course not, why ever would I call her?!'

Javorka was someone she had known years before, and who knows how the name had occurred to her?

'You meant Kaia, didn't you?'

'Well, I said I wanted to call Kaia, didn't I?' she snorted.

I understood her. Often when she couldn't remember a word, she would describe it: *Bring me that thingy I drink from.* I usually knew what her thingies were. This time the task was easy: it was a plastic water bottle she always kept at hand.

And then, she began coming up with ways to help herself. She started adding diminutive words like 'little', 'cute little', 'nice little', 'sweet', which she had never used before. Now even with some personal names, including mine, she would add them. They served like magnets, and sure enough, the words that had scattered settled back again into order. She was particularly pleased to use words like these for the things she felt fondest of (*my sweet pyjamas, my cute little towel, that nice little pillow, my little bottle, those comfy little slippers*). Maybe with these words and phrases, as though with spit, she was moistening the hardboiled sweets of words, maybe she was using them to buy time for the next word, the next sentence.

Perhaps that way she felt less alone. She cooed to the world that surrounded her and the cooing made the world seem less threatening and a little smaller. Along with the diminutives in her speech the occasional augmentative would jump out like a spring: a snake grew to be a big bad snake, a bird into a fat old bird. People often seemed larger to her than they really were (*He was a huuuuuge man!*). She had shrunk, that is what it was, and the world was looming.

She spoke slowly with a new, darker timbre. She seemed to enjoy the colour. A little crack showed up in her voice, the tenor became a touch imperious, with a tone demanding the absolute respect of the listener. With this frequent loss of words the timbre of her voice was all she had left.

There was another novelty. She had begun to lean on certain sounds as if they were crutches. I'd hear her shuffling around the house, opening the fridge or going to the bathroom, and she would be saying, in regular rhythm, hm, hm, hm. Or: uh-hu-hu, uh-hu-hu.

'Talking to someone?' I'd ask.

'No one, just me. Talking to myself,' she'd answer.

Who knows, maybe at some point she was suddenly unnerved by the silence, and to chase off her fear, she came up with her hm-hm, uh-hu.

She was scared of the dying and that is why she registered deaths so carefully. She, who was forgetting so many things, never missed mentioning the death of someone she knew, either close to her or distant, the friends of friends, even people she had never met, the death of public figures that she heard of on television.

'Something has happened.'

'What?'

'I am afraid it will be a shock, if I say.'

'Go ahead.'

'Vesna's died.'

'Vesna who?'

'You know Vesna! Second floor?'

'No, I don't. Can't say I've ever met her.'

'The one who lost her son?'

'No.'

'The one who was always wearing all that make-up in the lift?'

'Really, I don't.'

'It only took a few months,' she'd say, and snap shut the little imaginary file on Vesna.

Her neighbours and friends had been dying. The circle, mostly women, had shrunk. The men had long since died, some of the women had buried two husbands, some even their own children. She would speak without discomfort of the deaths of people who hadn't meant much to her. The little commemorative stories made therapeutic sense; relating them she fended off the fear of her own dying, I suppose. She evaded, however, any mention of the death of those nearest to her. Her close friend's death was followed by silence.

'She got so old,' she said tersely a little later, as if spitting out a bitter morsel. Her friend was almost a year older than she was.

She threw out all her black clothes. Before, she would never have worn bright colours; now, she was forever wearing a red shirt or one of two blouses the colour of young grass. When we called a taxi, she refused to get in if it was black. (*Call another cab. I'm not getting into this one!*) She tucked away the pictures of her parents, her sister, my father, which she used to keep in frames on the shelf, and set out the photographs of her grandchildren, my brother and his wife, pictures of me and beautiful pictures of herself from her younger years.

'I don't like the dead,' she told me. 'I'd rather be in the company of the living.'

Her attitude towards the dead changed, too. Earlier they had each held their place in her memories, everything was set out in a tidy manner, as in an album of family pictures. Now the album was disintegrating and the photographs were scattered. She no longer spoke of her late sister. On the other hand she suddenly began mentioning her father more often – who was *always reading* and *had brought books home*, and who was *the most honest man on earth.* Yet she was compelled to bring him down a peg. The memory of him was permanently tainted by the *greatest disappointment she had ever known*, an event *she would never forget*, and which she simply *could never forgive him for.*

The source of the memory was altogether disproportionate to the bitterness with which she spoke of it, or so at least it seemed to me. My grandparents had some good friends, a married couple. When Grandma died, these friends looked after Grandpa, especially the wife, Grandma's friend. My mother once happened on a scene of tenderness between the woman and my grandfather. Grandpa was kissing the woman's hand.

'I was sickened. And Mother said over and over: "Take care of my husband, take care of my husband!"'

It is highly unlikely that Grandma said anything of the kind. She had died of a heart attack. This pathetic plea – *Take care of my husband, take care of my husband!* – had been inserted into my dying grandmother's mouth by my mother.

There was one more image that overlapped with the 'sickening' scene of the hand being kissed, and this was an image that my mother could not easily dismiss. When she was in Varna for the last time, Grandpa asked Mum to take him back with her, but she – drained by my father's protracted illness and the gruesome throes of his dying, and then finally his death – feared the burden of the obligation, and refused. Grandpa spent his last years abandoned in a home for the elderly.

'He tucked a little towel, my gift to him, under his arm, turned and went back into the house,' she said, describing their last encounter.

It would seem that she had smuggled the towel into this last image. We always brought a pile of gifts every summer for my mother's Bulgarian relatives. It wasn't just that she liked giving things to people, she also liked this picture of herself: she would come back from the Varna she had left so many years before, feeling like the good fairy after distributing the gifts she had brought. I wondered why she had inserted that towel into the farewell scene with her own father. It was as if she was lashing herself with it, as if the towel he tucked under his arm was the most terrible possible image of a person's decline. Instead of undertaking the grand, sincere gesture, which would have meant jumping through troublesome and time-consuming bureaucratic hoops with little guarantee of success, she stuffed a towel into Grandpa's hand!

Her need to taint her dead was something new. These were not feasts but snacks, focused only on details, which I was hearing for the first time, and, indeed, she may have fabricated them on the spot to hold my attention and confide *a secret she had never told a soul.* Perhaps the fact that she was in possession of information relating to the dead gave her a glow of satisfaction. Recalling her late friends, sometimes, as if she'd just then decided to take their grades down a notch in the school records, she'd add importantly: *I never took to him; I never liked her much either; They didn't appeal to me; She was always stingy; No, they were not nice people.*

Once or twice she even made as if to taint the image of my father, who was, in her words, the *most honest man* she'd ever known, but for whatever reason she relented, and left him on the pedestal where she herself had placed him after his death.

'You weren't exactly crazy about him, were you?' I asked cautiously.

'No, but I did love him.'

'Why?'

'Because he was so quiet,' she said simply.

Dad was, indeed, a man of few words. And I remember my grandfather as being a quiet man. It hit me for the first time that both of them were not only *quiet*, but the *most honest men* Mum had ever known.

It may be that with this tainting of the memory of the dead she was easing her feeling of guilt for things she hadn't done for them but might have, her guilt for what she had let slip by. She camouflaged her lack of greater attentiveness to the people closest to her with a hardness in judgement. She simply seemed afraid of caring more for others. At some point she had been scared of life just as she was scared of death. That was why she held on so firmly to her place, her stubborn coordinates, and shut her eyes to the scenes and situations that moved her too deeply.

Onion should always be well sautéed. Good health is what matters most. Liars are the worst people. Old age is a terrible calamity. Beans are best in salad. Cleanliness is half of health. Always discard the first water when you cook kale.

It may be that she had asserted things like this before, but I had paid no attention. Everything had got smaller. Her heart had shrunk. Her veins had shrunk. Her footsteps were smaller. Her repertoire of words had diminished. Life had narrowed. She uttered her truisms with special weight. Truisms gave her the feeling, I suppose, that everything was fine, that the world was precisely where it should be, that she was in control and had the power to decide. She wielded her truisms as if they came with an invisible stamp of approval, which she smacked everywhere, eager to leave her mark. Her mind still worked, her feet still moved, she could walk, though only with the help of a walker, but walk she did, and she was a human being who knew for a certainty that *beans are best in salad*, and that *old age is a terrible calamity.*

Are You Alive and Well?

She often phoned the 'old witch', especially now that she was no longer able to go and visit her. Pupa was my mother's oldest friend not only in terms of age, but in how long the two had known each other.

'If it weren't for the old witch, you wouldn't be here today,' Mum would say and repeat the family legend about how Pupa, as a newly minted resident, assisted the obstetrician when my mother was in labour. (*'Lord, what a hideous child,' Pupa said when they pulled you out. My heart sank with fright. But you weren't at all ugly, that was just the old witch having a giggle!*)

'Ah, Pupa! Her life has not been easy,' Mum would say, pensively.

Pupa had been in the resistance movement, she had joined Tito's Partisans and fought in the Second World War. She went through all sorts of things; she nearly died several times, and was furious at her daughter, also a doctor, claiming that all her troubles were her daughter's fault. Without her, the old witch groused, I would have died quite nicely long ago.

She weighed barely eighty pounds, walked only with a walker and was half-blind – she saw the world only in blurred contours. She lived alone, obstinately refusing to go into a home for the elderly or live with her daughter and her daughter's family. Neither would she agree to having a paid helper live with her. There was nothing, it turns out, to which she would agree. So her daughter was forced to come by every day, and there was a cleaning lady, who she often replaced, who came daily. Pupa sat there in her flat, with her legs tucked into a huge furry boot, an electric leg warmer. Sometimes she would turn the television on and stare at the blurred images on the screen. And then she'd turn it off and sniff the air. Neighbours, ah, those damned neighbours were piping rotten gas into her flat again through the central heating system. That was her phrase, 'rotten gas', because the whole building stank of rot from it. She drove the cleaning lady to search every nook and cranny of the flat, to see if there wasn't something decaying somewhere, a dead mouse, or food, but the cleaning lady swore there was nothing. Except for the rotten gas there was nothing else which troubled her life. The problem was her death: it simply wouldn't come. If it had crawled in through the central heating system, she would have gladly given herself over to it. Death doesn't smell. It is life that stinks. Life is shit!

She'd sit in an armchair with her feet tucked into the big fur boot, sniffing the air. In time the fur boot merged with her and became a natural extension of her body. With her closely cropped hair, a birdish, beak-like nose, she'd elegantly curve her long neck and direct her grey gaze at the visitor.

'I have told her a hundred times, let me die,' she'd say, heaping the blame on her daughter. That was her way of apologising for her condition.

'Do you know what she has come up with now?' Mum said in a lively tone as she hung up the phone.

'What?'

'Every day she orders pastries by phone from a local pastry shop. She has been eating five big slices of cream pie at a sitting.'

'Whatever for?'

'I suppose she thinks the sugar in her system will rocket off the charts and do her in.'

'Surely she's not thinking that. She must still remember something from her years as a doctor.'

'I'm telling you, every day she eats slices of cream pie.'

'So, how are her sugar levels?'

'Nothing. Between five and six.'

'Rotten luck.'

'And she's fired the cleaning lady.'

'Why?'

'Must be the lady wasn't doing the job properly.'

'How could Pupa tell, she's half-blind!'

'Good point. There, I wouldn't have thought of that.'

Then she added gleefully, 'As far as cleanliness goes, the old witch used to be worse than I was. I don't remember anyone going into her house in their shoes. All of us were given rag pickers at the door.'

'Rag slippers?'

'Yes, I suppose the rag pickers have gone.'

Cleanliness is Half of Health

From our house, unlike Pupa's, guests left with their shoes cleaned! My mother would sneak out to nab the shoes that visitors had taken off and set by the door when they came in and she'd take the shoes to the bathroom, where she'd rinse the dust or mud off the soles.

She was obsessed with cleanliness. A glistening flat, freshly laundered curtains, a gleaming parquet floor, freshly aired rugs, a wardrobe in which all the clothes were neatly folded, perfectly ironed linens, clean dishes, a bathroom that sparkled, window-panes without a single smudge, everything in its place – all this gave her great satisfaction. She terrorised us – my father, brother and me – with cleanliness when I was small. Her daily cleaning rampages were accompanied by the phrase – *We don't want to smell bad the way . . .* – and then she'd give the names of people who, apparently, *smelled very bad.* Lack of cleanliness was invariably coupled with the word 'disgraceful' (*Disgraceful! That filth is disgraceful!*). When I was small she would box me into the corner with a crate, and on the crate she'd arrange my toys. I stood trapped in the corner until the daily cleaning was done.

The last time I heard that word (*Disgraceful!*) and that intonation was three years back, during our last visit to my father's graveside. We usually went there together, and if she couldn't go, she'd send my brother and me.

'It's disgraceful the way people treat their tombs,' she said pointing to nearby tombstones, and then she added,

'Here, let's rinse it one more time.'

To *rinse* it was to splash the tombstone with water. The whole job of cleaning the stone was arduous. You had to keep taking a bucket over to a water fountain that was not near by, and keep lugging bucketfuls of water back. Usually we scrubbed the tombstone with a brush and detergent, and she'd splash it with water over and over, but this time my mother was not satisfied.

'So, a little more,' she commanded.

The path from Dad's grave to the cab stand was a long one, and she was walking along it, leaning on me, for the last time, though we had no idea then.

'Now this one always sparkles,' she said at a tomb we always passed. 'But these others have been so neglected. Disgraceful!'

In hospital Mum confided in me that she'd sneaked out at night and gone back to the house.

'Impossible. How?'

'I slipped out and took a cab.'

'What did you do at home?'

'I quickly tidied everything up and then came right back here.'

'I was at home the whole time; if you had come home, I would have noticed. You dreamed it.'

'I did not,' she said, a little anxiously.

I came to hospital every day. The first thing she'd ask when I appeared at the door was,

'Did you tidy up the flat?'

* * *

Over the last three years we have often had to call an ambulance. It is the easiest and quickest way to sidestep the elaborate bureaucratic procedures and get my mother admitted immediately to hospital. We called an ambulance once when she was in a crisis. As the nurses, supporting her under the arms, were guiding her to the lift, Mum ducked down, spryly, and snatched up the plastic rubbish bag by the door, left there to be taken down and tossed into the bin.

'Ma'am, please!' shrieked the doctor, catching sight of her.

When I asked her to tell me something from her childhood, now she would answer curtly, describing it as *happy*.

'What was happy about it?' I'd ask.

'Everything was clean, and Mother did us up so nicely.'

In hospital, with a tube in her mouth and an IV in her arm, she never let go of her handkerchief. She was constantly dabbing her lips. When she had recovered a little, she immediately asked me to bring her a clean pair of pyjamas:

'Don't bring them if they're not ironed.'

Three years ago – when she sank quite suddenly into a lethargy – I took her first to a psychiatrist, probably unconsciously postponing the day I'd have to take her to hospital, which was what happened immediately thereafter.

The psychiatrist followed the routine.

'Your first and last name, ma'am?'

'Vacuum cleaner,' she said softly, her head bowed.

'Your name, ma'am?' the psychiatrist repeated, this time more sharply.

'Well . . . vacuum cleaner,' she repeated.

I was flushed by a wave of idiotic embarrassment: I cannot

say why at the time I felt as if it would have been easier to bear if she had said 'Madonna' or 'Maria Theresa'.

While she was in hospital – where instead of the harsh judgement of the psychiatrist (*Alzheimer's!*) her diagnosis turned out to be more 'amenable' – I began to wage my own battle, in parallel, for her recovery. I found someone willing to work from morning to night. He stripped the wallpaper that had nearly fused with the concrete. We painted the walls in fresh pastel colours. We redid the bathroom, laid new tiles and mounted a new mirror. I purchased a new washing machine, a new Hoover, I threw out the old bed in one of the rooms, and bought a bright-red modern sofa, a colourful new rug, a new pale-yellow wardrobe. On the balcony I set out potted plants in new flower pots (which were flourishing that year late into autumn!). I cleaned every corner of the flat and discarded old, useless things. The windows shone, the curtains were freshly laundered, the clothes in the wardrobe were neatly folded, everything was in its place. For the first time I felt I knew what I dared throw away, and what I should keep, and that is why I resisted the urge to toss out a homely old house plant with only a few leaves and left it where it was.

In the upper drawer of the dresser I left untouched the things she treasured: an old watch which had supposedly belonged to my grandfather, my father's medals (the Order of Brotherhood and Unity with Silver Wreath, the Order for Valour), an elegant box with a sizeable collection of compasses and a Raphoplex slide rule (my father's things), a key to the mail box from an earlier flat, an old plastic alarm clock with dead batteries, a box of *Gura* nails (judging by the design probably from East Germany), a silver-plated cigarette box, a Japanese fan, my old passport, opera glasses (from her trip with Dad to Moscow and Leningrad), a calculator with no batteries and a bundle of announcements of Dad's death, held with a rubber band. I carefully polished the old silver basket-shaped bonbon dish, in which she kept her jewellery: a gold ring, a pin with a semi-precious stone (a gift from my father) and costume jewellery, which she called her *pearls*. Mum's ikebana arrangement, the *pearls* tumbling out of the bonbon dish like writhing snakes, had stood for years in the place of honour on the shelf. I washed all of her dishes carefully, including the Japanese porcelain coffee service she never used. The service was intended for me. (*When I die, I am leaving the coffee service to you. It cost me a whole month's wages!*) Everything was ready to welcome Mum home, each thing was in its place, the house glistened to her taste.

My mother came home and walked importantly around her little New Zagreb flat.

'What have we here! This is the sweetest little surprise you could have given me!'

Come Here, Lie Down . . .

'Come here, lie down,' she says.

'Where?' I ask, standing by her hospital bed.

'On that bed.'

'But a patient is already lying on it.'

'What about over there?'

'All the beds are taken.'

'Then lie down here, next to me.'

Although she was delirious when she said those words, the invitation for me to lie down next to her stabbed me painfully. The lack of physical tenderness between us and her restraint with expressing feelings – these were some sort of unwritten rule of our family life. She had no sense of how to express feelings herself, she had never taught us and it seemed to her, furthermore, that it was too late, for her and for us, to change. Showing tenderness was more a source of discomfort than of comfort; we didn't know how to handle it. Feelings were expressed indirectly.

During her stay in hospital the year before, just after she'd turned eighty, my mother's false teeth and her wig got their little hospital stickers with the name of the owner. She asked me to take the wig home (*Take it home so it won't be stolen*).

When they removed the tube, I took her bridge from the plastic bag with her name and surname on it and washed it. Every day after that I washed her false teeth, until she was able to care for them herself.

'I washed your wig at home.'

'Did it shrink?'

'No.'

'Did you set it on the, you know . . . so it wouldn't lose shape?'

'Yes, on the dummy.'

My attention to her, to her intimate affairs, meant, I figured, far more to her than physical contact. I asked the hospital hairdresser to come and cut her hair short, and she liked that. The hospital pedicurist trimmed her toenails, and I tended to her hands. I brought her face creams to hospital. Her lipstick was her signal that she was still among the living. For the same reason she stubbornly refused to wear the hospital nightgown and insisted that I bring her own pyjamas.

We went to a café near her flat for her eightieth birthday. She went through her customary routine: she got carefully dressed, put on shoes with heels, her wig, her lipstick.

'Is it on right?'

'Terrific.'

'Should I pull it down a little more over my forehead?'

'No, it's better as it is.'

'No one could tell it is a wig.'

'Never.'

'So, how do I look?'

'Great.'

We sat in the café, outdoors, until a summer rain shower sent us inside.

'How could it rain on today of all days! My eightieth!' she complained.

'It'll pass in a minute,' I said.

'I get rained on for my eightieth birthday,' she protested.

We sat in the café for a long time, but the rain did not let up.

'We'll take a cab! I cannot allow myself to get wet!' she complained, though the chance that there would be a taxi willing to drive us 150 metres was slim. She was anxious about the wig. I protested that the wig would be fine.

'I could catch my death!'

We called a cab. Her inner panic burned down like the candles on the birthday cake, which she blew out several hours later, in the company of her friends.

For the last thirty years, since my father died, she has withdrawn into her home. She was left standing there, caught off guard by the fact that he was gone, at a loss for what to do with herself. Time passed, and she continued to stand there, like a forgotten traffic warden, chatting with neighbours, while with us, her children, and later, her grandchildren, she complained about the monotony of her life. She despaired, often her life seemed a *living hell* to her, but she didn't know how to help herself. She blamed us for a long time, her children: we had pulled away from her, we had left home, we no longer cared about her the way we used to, we had *alienated* ourselves (her phrase). Her list of refusals grew from one day to the next: she refused to live with my brother and his family (*Why? So I can serve them, do all the cooking and washing?!*), or to trade her flat for one in their neighbourhood (*I'd be doing nothing but babysitting every day!*), or travel with me while she still could (*I've seen it all on television!*), or on her own (*I'm not setting out, alone like a sore thumb, with everyone watching!*); she often refused to join us on short family get-togethers and excursions (*You go ahead, it is too much for me!*), spend significant time with her grandchildren (*I'm old and sick, I'd do anything for them, but they tire me out!*), with people her own age (*What am I supposed to do with those old biddies!*); she refused to talk to a psychologist (*I'm not crazy, I don't need a shrink!*), pursue a hobby (*What is the point? Consolation for dimwits!*), revive neglected friendships (*How can I socialise with them, with your father gone?*), until finally she made her peace. She settled into the house, venturing forth only to take walks around the neighbourhood, go to the market, the doctor's, a friend's for coffee. Ultimately she went out only for a brief stroll to a little café at the nearby open market. Her firmly held opinions on small matters (*Too sweet for my taste! I suppose I was raised to love spicy food!*), her pugnacity (*I will never wear those pads, I'd rather die. I am not some helpless little old lady!*), her demands (*Today we wash the curtains!*), her candour (*In hospital they were all so old and ugly!*), her lack of tact (*This coffee of yours smells awful!*) – all were signals of an underlying anguish that had been smouldering in her for years, an ever-present sense that no one noticed her, that she was invisible. She did her level best to fend off this frightening invisibility with all the means to hand.

Once, during a family Sunday afternoon, I took some pictures of all of us in relaxed poses. I photographed her, my brother, my brother's wife, the children, all of us together. And then I thought I'd take one of my brother's family, just the four of them. They lined up, and at the last moment, with breathtaking agility, Mum shouldered her way in.

'Me too!'

Every time I happened across that picture, it took my

breath away. Her face, thrust into the frame, and her grin, both victorious and apologetic, melted away the heavy doors of my forbidden inner sanctum, and I would dissolve, if the verb 'dissolve' can describe what happened inside me at those moments. And when all my strength, the strength of my every nerve, was spent in sobs, I would spit out a tiny breathing body, five or six inches across, no larger than the smallest toy doll, with a shapely skull planted on the spinal column, a slight forward stoop, eyelids lowered as if asleep and, hovering on her lips, the hint of a smile. I'd study the fragile tiny body in the palm of my hand, all wet from tears and saliva, from some vast distance, with no fear, as if it were my own small baby.

The Cupboard

The first thing that caught my eye was the cupboard. I had picked it up by chance, during a previous visit, at a Sunday antiques fair. An old piece of homely, country furniture, with one of its sides fashioned at an angle. The old paint had been stripped, and in that lay its only value, in the old wood, stripped of paint. The cupboard had now been painted clumsily in off-white oil paint, and it stood there in the room like an admonishment.

'This is the little surprise I told you about.'

She had mentioned in several phone calls that *a little surprise* was waiting for me at home, but I had paid no attention. This was a ploy of hers, she often used *little secrets* and *little surprises* as a lure, so I generally assumed that there was not much behind these promises.

'Who painted it?'

'Ala.'

'Ala who?'

'The young Bulgarian woman you sent me.'

'As I remember, her name is Aba?'

'Like I said, Ala.'

'Not Ala, Aba!'

'Fine, but why so angry?'

'I'm not angry.' I lowered my voice.

* * *

In fact, it bothered me. Not because of the cupboard, but because of the whole strategic operation she had undertaken out of her dislike for it. She could not bear the thought that this *unpainted piece of junk* was standing there in her flat; this was something out of her control, and she didn't dare say so to me. In the past she would never have let things like that come through the door. Now, what with the new situation, she was more tolerant. But when the young woman showed up from Bulgaria, the first thing Mum came up with was this brilliant idea. She let Aba think, I assume, that I had intended to paint the cupboard myself, but had been pressed for time; how she would already have painted it herself, but, regrettably, she was no longer able to because of her illness. I assume she added that I would be so pleased when I saw the cupboard painted exactly the way I'd wanted it. I was guessing that she managed to talk the startled guest into painting it for her. It turned out that it was Aba, not Mum, who had done it – actually the two of them decided to cook up this *little surprise* for me.

'I can't imagine why she hasn't been in touch lately,' she worried.

'Why would she?'

'Since she left she has written several times. I got a few postcards from her.'

'Really?'

'She even called.'

Aba was a young woman from Bulgaria who had written to me a few months earlier by email. A Slavic scholar, apparently a fan of mine, she had read everything I'd written, spoke Croatian well, or Serbo-Croatian, or Croato-Bosno-Serbian, and by the way she was eager to hear what I thought of all that, since language is, after all, the writer's only vehicle, *n'est-ce pas*? (N'est-ce pas? What was with the French?!), and she would love to talk to me about the language question, and about so many other things, of course, should I find myself in Zagreb over the summer. All in all, she hoped I would set aside some time for her. She was going to have loads of time. She had been given a grant to spend two months in Zagreb and had been invited to participate in the summer Slavic seminar in Dubrovnik. She would absolutely love to meet me, she had been dreaming of the moment ever since she read my first book. No, she didn't know a soul in Zagreb, this was going to be her first time in Croatia.

The first thing that occurred to me was that this young woman from Bulgaria might be just the person to keep my mother company. Mum had been moving in a narrow circle for far too long; a new face would perk her up. She would love having the chance to speak a little Bulgarian, I wrote in my email. And moreover, I added, if Aba was having trouble finding a place to stay, she could stay in 'my' room in my mother's flat. I sent her Mum's phone number and address. I, regrettably, was not going to be in Zagreb during Aba's visit. My suggestion should not obligate her in any way, of course, and I would understand if it might even sound a little insulting since my mother is an elderly woman, though that was in no way my intent.

Evidently it turned out quite differently. Aba stopped in frequently to visit, as Mum boasted, and the two of them became fast friends.

'Ala is so wonderful, such a shame you weren't here to get to know her. I have never met such a marvellous creature.'

By her voice I could tell she meant it.

'She is very, very kind,' she said, touched.

* * *

The habit of repeating a word twice when she wanted to draw attention to it was new, just as was her custom of dividing people into *kind* and *unkind*. The ones who were kind, were kind, of course, to her.

'Look what she gave me.'

'Who?'

'Why, Ala.'

She showed me two wooden combs with folklore motifs and a bottle of Roza rose liqueur. A little card dangled from the neck of the bottle on a golden ribbon, and on the card were the words:

'*Springtime is upon us, the trees are decked in tender young leaves, the fields are a riot of flowers, the nightingales are singing sweetly and amid it all, like Venus among her nymphs, the rose gardens glow the reddest of reds,*' I read out loud.

'Why are you rolling your eyes?' she asked.

'I am not.'

'That is just the way it used to be,' she said, taking a staunchly defensive tone. 'Roses bloomed everywhere. Your grandmother made special preserves every year from rose petals.'

In the wardrobe she kept several hand-embroidered tablecloths. They were gifts from her Bulgarian relatives and friends, and she knew precisely who had embroidered each one: Dia, Rajna, Zhana. The fabric had yellowed and was threadbare along the folds, but the tablecloths, in Mum's opinion, were priceless.

'Do you have any idea how many stitches there are here?' she would ask me, and with solemn importance she would announce a random six-figure number she had plucked from the air.

* * *

For years she had an unsightly reproduction hanging on the wall showing an old man in Bulgarian folk costume, smoking a peasant pipe.

'Throw that out, it's awful,' I'd tell her.

'I am not letting go of the picture! It reminds me of Dad!' she'd answer, meaning her own father. Grandpa didn't look at all like the man in the picture. Later, in order to keep the picture from my grasp, she said that Dad (this time meaning my father) had bought her the picture during one of our summer visits to Varna. The picture was deteriorating. I finally used one of her sojourns in hospital to throw it out. She didn't notice it was gone, or pretended not to.

She kept a wooden doll on her television set dressed in Bulgarian folk costume. The doll often toppled off the TV, but she insisted on keeping it there and nowhere else.

'To remind me of Bulgaria,' she said.

The Bulgarian woman had served a function far more important than the chance to speak Bulgarian now and then: she had painted the cupboard. The souvenirs, the ones that were supposed to remind my mother of Bulgaria, could not be compared to the thrill of the cupboard.

Her home had always been her kingdom. When I moved out of Zagreb I no longer had a flat of my own there. Whenever I came back, I stayed with her. More than anything she loved having people visit, yet when they left she would mutter about how they had littered the place with unrinsed coffee cups. She adored her grandchildren, her eyes would well with tears at the mere mention of their names, but after they left she would moan about how long it would take her to get the flat back into order. Whenever I left the country, I would leave some of my things, mostly clothing, there with her. She let me leave only clothes. With time I noticed that even the clothes were disappearing. It turned out she'd given my coat away to a neighbour, a jacket to another, shoes to a third.

'You didn't need them any more, and people here haven't money for nice things,' she protested.

It wasn't the things I cared about, it was her obsessive cleaning that bothered me, her maniac insistence that she could not permit anything in her territory which was not to her liking and was not her choice, which was, after all, the real reason why she was so generous in giving my things away.

If I bought a newspaper in the morning it would be gone by afternoon.

'I lent your paper to Marta, my neighbour. She hasn't the money to buy a paper. She'll bring it back. But you'd read it already, anyway.'

When I bought myself food it, too, would end up at the neighbour's.

'That cheese you bought – didn't suit me,' she'd say. 'I gave it to Marta's sister.'

'And the biscuits?'

'I tossed them out. They were nasty, the look and the taste.'

She would object if I ever hung any of my clothes in her wardrobe. She left the bottom-most shelf in the shoe cabinet for my shoes. My things in the bathroom took up only a small corner, and she'd immediately protest if by any chance my things mingled with hers.

'I haven't touched a thing since you left. Everything is where it is supposed to be!' were her first words to me whenever I came back.

This only meant that she had fought off the urge to tidy up and put everything in order.

I came often. She couldn't spend her summer alone, or her Christmas holidays, or, of course, her birthday.

'You'll be here for my birthday, won't you?'

Ever since she'd got sick I came more often and stayed longer. Each time I arrived I could see her beaming with genuine delight. Tears would fill her eyes when I left as if these were our very last goodbyes. But as soon as I was out the door, I knew she would head straight for the broom cupboard, roll the Hoover out, hoover 'my' room, put everything back where it was supposed to be, go to the bathroom, take all 'my' bits and pieces, the toothbrush, toothpaste, face cream, shampoo, and arrange them in 'my' cupboard. She was undoubtedly sniffling all the while, dabbing at the tears, and berating cruel fate for dealing her the destiny of an old age lived alone.

She had lost her feel for cooking, she no longer had the will or the strength, so I took over. But she couldn't leave it be. She'd come into the kitchen, elbow me in the cramped space, rinse a few dishes, carp that I should do it this way, mutter that I would never learn a thing. The kitchen was the realm of her absolute authority, and she was defending it with her last ounce of strength.

When she heard me on the phone with someone, she'd come into 'my' room, she'd ask or say something, raising her voice like a parakeet in a cage, so that I would have to hang up. She did this without thinking, as if not aware of her actions.

'I have to call the old witch,' she said, seeing me holding the receiver.

'Sure, let me finish this.'

'I called her a couple of times and no one is picking up.'

'We'll call her.'

'Ask Zorana, she'll know.'

Zorana was Pupa's daughter.

'I'll ask, just let me finish this.'

She stood, clutching the cupboard, and watched me.

'And Ada hasn't called.'

'Aba.'

'She hasn't called, either.'

'She will.'

'We really ought to call them.'

'Them' is her way of referring to my brother and his family.

'We called them this morning!'

'Open the balcony store, the room is stuffy,' she said and padded over to the door.

'The balcony door,' I said.

'There, I've opened it.'

She had tidied everything and set it to rights, including the *homely piece of junk*, the cupboard, which I had brought into the apartment, just as she had been cleaning up and tidying her whole life. Only once, in a conversation about our first house, with its capacious garden, did she admit,

'I was more anxious that the vegetable beds be hoed in straight lines than I was with what I'd plant or how it would grow.'

Her instalments to the funeral fund had been made regularly for years, so her funeral was fully paid for: her burial with all the formalities was guaranteed. Her mental and emotional territory had narrowed, it was all set out – like a box. Here, in this box, her two grandchildren, my brother and his wife were knocking about, along with two or three old friends (in that order of importance).

I was in there, too, of course. Sometimes she seemed to love our talks on the phone even more than our conversations in person. As if she felt freer over the phone.

'I am sitting in your chair,' she'd say, referring to my desk chair, 'and looking at the flowers on the balcony and thinking of you. If you could only see how the flowers are blooming! It's as if they're weeping because you left.'

And then, as if shaken by her giddy sense of freedom, she would add in an unnaturally bright tone,

'Goodness, how empty my life is!'

She had snapped shut almost all of her emotional files. One of them was still slightly open: it was Varna, the city of her childhood and youth. That is why she let the unknown woman from Bulgaria into her realm with such ready warmth.

Mother's Bedel

I.

Everything was badly organised. Contact with the organisers of the literary gathering 'Golden Pen of the Balkans' in Sofia had reached a dead end. They left me to make the reservations and buy the plane ticket myself. At least Aba responded to my emails. The real goal of my trip was to visit Varna. My participation in 'Golden Pen of the Balkans' had simply been a handy excuse. Aba replied quickly that she would join me, if I didn't mind; she had a cousin in Varna she hadn't seen for years and several friends. I didn't mind.

Mum wound me up and set me moving in the direction of Varna; she guided me by remote control like a toy, dispatched me to a place she could no longer travel to on her own. Centuries ago the wealthy would send someone else off on the hajj or to the army in their stead, as a *bedel*, a paid surrogate. I was my mother's *bedel*. She said I must look up Petya, her closest friend from childhood and her teenage years. Petya had been stricken by Alzheimer's, and to make matters worse she was being looked after by her son, an alcoholic. Petya's address, however, had vanished, strangely, from Mum's address book.

'Ask the police,' Mum insisted.

'And Petya's last name?'

'Well, her husband's name was Gosho.'

'His surname?'

A shadow of distress flitted across her face.

'Fine, I'll enquire with the police; they will be sure to know,' I hastened to add.

She did not ask me to seek out my grandmother's grave. Grandma and my mother's sister were both buried at the city cemetery in Varna. At one point Mum had let Grandma's friends also use the gravesite. Graves were, apparently, expensive, and there had been a lot of deaths.

'I am so foolish. I let them use the grave, and later none of them thanked me,' she complained.

Neither did she mention Grandpa's grave. She couldn't. She didn't know where exactly he was buried. She had received the death notice too late. Those were hard times, two different countries, there wasn't much she could have done about it. Except for Petya, who had sunk into dementia, there was no one left in Varna. The main task of my mission as *bedel* was to take photographs of Varna and show the pictures to Mum on my new laptop. It was my idea to take the pictures, and for that purpose I had purchased a little digital camera.

I asked Aba to reserve a ticket for my flight. At the Bulgarian Airlines office in Amsterdam they explained it would be cheaper to buy the ticket for Varna in Sofia. Aba replied that the flight was very expensive and suggested we go by train. I refused; I had heard all kinds of stories about dilapidated old Bulgarian trains plagued by thieves. I insisted on the plane. Who could bear the prospect of jouncing for seven or eight hours in a bus from Sofia to Varna! She answered politely that the plane would be too expensive for her. She would take the bus, but she had reserved a plane ticket for me. She put me to shame. I agreed, of course, to take the bus, why not. The hours of trundling through the late autumnal Bulgarian countryside would certainly have their charms. We sparred over the hotel. Aba suggested several less expensive versions. I immediately envisioned rundown communist hotels, with broken heating systems, and answered that I preferred a decent hotel in the centre of town and that I didn't care about the price.

'I can hardly wait to meet you, you have no idea how much your books have meant to me,' she added in her email. She insisted she would meet me at the airport. 'There is really no need, I'll take a taxi to my mother's relatives,' I wrote back. 'No, no, I will be there to welcome you. You wrote somewhere that a foreign country is a place where there is no one to greet you when you arrive.' I could not recall where I might have written such a thing, or whether I had, indeed, written those words – even if I had, they now sounded alien to me.

When I arrived at the airport I didn't see her at first. I looked everywhere in the waiting area, hung around for a while, stood in line to change my euros into levs, then made my way through the waiting area once again, and finally caught sight of a diminutive girl standing pressed in a corner, clutching a nosegay of flowers, watching each passenger coming through the exit gate. At last she caught sight of me. She dashed over and kissed me warmly on the face. Oh, how stupid, I must think she is a total idiot, but she was so sure it would work best to stand right on that spot, because if she were to move, I'd come out and she'd miss me, and from there she had absolutely had the best view, she had sussed it all out, and she couldn't work out how she'd missed me.

She was petite, slender, so thin that she was slightly hunched over. Her over-sized glasses with frames too large for her tender face (a book worm!) were the first thing to notice on her. She had a spotty complexion masked by a thick layer of foundation, her hair was shoulder length, with a reddish L'Oreal glow. She had an unusually disarming smile. All in all, a little girl, a little Bulgarian girl. I could see at once why my mother had taken such a liking to her.

She immediately asked about Mum, how she was doing, what she was up to, were the pelargoniums on the balcony still blooming? (So, they had planted flowers together on the balcony!) And then she said we must give my mother a call and send her a postcard. We? I was a little startled by her use of the plural. She added that my mother was a marvellous person, that she was the only warm, human contact Aba had had while she was in Zagreb, and she had spent two months there! The young Bulgarian woman was very young, or at least looked young. She could have been my daughter. Her questions about my mother sounded sincere enough, and for that reason she aroused my suspicions all the more. What she had had in common with my ailing old mother puzzled me.

We took a cab. She insisted on seeing me off to my mother's relatives. She insisted on paying for the cab.

'And you, where are you going after this?' I asked her.

'I'm not sure,' she said. 'I'll go on home.'

She seemed reluctant to leave, as if she didn't know where she was going.

'I'll give you a call tomorrow morning. We can discuss what happens next,' I said, slammed the taxi door, and immediately felt a dull stab of guilt. The taxi moved away. She waved. She was still holding the nosegay of flowers she had clearly forgotten to give me.

2.

'The hotel is in the centre of town,' she said confidently.

'The hotel is next to the train station,' said the taxi driver.

'Well, the station is in the centre,' she added.

The hotel was called the Aqua, and judging by the little map printed on the hotel card it was indeed very close to the train station. Aba, who had obviously failed to inform her cousin or her friends that she was coming, waited quietly by the front desk while I made the arrangements for the room, as if this was something to be expected. This made me bristle, but I had nowhere to go with it. She had me over a barrel, and she made no effort to apologise. She has a cell phone, damn it, I muttered to myself, why doesn't she call that cousin?

We brought our things up to the room, pulled the joined single beds apart. I pulled back the curtains. Black shadows of loading cranes were outlined against the dark sky. We must be near the port, I thought, but I couldn't visualise where the port was and where the train station was. I suggested to Aba that we take a walk and find a place to eat. The man at the main desk warned us it was late, and that we'd be hard pressed to find a place to eat so late. I looked at my watch. It was only ten p.m.

* * *

We wandered through the empty streets. She had no idea where we were either. I began to seethe: everything was wrong. We had travelled for eight hours instead of six, with only one stop along the way. The bus was admittedly a nice one, with screens, and there were movies showing which were not half-bad. I spent the whole ride with my eyes glued to the screen. Aba stared out at the yellowing late-autumn scenes gradually slipping into dusk and ultimately fell asleep. She woke up just as we were arriving in Varna.

The wind was gusting outside and rubbish tossed around on the streets. The town was nightmarish. It bothered me that I hadn't recognised a single detail. Then we finally caught sight of a little restaurant with lights on so we went in and sat down. I was tired, I wanted us to get something to eat as soon as possible and go back to the hotel. I had decided I'd change hotels the next day, and presumably Aba would go looking for her cousins and friends.

'Aba, what is the origin of your name?'

She perked up. Her mother had been a fan of the Swedish pop group Abba, which had not been easy in communist Bulgaria; there were many shortages at the time, and one of them was vinyl LPs. Aba was born just when Björn, Benny, Agnetha and Anni-Frid were performing for the last time, perhaps it was at the very moment when they were belting out their last 'Knowing Me, Knowing You' on a stage somewhere in Japan. She was born in March 1980 and her mother chose to call her Aba. They wrote the name with a single 'b' in the Registry of Births, which they would have done anyway, with her mother's intervention or without it. Her father was a Hungarian by background, but her parents had long since divorced.

'If Mum had been into Nabokov instead of Abba, I'd be Ada now, not Aba.'

'They both sound perfectly fine to me,' I said.

The Nabokov thing touched me; it was a naively pretentious comment. I smiled. And she smiled. Without a smile on her face she looked older and darker. Her smile, clearly, was her strong point. Yes, she could have been my daughter. Back then I, too, had had a weak spot for Abba.

'What are you engaged in at present? Any employment?' I said, rather stiffly.

'Why so formal?' she asked, edgily. 'Aren't we friends?'

'Are you a student at the Slavic Department?'

'Oh, no. I'm finished!' she said, importantly.

'What are you pursuing now?'

'You'll never guess!' she said.

We could not get beyond the stiltedness.

'You were saying?'

'Just now I'm deep into folklore studies.'

'And the doctorate and all that? You've completed it?'

'Piece of cake!' she said.

If there was something I could not abide, it was folklore and the people who studied folklore. Folklorists were inane, they were academic infants. They snuggled into their academic nooks and crannies, quiet, in nobody's way. In my day, through all those zones so rich in folklore – Yugoslavia, Bulgaria, Romania – it was mostly folklorists nosing around. They were interested in only two things: folklore and communism at the level of folklore (political jokes, *chastushkas*, *ganga* singing, communist legends). These days I could no longer swear that there was anything more to it, but at the time their interest struck me as intellectually second-rate. Domestic folklorists were generally closet nationalists, as became abundantly clear later on, once the hatred had surfaced. Then the war came. Foreigners, western Europeans and Americans imposed their academic colonialism without risk: there was no danger that the 'natives' would boil them and eat them for dinner. That is why so many foreigners, despite the rich pickings of Renaissance literature, the baroque, Modernism, the allure of the Avant-garde, even Postmodernism, latched on to folklore and would not let go. When Yugoslavia came undone, there were many disappointed, perceiving the collapse as a plot levelled against them, personally. The lively international meetings suddenly vanished, where the *šljivovica* had flowed in streams and the lambs had turned blithely on the spit; there were no more embroidered towels, naive painters, fervent circle dances, ethno-souvenirs and chatty local intellectuals who always had time for every one and every subject. Once the war had erupted, there were new 'folklorists' who hurried to this new zone, and the hatred became an engaging field for study in anthropology, ethnology and folklore. From the legend of Kraljević Marko, they moved on to the latter-day legends of murderers, criminals and mafia bosses, the Serbian hero Arkan and his maiden Ceca, and the Croatian hero and playboy Ante Gotovina. The victims were of little interest to anyone.

'Well, folklore studies certainly are a discipline,' I said, to be kind.

I had her pegged, she was a bookworm, she had finished her university studies and earned her doctorate in record time. Maybe one day she would become Bulgarian minister for culture. When the need arises in countries like this, folklore scholars are at the top of the list, I thought.

'Where do you work?'

'I'm in transition at the moment,' she said, placing special emphasis on her answer. It was a little signal to me, as if she were cajoling me with the quote. In one of my texts I had spoken of the newly coined euphemisms of our age. To be in transition meant to be out of work. I pretended not to notice. These occasional quotes of hers grated on my ear. She was using the wrong tone.

'And now you're looking for a job?'

'Well, yes.'

'In Sofia?'

The question was pointless; I was stretching the conversation out like chewing gum. Luckily the dish we'd ordered had arrived. I noticed that Aba had ordered the same thing I ordered.

On our way out of the restaurant I recognised where we were. An empty square with a fountain in the middle stood before us. I hadn't noticed it at first, probably because I was so tired. There was a theatre on the square and some ungainly exemplar of communist architecture, the municipal offices, or something similar. My eye caught sight of a neon sign for the City Hotel and I hurried over to it. The entrance to the hotel was from a side street.

'Have you any rooms available?' I asked the young receptionist.

'Yes, we do.'

'Do I need to make a reservation tonight if I need a room tomorrow?'

'No.'

'Tomorrow I'll be back,' I said.

The receptionist nodded courteously, from right to left, as the Bulgarians do.

Aba and I went back to Hotel Aqua. Stray dogs wandered through the poorly lit streets. Aba stopped from time to time to pat one. The dogs licked her hand obediently. I trembled, partly from fear, and partly from exhaustion.

3.

The next day we moved over to the little hotel on Independence Square. I couldn't recall whether this was a new name for the square, or if it had been called that before. Again I took a room with two beds. Standing to one side, as if she was a policewoman who had had me brought to the hotel, Aba silently left me to see to all the formalities at the front desk. Again she showed no inclination to call her cousin or friends. I was furious, but I could not bring myself to spit out the sentence: 'Isn't it time you called that cousin?' Or: 'Your friends must be concerned that you haven't called them yet, since they know you are in Varna.' I was less bothered that she would be sharing the room with me, and least of all that she hadn't offered to shoulder her part of the expense. Maybe she had no friends, maybe there was no cousin, maybe she had never been to Varna, maybe she was broke, maybe she had made it all up so she could travel with me. All of that would have been fine. It was her constant presence that grated on me, and that she had not been clear about when she would be detaching herself from me next. What was I doing going everywhere with this child!? Where was the cousin, damn it, where were the friends?! I was here on my own 'special mission' – I muttered to myself – and under your watchful gaze I cannot recall a single detail of a city where I spent so much time! True, I was a teenager back then, but I'd crossed this damn Independence Square dozens of times! And that washbasin of a fountain, which looks as if someone abandoned it years ago in the middle of the square, it worked back then with those same jets of water every bit as weak and erratic as they were now!

'Come on, let's leave our things up in the room, and then we can get a cup of coffee somewhere. We need to pick up a map of the city, too,' she said.

I snorted. Her use of the plural infuriated me. And her 'we need to pick up a map of the city' grated on my ear. Wasn't she at home here? Why would she need a map?!

4.

We sat in a restaurant next door to the hotel and had coffee. The restaurant was part of a new chain, with fast and tasty food, something like a superior Bulgarian take on McDonald's. We were served a Bulgarian version of Chinese 'fortune cookies' with our coffee. They were the fortunes without the cookie, advertising Lavazza. The new advertising gimmick was called *kastmetche* – a little fortune.

For her fortune Aba had got a quote from Winston Churchill, which sounded like a verse from some turbo-folk song. *Never, never, never, never surrender.*

'And what does yours say?'

'*Know that only matchstick boats sink in a tempest in a tea cup.*'

'Who said that?'

'Kukishu.'

'Who is he?'

'No idea. A Japanese writer, maybe?'

I watched her. She smoked a cigarette with the gestures of an adult, self-confident woman. We conversed in Bulgarian. True, my Bulgarian was awkward, the way I'd picked it up as a teenager when I spent my summers here. Her Bulgarian seemed, rightly or wrongly, a little hobbled. With her language, as if with a wooden clothes peg, she was holding together bits and pieces that were jostling and bumping against each other. The bigger picture was eluding me.

'So what is simmering these days in the author's kitchen?' she asked suddenly.

The wrong tone, again she went for the pretentious tone.

'Soup with pudgy little children's fingers floating in it,' I said, feigning severity, and summoned the waiter so we could pay.

She grinned. She wasn't hurt that I had evaded her question.

We must have looked odd on the street, the two of us. In a city abandoned by tourists we set out with our cameras on the lookout for interesting shots. I was looking for my subjects, or rather ones I thought my mother might like, while Aba was looking for – mine. I took a picture of the display window at a restaurant that announced they served two roasted suckling pigs on Tuesdays, and on Thursdays two roasted lambs. Now that would give Mum a chuckle, I thought. Aba took pictures of the same display. I took a picture of a bakery where there were trays of fresh *burek* cheese pies, *gevrek*, boiled or baked, with or without sesame seeds, cheese crescents, *mekitsa* and *banitsa* cheese pastries. Aba took pictures of them, too. I took pictures of sad elderly people selling whatever they had on the pavement, to earn a little loose change: knitted slippers, homemade honey, a basket of apples, a few cucumbers, a head of cabbage, a bunch of parsley. Aba, too, snapped a picture of the scene. I took a picture of a kebab shop with the large-sized Bulgarian kebab in the window.

Aba purchased a kebab. I took a picture of Aba holding the kebab. I snapped a shot of peeling pastel paint on a building. Aba also found the peeling façade intriguing. 'Stuck like glue, stuck on you,' I muttered to myself, the girl was suffering from 'mental echolalia', and I happened to be her victim.

We strolled along Knyaz Boris Street, heading for the beach. The street was crowded with stands selling all sorts of things. We turned into Slivnica, the street that came out at *Morskata Gradina* and the city beach. The ugly concrete building of the Black Sea Hotel, formerly a luxury hotel under the communists, was now plastered with billboards. The hotel had obviously been occupied by people who were not troubled by the aesthetic of communism: transition thieves, thugs, criminals, smugglers and prostitutes. Their bodyguards were dressed, just like policemen, in 'uniforms'. They strutted around the expensive cars in front of the hotel in their black suits, black t-shirts, black glasses, decked out in gold chains, cell phones and ear buds, slender wires dangling from their ears. A persistent advertisement for a real estate agency, Bulgarian Property Dream, followed us from the peeling façade to the entrance to *Morskata Gradina*.

Along the way we stopped in at a cafeteria.

'This is so awful. Is it a lack of cash that has made them plaster the buildings with billboards?' I asked, staring at a façade which was as flashy with ads as a porno website.

'Well, New York is one big advertisement!' said Aba, following my gaze.

I was certain she had never been to New York.

'Yes, but everything developed there at a natural pace,' I said.

'And so it will here as well.'

'This used to be a lovely town. But now it has been turned into a way station for transition gold diggers. Everything is falling apart, abandoned, it all looks so vulgar.'

'It is the transition that is vulgar,' she said assertively.

Her certainty was aggravating. Especially because I was in bad shape myself.

The waitress, having brought the coffees and a pastry for Aba, demonstrated a new brand of 'have a nice day' courtesy.

'*Kak ekler no vkusnee!*' Aba declared in Russian and thrust her fork into the elongated pastry covered in chocolate sauce and filled with confectionary cream. She had quoted me again. I had used that line in one of my essays. Apparently this was her way of trying to coax me into a better mood. I pretended not to notice. I unwrapped my *kastmetche.*

'Well?' she asked.

'*De nihilo nihil fit.* Xenophanes. What did you get?'

'Though the world may be crowded the mind is spacious. Thoughts coexist without effort, but objects collide painfully in space.'

'Who said that?'

'Friedrich Schiller.'

I squirmed. It was now painfully clear that Aba was getting on my nerves. What a know-all!

'Let's carry on to the beach. I can hardly wait to see the sea!' I hissed.

'*Varietas delectat!*' she announced cheerfully and got up from the table.

I didn't recognise the entrance to the city beach either. The building we used to go through to get to the strand had melted like ice cream. The terrace, with the year 1926 carved in it, was paved in stones from which steps led down to the sand.

'That is the year my mother was born.'

'I know,' she said.

Wow, you know even that! I huffed to myself and felt the swell of misery and despair rising. We passed by a row of cabins and came out on the strand. The sandy beach which had seemed endless to me before was now cluttered with ramshackle stands and plastic awnings. Everything was a jumble, with no order, as if all this was detritus tossed up on the beach by the waves. Apart from an old fisherman and the two of us, there was nobody there. The sea and sky poured into dark-grey stains. Two tankers floated motionless, off on the horizon, tiny as a child's toys. Nervous seagulls zigged and zagged across the sky in sharp flight.

The entire landscape was taut with suppressed anxiety. While I searched for a consoling detail, Aba, having held on to the kebab purchased for the purposes of photography, fed it to a stray dog.

There were sudden strong gusts and the sky grew darker still. We hurried to catch a taxi. As soon as we got into the cab, big drops of rain began pounding on the windscreen. The looming billboard BULGARIAN PROPERTY DREAM, like some obstinate mystical signal, stared at me through the foggy glass. This city was not my property, but my mother's, I thought. Property, which she had given over, like Grandmother's grave, to others. Nothing here was hers any more, except the dream, and it had faded over the years. Why had the feeling of despair grown in me so and filled me like beer foam in a mug, I wondered. Was it because I had taken it upon myself to be my mother's *bedel*?

5.

A powerful storm blew in. I watched through the window as the wind snapped the tree branches. White plastic bags flitted through the air like little phantoms. The rain whipped the windowpane so powerfully it seemed likely to smash the glass. The hotel room was freezing cold. I started shivering. I pulled on a sweater. I wrapped myself in my blanket, and finally, teeth chattering, slid into bed.

'Could you please go down to the main desk and ask them for extra blankets? And ask them to turn the heat on!'

Aba decided she would turn the heat on herself. She spent ages fiddling with the heating unit in the wall, but to no avail. Then she searched every corner of the room to find extra blankets. She threw her own blanket over me. It didn't help. I was still shivering. I was certain that her reluctance to go downstairs lay in the prospect of a confrontation with the hotel staff, a vestigial reflex from communism, the fear that they would dismiss her out of hand, the potential for humiliation. Hence her exultant expression when she came back. No one had hurt her feelings, and furthermore she had come through victorious: she was carrying two woollen blankets, and a young man came in behind her who turned on the heat.

'Is that better?' she asked, all important.

Warm air soon began to flow from the heater and I – grumbling that I would be getting out of this hostile, stormy place as soon as I could the next day – dropped off to sleep.

When I woke up I saw Aba sitting before the mirror, massaging lotion into her hair. The storm was still raging outside, but the rain had stopped.

'Aba?'

'Yes?'

'Is Lili Ivanova still alive?'

'Yes, she is. Why do you ask?'

'I just thought . . .' I muttered.

'Whatever made you think of her?'

'When I was a teenager she was the biggest Bulgarian pop star.'

I sat up. It was like a steam bath in the room. Aba had little bottles, tubes, lotions piled on the table in front of her.

'What are you doing?'

'My hair has been falling out lately.'

'It couldn't be.'

'It really is.'

'You seem to have plenty of hair.'

'Well, I used to have more.'

'Have you been to see a doctor?'

'What can a doctor do for me? It's falling out, that's all. I rub my scalp with lotions and take vitamins B and E.'

'Things like this may be due to stress. But it will grow back, I am certain of that. Only ageing women go bald.'

'I am an ageing woman.'

'You are just a baby still.'

'Babies are ageing women.'

'OK, so you are a bald baby. Could there be anything nicer?'

'Yes, there could.'

'What?'

'A baby with long pigtails.'

She was not without a sense of humour, when she felt like it. I glanced at my watch. It was eight thirty. I wondered how we would get through the evening. I got up and looked out the window. Going out was not an option. Unless we dashed to the restaurant just around the corner.

'Are we really going back tomorrow?' she asked me as we surveyed the menu. She was insisting again on that plural of hers.

'No point in me staying on here,' I answered in the emphatic singular, 'the weather being as it is.'

'Perhaps the sun will shine tomorrow.'

'Very little likelihood that the sun will shine tomorrow.'

Aba had pulled a black woollen cap over her head to hide her greasy hair. When she took her glasses off for a moment, I noticed that her eyebrows met in the middle. She had something around her neck, a leather thong with a round grey pebble hanging from it.

'What's that?' I asked.

'Oh, nothing. I found the pebble with a hole in it somewhere and strung it on the leather.'

I ordered warm cheese and honey pastries, lamb stew served in a little ceramic pot and feta cheese baked in parchment. The storm was raging outside, the restaurant was cosy, and my firm resolve – especially at the prospect of jouncing for eight hours back on the bus – began to weaken.

'Aba, do you have a boyfriend?'

Again I was forcing the conversation. This was the kind of question with which doltish adults ply children. I used the word *gadzhe* for sweetheart, old-fashioned slang that had been current back in my teenage years.

Aba grinned.

'Don't people say *gadzhe* any more?!'

'No, no, they still say it.'

'So, do you have a *gadzhe*?'

'May I tell you a story?'

'A real story?'

'Yup.'

'Go ahead.'

'There is a Russian fairy tale in which the Tsar-maiden and Ivan, the merchant's son, fall in love.'

'The Tsar-maiden?'

'Yes, that is what the story is called, 'The Tsar-maiden'. So every time the two of them are supposed to meet, Ivan botches it by dropping off to sleep like a log. Ivan has this evil, jealous stepmother. She knows a trick: when she pricks Ivan's clothes with a needle, he falls asleep. The Tsar-maiden is angry and returns to her empire, far away beyond seven hills, seven mountains, and . . .'

'Seven seas!'

'Ivan goes off after the maiden. He travels and travels, and finally reaches her, but not her heart. To reach her heart, Ivan still has to cross the sea. On the other shore grows an oak tree, in the oak there is a box, and in the box is a rabbit, and in the rabbit is a duck, and in the duck there is an egg. In that egg is hidden the love of the Tsar-maiden.'

'And then?'

'That is still not enough. The maiden must eat the egg. Once she eats it, the love for Ivan will return to her heart.'

'So, does she eat this egg?'

'She does. She is tricked into it, of course.'

'Jesus! Who could walk that vast distance, then cross a sea, and then climb an oak. And then the egg! Hardboiled, no less? Ugh!'

'Precisely. That is the whole point,' said Aba, with a wry smile.

'Now I know what this folklore of yours has taught you!'

'What?'

'High standards!'

We both burst into giggles. I liked the way she had packaged her answer. For the first time the conversation between us relaxed, and the whole situation acquired a rosy hue like a girl's school excursion. Perhaps the unexpected weather contributed to this as well, perhaps it was I, not she, who had been tense to begin with, insisting on the rules of a 'genre' that I had defined in advance, and so forced her to adopt. Lord, she was so young! I tried to put myself in her shoes: yes, the 'little girl' had been adapting all the while to me, and truth be told, had been handling the situation with more style than I had. A girl's school excursion, why not: when had I last had a chance to do something like this?! Perhaps I should stay on a day or two longer? After all, the 'Golden Pen of the Balkans' didn't start for another few days.

'And so. Tomorrow our story ends,' she said, with a touch of irony.

The 'our story' rang like a shattered glass. She had used the Bulgarian phrase *nashiyat s tebe roman.* Russians say the same. The word *roman* can mean two things: the novel as a literary form, or a romantic liaison, an affair. The phrase *to have a story with someone* means to be in love. This was an awkward moment on her part: she had wanted to use a pun, she meant to use both meanings ironically, or maybe, who knows, had simply hoped to say something witty. I could understand all of that, the semantic overtones didn't bother me. Something else was grating on my ear. That tone. Ding-ding-ding – dong! That tone.

* * *

It was the ring of hunger. I recognised that brand of hunger. She had a hunger for kindness that clung like a magnet to a kindred hunger for kindness and fed on it; a hunger for attention which attracted the same sort of hunger for attention; a blind hunger which sought to be led by the blind; a crippled hunger which sought an ally in the crippled, the hunger of a deaf mute cooing to a deaf mute.

Aba had stumbled onto the truth by chance: yes, she was an ageing little girl. She was born with the invisible mark of the unloved child on her brow. It made no difference whether they'd really loved her or not, would love her or not; the hunger was born with her, and with her it would vanish. There was little that could assuage that hunger; many had worn themselves ragged trying. Was it this, rather than genuine hunger, that punished mythical Erisychthon, who ended up gnawing at his own bones?

Aba found a common, secret language with my mother immediately. Perhaps they were made of the same stuff, and recognised each other without realising they had. They were bound by the same fear of vanishing, an unconscious desire to leave their mark behind them, to inscribe themselves on the map. They did not choose the means or the map in the process; it could have been the skin of their own children, the hand of a stranger. It was not their fault, nor was it anything they had done wrong. As if a capricious and thoughtless fairy had branded them at birth and made them think they were invisible. The sense that they were invisible acted on them like stomach acid and made them hungrier yet. There was nothing to assuage a hunger like that, not a giant magnifiying glass, or powerful spotlights, or the lavishing of attention. The hunger whimpered in their stomachs like a stray dog. This was a cunning hunger, gluttonous, capable of proudly refusing food, a sly foe able to hide and keep from being discovered, a tremulous foe who dared not raise a hand against itself, a lying and cheating foe, who knew how to make its whimpering sound like a siren song and left its saliva.

I looked at her. The kind face shaded with melancholy, which immediately provoked a feeling of guilt in the onlooker. She did everything she could to get others to like her. She loved her parents, if she had them, her friends, which she most certainly had. Because she was the one who never forgot a birthday, she was the one who sent courteous notes, postcards and emails, she was the one who was always first to pick up the phone and dial the number. She had never harmed anyone else; she had never kicked anyone in the shins; she never cheated in school; she was always a good pupil and a good student; she helped others; she never, or almost never, lied; she was kind to everyone; and in her bartering with emotions she always felt the loser. She watched me. She was interested in figuring out how the wheels and gears of my clock worked, and for the sake of discovery she was prepared to take the clock apart. Because why was it that everyone else in this world ticked and tocked so regularly, while only she was on the wrong beat?

I recognised the seductive whimper. I had been feeding my mother's hunger for too long. After all, wasn't I serving one of them here as a *bedel*, and the other as a potential morsel? Yes, love is on the distant shore of a wide sea. A large oak tree stands there, and in the tree there is a box, in the box a rabbit, in the rabbit a duck, and in the duck an egg. And the egg, in order to get the emotional mechanism going, had to be eaten.

6.

The next morning dawned a quiet, grey day. I learned that the storm the night before had wreaked terrible damage, brought down electric lines, roofs had been ripped from houses, some of the local roads were blocked.

I kept to my decision to leave. The afternoon bus was going to go at four thirty.

'You can stay if you like,' I said, 'and spend a few days with your cousin,' I added cautiously.

'No, we haven't seen each other for years.'

She said it without pretence. There was no longer any point in pretending that she had come here to see her cousin.

'I'm leaving. I'm going to see if I can find the street where my grandparents lived.'

'I am going with you,' she said. A childish determination rang in her voice.

'No,' I said.

She pressed her lips together as if she were a little insulted. All the more so because it was clear that we'd be skipping *our* morning cup of coffee. We parted ways in front of the hotel, agreeing to meet back there at three o'clock. I didn't ask her what she would do.

'*Priyatno snimane!*' she shouted in the tone of a child who is being left behind. Perhaps this is a common phrase in Bulgarian, but it, too, grated on my ear. *Have a great time with the picture-taking!*

I was suddenly awash with relief. It was as if only now – once I'd finally got rid of Aba's presence – I had arrived in Varna. I set off down Vladislav Varnenchik street (was this what the street had been called before?), trying to retrieve a living image from memory. This was the route I used to take to the city beach and I would come back, sun-burned and groggy, dragging my feet on the hot asphalt. The only place I recognised, however, was the main post office. Everything else seemed confused. My grandparents lived on Dospat Street, one of the smaller streets off to the left. Earlier they had had a house of their own with a garden by a lake just outside of Varna. That is where my mother spent her childhood and early youth. There was a train station there on the lake, long since abandoned, where Grandpa had worked. Mum remembered the station with special tenderness. During summer evenings the neighbourhood children gathered there. *We'd meet down at the station in the evening, after all the trains had passed* . . . I remembered that phrase – *in the evening, after all the trains had passed* – because she must have repeated it. Having adopted the phrase, I further embroidered it with my own colours. Dusk, fireflies, a quiet train station, the warm tracks gleaming in the dark, croaking frogs, a moon in the sky – and my mother's young, eager heart pounding with excitement.

Now I wondered why it was that although we had come to visit my grandparents so many times, we never went to see the old abandoned train station and the house they'd lived in. When Grandpa retired, my grandparents moved to a school where they lived as custodians. They stayed in a little house in the school yard. The house had only two rooms, but the yard was large and part of it was covered, so we were out all day during the summer, even when it rained. The school was empty over the summer; there was plenty of space.

I found the school. The gate was locked. I hadn't remembered a brick wall, it must have been built since then. I remembered an iron gate with bars. The gate was painted an ugly green colour. The word *Kotelno,* 'furnace', was written on it in black. I tried the handle. It was locked. This was upsetting. A familiar sense of panic swelled in me, a feeling I sometimes have when I can't get out of a place. I stood there at the door as if hypnotised. How small everything looked! The roof of the little house by the wall was dilapidated, the wall on the outside was cracked, damp stains spread along its base. And the yard – that spacious sunny yard with the vast piece of blue sky – how tiny it had become! How did all of us fit here? Dad, Mum, my brother and I? Had my grandparents slept at the home of friends across the way during the times when we visited? Or in one of the classrooms in the school building on improvised beds?

What had once been a charming little street with cosy houses and gardens was no longer recognisable. The street had become a construction site; new homes were sprouting on all sides. I walked around the school, found the entrance and bumped into a man and two women in the corridor. I explained that I would like to see the yard, and had tried to let myself in, but it was locked.

'Why are you interested in the yard?' the man asked.

'My grandparents used to live there years ago.'

'You cannot go in. The furnace for the school is there.'

'I would just like to peep into the yard for a moment.'

'Madam, there is no yard there! There is nothing there! It's the furnace for the school. And it has always been there as far as I know.'

The women agreed and nodded, right to left, as the Bulgarians do.

* * *

I left the school building and went back to the green gate. It was standing there in front of me like a forgotten password. If I could only open the gate a crack, I thought, everything would come back to me. Some images were surfacing: the dynamic figure of my grandmother, who was always busy with something – cooking, cleaning, washing, ironing – and the static figure of my grandfather, who sat in the school yard and smoked. Everything else tumbled and mixed in the furnace behind the green gate.

I looked over at the little house across the way, which, surprisingly, was still standing. My grandmother died in that house while she was over visiting her friends, who, themselves, are no longer alive. They were watching television together, Grandma, suddenly agitated, asked, 'Why did it get so dark?' and then she died. That was Mum's most recent version of Grandma's dying words.

Gulping breaths of air I went back to the main street and there I flagged down a taxi that saved me. The ride was an instant sedative. I decided to take the route of this pointless and troubling pilgrimage all the way to its end.

'Can you take me to the old train station by the lake?' I said.

'Why?' The taxi driver was astonished. 'There is nothing there!'

Beyond the tangle of rusty tracks, in front of me stood the lake. It stood – precisely that and nothing more. The sky was intersected by electric wires, the tracks were covered in grass. The grass was a dark green, the sky and lake a greyish blue. The place was ugly, but not entirely without appeal. The appeal lay in the sense of total desertion that radiated from all sides. I turned around. Across, on the other side of the road, where the house with the garden was supposed to have stood, the one we'd never gone to see, there was a slope with a few run-down little houses along the top. The slope was dangerously eroded, so much so that the little old houses looked as if they might come tumbling down at any minute. At the foot of the hill, along the road, were more run-down buildings with advertisement signs: Car Mechanic, We Change Oil, and so forth.

'Love, I told you there is nothing here but ghosts! Unless you are looking for a part for a car. And a very old one at that!' the taxi driver said kindly.

When we turned around to return to the centre of town, I looked back once more at the lake. It seemed as if I could see a barely visible bluish shimmering, ghosts shimmering in the air over the lake.

7.

Walking towards the hotel, I saw Aba standing by the fountain, feeding seagulls. The water spraying in spurts behind her looked a little more lively than it had that morning. Lit by sunshine that was breaking through the clouds, the jets of water glistened in all the colours of the rainbow. And the seagulls, it was as if the gulls had gone mad: they swooped in great loops in the air, flapped their wings and then slowly, like parachutes, they descended to Aba's interlocked open hands and they pecked at the crumbs of bread.

Passers-by stopped and watched the scene: there was something marvellously acrobatic and, at the same time, natural in Aba's performance. Aba inscribed herself perfectly into the space. This time there was no 'wrong tone'. If Aba was sending a message, that message was not directed at those of us who were watching her on the square, I was sure of that.

I did not go over to her. I loathe feathered creatures. I watched the scene from the side. She caught sight of me, tossed the rest of the bread into the air, clapped her hands together to wipe off the crumbs and came over to me.

We brought out the bags that had been left at the main desk that morning. While we waited for the taxi in front of the hotel, I asked her how she had spent her time.

'Nothing much, I wandered around town a bit.'

And then she looked at me carefully, and said,

'Ah, yes, I went over to your grandmother's – Dospat Street, *n'est-ce pas*?'

She had deliberately stabbed me in the flesh with her sharp little claw, there could be no doubt. Fury bubbled up in me in an instant. I quietly sucked the blood from the invisible wound and said,

'Why? There is nothing there!'

At that moment the taxi arrived.

As They Came, So They Went Away

'I can hardly wait for you to come to Zagreb and tell me all about how it was in Varna! I can hardly wait,' she repeated excitedly during every phone conversation. I could recognise in her voice the routine excitement she always expressed the same way: *I can hardly wait.*

I rehearsed versions of my report in my mind. Maybe it would be better to tell her I had stayed in Varna for two days, that the weather had been bad, which was true, and that I had hardly seen anything. Or should I tell her that with the help of a kind Varna policeman I had been able to locate her Petya, who looked well, beautiful in fact, had sent her regards, but, unfortunately, couldn't write, because she was having difficulties writing. Her son, Kostya, who, by the way, had stopped drinking, was looking after her with genuine devotion. And Varna, Varna was so wonderful, but I hadn't brought her any pictures because I pressed the wrong button on that new digital camera.

'I don't recognise anything here,' she said, peering at the images on my computer screen. 'Is that Varna?'

She was surprisingly cool and collected. Of the wall that

separated the school yard from the street, she said, 'No, that wall wasn't there before. Something new.'

Amazingly she was not as disappointed by the grey scenes of the city beach as I had been.

'That city beach was never very nice. Do you remember how we always preferred to go to Asparuhovo and Galata? The water was cleaner there.'

When I next visited I urged her to look at the photographs again. She seemed to have forgotten she'd seen them the first time. Her comments were identical, and her indifference troubled me. I had not received the anticipated 'payment' for my service as a *bedel,* the emotional reciprocation from her end. Then again, maybe I hadn't deserved it. I had clearly done the job badly. I had brought back nothing from my pilgrimage, and received nothing in return. I can't tell whether she had erased the Varna file in her memory, or had saved it somewhere else, but I was sure that neither she nor I would be opening it again any time soon.

This time I noticed that she had changed the way she walked. She was trying to stand a little straighter when she pushed her walker, and to lift her feet a little more with each step.

'That is what Jasminka told me, to lift my feet.'

Jasminka was her physiotherapist.

We went, as usual, to her favourite café at the marketplace for coffee. She went in with the walker, stubbornly refusing to leave it outside (*I don't want anyone stealing it!*). People had to get up and move their chairs to let her pass. I think she was not unaware that her arrival at the café with the walker was causing a fuss.

'When you aren't here with me, the waiters lend me a

hand. They are all very, very kind. People are generally very kind, especially when they see me with the walker,' she said.

She always ordered the same thing, a cappuccino, and Kaia or I would bring her a cheese turnover, a triangular piece of pastry, from the shop two steps down from the café. Without her ritual turnover and the cappuccino, the day wouldn't function. If the weather was bad and she couldn't go out herself, someone else would bring the turnover, and the cappuccino would be made at home.

After she sat for a bit, she had to go to the bathroom. She came back from the bathroom upset.

'How could that happen to me! The prettiest little old lady in the neighbourhood!' she grumbled.

She refused to wear the incontinence pads with the same obstinacy that she refused to wear flat-heeled orthopaedic shoes for the elderly (*I can't bear them! I have always worn heels!*). Someone had told her she was the prettiest little old lady in the neighbourhood. A year earlier she would have been insulted by a similar sentiment, but now she was pleased to say it over and over: *Everyone says I am the prettiest little old lady in the neighbourhood!* It is true that she said it with a hint of irony. She used the phrase as an apology for her clumsiness and as a request to respect her 'exceptional' age. The incontinence was the worst insult her body had come up with for her. And she was irked by her forgetfulness (*No, I did not forgot!*) yet ultimately she relented (*Maybe I forgot after all?*) and finally she made her peace with it (*It is hardly surprising that I forget things nowadays. I'm eighty years old, you know!*).

'If this happens again, I'll kill myself straight away,' she said, indirectly asking me to say something to console her.

'It's perfectly normal for your age! Look on the bright side. You are over eighty, you are up and about, you are in no pain, you live in your own home, you go out every day and you socialise. Your best friend, with whom you drink coffee every day, is ten years younger than you. Jasminka visits you three times a week. Kaia brings you breakfast, lunch and dinner every day, and she is an excellent cook and keeps you on schedule with your medical check-ups. Your doctor is only five minutes' walk from your house, your grandchildren visit you regularly and love you, and I come to see you all the time,' I recited.

'If I could only read,' she sighed, although she had little patience for reading any more, aside from leafing through newspapers.

'Well, you can read, though, it's true, with difficulty.'

'If only I could read my Tessa one more time.'

She was referring to Hardy's *Tess of the d'Urbervilles.*

'As soon as you decide, we'll go ahead with the operation. It is a breeze to remove age-related cataracts.'

'At my age nothing is easy.'

'I said a breeze, not easy. Do you want me to buy you a magnifying glass?'

'Who could stand reading with a magnifying glass?!'

'Do you want me to read you *Tess* out loud? A chapter a day?'

'It's not as nice when someone else reads to you as when you read for yourself.'

She responded to all my attempts to cheer her up with obstinate childish baulking. She'd give way for a moment (*Maybe you're right*), but the next instant she would clutch at some new detail (*Ah, everything would be different if I could only walk a little faster!*).

'I have changed so much. I barely recognise myself.'

'What are you saying? You haven't a single wrinkle on your forehead.'

'Maybe so, but the skin sags on my neck.'

'The wrinkles on your face are so fine they are barely visible.'

'Maybe, but my back is so hunched.'

'You've kept your slender figure.'

'My belly sticks out.' she complained.

'Sure, a little, but nobody notices,' I consoled her.

'I have changed. I barely recognise myself.'

'Can you think of anyone your age who hasn't changed?'

'Well, now that you ask,' she'd relent.

'What were you expecting?'

'I don't know.'

'Your beloved Ava Gardner, for instance.'

'Ava was the most beautiful woman in the world!' she said firmly, but with a hint of melancholy, as if she had been speaking of herself.

'Ava died at the age of sixty-eight.'

'You're kidding!'

'No, really, she had a stroke. Half of her face was paralysed. Near the end of her life she was penniless, so Frank Sinatra paid for her medical expenses.'

'She? Broke!? I can't believe it.'

'Yes, she moved from the States to London. She was isolated there, she was probably no longer able to earn anything. Her last words to her servant Carmen were: "I am tired,"' I said. 'Story has it that Frank Sinatra locked himself up in his room for two days when he heard that Ava had died. They say he sobbed uncontrollably.'

'Well, and so he should have!' she said. 'Such a little man, nothing much to look at, scrawny, a shrimp. Next to her he looked like a frog!'

'What about Mickey Rooney?'

'Why Mickey Rooney?'

'Well, he was her first husband.'

'Well, that Rooney was a shrimp too! Such an exquisite woman and around her she had only dwarves.'

'Ava was only four years older than you.'

'Ava was the most beautiful woman in the world!' she repeated, ignoring the comment about the difference in their ages.

'Take, for instance, Audrey Hepburn.'

'That little woman? The skinny one?'

'Yes. She died at sixty-four.'

'I didn't know.'

'And Ingrid Bergman?'

'What about Ingrid Bergman?'

'She died when she was sixty-seven.'

'She was a little clumsy, but still exquisite.'

'What about Marilyn Monroe? Marilyn was a two-month-old baby when you were born! And she died at thirty-six!'

'Marilyn was my age?'

'Your generation! You were both born in 1926!'

It seemed that the fact that she shared her year of birth with Marilyn Monroe left her cold.

'What about Elizabeth Taylor?' she asked.

'She just celebrated her seventy-fifth. They wrote about it the other day in the papers.'

'I can't believe Liz is younger than me.'

'A full six years!'

'She, too, was a beautiful woman,' she said. 'There aren't any more like her today.'

'You should see her now!'

'Why?'

'They took a picture of her in her wheelchair for her birthday.'

'How much older am I?'

'Six years.'

'Five and a half,' she corrected me.

'Just think how many operations she had,' I added.

'She had trouble with her spine.'

'And alcohol, then those unhappy marriages.'

'How many times was she married?'

'Nine. When they reported her birthday celebration they said she may marry a tenth time.'

Mum grinned.

'Hats off to her!'

At last we were talking. We chatted about Liz as if we were two good friends chatting about a third. I'm supposing that Mum was pleased to hear all that information. Liz was seventy-five and had her picture taken in a wheelchair. Mum would be turning eighty-one in another month or so, and she was not in a wheelchair. She wasn't even fat.

'I suppose beauty and fame don't mean a thing,' she said, relieved.

The expression on her face suggested that this time she was satisfied with the balance in her life.

'Do you know what Bette Davis said?'

'What?'

'That old age is no place for sissies.'

'Well, it isn't,' she said, heartened for a moment.

She often thought of herself as younger than she was. Once when she slid like this into a different, younger age, she addressed me as 'Grandma'.

'What, are you asleep, Grandma?'

She slid back and forth in time. She no longer knew exactly when different things happened. She would have been happiest to stay in her childhood, not because she thought of those years as the brightest period of her biography, but because her feelings in that period were 'safe', long since formulated, sealed, related many times over, chosen to be a repertoire which she was always able to offer her listeners. She retold the little events and details from her childhood in the same way, with the same vocabulary, ending with the same points or more often with the same absence of a point. It was a sealed repertoire which could no longer be corrected or changed, at least that was the way it seemed, and at the same time it was her only firm temporal coordinate. Sometimes, it's true, harsh images would surface which I was hearing for the first time.

'I was always afraid of snakes.'

'Why?'

'Once we went on an excursion to a wood and stumbled on a big old snake. Dad killed it.'

'I hope it wasn't poisonous!'

'It was a price snake.'

'You mean a dice snake?'

'Yes, it was a big bad old snake and Dad killed it.'

She used to call my father, her husband, Dad, while she usually referred to her own father as Grandpa. Now she was using Dad to refer to her father.

Three years had passed since she'd been given the 'ugly diagnosis'. Would there be another year? Two? Five? Bartering with death suited her (*If I could just stick around for my grandson's birth! If I could see my grandson start first grade! If I only have the chance to see my granddaughter start school!*). There was one thing for certain: she had taken care of it all, wrapped everything up, everything was ‘neat and tidy’, it was ready. She sat in life as if she were in a clean, half-empty doctor’s waiting room: nothing hurt, nothing moved much, she was waiting to be summoned and it was as if she no longer cared when it would happen. All that mattered was her everyday rhythm: Kaia came over at 7:30 a.m., she ate her breakfast while watching the morning television programme *Good Morning, Croatia*, then she got dressed and went out to the café for her cappuccino and cheese turnover, her slow return home with little chats along the way with neighbours, then waiting for Kaia to bring her lunch at about 1:30 p.m., then an afternoon nap, then Kaia with her dinner at about 6:30 p.m., dining with her favourite television show, *The Courtroom*, and then the television news, then off to bed. Kaia came three times a day and went with her for the walk to the café where they had their coffee together. Jasminka came three times a week, helped her with little exercises and to bathe, neighbours dropped in every day, she saw her grandchildren once a week, usually on Sundays. I called her at least three times a week, and I often came to Zagreb, staying several days or more.

She was sleeping more than she used to. Sometimes she slept so soundly that she wasn’t even wakened by the phone ringing or my banging on the door. When she lay down she took the same pose as on her CAT scans, her head tilted a little forward. She lay there peacefully, relaxed, with a hint of a smile on her lips. Sitting in the armchair she would often dip into a brief, deep sleep as if slipping into a hot bath. I happened upon her when she was asleep, sitting in front of the blaring television, her head bare, duster in hand. Then she opened her eyes, slowly lifted the duster, a small brush on a long handle around which she’d wrapped a soft rag, and wiped the television screen clean of dust. Then, spotting a smudge on the floor, she got up and slowly, shuffling, she went to the bathroom, moistened the rag, wrapped it around the brush, went back and sat down in the armchair again, and from there she wiped up the smudge.

'Buy me those sphincters, they are the best,' she'd say.

'You must mean Swiffers, Mother.'

'Yes, we're out of them.'

I had been bringing her those boxes with the magical soft cloths, which were 'death to dust' (*Those cloths are death to dust!*). Shuffling around the house, she wielded the light plastic handle with a Swiffer cloth wrapped around the rectangular base, and with slow movements she wiped the dust off the walls, the furniture, the floor. The bright sun shone through the lowered blinds and splashed the floor with golden specks. She stood there in the middle of the room sprinkled with shafts of sunlight, her hair cropped close to her shapely head, her pale face with slightly slanted light-brown eyes and her lips surprisingly still full, awash in the sun as if it were an abundance of gold coins. A million particles of dust were afloat in the air around her, shimmering. She'd wave the handle through the air to chase them away, but the golden particles remained. And then she'd sit in the chair again and sink back into sleep. The golden dust swam around her. Sitting like that under an array of sun specks, surrendered to sleep, she looked like an ancient slumbering goddess.

Once, when she started awake, she said, groggily,

'Do you know what my mother once told me?'

'What?'

'That when she was giving birth to me there were three

women standing there by her bed. Two were dressed in white, and the third was in black.'

'Do you suppose those were the Fates who determine your destiny?' I asked, cautiously.

'Nonsense,' she said. 'Most likely mother was suffering from the labour and hallucinated them. Two in white, one in black,' she mumbled, and sank back to sleep.

During those fifteen days in March 2007, the sunrise was so lavish and bright that we had to lower the blinds every morning. The air had the smell of spring. My mother's balcony was neglected; the soil in the flower boxes was dry.

'We should buy some fresh loam and plant some flowers,' I said.

'We will be the first to have flowers in our building!'

'Yes, the first.'

'Yes, pelargoniums.'

Sparrows settled onto the balcony railing. That was a good sign; Mother was convinced that this year there wouldn't be a swarm of starlings.

'Those pests are gone,' she said.

'Which pests?'

'You know, the darlings!'

'Starlings are birds, darlings are your grandchildren.'

'That's what I said.'

'What did you say?'

'That the pests are gone.'

Then she added, with an air of mystery,

'As they came, so they went away.'

PART TWO

Ask Me No Questions and I'll Tell You No Lies

Day One

I.

As soon as the receptionist, Pavel Zuna, caught sight of the three figures approaching the desk, he became aware of a slight current running upwards from his left big toe and stopping somewhere in the small of his back. Or the other way round: running downwards from his back to his toe. Pavel Zuna was not a neurologist but a receptionist, and a receptionist rather than a poet, so he did not abandon himself to contemplating this unusual sensation, especially as the picturesque appearance of the approaching figures occupied his full attention. In a wheelchair sat an old lady with both feet tucked into a large fur boot. It would have been hard to describe the old lady as a human being; she was the remains of a human being, a piece of humanoid crackling. She was so little and so crumpled that the boot appeared more striking than she did. The old lady had a tiny face that consisted of a skull and aged skin stretched over it like a nylon stocking. She had thick, closely cropped grey hair and a hooked nose. Her lively grey eyes sparkled brightly. The old lady was holding a big leather bag on her lap. The other one, the one pushing the wheelchair, was exceptionally tall, slender and of astonishingly erect bearing for her advanced years. Although Pavel Zuna was not a particularly short man, a quick glance suggested that he would barely reach the tall woman's shoulder. The third was a short breathless blonde, her hair ruined by excessive use of peroxide, with big gold rings in her ears and large breasts whose weight dragged her forward. Pavel Zuna's career as a receptionist had been neither brief nor unsuccessful, nor indeed uninteresting, that is to say he had seen all kinds of things – even more intensely bleached hair and even bigger earrings. But still, Pavel Zuna did not recall ever, either behind the reception desk or in his entire life, seeing women's breasts larger than those of the breathless blonde.

Pavel Zuna was an experienced receptionist with a particular talent. He was endowed with a built-in financial scanner, which had, up to now, proved infallible: Zuna was able to guess at once to which class a given person belonged and his or her financial status. Had Pavel Zuna not loved his receptionist's job so much, he could have been head-hunted by any tax department in the world, so infallible was his estimate of the depth of other people's pockets. In short, Zuna could have sworn that this unusual troika had just wandered into his hotel by mistake.

'Good morning, ladies. What can I do for you? Might you have lost your way?' asked Zuna in that patronising manner adopted by medical personnel in hospitals and old people's homes when addressing their older patients.

'Is this the Grand Hotel?' the tall lady addressed Zuna.

'It is indeed.'

'Then we have not lost our way,' said the lady, handing Pavel Zuna three passports.

Pavel Zuna felt that current in his toe again, this time so

forcefully and painfully that it took his breath away. However, in the practised manner of a supreme professional, Zuna smiled agreeably and went to verify their names on the computer. Pavel Zuna's face illuminated by the light of the computer screen turned pale, partly with pain, partly with surprise: the two best and most expensive suites in the hotel had been reserved in the names on the passports.

'Excuse me, how long will you be staying? I don't see the date of your departure here,' said Pavel Zuna in the tone of a man whose professional pride has just been bruised.

'A couple of days, maybe,' said the little old lady asthmatically.

'Or maybe a week,' said the tall lady drily.

'Or maybe forever,' chimed the blonde.

'I see,' said Zuna, although he didn't see at all. 'May I have your credit card, please?'

'We're paying in cash!' said the blonde with the large breasts, smacking her lips as though she had just consumed a tasty morsel.

The little old lady in the wheelchair silently confirmed the authenticity of the blonde's statement by opening the zip of the leather bag that was lying limply on her knees. Pavel Zuna bent slightly forward and caught sight of the fat bundles of euro notes arranged tidily in it.

'I see . . .' he said, feeling a little dizzy. 'Ladies of a certain age always pay cash-in-hand.'

There had clearly been a serious malfunction of Pavel Zuna's inner scanner, and that troubled him. He waved a hand feebly and at the same instant three young men in hotel uniforms appeared.

'Help these ladies to their rooms, lads. *Presidentske apartma! Cisarske apartma!*' Zuna commanded, handing them the keys.

* * *

Surrounded by hotel personnel of the male gender, the three female figures glided away towards the lift. Pavel Zuna just managed to observe a sudden breeze blow petals off the luxuriant floral display in a Chinese vase on the reception desk, before his eyes clouded over. The pain from his left big toe swept upwards. It struck him in the small of the back with such force that he simply collapsed.

This whole scene was observed out of the corner of his eye by Arnoš Kozeny, as he sat comfortably sprawled in one of the lobby armchairs. Arnoš Kozeny, a retired lawyer, was a kind of fixture in the Grand Hotel. He came here every morning for a cappuccino, to leaf through the fresh newspapers and smoke a cigar. He would reappear in the hotel about five in the afternoon, in the café, and in the evening he would hang around the hotel casino. Arnoš Kozeny was a well-preserved seventy-eight-year-old. He was wearing a sand-coloured suit, a freshly ironed light-blue shirt and a bow tie of a bluish hue, with canvas shoes that matched the colour of his suit.

As he leafed through the papers, Arnoš was struck by the news that Czech vets had found an unidentified strain of bird 'flu on two farms near the town of Norin. The vets had confirmed that it was the H5 virus, but they were not sure whether it was the H5N1 type, which, if measures were not taken in time, would be as deadly to humans as the Spanish 'flu of 1914. The article suggested that, in the course of the last year, the virus had appeared in some thirty countries. Josef Duben, spokesman for the Czech Veterinary Service, announced that, as far as the Czech Republic was concerned, it had not yet been decided whether or not to decontaminate the two farms where the H5 virus had been detected. For the time being there was a three-kilometre quarantine.

The item caught Arnoš's attention because of Norin, where his first wife, Jarmila, lived. He hadn't called her for more than a year now. This would be a good excuse for a little chat, he thought, puffing the smoke from his cigar with relish.

What about us? We carry on. While the meaning of life may slip from our hold, the purpose of a tale is to be told!

2.

Beba was sitting in the bath weeping bitterly. No, she had not burst into tears as soon as she entered the suite, because it took her some time to produce the quantity of tears she was going to shed. When she first came in, she swept her eyes slowly over every detail, exactly like a diver examining the seabed. She ran her hand over the snow-white linen in the bedroom, opened the cupboards, went into the bathroom, removed the disinfectant tape from the toilet, examined the little toiletries by the washbasin, stroked the soft white towelling wrap. Then she opened the curtains and before her eyes stretched a magnificent view of the spa and the wooded hills around it. Here Beba suddenly remembered a Bosnian she had asked to redecorate her flat. It was long ago. Beba had asked for it all to be painted white. When he finished the job, the Bosnian had said: 'Here you are, my dear, now your flat is like a swan!'

And now everything congealed in that stupid word *swan*. The word stuck like a bone in her throat – and Beba burst into tears. And what exactly was the matter? In that hotel with its white façade, spreading its wings over the town like a swan, in the soft space of the imperial suite, wrapped round her like an expensive fur coat, Beba was forcefully struck by a sudden awareness of how ugly her life was. As though under powerful police searchlights, all at once the image of her Zagreb flat appeared before her eyes. The miniature kitchen where she had pottered and fiddled about for years, the fridge with the broken handle and its plastic interior now grey with age, the rickety chairs, the sofa and worn armchairs that she covered with rugs and cushions to make them look 'jollier', the moth-eaten carpet, the television set in front of which she sat mindlessly more and more often and for ever longer periods. And then the licking and cleaning of all that junk and trembling at the thought that something might stop working – the television, the fridge, the vacuum cleaner – because she could no longer buy anything much. Her pension was barely enough to cover her basic outgoings and food, while her meagre savings had vanished with the Ljubljana Bank some fifteen years before, when the country fell apart and suddenly her bank was in a different state, and everyone had been rushing headlong to steal from everyone else. Had she wanted, she could have derived some bitter satisfaction from it all: in comparison with many other people's losses hers were negligible, because she had simply had nothing in the first place.

Then all at once, everything had turned ugly. The people around her had grown ugly with hatred, and then with self-pity and the realisation that they had been cheated. They had all developed a rat-like expression, even the young, those who had begun to come of age breathing in their parents' poisonous breath.

* * *

Beba was weeping because she could not remember when she had last had a holiday. She used to go in both summer and winter. Winter holidays on the coast had been especially cheap. Now they were out of the question, now everything was out of the question. The coast had apparently been bought up by wealthy foreigners and local tycoons.

When Beba opened her suitcase to put her things into the wardrobe, and when the salami wrapped in foil that she had brought along 'just in case' rolled out, it unleashed a new torrent of tears. That salami made her look like a comic figure from some other age who had accidentally found herself in this one. A glance at her cosmetic bits and pieces, her toothbrush and toothpaste (especially her worn, frayed toothbrush!), by contrast with those that awaited her in the hotel bathroom, provoked a sharp pain under her diaphragm. And, as though she were performing some kind of ritual murder, Beba threw all her bits and pieces – one by one – into the bathroom rubbish bin. Bang! Bang! Including the salami in its foil. Bang!

Although she had brought with her all the best things she possessed, Beba's clothes now seemed shoddy and vulgar. She was used to poverty, she bore it cheerfully, as though it were an unavoidable downpour. Besides, hardly anyone lived better. She was the daughter of working people from the suburbs of Zagreb who, instead of training as a hairdresser or retailer, had insisted on going to art school. And she graduated, but, for various reasons, was obliged to get a job. She worked for years at the Zagreb medical faculty, drawing anatomical sketches for professors, students and medical textbooks. In those days there were no computers, but everything changed when they came on the scene. Beba continued to carry out administrative tasks, and then she retired. It was through the faculty that she had come by her little apartment, some forty square metres in size.

Beba sat in the bath wrapped in lacey foam. She could not remember the last time anyone had treated her with greater warmth or tenderness than this hotel bath. This was the kind of painful realisation that drives the more sensitive to put a bullet in their temple, or at least to look around to see where they might attach an adequately strong noose. Now her decision to come on holiday with Pupa and Kukla seemed a mistake. It would have been better if she had stayed in her burrow. All the more so since she could not see the point of their coming here. Who goes on holiday with an eighty-eight-year-old lady with one foot in the grave?! Pupa had stubbornly insisted that they should go 'as far away as possible'. They could have gone to a spa in Slovenia, but that wasn't far enough for Pupa. They could have gone to Austria or Italy, but at a certain moment Pupa had latched onto this place. It was true that the journey had gone without a hitch; Beba even had the enduring impression that an invisible hand was carrying out all the actions for them, guiding them towards their destination. She did not understand how Pupa had come by so much money. Pupa was a doctor, a gynaecologist, who had retired long ago, and pensions had not increased – on the contrary, they were lower with every passing year. Beba had several times stopped herself from calling Zorana, Pupa's daughter, to tell her about the situation, but she held back, because she had given Pupa her word that she would say nothing. Pupa had asked them not to tell anyone where they were going, which was a little strange, but could be explained by Pupa's old lady's paranoia. And then, even if she had wanted to, Beba had no one to whom she could boast, or complain, and that was the most sorrowful thing of all.

* * *

Beba gave a start when a telephone rang right by her ear. And when she realised that the handset on the wall was not an additional shower-head but a telephone (Heavens! A telephone in the bathroom!), Beba burst into tears again.

'Yes . . . ?' she said, her voice cracking.

'We're meeting in an hour. We're going to dinner,' Kukla's voice poured through the telephone receiver.

'Fine,' said Beba without conviction and slipped back into the bath.

There was plenty of time for suicide. Dinner first, and then she would make a plan with herself. For the time being it was more sensible to stop tormenting herself, to try to get at least a little pleasure out of this 'swan', for heaven's sake, and stop this snivelling right now, because there'd be lots of time for that when she got home.

That's what Beba was thinking. What about us? We carry on. While life like a seal wallows in glee, the tale sails off to the open sea.

3.

Mr Shaker, an American, was one of those people who could be called 'a man of his time', the right man in the right place at the right time, one of those people with whom our modern world abounds; those numerous stars, artists, pop singers, male and female, those con men and bullshit artists, those gurus who hoodwink us daily, those numerous prophets, swindlers and 'designers' of our lives in whose power we choose to place ourselves.

Long ago, this seventy-five-year-old had used his small inheritance to purchase a Chinese man's run-down drugstore together with a vast number of vitamin preparations that were passed their sell-by date. Mr Shaker had stuck new, alluring labels on the old bottles and the vitamins were selling like hot cakes. At first Mr Shaker had not believed that people were so naive, but after the cheerful clink of the first cash, he came to believe not only in people but also in the fact that he was a man with an important mission in this world. And Mr Shaker's mission could be condensed into a simple slogan: Pump it up! To cut a long story short, with time Mr Shaker had grown into the king of an industry of magical powders and potions, bearing the label food-supplement. Those whose job it is to monitor such products had long since realised that it was better for these things to be sold legally, because otherwise they were only going to be sold illegally. From vitamins that had passed their sell-by date, Mr Shaker moved on to mixtures, or, to put it another way, he moved from fiction to science fiction, from grammar to mathematics, from physics to metaphysics. Like every successful tradesman, what Mr Shaker actually sold was ideological hot air, in this case the hot air of metamorphosis. His products suggested to frogs that they would turn into princesses. His customers believed that the body was a divine temple, that his magical powder was the sacred host and that only a transformed body was a valid visa for a life in paradise on earth. Mr Shaker's advertising slogans contained the words nutrition, transformation, form, reform, shape, reshape, model, remodel, tone and tighten – suggesting that the human body was a heap of Lego pieces, and that it could therefore become its owner's favourite toy. Mr Shaker activated the acupuncture point of the archetypal dream that slumbers in each of us, a dream in which, with the aid of a magic potion, the dreamer can become as small as a poppy seed, pass through any keyhole, become invisible, be transformed into a giant, vanquish a terrible dragon and win the heart of a beautiful princess. More by chance than design, Mr Shaker had put his finger on the fundamental obsession of our age, which explained his success. In the absence of all ideologies, the only refuge that remains for the human imagination is the body. The human body is the only territory which its owner can control, thin, reduce, pump, increase, shape, firm and adapt to its ideal, whether that ideal is called Brad Pitt or Nicole Kidman. Yes, Mr Shaker successfully milked that obsession.

While the contents of Mr Shaker's preparations stirred respect (creatine monohydrate, creatine phosphate, alpha-lipidic acid, glycogen, taurine, argol, aminogens), their names evoked real reverence: AS, C-250, Powermax, Aminomax, Myo Maxx, Trans-XX, Volume 35, Sci X, Iso X, WPC, Ultra AM, GLM, ALC, CLA, HMB, HMB Ultra, Carni Tec, Mega AM, Uni Syne, Yohimbe, Gro Now, Carbo Boost, Cyto For, Hyper M, Cy Pro, Cyto B, Animal Mass.

Mr Shaker's kingdom began gradually to implode when the newspapers published a few dubious reports, and then serious articles as well, suggesting that his powders may have helped pump up muscles, but their hormonal ingredients reduced potency. Mr Shaker watched in despair as everything he had built up over the years deflated like a balloon. And that was how he had ended up here, to kill several birds with one stone: to soothe his nerves and at the same time have a good sniff round the post-communist market, to see whether there were any crumbs for him there, and if there were, to drive the 'easterners', stodgy with beer, yellow with smoking and bloated with alcohol, to reshape their bodies from what had been commercially incompatible to what was compatible.

* * *

And since we have mentioned compatibility, Mr Shaker had yet another burden on his shoulders. That burden was called Rosie. Mr Shaker was a widower, and Rosie was his daughter. And his daughter, who he hoped would inherit his kingdom, represented a constant mockery of Mr Shaker's ambitions. It could not be said that she was not pretty, but, at least in American lifestyle terms, she was simply too chubby. And what was worse, she seemed to be entirely indifferent to the fact. Mr Shaker knew the reputation of this spa and its Wellness Centre under the creative management of Dr Topolanek, and he hoped that he would be able to refresh his brain with new business ideas, and that Rosie would lose the odd pound. And as far as business ideas went, there was something else nagging at him. From acquaintances who had recently been on holiday here, Mr Shaker had learned that there was a young masseur working in the Wellness Centre who was not only physically attractive but also apparently uniquely sexually endowed. If he were able to persuade such a young man to be the potent advertising mascot of his products, Mr Shaker would once again sail off at full steam.

Such were the dreams Mr Shaker wove as he sat in the hotel restaurant. And when he caught sight of a tall, slender woman of his own age, accompanied by two others, yet another of his dreams suddenly leapt into life: old age *à deux*. It was quite possible that this whole world of crackling, explosive physical energy, which had surrounded Mr Shaker for years, had after all damaged his nerves. That is why a mere glance at the lady with her tranquil way of moving had a beneficial effect on him, like good old valium.

Somewhat later, Mr Shaker summoned up his courage, approached the table where the three ladies were sitting and invited the tranquilising lady to dance. To his great surprise, the lady did not refuse. What is more, she spoke very decent English.

There, that's enough about Mr Shaker for the time being. As for us, we carry on. While life's road may twist and bend, the tale hurries to reach its – end!

4.

Pupa kept urging them, in her disarming way, to be her surrogates. She did not actually use that word, but she would say: you drink, and I'll get drunk. You eat, and I'll love the taste. You have a massage, and my bones will be rejuvenated. You dance, and I'll enjoy it. She herself, poor thing, no longer had the strength for anything at all. She spent most of the time dozing in her wheelchair. From time to time she would open her eyes just to 'check on things'.

'I'm just checking, to make sure you're having a good time.'

And, what do you know, just a few hours after they arrived, Kukla had already found a dancing partner. 'Where does she get the energy?!' thought Beba, endeavouring to suppress her fresh sense of affront. After dinner an elderly guy had come for Kukla, rather than for her, which was an insidious blow in the plexus of Beba's already shattered self-confidence. Although Kukla was ten years older than Beba, it was Kukla the guy had chosen. Admittedly Beba did not find him remotely attractive, and that was some small consolation.

'What are they doing?' Pupa roused herself from her slumber.

'Dancing,' said Beba.

'Aahaaa,' said Pupa, nodding off again.

* * *

That was why Beba came suddenly to life when she saw an older man, far better-looking than Kukla's dancing partner, approaching their table.

'Allow me to introduce myself. Doctor Topolanek,' said the man, squeezing Beba's hand vigorously. 'Would you have any objection to my joining you?'

'No indeed, by all means sit down,' said Beba cordially.

Pupa roused herself again and squinted in their visitor's direction.

'Allow me to introduce myself, Doctor Topolanek,' the man repeated.

Pupa simply smiled. She did not offer him her hand. She knew that she was already so old that no one expected anything of her any longer, and that everything was forgiven her in advance, like a child. So she relaxed into her role, not even saying 'pleased to meet you' and – drifted off again.

Of course going through life was not the same as walking across a field – in the words of the Doctor's favourite poet Boris Pasternak, with whose hero, Doctor Zhivago, Topolanek had identified in his early youth. Of course going through life was not the same as walking across a field, but since the tale always pleases itself, we shall, to please the tale, say a word about Dr Topolanek.

When the velvet Czech revolution took place, Dr Topolanek felt that his moment had come. In fact, the revolution was more than a little late, but nevertheless it happened in time, at least as far as Topolanek was concerned. He was exasperated with the communists, but communists were the only people he knew, and then he quickly became exasperated with anti-communists when anti-communists were the only people he knew. Both sides just talked hot air, there was nothing to choose between them. The revolution had dawned like a peacock, or that was how it seemed to Topolanek. Now it was all an unholy mess of wounded revolutionary vanity and the first things to rise to the surface were greed and stupidity. In the general transitional turmoil, Topolanek made a firm decision to grab a little of what was going for himself. His colleagues, outstanding practitioners, were all languishing in hospitals on miserable salaries, while he, who had begun his career without ambition, as a GP in a spa, had made it to the position of manager of the best-known Wellness Centre in the country and beyond. Yes, he could be called an amateur surfer, skating over the waves. Some people are helped by their genes – you can clobber them as much as you like, but you'll never do them in – and others by their character. Topolanek was not burdened with a surfeit of character, and this little handicap saved his life. Mild as grass, he bent whichever way the wind blew. Only oaks are destroyed by storms, thought Dr Topolanek poetically, while grass just keeps on growing.

Topolanek knew something about that, about flora and survival – his parents had been intellectuals and dissidents, and some of that had rubbed off on him. And then came the moment of freedom, and, what do you know, freedom behaved like a capricious Santa Claus, bringing his parents nothing. More exactly, they had possessed nothing that could be restored to them, so they gained nothing. What bothered them most was that they had been bypassed even by moral acknowledgment. No one so much as mentioned the underground struggle they had waged for years. All that was left for them was to confront every day the results of the freedom for which they had sacrificed their youth. Their surroundings changed, while they themselves stayed the same: living in a small flat, on a small pension, with two or three remaining friends, losers like themselves. They had struggled and beaten Big Brother, and now they watched it on television every day. The Russians embarked softly on a new kind of occupation, not with tanks as before, but with crinkly banknotes. But in fact the Russians were unimportant in the whole story, money has no nationality, only people do, and generally speaking those are people who have nothing else. All that was left for Topolanek's parents was senile grumbling and they sank into that grumbling as into quicksand. They grumbled at their former co-fighters, dissidents, who had, allegedly, got everything, while they got nothing; they grumbled at their friends who had made it, at emigrés who had returned, at foreigners who were overrunning the Czech Republic, at Slovaks, for whom things were, allegedly, going quite well, at everyone and everything. The freedom for which they had fought turned out to be fatal. It destroyed them the way oxygen destroys buried frescoes when they are suddenly brought into the light.

In the first capitalist commotion, Topolanek realised that the easiest way to make money was out of human vanity, without harming a hair on anyone's head. His clients were satisfied, and his Wellness Centre brought in far more than the hotel itself. They were in competition; they sold the radiance of Central-European Europeanness, which, against the background of former communism, had looked more attractive than the West-European version. The medical institution, a communist leftover, stood on firm foundations: the prices of minor medical services were lower than in Western Europe, and those same services were here, on the spot and within reach.

* * *

Dr Topolanek was not one of your transitional cynics. He had his own revolutionary dream, only his revolution, unlike that of his parents, was played out in a more profitable, more beautiful and softer place – in the human body. Dr Topolanek was concerned with the theory and practice of longevity. That was why he had approached the table where the ancient lady was sitting in her wheelchair, beside her agreeable companion. Topolanek considered it his duty to greet them, to invite them to make use of the services of his Wellness Centre and to attend, if they wished, a series of his lectures on the theory and practice of longevity.

Beba listened to Dr Topolanek with great interest, while Pupa dozed.

'Why don't you dream up a way of dispatching old people comfortably, instead of tormenting them by dragging out their old age?' Pupa emerged from her slumber.

'Forgive me, I don't understand . . .'

'Crap! Prolonging old age indeed! It's youth you want to prolong, not old age!'

Dr Topolanek could not believe that these resolute words should have issued from such a tiny, frail body. But, just as he opened his mouth to say something in defence of his theory and practice, an elderly lady came up to the table with her companion.

Mr Shaker was pleased to meet Dr Topolanek. He promised that he would be sure to visit the Wellness Centre the following day and attend the lecture. Pupa and Beba learned that Kukla's dancing partner was called Mr Shaker, that he was American, that he was staying in the same hotel and, like them, had arrived that day. However, by then it was quite late, so Kukla suggested that they go their separate ways.

'Goodbye!' said Beba and Kukla to Dr Topolanek.

Beba shook hands with Mr Shaker.

'See you, die!' she said.

The American took a step backwards. There was an uncomfortable silence.

But here we should explain that Beba had some unusual traits and one of them was a tendency to linguistic lapses. So she did not understand why Kukla was apologising to the American, when she had simply bid him farewell with the usual: 'See you, bye!'

Kukla took hold of Pupa's wheelchair and set off towards the lift without a word.

'What's wrong?' asked Beba, scurrying to catch her up. 'Why are you angry with me? What have I done now?'

Pupa woke up for an instant and asked:

'Has that Dr Bullshit gone?'

She meant Dr Topolanek.

What about us? We carry on. We wish Pupa, Kukla and Beba pleasant dreams, while we hasten to reinforce our story's seams.

Day Two

I.

The girls were indifferent to the Wellness Centre's seductive offers. Pupa was like an ancient porcelain cup that had been shattered and stuck back together again repeatedly and now had to be stored in one place and 'used' as little as possible, in order to be kept whole. Unlike Pupa, Kukla was in an enviable physical state, and Beba could not understand her resistance. Kukla, who shared a suite with Pupa in order to be on hand instantly, should, heaven forbid, anything untoward occur, apologised that she could not leave Pupa. But they both encouraged Beba warmly. In any case it was high time Beba finally tried to make friends with her own body, with which she had lived far too long in mutual hostility. But, as life is lived slowly and tales are told swiftly, we're going to fast forward a bit here, and we'll slow things down later to relate the brief history of intolerance between Beba and her body.

As she ran her eye over the list of massages with picturesque names, Beba resolutely crossed out the 'Sweet Gallows', a massage in which, according to the brochure, the masseur hung from a rope, swinging to and fro and scampering lightly over the back of the client on the massage table *(As though I'm about to let some Tarzan use my back as a springboard!).* Beba eyed the Thai hot-rock massage, the 'Sweet Dreams' treatment – and in the end opted for the 'Suleiman the Magnificent Massage'. She chose 'Suleiman' because in the ambience of Czech spa culture and post-communist tourist recreation it sounded the most bizarre. The photograph in the brochure was appealing: it showed a naked female body lying covered in a cloud of soapy foam, like a sponge-finger in cream. Pupa and Kukla approved Beba's choice. They both also thought 'Suleiman' sounded exciting.

A woman in a white uniform led Beba into a not particularly large room lined with tiles of oriental design. In the centre was a stone massage table. The woman asked Beba to undress and lie face down on the table.

'I'll freeze on that stone.'

'Don't worry, it's a special table with built-in heating,' said the woman kindly.

Beba climbed up the little steps onto the table, but the idea of lying face down was simply out of the question. With an apologetic expression on her face, Beba pointed to her large breasts.

'Don't worry!' said the woman sympathetically and disappeared. She came back with a special aid in the form of a small hill, lined with soft sponge, with two large openings in the middle. Now Beba was able to lie face down, while her breasts slipped through the openings and were not pressed painfully against the table.

Beba hugged the little hill. The position was comfortable. Soft, agreeable, vaguely oriental music trickled out of invisible speakers. Lying on her little hill, Beba felt like a gigantic slug on a mushroom.

The woman in the white uniform reached under the table, drew out a nozzle like the ones used for washing cars and delivered a cloud of aromatic soapy foam to Beba's back.

'Don't worry, Pan Suleiman will be here in a moment,' she said, and went away.

Pan Suleiman? Covered in the warm foam, Beba waited for what was to come.

A young man came into the room. He was wearing a rainbow-coloured turban, and his upper body was bare, if you did not count his tiny, extremely short waistcoat. Instead of trousers, he was wearing wide silk oriental pants, gathered at the ankle. The young man had a virile body, nicely formed muscles in his arms, a flat stomach and satin skin. His face was oriental, or at least so it seemed to Beba, with a prominent nose, fine teeth and full lips, large brown eyes and a little moustache, which struck her as a trifle old-fashioned and therefore attractive.

'Hai, mai neym iz Suleiman. I em yor maser!' he announced huskily, in beginner's English.

'Hi! My name is Beba!' said Beba.

At that moment, Beba's head, poking out of the cloud of foam, happened to be right beside the young man's pants, that is to say the young man's pants were right beside Beba's head, and Beba came face to face with the part of them that was about eight inches below his navel. Beba's face flushed red. That below-the-navel part of the young man's pants was peaked like a tent. 'Whatever is the old woman thinking of . . .' Beba reproached herself silently.

'Reeleks!' said the young man, running his hands over

Beba's body. Beba tingled all over with pins and needles, as though she had been given a slight electric shock. Plunging his hands into the foam, the young man began to massage her body.

The space was filled with quiet. The oriental music from the invisible speakers was barely audible. Beba thought that the young man was not saying much because his English was bad.

'Mmmmmmm,' moaned Beba with pleasure.

At that moment the young man happened to brush against Beba's thigh with that below-the-navel part of his pants and now there was no longer any doubt – or so it seemed to Beba. 'Good lord! What now?' she thought.

'Reeleks!' said the young man.

Beba could not remember when this had last happened to her, that a young, attractive, half-naked male body had stood before her, in full battle readiness. Beba's face was lit up with a dreamy smile. She pressed herself into the little hill lined with soft sponge and licked the aromatic soapy foam. Her body was tingling with expectation. As he massaged her, the young man came round the table and now he was again standing beside Beba's head so as to reach the back of her neck. Through her half-closed eyes, she could see the young man's smooth stomach muscles. That tent-like part of his pants was still taut. 'Shame on you! You female Gustav von Aschenbach!' Beba silently chastised herself.

Perhaps it should be said at this point that Beba, who considered herself stupid – and those immediately around her did not exactly fall over themselves to disabuse her – often chose intellectual comparisons, without herself fully understanding why she did so, and when she did understand, she had no idea where that knowledge came from. No matter, we have to move on. Because in life we each have our cross to bear, while the tale makes obstacles disappear.

'Veer yu from?' asked the young man.

'Croatia,' Beba muttered reluctantly. The young man's appalling English acted on her dreamy mood like an icy shower.

The young man's hands stopped moving.

'One of us!' said the young man in his own language, gaping.

'A fellow countryman!' said Beba, gaping.

'Yes, of course, what did you think I was?'

'A Turk!' said Beba, although she had really thought that the young man was a Czech in disguise.

'Turk indeed! Not on your life! I'm Bosnian!'

'Where from?'

'Sarajevo!' the boy burst out, with the stress on the 'e', evidently imitating foreign war reporters.

'What are you doing here?'

'Massaging, of course. As you see.'

'I mean, how did you end up here?'

'I was a refugee.'

'When?'

'A bit before Dayton . . .'

'So how long have you been here? Twelve years?'

'About that . . .'

'So how old are you?'

'Twenty-nine . . . Well, am I going to massage you or what?'

'I don't know, I feel a bit awkward now. I could be your mother . . .' said Beba, trying to get off her little hill. The young man hurried to help her.

'Why should it be awkward? I've had all kinds of bodies through my hands, since I've been doing this.'

'But even so . . .' Beba mumbled, embarrassed.

Somehow Beba clambered up and sat on the table, but the aid remained stuck between her breasts. Seeing Beba in a cloud of soapy foam, with the aid, and her breasts sticking out of the openings like two watermelons, the young man began to roar with laughter. Realising what a ridiculous situation she was in, Beba too burst out laughing. Her laughter sent the foam flying in all directions.

'Oh, my! Now you look like a Yeti!' said the young man, in his Bosnian accent, trying to suppress his laughter.

The young man helped Beba remove the pillow and brought her a towelling robe. Wrapped in the white robe, Beba wiped the foam from her face with a towel.

'Fancy a fag?' said the young man in his characteristic Bosnian accent.

'Sorry?'

'Shall we have a smoke?'

'Here?'

'Well, why not?'

'Oh, all right.'

'I call the shots here, love. I'm untouchable! And what kind of a Suleiman would I be if there wasn't a smell of tobacco round me, eh?'

Beba and the young man lit their cigarettes.

'Eh, I haven't had a good laugh like that in years!' said the young man warmly.

'Eh, my Suleiman . . .' Beba sighed cheerfully.

'My name's not Suleiman!'

'What is it?'

'Mevludin.'

'Muslim?'

'Hardly, love! I'm like the former Yugoslavia, like a Bosnian stew, I'm a bit of everything. My dad was Bosnian and my mother half-Croatian, half-Slovene. And there were all sorts in the family: Montenegrins, Serbs, Macedonians, Czechs . . . One of my grandmas was Czech.'

'Eh, Mevludin . . .'

'You can call me Mevlo. I'm known as Pan Mevlička here. Suleiman is my professional name. It was the Czechs who dressed me in these pants, they say Turkish massage is great for tourists. They haven't a clue, it wasn't them who had the Turks breathing down their necks for five hundred years.'

'You strike me as something of an actor.'

'Sure, I'm an actor. But I'm trained as well, as a physiotherapist. People say I have golden hands.'

'It's true, you do,' said Beba solemnly.

'What good are they to me . . .?' sighed the young man, frowning.

'What do you mean, what good are they?'

'What's the use if I don't have anything else?'

Beba didn't know what to say. As far as she could judge, the young man was fine in every way. More than fine.

'This thing of mine stands up like a flagpole, but what's the use, love, when I'm cold as an icicle? It's as much use to me as a cripple's withered leg. You can do what you like with it, tap it as much as you like, it just echoes as though it was hollow.'

'Hang on, what are you talking about?'

'My willy, love, you must have noticed.'

'No,' lied Beba.

'It happened after the explosion. A Serbian shell exploded right beside me, fuck them all, and ever since then, it's been standing up like this. My mates all teased me, why, Mevlo, they said, you've profited from the war. Not only did you get away with your life, but you got a tool taut as a gun. Me, a war profiteer? A war cripple, that's what I am!'

The young man looked dejected. Out of the corner of her inquisitive eye, Beba observed that the relevant part of his anatomy was still just as perky.

'I'm sorry,' she said.

'I'm hiding here in these wide pants. I act the part of a Turk, and keep waiting to get better. I've asked some doctors. They've examined me; they laugh and say there's nothing wrong with your tool, Pan Mevlička. That's how it is in life, love, everyone wants to push and shove, but no one to cuddle and snuggle . . . I'd go back to my Bosnia, I felt really great in Bosnia, even during the war, but they'd all make fun of me there. Mevlo the Superman, Mevlo the Golden Tool, you know what our lot are like. That would really do my head in. I can't go back like this, I'm not a man, or a woman, I'm nothing . . . I've had some women after me here, actresses, all sorts, you know what working in a hotel means, you're on room-service twenty-four hours a day, everyone thinks they've got a right to pester you. Some people tried to talk me into making a porn film, some Germans, Russians, Yanks . . . I gave one of them a proper hammering, I broke all his bones, I got a bad reputation, but at least that means people leave me alone. Maybe it would be easier if I was gay, what do you think?'

'The main thing is that you have a good heart,' said Beba gently and at the time she sincerely believed what she said.

'I've got a heart as big as a mosque, but what's the good of that!'

Beba smiled.

'And I'm sure you've got brains as well.'

'Well, now, that's something I haven't got,' the young man

brightened up. 'I'm a fool, love. And once a fool, always a fool.'

'It'll all get sorted out somehow, I'm sure,' said Beba compassionately.

'Well, if only this boa constrictor down there gets sorted out. I'm sick of the sight of it! It's as though that Serbian shell put a spell on me, fuck it to hell!'

The young man looked at Beba and a gentle smile spread over his face.

'Hey, sorry for swearing like that.'

'It doesn't bother me.'

'And sorry for all the stuff I've offloaded on you. If only someone could unwitch me, the way the shell bewitched me. That's what I dream about every day, love . . .'

There was a knock on the door. The woman in the white coat came into the room.

'Pan Suleiman, there are two clients waiting for you outside.'

The young man helped Beba to get off the table and accompanied her to the door.

'How long are you staying?' he asked.

'I don't know.'

'Will you come again?'

'For sure.'

'Do. Don't forget. Call by after work, and we'll go for a beer . . . You'll find me easily, I live here in the hotel. Just ask for Pan Mevlička. Everyone knows me.'

'I'll do that!'

And then in eloquent Czech, he turned to the woman in the white coat:

'*Napište masaž teto damy na muj učet.*'*

* * *

* *'Put this lady's massage on my account.'*

And what about us? While life gets tangled in the human game, the tale hastens to reach its aim!

2.

Dr Topolanek was standing in front of a colour photograph projected onto a screen. It was the portrait of an old woman sitting in an armchair, dressed in a suit, a white shirt with its collar and cuffs emerging from the jacket sleeves, and with a brightly coloured pullover thrown youthfully over her shoulders instead of a shawl. The old woman had curly grey hair, blue eyes sunk deep into their sockets and lips that were completely sucked in. The most striking things about her were her hands, with their fat, misshapen fingers, exactly like claws.

'They could at least have put lace gloves on her,' thought Beba, looking at the photograph.

Dr Topolanek handed everyone in his audience a list of people over a hundred years old. Beside their names were their race, gender, nationality and the number of years they had achieved.

'You are wondering,' said Dr Topolanek, 'who the woman in this photograph is. If you take a look at the list, you'll find her name at the very top. Jeanne Calment has been proclaimed the oldest person in the world. Mrs Calment died at the age of one hundred and twenty-two years and sixty-four days! "I've only ever had one wrinkle and I'm sitting on it! *Je n'ai jamais eu qu'une ride et je suis assise dessus*," she announced to the press. Mrs Calment rode her bicycle until she was a hundred!'

Dr Topolanek continued: 'Sarah Knauss, Lucy Hannah, Marie-Louise Meilleur, María Capovilla, Tane Ikai, Elizabeth

Bolde, Carrie C. White, Kamato Hongo, Maggie Barnes, Christian Mortensen, Charlotte Hughes – I could go on. These are all the names of ordinary people, heroes of longevity. Or more accurately: heroines. Take a closer look at the list. Ninety of the people there are female, and ten male!'

Dr Topolanek looked significantly at his audience.

'We men are called the stronger sex. But has it ever occurred to anyone that we are apparently stronger than women simply because somewhere deep inside us we have a built-in biological alarm, the realisation that we will leave this world far earlier than our female companions? The future belongs to women: both metaphorically and literally. And once we are no longer needed for reproduction, which will happen very soon, the whole male gender will be definitively thrown onto the rubbish heap of history.'

Mr Shaker was the only man in the anyway sparse audience. Beside Beba, Kukla and Pupa, who was dozing in her wheelchair, and a few other old women, Mr Shaker was definitely in the minority. And when Topolanek explained in such a picturesque way that he was about to be thrown onto the rubbish heap of history, Mr Shaker got up and left the hall.

'If the gentleman affected by the near future of his gender had not left the hall, he would have heard the consoling fact that things are quite different in mythology. There it is exclusively the men who are long-lived, which makes sense since the creators of that mythology were men. So, Methuselah, the oldest being in the history of the human imagination, is credited with a life of nine hundred and sixty-nine years. Our forefather Adam lived nine hundred and thirty years, his son Seth nine hundred and twelve and Adam's grandson Enoch nine hundred and five years . . .

'We will not find any information about Eve and her age in the Bible,' said Dr Topolanek significantly. 'Eve was made from Adam's rib. That mythological fact gave Eve and the whole female gender a secondary status, which is why women from Eve on have on the whole been treated like – ribs.'

There was a giggle from the audience. It was Beba, who was amused by Topolanek's dramatic performance, and his observation about rib-women.

'Noah lived to be nine hundred and fifty, which is the first confirmation that genetics play a major role in longevity,' continued Topolanek. 'Noah was Methuselah's grandson, and probably the last long-lived man in the history of humanity. After the Great Flood, human life was no longer measured on a heavenly but a human scale, no longer by the gods, but by mortals. The Great Flood divided the two worlds once and for all: from then on the divine was to belong exclusively to the gods, while the human was left to human beings. In the human world, longevity was achieved only by important people: saints, prophets and rulers. Thus Abraham lived to be a hundred and sixty-five, and Moses a hundred and twenty, while ordinary mortals lived out their brief human lifetime . . .

'And the idea of longevity,' continued Dr Topolanek, 'was transferred into Utopias and legends about paradise on earth, about healing springs, fountains of youth, living and dead water, about the tree of life, about special races, tribes, islands and places usually situated in far-flung areas of the globe. There are legends about the "golden age" and people who lived young and carefree for many years, and when the time came for them to pass into the next world, they would simply fall asleep. There is a legend about the Egyptians who, according to Herod, were the most handsome and tallest people in the world, and who lived on average a hundred and fifty years, in great cheerfulness, happiness and friendship with their gods. The ancient Greeks believed that there were people in India with the heads of dogs, the Cynocephali, who lived some two hundred years, unlike the Pygmies, who, according to the ancient Greeks, lived barely eight years. There is a legend about long-lived people in Africa, called the Macrobi, and a legend about the Hyperboreans, who lived in the far north, and whose lifespan was a thousand years. One of the most entertaining legends was spread by the Greek Iambulus. He was borne by the sea onto an island in the middle of the Indian ocean, inhabited by beautiful people over six feet tall. These people spoke the language of birds and had the ability to talk to two people simultaneously, because their tongues were pronged like forks. They did not practise monogamy, but shared their women, they cared for their children communally and lived well and happily for a hundred and fifty years . . .'

'This doctor of ours has hardly started. By the time he reaches Bulgarian yoghurt, botox and anti-oxidants, we'll all be skeletons,' Beba whispered to Kukla.

At this moment Pupa also woke up.

'Are we staying or shall we call it a day?' she asked.

'Let's call it a day!' all three agreed.

Kukla apologised to Dr Topolanek, inventing a reason why they could not stay for his lecture.

'That's absolutely fine,' said Dr Topolanek. 'But you will come tomorrow, won't you?'

'But of course!' said Pupa, Beba and Kukla sweetly in unison.

As soon as they were outside, Pupa said resolutely: 'Not on your life!'

Here we have to say that Pupa, Beba and Kukla were unfair to Dr Topolanek, and it really was a shame that they left the hall: they missed hearing all kinds of interesting things, for instance Plato's idea of a happier world, which would come into being as soon as the whole universe started moving in the opposite direction. Instead of being born from sexual union, people would spring out of the earth like plants, straight into their adult form, and then they would steadily become younger, and in the end return to the earth. Life might not be longer than ours today, but it would certainly be happier, because it would be free of ageing and death. Pupa, Kukla and Beba missed hearing the interesting story of Medea who, in order to make Jason's father younger, carried out the first transfusion in the history of medicine. Medea slit the old man's throat with a sword, let the blood run out and then filled the old man's veins with her own concoction, consisting of many spices, plants, roots, seeds, deer's liver and vampire's entrails. The old man's white hair darkened, his wrinkles were smoothed out, his limbs twitched into life, his heart began to beat faster and the burden of some forty years slipped from his ancient body.

Yes, the three old girls had missed learning a lot more, but we too, unfortunately, must press on. While people yearn for what they cannot get, the tale hastens on, with no regret!

3.

The son of one of Pupa's patients told her that he had once taken his mother out in her wheelchair, to sit outside the house for a while and breathe in the fresh air. It was the end of November, and he had snuggled her up in blankets so that she wouldn't catch cold. He went back into the house for a moment to get his cigarettes, then forgot what he had gone for, so sat down and smoked a cigarette . . . In the meantime, it began to snow. And when it was getting dark and the old woman was covered in snow like a haystack, the son remembered to his horror that she was still outside. The old lady was so senile that she did not understand what was going on. She had enjoyed watching the snowflakes and had not even caught a cold.

Pupa often dreamed about how nice it would be if someone were to take her to Greenland and forget about her, lose her the way one loses an umbrella or gloves. She had reached a stage where she was unable to do anything any more. She was like a rubber plant, moved from place to place, carried out onto the balcony to have its fill of air, brought into the house so as not to freeze, regularly watered and dusted. How could a rubber plant make decisions or commit suicide?

All primitive cultures knew how to manage old age. The rules were simple: when old people were no longer capable of contributing to the community, they were left to die or they were helped to move into the next world. Like that Japanese film in which a son stuffs his mother into a basket and carries her to the top of a mountain to die. Even elephants are cleverer than people. When their time comes, they move away from the herd, go to their graveyard, lie down on the pile of elephant bones and wait to be transformed into bones themselves. While today hypocrites, appalled by the primitive nature of former customs, terrorise their old people without the slightest pang of conscience. They are not capable of killing them, or looking after them, or building proper institutions, or organising proper care for them. They leave them in dying rooms, in old people's homes or, if they have connections, they prolong their stay in geriatric wards in hospitals in the hope that the old people will turn up their toes before anyone notices that their stay there was unnecessary. In Dalmatia people treat their donkeys more tenderly than their old people. When their donkeys get old, they take them off in boats to uninhabited islands and leave them there to die. Pupa had once set foot on one of those donkey graveyards.

She who had helped so many babies into the world, cut who knows how many umbilical cords, who had so often heard a child's first cry, she at least deserved to have someone sensible *extinguish* her, the way lights were extinguished in houses so as not to waste electricity. That is what she kept trying to explain to Zorana, but Zorana had resolved to respect medical rules rather than show any empathy.

Zorana did not understand her. Zorana, who had spent her whole life accusing her, Pupa, of not understanding her. To start with Pupa had resisted and defended herself, then for a long time she had felt guilty, then finally she admitted that Zorana was right, at least in one respect: no, she really did not understand. She could not, for example, understand why Zorana agreed to live with a husband who was a notorious creep. Some eighteen years ago something in him had responded to the call of Croatian nationhood, and he had vehemently supported the government of the time, shouting from the rooftops that all Serbs should be slaughtered, and suggesting in passing that neither Muslims nor Jews had much more appeal. Overnight, the man had become an anti-communist and a devout Christian, hung Catholic crosses round Zorana's and the children's necks, and a portrait of one of his ancestors, an Ustasha cut-throat, on the wall, and, what do you know, his zeal paid off. He was appointed manager of a hospital, slipped deftly into some kind of financial embezzlement, and they – Zorana and he – became part of the newly minted Croatian elite, who Pupa had watched on television, while she still could, at New Year receptions hosted by the President of the state, at concerts and at exhibition openings. And the creep went so far as to accuse her, Pupa, 'and her commie friends' of being to blame for everything, being part of 'a bloody Yid conspiracy'. And when he said something ironic about Zorana's father, calling him his 'stupid Serbian father-in-law, who had the good fortune to be in his grave' – Pupa threw him out of her house. This was more than fifteen years ago, and the creep had never set foot there again.

Sometimes she felt that Zorana was punishing her, that she was keeping her alive so that she would at last 'open her eyes' and realise how much things had changed and that her life and values no longer had anything to do with the new reality. Meanwhile she, Pupa, was spared 'the great revelation' by ordinary old-age cataracts. She could no longer read or watch television; she felt as though she was living at the bottom of a well. And it was not only that the world around her had become invisible: she herself had become invisible. And only one sweet creature in this world was able to see her . . .

She sat in her wheelchair, imagining that snow was falling round her. She watched the fat flakes in the air and was surprised not to feel cold. The snowflakes kept on and on falling, and she imagined hibernating under a snowy blanket, until the spring, until it got warm and the snow melted. And she could already see a little heap of her own white bones, appearing out of the melting snow.

4.

Beba and her body lived in a state of mutual intolerance. She could not remember exactly when the first hostile incident had occurred. When she put on the first ten pounds? Perhaps her body had already taken control by then and nothing could prevent it from continuing to conspire against her. And she had imagined that taking ten pounds off would be a simple matter; she would start the campaign the very next Monday. Or was it when she came face to face with her image in a mirror and discovered to her great surprise that she was in a body that was not her own, and that it was a body that she would have to continue to bear as a punishment? Her breasts, which had been neither large nor small, had become big and then too big, and then so huge that things happened like this morning, when she was leaving her massage . . . A sullen Russian jerk with spiky hair, flanked by two similar jerks, had remarked: '*Ai, mamaaa, tytki kak u gipopotama!*'* confident that she would not understand Russian. But Beba had understood; insults don't need translation.

Her shoulders were deformed by the weight of her breasts, and had acquired deep clefts; her upper arms were as bulky as a dock-worker's and dragged her neck after them. She had always had a neck of a respectable length, and now all of a sudden it had completely disappeared. The upper part of her body had begun to swell, a thick layer of fat had built up round her waist, like an old-fashioned rubber ring, on the upper part of which big Beba was wedged, while the lower part of her body, from the waist down, had begun to taper off. Beba had also acquired a new behind, one of those sad, flat behinds that could belong to an old woman or an old man. The only thing that had not changed were her calves, and her forearms, from her elbows to her wrists. Beba's face, which until a few years before had been appealing, oh, it too was taking its revenge! Fatty sacks had formed round her eyes,

* '*Wow, mamma, tits like a hippopotamus!*'

and her once lively blue eyes had sunk dully into subcutaneous fat. Jowls had appeared on her lower jaw, dragging her mouth downwards. Her hair had grown thin, and her feet had become two sizes larger. Originally a thirty-eight, Beba now took size forty shoes. The only thing that she took a bit of care over were her toenails, and had she not gone regularly to a pedicurist, her feet would have turned into – hooves. And her teeth?! What had they done to her? She had spent her whole life in a dentist's chair, in the hope of preserving healthy teeth, but she had not succeeded. Yes, her body was exacting cruel revenge, nothing belonged to her any longer.

To be fair, she was still trying to improve the situation. She had begun to wear a 'minimiser' corset, which reduced the size of her bust, then large earrings, strikingly long scarves, big brooches, big rings, all with the intention of deflecting the critical observer's gaze from her bust to these details. She was rarely parted from her necklace, a ribbon with a large, round, flat stone with a hole in the middle hanging from it. And the strategy worked; most people would tend to fix their eyes on that stone. Yes, she was gradually turning into what she found repellent: one of those bleached old hags with cropped hair, their faces overcooked from tanning in cheap solariums, their hands mottled with swollen veins and aged freckles, decorated with strikingly cheap rings and thick rhinestone bracelets. And as for their ears, those sorrowful, elongated ears drawn down by wearing too many heavy earrings . . .

On the other hand, what is left for women when they stumble into old age? One rarely sees those few fortunate ones with *übermensch* genes, such as that crone of Hitler's, Leni Riefenstahl, who lived to be a hundred and one, and showed everyone the meaning of 'the triumph of the will'! She carried on climbing mountains and skiing until her hundredth year, at ninety she learned scuba-diving, travelled through Africa, photographed the poor Nubians and slept with them, sucking their blood – it kept her fit! And what other, worthy examples are there? Jessica Fletcher? Gloria Swanson in the film *Sunset Boulevard*? Bette Davis and Joan Crawford in *Whatever Happened to Baby Jane?* But most are left with the 'old-lady in good-health look'. These are desexualised old hags with short, masculine haircuts, dressed in light-coloured windcheaters and pants, not differentiated in any way from their male contemporaries, and noticed only when they are in a group. Yes, perhaps that is the way out: perhaps one should disguise oneself as a third sex, a sex without a sex, and live an unnoticed, parallel life: climbing mountains, walking with Nordic poles, travelling in organised tour groups of opera lovers, lovers of Alsatian wines, lovers of Mediterranean cheeses . . . Because what other variants are there in the typology of old women? Those dotty old creatures surrounded by cats, whose neighbours break into their house one day and find them dead, in a stench of cat pee? Those greedy old hags of unquenched sexual appetite who each spring visit geographical zones in which the local young men prostitute themselves for money? Those wealthy old women who submit hysterically to treatments – face-lifts, liposuction, hormone therapy, shit therapy if necessary – just to delay by a little the inexorable onset of age? Are spas not places which offer the illusion that they delay ageing? Yes, spas are the natural habitat of old hags, except that what used to be called a spa is now – same crap, different packaging – a wellness centre.

With the white towelling robe draped over her naked body, Beba looked at herself in the mirror. Everything was hanging out, everything was old, everything was distorted, and only that 'little bush' down below, sprinkled with grey, was still luxuriant. Come now, why this idiotic pride in the 'luxuriance' of her 'little bush'? As though it were treasure! As though the other parts of her body were police, accountants, porters – existing only in order to attend to the treasure! But what was this, why this sudden moralistic protest? Had not her 'little bush' been her 'treasure' for many years, had not everything revolved around sex for a major part of her life? When she was younger, she would have sold her soul to the devil for that, for the simple mechanism of the snap fastener. 'Men and women are like snap fasteners', one of her lovers had once said. She no longer recalled his name, but she remembered the sentence. At the time, she had found the image irresistibly comic. Click-clack! Click-clack! Now she felt it was inappropriate. But if she really thought about it, was there anything apart from that click-clack? Was everything else not mere fog to soften the truth and make the human snap-fastener mechanism appear less frighteningly simple? Of course, it was all a matter of perspective. Now it seemed to her that before, when she was younger, she used to think the opposite. She was prepared to die for that damned 'snap fastener'.

Beba plucked at her 'little bush' down below in a desultory fashion. But just as she was about to go into the bathroom, it seemed to her for an instant that instead of that dry, greyish 'bush', she saw sleek, black feathers. Beba went up to the mirror and – oh my! – now it seemed that a bird's eye was observing her from that place and, what is more, that gleaming, malicious bird's eye was winking at her. 'Shoo, you fiend!' muttered Beba, and, wrapping her robe tightly round her, made her way to the bathroom.

What about us? We carry on. While life can at times be hard and rough, the tale shies away from anything tough.

5.

Mr Shaker, who was lying on the stone massage table, pasted with soapy foam like a car in a carwash, saw it at once: the young man could have been Clooney's son. Olive skin, large, dark eyes, but a fuller and more finely shaped mouth, a natural smile, which did not, like Clooney's, end in a fan of lines at his temple. And he was far taller than Clooney! But why was he so stuck on Clooney? The young man was simply good-looking and would appeal to both women and men, regardless of their age, which, from a marketing perspective, was the key. And those wide oriental pants, imposingly taut in the right place, hinted that the rumours of the young man's sexual prowess may have been well-founded.

'Hi, mai neym iz Suleiman. I em yor maser!' muttered the young man through his teeth.

'Hi! I'm Mr Shaker,' said the American warmly, offering the young man his hand, but he did not manage to shake it. The young man pinned him to the table with a deft movement of his arm.

'Reeleks!' said the young man.

The young man's dreadful English would not be a problem, thought Mr Shaker, he was bright, he'd learn the language . . . Mr Shaker squirmed nervously on the massage table. The foam was suffocating him, and he felt extremely uncomfortable in that whole soapy set-up.

'Where are you from?' he asked the young man.

'Sarajevo,' snapped the young man.

This information stimulated Mr Shaker's business imagination. The young man was Bosnian; that should be exploited! Because, for instance, Havel and the Czechs didn't mean anything any more to the average American. But Sarajevo still rang in the average American ear. Or more accurately, Mr Shaker hoped that it still rang.

'Listen,' Mr Shaker tried to lever himself up, but the young man glued him back to the table.

'Reeleks!' said the young man and began massaging the vertebrae of the American's neck.

At a certain moment the young man's attention lapsed and Mr Shaker flapped like a tuna and straightened up to a sitting position.

'Listen, young man, there's been a misunderstanding, I didn't come here for a massage, but to offer you a job.'

The young man listened to the middle-aged American in amazement. He was quite baffled. 'Could he be gay?' he wondered. All that he managed to grasp from the American's tirade were figures: tventi tausand, then fifti tausand, then hundrd tausand, then hundrd tventi tausand . . .

'What's he on about? I don't get a word of it,' grumbled the young man in Bosnian. 'Are you listening to me? He's not listening, why should he, Yanks never listen, they just press on with their own agenda. Leave me alone, I've already been called by the Viagra people . . . Oh, but you, you don't give up, you're like NATO! Why didn't you come when they were shelling Sarajevo, and when that bomb exploded near me, instead of coming to harass me now?'

'I have to find an interpreter! Yes, an interpreter,' said Mr Shaker resolutely. He leapt from the table and, almost slipping, ran out of the massage room.

'What a performance! What will these idiots think of next? . . . Hey, my Mevlo, what else have these hulks got in store for you?' sighed the young man.

* * *

What about us? We carry on. While life may beguile and tempt like a gift, the tale is decisive and above all swift!

6.

Kukla went down to the hotel computer for a moment, to check the Croatian newspapers on the Internet. She could have done this in her room, but she felt like stretching her legs. At home she amused herself every day leafing through local and foreign newspapers. The Croatian one she usually took was *The Morning News.* Its format was predictable: embezzlement, corruption, quarrels between political parties and their opponents, articles about the unjust conviction of 'Croatian heroes' by the Hague Tribunal, financial scandals involving people who had earned small fortunes through Croatian patriotism and the war. Kukla clicked on the cultural section and was surprised to see a fairly lengthy review of Bojan Kovač's new novel *Desert Rose.*

The novel Desert Rose *by Bojan Kovač will disappoint all those who think that it has any connection with Sting and Cheb Mami's 'Desert Rose', or with popular romances,* said the article. Kukla hadn't a clue who Sting and Cheb Mami were so for a moment their names sounded threatening, but the way the review went on cheered her. Desert Rose *is the greatest event on the Croatian literary scene for the last fifteen years, if not longer,* the review went on. *It is a book through which this prematurely deceased Croatian classic writer has earned the right to a second life and places himself at the very peak of Croatian literature. The novel of unusual structure, reminiscent of a rose, is rooted in the deposits of time, the biographies of ordinary people, reality and dreams, essayistic and fictional passages which treat events from the recent wartime past, from contemporary Croatian reality, and the time of the Second World War. A novel left as a legacy by a writer who lived in the shadows, far from the lights of the literary stage, is a great lesson for today's instant products of the literary-entertainment industry. This unusual book is like a solitary rose blooming in the desert of Croatian literature.*

The Evening News announced that a review of this '*first class work by Bojan Kovač*' would appear in the Sunday edition, while a weekly magazine advertised '*a masterpiece of Croatian literature on a par with Marquez's novel* One Hundred Years of Solitude.'

'Blah-blah-blah,' muttered Kukla and logged off. Passing through the hotel lobby, she caught sight of Beba and an elderly man in the hotel café. Beba waved to her, inviting her to join them. Kukla declined, as she had promised Pupa that she would take her out in her wheelchair for a spin through the town. A little fresh air before dinner would do them both good.

What about us? We carry on. While humans long for fame and glory, the tale just wants to complete the story.

7.

Arnoš Kozeny adored the Grand Hotel. In fact, for him it was not a hotel, but a metaphor for human interaction with other people. The hotel stood in its place, everything else changed: the times, fashion, political régimes, people. The hotel rooms were ears through which a thousand and one human stories had passed. And not one was complete: they were just the exciting sounds of human lives. As he sat in the hotel lobby, Arnoš Kozeny would for a moment close his eyes and listen in. He would go back to his childhood and the moment when he had turned the knob on the radio for the first time and tuned in to the din of the world: noises, tones, sounds . . . And when he opened his eyes, it seemed to him that he was holding an invisible television remote in his hand. For the most part there was no volume and Arnoš Kozeny would fix his gaze on a scene: two people at the reception desk talking about something, opposite him a tubby man reading a newspaper and sipping cognac, a young couple in the restaurant, whose outlines flashed in the glass, hotel employees scurrying outside to meet some important person, the important person coming into the hotel and going to the desk without looking round. Arnoš would zoom in on a gesture, a movement, a detail, a shadow, someone's hand, someone's smile, a ray of sunlight that suddenly revealed the gleam of someone's false teeth, an ear lobe with an earring, a high heel, the line of a leg, a mouth, the rim of a coffee cup with a lipstick stain. Arnoš Kozeny read the signs, signals and gestures, just as in his youth he had read books, with great attention and great enjoyment. And that reading filled him with his old youthful excitement.

Now that he had retired, he could not imagine life without the hotel. Compared to the great satisfaction he felt when he was there, all other options for spending the modest remains of his lifespan seemed unappealing. At one point, Arnoš Kozeny had bought a small flat in the town. That flat, which had served in his younger days as a secret refuge, now became his permanent address. All the assets he had acquired in the course of his life as a lawyer had gone to his wife and children. Arnoš had married and divorced several times and this bachelor flat was the only thing he had left. But Arnoš Kozeny was not complaining; he no longer needed anything more.

Now he was sitting at a table with three ladies, with whom he had immediately felt at ease. He knew their country, admittedly from a time when it had been in one piece. He had often spent his family summers (not always only with his family) on the Adriatic coast. Enchanting Opatija was one of the significant topoi on the modest geographical map of Arnoš's otherwise rich amorous biography.

'Such a shame,' said Arnoš Kozeny. 'Do you know that I followed the events in your unhappy country for days on end? What a shame! Hey-ho, what can we do, the country fell apart, but maybe that's how it had to be. Maybe it was no good . . .'

'The country was good, perfectly good, it's just the people who are shit!' snapped Pupa.

'Which just goes to show that we never learn anything from history, as our forebears would have us believe,' said Arnoš Kozeny in a conciliatory tone.

'Indeed not!' said Beba, blushing. (Oh God, she thought, why must I always blurt out stupidities!?)

'Which might even be good, because otherwise there'd be no life!' said Arnoš Kozeny brightly.

'How do you mean?' asked Kukla.

'Simple. Many people don't have the best of experiences with their parents, but they still have children, don't they?'

'That's not a choice, it's our biological code. We exist only in order to procreate,' said Pupa, who had surfaced for a moment from her doze.

'And love? Where is love in all of this?' asked Beba.

'A complicated question,' said Arnoš.

'In the egg!' exclaimed Kukla.

'What egg?' Beba and Arnoš perked up.

'You know that Russian fairytale . . . Ivan falls in love with a girl, but to make her fall in love with him, he has to find out where her love is hidden. And he sets off over seven mountains and seven valleys, and reaches the ocean. There he finds an oak tree, in the oak there is a box, in the box a rabbit, in the rabbit a duck and in the duck an egg. It is in that egg that the girl's love is hidden. The girl has to eat the egg. And when she eats it, the flame of love for Ivan flares in her heart.'

'The message of that fairytale is that love does not exist. Because no one has the strength or time to make that journey,' said Beba.

'That's why people have sex,' said Arnoš.

'Sex is instant love,' said Beba.

'Sex is a quick lottery, a shortened version of the search for the egg,' said Arnoš.

'Oh, don't say that, I'm a child of the sexual revolution . . .' said Beba, biting her tongue.

'Just as well that revolution didn't catch you as a child,' said Kukla wickedly.

'Every revolution devours its children,' said Arnoš.

'I am the victim of the sexual revolution,' Beba corrected herself.

'You don't look like a victim to me,' said Arnoš agreeably.

'What do you know about victims and sacrifice? You're a man. Sacrifice is a strictly female accessory,' said Kukla.

'Perhaps. But since you've mentioned Russian fairytales, here is another Russian example. Pushkin's poem *Ruslan and*

Lyudmila. You know the story: brave Ruslan sets out in search of the beautiful Lyudmila, who has been snatched by the magician Chernomor. But actually I've always been intrigued by a secondary story in the poem,' said Arnoš Kozeny.

'Which one?' asked Beba, although she hadn't the remotest knowledge of either Pushkin or his poem.

'On his journey Ruslan comes to a cave,' Arnoš went on, 'and in the cave there is a wise old man. The old man tells Ruslan his life story. When he was a young shepherd, he fell in love with the beautiful Naina. But Naina rejected his love. In despair, the shepherd left his homeland, founded a fellowship, put out to sea and fought wars in foreign lands for ten years. And then, tormented by longing, he returned and brought Naina gifts: his bloodstained sword, coral, gold and pearls. But Naina rejected him again. Humiliated, the "parched seeker of love" as Pushkin calls him, decided that he would conquer Naina with spells and so he spent his time alone, learning the secret art of wizardry. And when he finally discovered the last "terrible secret of nature", there was a flash of lightning, a fearful gale began to rage, the earth shook beneath his feet – and before him appeared an old hunchbacked woman with sunken eyes and grey hair. "The embodiment of senile blight," says Pushkin. That was Naina,' said Arnoš, pausing significantly.

'And what happens next?' asked Kukla and Beba impatiently.

'Horrified, the old man bursts into tears and asks whether it is possible that it is her, and where has her beauty vanished, is it really possible that the heavens have changed her so terribly? And he asks how much time has passed since their last meeting. Naina replies:

"Just forty years"
The maiden's faithful tones responded;
"My age is seventy today.
Such is the way of things," she quavered,
"In swarms the years have flown away.
My spring, or yours, will not be savoured
Afresh – we both are old and grey.
But friend, is life without allure
Because inconstant youth forsook it?
My hair is white now, to be sure,
Perhaps I am a little crooked,
A trifle slower to entice,
Not quite as lively, quite as nice;
But then (she mouthed) let me confess:
I have become a sorceress!" '*

Arnoš recited in Russian with a strong Czech accent. Perhaps it was because of the accent that Kukla and Beba had no problem understanding him.

'And what happens next?' they asked.

'Next? Um . . .' said Arnoš, 'next we have an interesting and psychologically most satisfying situation. Naina says that she has only now realised that "her heart was fated for tender passion" and invites him into her embrace. However, the old man is profoundly revolted by the physical appearance of his "wizened idol":

My wizened idol warmed to me
With passion, started to importune,
On withered lips a ghastly smile,
In churchyard tones she would beguile,
Avowals, hoarsely wheezed, she offered . . .

* *Ruslan and Ludmila,* transl. by Jenni Blackwood (www.sunbirds.com/lacquer/readings/1015)

'The old man refuses to acknowledge reality,' continued Arnoš. 'He flees from Naina and resolves that he would prefer to live as a hermit. What is more he accuses Naina in front of Ruslan of transmuting "thwarted love's belated flame to ire".'

Arnoš puffed impressively on his cigar.

'Why yes, the old witch!' said Pupa, rousing herself from her slumber.

They all laughed, apart from Beba . . .

'Naina apologises for her ugliness. But the old man does not see himself as either ugly or old!' said Beba.

'What misogyny!' said Kukla. It seemed that she too had taken Naina's story to heart.

'I agree,' said Arnoš.

'Women are more compassionate than men in every way!'

'You're right,' said Arnoš.

'What a moron!' said Beba bitterly, still mulling over the character of the wise old man.

'What else could she do but become a witch!' said Kukla, who was still protesting in Naina's name.

'Our whole life is a search for love, which you, Kukla, based on the example of a Russian fairytale, have identified as – an egg,' concluded Arnoš. 'Our search is frustrated by numerous snares that lie in wait for us on our journey. One of the most dangerous snares is time. We need only be one second late and we will have lost our chance of happiness.'

'That right moment is called death, my dear Arnoš, an orgasm from which we no longer awaken. Because the logic of love is to end in death. And as none of us accepts that option, we all bear the consequences. Old age is simply one of them,' said Beba.

They were all astonished by Beba's eloquence.

'All that is left us is the art of dignified ageing,' said Arnoš.

'Dignified ageing is crap!' announced Pupa, putting an end to the discussion.

It was already quite late and the little group decided to disperse. Arnoš Kozeny saw the ladies to the lift, kissed each one's hand and, before the lift door closed, he blew them a kiss for good measure.

In the lift Beba said:

On obol'stil menya, neschastny!
Ja otdalas' lyubvy strastnoy . . .
Izmennik! Izverg! O pozor!
*No trepeshchi, devichiy vor!**

Kukla and Pupa listened in surprise.

'You know Russian?' asked Kukla.

'No. Why do you ask?' asked Beba.

Beba had quoted a stanza from Pushkin's *Ruslan and Lyudmila.* Aside from her occasional lapses, this was another of her quirks: she would from time to time blurt out something in languages she otherwise had no mastery of. These attacks occurred to Beba out of the blue, as in a dream, and so Kukla and Pupa did not wake her.

And what about us? We carry on. While in life we stop to greet a friend, the tale speeds to embrace its end.

* *'He flattered me, seducer fashion! / And I succumbed to reckless passion . . . Deceiver, profligate! Oh shame! / But tremble, heartless libertine!'*

8.

A girl was standing beside the town fountain. Her head was turned towards it and she was leaning all her weight on one hip. The young man could see her luminous complexion, pink ear, which seemed to him as fresh as a segment of orange, and a copper-coloured curl that had caught on her ear like an unusual earring. The girl was wearing a simple little floral sleeveless dress. The dress revealed the girl's plump shoulders sprinkled with rusty freckles, her broad hips and the chubby calves of her legs.

All around, in the tops of the old plane trees, whose leaves had acquired a pale grey-green colour in the bright sun, birds were chirping. The young man walked round the fountain and stopped opposite the girl. Now he could see her face. She had a regular, full little face, almost child-like, with bright green eyes, quite wide set. The neckline of her dress gave the young man a glimpse of her ample bosom and the freckles, like an army of pale orange ants, disappearing into the shadowy dip between her breasts. The girl was licking ice cream out of a crunchy cornet. She ran the tip of her tongue round its edge, as though she were making a little pit, tidily licked up the drips of ice cream that were sliding down the outside of the cornet, pushed the foamy mass towards the top with her tongue, and then, with her full, pink lips, she sucked up the peak. The girl was licking her ice cream so carefully and with such concentration that she might have been solving a difficult mathematical problem. From time to time she took her right foot out of her clog and scratched her left ankle. And then she tucked her right foot back into its clog, took out her left foot and used it to scratch her right ankle. All this time, she did not for a moment lose her focus on the ice cream. As though the ice cream was a tiny wild animal she had caught. She played with the ice cream like a cat with a mouse.

The air was glowing with the setting sun, birds rustled in the surrounding treetops, paled by the sunlight, the water in the fountain sputtered in short comic spurts. Everything seemed to have been numbed by the heat which was slowly settling into the ground; there was not a breath of wind, the leaves of the plane trees hung as though turned to stone. But nevertheless, the young man seemed to feel a vague current of air. At a certain moment the girl raised her eyes and looked straight at him. Her slanted, light-green eyes met the young man's. A little blob of ice cream was melting on the girl's lip. The young man felt a sudden longing to be that little blob.

Day Three

I.

Kukla was nearly six foot three, slim, with an exceptionally straight back and an easy gait, all of which made her seem younger than she was. What stood out on her regularly featured face were her strong cheekbones, slanting eyes of indeterminate colour, usually called 'almond', and her shy smile. That smile was also unusual for her age. She had broad, bony shoulders, as though she had done a lot of swimming in her youth, although she despised every sport apart from walking. Her 'uniform' contributed to the refinement of her appearance. That was what Kukla called her simple outfit: a dark straight skirt, light silk blouse, usually white, and a fine woollen cardigan, usually grey. She always wore a small necklace of real pearls. Her hair was dark, well streaked with grey, secured at her nape with an ordinary little comb. The only unharmonious parts of her body were her feet. She wore men's size shoes, forty-four. When she was younger it had been hard to find anything in her size, so she had simply begun to buy men's. But she successfully disguised her handicap through the lightness of her stride. Unlike many of her contemporaries, Kukla was not afraid of death. However, she had the feeling that she would live a long time: all the women in her family had been centenarians. And there was something else: those who came near her were inclined to think they could feel a vague current of air, something like a gentle breeze.

'Please explain to him,' Mr Shaker was saying, 'that I am prepared to take on all the financial obligations, that is travel costs, hotel accommodation while he is in Los Angeles and a rapid course of English. Dr Topolanek assures me that he would give Mr Mevličko unpaid leave, if, that is, the gentleman decided not to remain in America.'

Kukla translated all of that for Mevludin.

'Ask him what he wants me there for,' said Mevlo.

Mr Shaker began by explaining at length the purpose and importance of his industry of potions and powders, and then said that Mr Mevličko's job would be to advertise his products. He, Mr Shaker, had a whole team of experts in marketing. They would see to it that Mr Mevličko became a great star of promotional videos, posters, websites and other advertising material.

'Tell him I won't have my picture taken, not at any price,' said Mevlo, but Kukla interrupted him.

'And what would Mr Mevličko's salary be?' she asked Mr Shaker.

'A thousand dollars for an hour of filming,' said Mr Shaker, and added: 'that's a very high rate, I hope you realise.'

Kukla translated all that for Mevludin.

'Tell him to forget it,' said Mevlo.

'Three thousand!' said Mr Shaker.

'I'm not interested, what good are dollars to me? Just look at it, it's stuck and it won't go down,' said Mevlo, directing his message to no one in particular.

'Five thousand.'

'Are you deaf or do you just need your ears cleaned!? I'm not interested; that's all there is to it!'

Now Mevlo was addressing Mr Shaker, who was looking to Kukla for help. Kukla, of course, did not translate what Mevludin had said.

'He says he's a bit nervous about the offer,' she said.

'Seven thousand!' said Mr Shaker, adding, almost angrily: 'tell Mr Mevličko that one job leads to another. I have connections in Hollywood. I'm sure that a man of his appearance will easily make a career in film as well.'

'A career! In your dreams! I won't have my picture taken, I won't have folk in Bosnia seeing me like this and taking the piss,' Mevlo dug his heels in.

'Ten thousand!' said Mr Shaker angrily. 'For God's sake, not even Naomi gets more!'

'Naomi who?' asked Mevlo.

'Naomi Campbell, the model,' explained Kukla.

'Oh yeah, Naomi wouldn't get out of bed for less than twenty thousand,' said Mevludin impassively.

'How the hell do you know, if I may ask?' said Mr Shaker, who was quite furious by now.

'Whoopi told me.'

'Whoopi who?' asked Kukla.

'Whoopi Goldberg.'

It sounded unlikely, but in fact the name of Whoopi Goldberg had caught Mr Shaker's eye when he was examining the list of famous guests at the Grand Hotel.

At that moment a young girl in a flowery summer dress, with clogs on her bare feet, approached the table. She had a pale round face scattered with light orange freckles and thick copper-coloured hair, which sprang round her neck in lively curls. Holding an ice cream cone in her hand, the girl sat down and, parting her legs a little, began rubbing her right ankle with her left foot.

'My daughter Rosie,' said Mr Shaker testily. His face showed the inner fleet of his hopes slowly sinking.

The girl, staring more at the ice cream dripping down the sides of her cornet than at those present, shifted the cone from her right to her left hand and offered her right hand to Kukla, then to Mevludin. A drop of ice cream slipped out of the cornet and fell onto Mevludin's hand. Mevlo gave a start, gazing at the little drop like a gold coin that had fallen from the heavens straight onto his hand, and then he licked it attentively and smiled.

'Tell him,' he said quietly, 'that I accept . . .'

And then he came right up to Mr Shaker's face and repeated: 'I em in!'

Mr Shaker hastily took out his chequebook, wrote a cheque for a considerable advance and handed it to Mevludin. Admittedly, he did this more to impress Kukla than the stubborn young Bosnian.

And what about us? We push on. Life may linger, lurking for the attack, but the tale moves on, without looking back.

2.

After a cosmetic treatment for her face, Beba decided to try something else from the rich array on offer. The promotional brochure offered bathing in hay made from meadow grasses, bathing in a mash made from oat flakes (That must be quite disgusting, thought Beba), bathing in seaweed, then various kinds of massage . . . Beba finally chose 'Sweet Dreams' – a special treatment, consisting of being steeped in a bath of warm chocolate followed by a massage. First, of course, she asked Pupa whether she could put it all on the room bill. Pupa had no objection, on the contrary:

'Just you go and have a good soak. When you come out you'll be like a chocolate truffle!' she said.

A young woman in a white hospital gown led Beba into a space that looked like a film set. It was a small room with an antique copper bath in the middle. The walls were covered in greenish silk wallpaper, on one wall there was a reproduction of Renoir's *Woman with Parrot*, and under it, on an old-fashioned flower stand, there was a fern. How kitschy, thought Beba. What had induced the designer to connect the greenish wallpaper, the bath and its function – with the reproduction on the wall?

Here one might add that the presence of fine art in all the rooms was one of the most striking features of the Wellness Centre. It was Dr Topolanek's doing. He considered that agreeable and unobtrusive education delayed the process of ageing just as moderate exercise did, so he had arranged for the Wellness Centre to be literally 'clothed' in reproductions of well-known paintings, mostly classic art. For instance, at the entrance to the Centre he had placed a reproduction of Lucas Cranach the Elder's *Fountain of Youth* – a painting that was the symbolic representation of the fruits of Topolanek's professional efforts.

Now Beba was lying back in the tub filled with warm chocolate. A loudspeaker was emitting that irritating new age music that is supposed to induce relaxation. Beba's gaze was focused on the reproduction on the wall. And, hey, the living fern on the stand seemed to be imitating the fern on the right of

Renoir's painting. Beba also felt that the wallpaper echoed the blue-green tone of the walls in the picture. And, thanks to the fertile imagination of the hotel designer, the golden cage in Renoir's painting was given form in reality in – the copper bath! The young woman in the sumptuous black dress, with a long red bow behind, had dark hair and a homely, girlish face. The woman was holding a parakeet on the finger of her right hand, while she fed it with her left. The whole of the woman's body was bent towards the parakeet, and she appeared to Beba to be completely spellbound by the bird.

As she looked at the picture, Beba suddenly recalled a word from her childhood that she had hated more than any other: *fanny!* Little boys had *peckers,* and girls had *fannies.* That would have been all right if Beba had not once stayed as a little girl in the country with a relative who kept fan-tailed chickens in her garden. The fans of their tails had somehow got caught up in Beba's child's mind with that hated word *fanny* and their persistent pecking with the idea of little boys' *peckers.* One day her relative wrung the neck of one of her *fantails* and they had chicken soup and meat for lunch. *Peckers* and *fannies* . . . Why hadn't all this occurred to her before? That all this sexual business is connected in the male imagination with – ornithology! In the history of the male sexual imagination the role of women was constantly to pull onto themselves, and then push off, birds of all shapes and sizes. From Zeus who forced himself on Leda in the form of a swan onwards. And, in the seventeenth, eighteenth and nineteenth centuries, the swan – that unambiguous companion of women – transformed itself into a more discreet and smaller companion, a parrot!

A slide show now got underway in Beba's head, fuddled by the sweet aroma of chocolate. That famous painting by Tiepolo of a half-naked woman with a parrot . . . The beauty has astonishing skin, which seems to be made of milk, mother-of-pearl and blood. The young woman is wearing a pearl necklace. It is placed high on her neck, right under her jaw bone, so that it looks more like an expensive bridle than a necklace. She has a rose in her hair. Her dress has slipped off one of her shoulders, exposing her breast. The young woman is holding a copper-red parrot in her arms. Large as a hen, the parrot has gripped the woman's hand with its claws, while its sharp beak has come dangerously close to her nipple with its mother-of-pearl sheen.

Then that Dutchman, Quirijn van Brekelenkam, from the seventeenth century. In the background of his painting a young lute-player is sitting at a table, completely absorbed in his playing, while in front of him, in the foreground, a young woman is sitting, with a parrot on her finger. She sits straight as a rod, her left hand lies relaxed in her lap, which is covered with a long white apron, while on her right hand there is – a parrot. The parrot has gripped the woman's finger with its claws and is looking at her, while the woman gazes at the lute-player. On the floor, beside the woman's feet, there is a jug. It is unclear whether the woman is mesmerised by the parrot on her finger, the music she is hearing or its young performer.

And then Courbet. That painting of Courbet's of a lascivious, naked woman's body on a crumpled bed. The woman's legs are partly open, her luxuriant brown hair is spread sumptuously over the bed. The woman is relaxed, exhausted, as though her passionate lover has just left the room. In the background is a stand for a parrot, with a water dish on the top and crossbars at the sides. While the woman is lying there, the parrot has left its observation post – its perch – and landed on its owner's hand. The parrot has spread both its wings wide, as though it were in a state of total ecstasy. And again, a riddle. Perhaps there was no lover, perhaps the parrot is that perfect lover, a flying penis, the tool of the male painter's imagination, which has satisfied the woman and is now spreading its wings in satisfaction.

In Delacroix's painting, a naked beauty is sitting on a sofa, although it looks as though she is sitting on open bales of silk. One would not notice the parrot had the beauty not let her hand dangle, followed by her sleepy face with its half-closed eyes, towards the foot of the sofa, towards a parrot crouching in the dark shadows. The naked woman is evidently playing with the parrot and seems to be about to stroke the feathery crest on its head. And again, it is not clear: is the parrot a toy, a living vibrator, a substitute for a lover or is it the lover himself? Or could it be that the woman is playing with her own genitals, embodied in – a parrot.

Then Manet's *Woman with Parrot*, painted in the same year as the Courbet! Olympia is dressed from head to foot in a peach-coloured habit almost as ascetic as a nun's. On a tall perch is her companion, a grey parrot. The parrot has bowed its head, it seems despondent. Olympia is holding a small bunch of flowers, which she has moved a little away from her nose, or perhaps she is just about to smell them. Her gaze is directed straight at the observer. At the bottom of the parrot's perch lies a large, half-peeled orange – the one licentious detail in the painting. Who is the parrot in the picture? The woman's grey dejected genitals or her unsatisfied companion, whose rival is that ecstatic parrot in Courbet's painting? Or are the two painters – Manet and Courbet – sending each other secret messages about the length of their respective penises?

And then Marcel Duchamp, who paints a woman in stockings – as Courbet does in one of his paintings! The woman's legs are parted, but, unlike Courbet, Duchamp places his parrot unambiguously at the very entrance to the woman's vagina.

Frida Kahlo also uses parrots as a decorative detail! In one picture she puts a green parrot on her shoulder, like a pirate; in another she paints herself with four parrots, one on each shoulder and two in her lap. And she is holding a cigarette at the same time.

And René Magritte? His painting is the portrait of a young woman with loose copper-red hair. The woman has a dress with a collar made of rich white lace. There is lace also at the end of her long sleeves, like gloves. The woman is standing beside a tree in which birds are perched. One bird with a luxuriant coppery crest and a long slender beak is particularly striking. The woman has picked up another bird with both hands and is eating it as though it were a ripe fig. We can see the bird's dark red insides, its heart and liver, but surprisingly there isn't a drop of blood! The lace collar and cuffs remain astonishingly white. The woman has a lascivious look on her face and the painting has the unambiguous title *Pleasure*.

Women and their enchantment with birds . . . Apart from bisexual Frida Kahlo, a woman who appears in the picture as a man with a moustache and a cigarette in her hand, the authors of this implicit eroto-ornithological debauchery are all men. And, were the women to be asked, their choice of favourite bird would certainly not be a parrot but – Superman! Is it a bird? Is it a plane . . . ?

Beba was feeling somewhat faint from the slide show in her head and the aroma of the chocolate. So she got out of the bath and went to look for the shower. In passing she caught sight of her reflection in a mirror and gave a start. She looked like a gigantic chocolate owl.

'What about your massage, madam?' the woman in the white coat called after her.

'We'll leave the massage for another time,' said Beba, getting into the shower. Instead of raising her spirits, the bath had had quite the opposite effect. Beba felt as though she had emerged from a whirlpool which had drained all her energy.

Hurrying to tell Pupa what that stupid 'truffle' was like, Beba nearly collided with Mr Shaker. Catching sight of an unappealing woman, spreading a disagreeable sweet smell round her, Mr Shaker scowled.

'Have a nice lay,' said Beba pleasantly.

Mr Shaker said nothing, just rolled his eyes and hurried on his way.

Heavens, what an unpleasant guy! thought Beba. Because Beba, knowing that Mr Shaker and Kukla were going to play golf that afternoon, had simply wanted to wish him a nice day.

What about us? We hasten on. While life mocks us, often seeming absurd, the tale flies on through the air – like a bird!

3.

Yes, man has developed a terrific appetite for life. Since it became likely that no other life awaits him in the skies, man has decided to stay where he is for as long as possible, or in other words to chew the chewing gum of his life as lengthily as possible and amuse himself the while by blowing little bubbles. If the statistics are to be believed, the difference is truly impressive: at the beginning of the twentieth century the average lifespan was around forty-five years, in the middle of the century it had increased to sixty-six, while today, at the very beginning of the twenty-first century, the average age achieved is the fine figure of seventy-six. In the course of a mere hundred years, people have extended their life expectancy by nearly fifty per cent. Admittedly, this statistical boom has occurred in the more peaceful and richer parts of the world. Because in Africa people still die like flies, probably more quickly and effectively than ever before.

Dr Topolanek was sitting alone in the hotel lecture hall, thinking. A photograph of Joseph Vissarionovich Stalin was flickering on the projection screen. Today Dr Topolanek wanted to say something about the communist idea of longevity, but he had no one to say it to. The lecture hall was empty.

Yes, the communists were skilled. The new communist man had to live long, collectively and industriously, by the strength of his own will, rather than genetic inheritance. For inheritance, even genetic, was not acknowledged. Illness, depression, suicide, physical weakness – that had all been dreamed up by the bourgeoisie, defeatists and deserters from the frontline of life. Belief in a better, hybrid tomorrow permeated all the pores of communist society. Michurin and Lysenko were concerned that what the communist masses might one day eat should be as good and abundant as possible. Later everyone laughed at them. And today everyone devours those gigantic smelly strawberries blown up with gas, but strangely no one laughs any more, nor does anyone ask any questions. Not to mention those white Dutch aubergines, which seem to have grown up in Michurin's garden! The famous Caucasian Nikolai Chapkovsky lived under communism and died at a hundred and forty-six. Centenarians sprang up in those days like mushrooms after rain, mainly in the Caucasus, their longevity confirming the idea that their countryman, Stalin, would live if not long, then forever. He did not live especially long, or forever. Alexander Bogomolets, the author of *Extending Life*, invented the famous serum named after him. The serum combined with regular transfusions was his recipe for rejuvenation. Everyone laughed at him too, later: it was all part of the megalomaniac communist delusion. Today clinics offering complete blood transfusions are springing up everywhere, but only those with deep pockets can indulge themselves in a change of blood. Serums too, somewhat more advanced, are on the daily menu of those who can afford them. Gerovital, a cream made from the placenta, could only have been invented under communism, when abortion was the most common means of contraception, and here the Romanian Ana Aslan should be acknowledged . . . Whether the cream really was made from placenta or not no one knows, but Charles de Gaulle, Pablo Picasso, Konrad Adenauer, Salvador Dali, Charlie Chaplin, John F. Kennedy, Omar Sharif and many others made a pilgrimage to Ana Aslan, and communism did not bother them in the slightest. Mankind has always been obsessed by death, immortality and longevity.

Battles have always been waged on that territory, and they are still being waged today, that is where things were always liveliest. One vast army of people – in medicine, pharmaceuticals, cosmetics – serves another army which has taken on the task of living as long as possible and looking as good as possible. They are both firmly connected, like organ donors and their recipients.

There was nothing wrong with Topolanek's 'theory'. The theory, as always, was frustrated by brazen, disobedient and unpredictable life. In addition to the insultingly empty hall, that 'life' now appeared in the doorway in the shape of an unexpected visitor, a tall, agitated old woman, who demanded, more with gestures than words, that Topolanek accompany her urgently to the golf course! Dr Topolanek turned off the projector, grabbed his doctor's bag, which he kept with him at all times, and set off after his flustered visitor.

And what about us? We shall hurry after them. While in life one may often demur and dither, the tale hurries on – we all know whither!

4.

As they made their way to the golf course, Mr Shaker had given Kukla a vivacious account of the meaning of his existence. He was like the drawer in an old-fashioned lady's dressing table, which emits clouds of powder when opened. Mr Shaker choked on his own words. Kukla felt sorry for him, as she did for everyone who saw their work as the only reason for their existence. She found this human machine producing words, movements and gestures amusing, until the moment when the conversation snagged on Rosie, Mr Shaker's daughter.

'Rosie is, unfortunately, incompatible.'

'How do you mean, incompatible?' asked Kukla.

'It is our duty to make ourselves into better and more perfect beings than God made us, is it not?' said Mr Shaker.

'I can't see what your daughter's lacking,' said Kukla.

'There's nothing lacking, unfortunately; on the contrary, there's altogether too much of her.'

'That's just a bit of puppy fat, youthful sturdiness.'

'Sturdiness could be the source of her future unhappiness. Unfortunately, we live in a time when even a little excess weight determines our life's course.'

It could not be said that Mr Shaker was not concerned about his daughter. But his concern was for the product, and, in Mr Shaker's eyes, although of course he would never have admitted it, Rosie was a kind of reject.

'What about your wife?'

'My late wife . . . She was perfect. Like you,' said Mr Shaker.

She was perfect until she broke down. Of course Mr Shaker did not use the expression 'broke down', he said 'fell ill', but he meant 'broke down'. The mechanism stopped working properly, and Mr Shaker had done everything in his power to get the mechanism mended. But, unfortunately, there was nothing to be done.

'Strange,' said Mr Shaker.

'What's strange?'

'Well . . . When I'm with you I feel as though I were beside a fan,' he said.

Mr Shaker became exceptionally animated when they reached the golf course, evidently because the role of teacher appealed to his vanity. Kukla didn't have a clue about golf and Mr Shaker endeavoured to explain the rules. What had always seemed to her pointless – strolling around a grassy expanse with a stick in one's hand and knocking a little ball into a hole – did after all have some point: being outside in the fresh air.

They were an incompatible couple. The tall, bony woman with large feet and a golf club in her hand strode across the sun-drenched grassy expanse like a kind of female knight. Her partner, a short, breathless man, rushed energetically over the grass like a lawn mower. Kukla watched him: he was saying something, waving his club, gesticulating, demonstrating movements, making her imitate them, waving his arms and hitting the ball energetically with his club.

While Mr Shaker was preoccupied with the idea that all incompatible bodies must be transformed into compatible ones, Kukla had always thought that there was too much noise in this world and amused herself imagining how nice it would be to be able to control that noise, to turn off talkative people like radios, to put silencers on sharp sounds, to turn down the shrill din of ambulance sirens and amplify birdsong. As she waited for the green light at crossings, she imagined stopping the traffic completely for a moment and serenely crossing the road. These were childish imaginings, *daydreams,* her mental exit lights. Sometimes those daydreams were so strong that they seemed quite real. When she was a little girl, the sheer force of her intentions had sometimes made things happen: something would shift, scrape, collapse, fall onto the floor. With time she learned to walk cautiously through the world, as though on eggshells, quiet and silent as a shadow, accompanied by currents of air whose origin she could never fathom.

* * *

Come on, gesticulated Mr Shaker, hit the ball. Kukla thought he was far further away than he really was. For God's sake, come on, the man on the green horizon waved his arms, and Kukla finally swung her club, hit the ball, the ball spun in the air and took flight. The man jumped up and down with delight, bravo, a perfect shot, he made a fist with his thumb pointing up and waved it at Kukla, congratulating her. The little ball hovered for a moment in the air, or at least so it seemed to Kukla, and then with all its force it plummeted and lodged in the man's wide-open mouth. The man dropped to the ground, as though felled.

When Kukla reached him, Mr Shaker was lying motionless on the grass. The little ball had trickled out of his mouth like saliva and was now calmly settled by his head, like a miniature gravestone. Mr Shaker's death had been crouching inside an innocent golf ball.

Kukla rushed to the hotel to find Dr Topolanek. They went back together to where Mr Shaker's body was lying. It seemed to Kukla that in the meantime his body had shrunk. In the course of those ten minutes it had taken her to go and fetch Dr Topolanek, Mr Shaker's body had condensed and, if it was true that there was a soul which parted from the body after death, then Mr Shaker's soul weighed as much as ten golf balls.

'Heart attack!' announced Dr Topolanek.

And then, smoothing his hair, ruffled by an invisible fan, he turned to Kukla and added:

'I do hope that this disagreeable incident will not have put you off golf forever. Golf is an exceptionally fine sport.'

* * *

And what about us? We carry on without hesitation. While we may all be targeted by a drawn bow, the tale speeds like Hermes and is never slow.

5.

While everything in a story goes quickly and easily, it's not usually like that in real life. This time, however, real life surpassed the story in speed and ease. Here's what happened. Before she set off on this trip, Beba had taken out her pension and meagre savings, and changed it all into euros. The bank gave her a five-hundred-euro note and some change. Beba took the note without thinking. How could she possibly have known all the problems that she would encounter in an EU country, when she tried to change that cursed euro note?

At the hotel reception they told her to try the hotel bureau de change, while the hotel bureau de change directed her to the local banks. She tried two or three banks, and they all gave her the same answer: why didn't she change the note at a branch of her own bank?

'But my bank's in Zagreb!'

'So why didn't you change it in Zagreb?'

'That's where they gave it to me.'

'Why don't you use a credit card?'

'I haven't got one.'

'You're travelling abroad and you don't have a credit card!'

'Not everyone has a credit card, you know!'

'It's just as well you told us, because otherwise we might have changed that note, but only if you had shown us a credit card.'

'I've got a passport.'

'A passport isn't a relevant document any more. You know how it is with passports, anyone can get an illegal one nowadays for just a few hundred euros!'

'So, what should I do?'

'Try an exchange bureau.'

Beba tried several. They told her that five-hundred-euro notes were notorious.

'Why?'

'They've been forged.'

'Well, you presumably have those machines that verify notes.'

'Yes, but they're no use, since the North Korean forgeries came on the scene.'

Beba was going to ask what on earth North Korea had to do with it all, but she decided against it. Obviously, nothing was going to help.

And it had all started with Beba wanting to buy some hair dye, to fix those grey hairs of hers which had flashed that morning in the Wellness Centre mirror after her chocolate soak. She really could not have asked Pupa for something so trivial. But, apart from that, Beba wanted to have a bit of money of her own, for little needs, for coffee and fruit juice, or hair dye.

In short, when she reached the hotel having got nowhere, Beba found herself breezing into the casino, more by chance than design. At the entrance, she was met by a wave of clamouring voices mingled with the metallic sounds of the roulette wheel, so that for a moment she felt as though she had wandered into a monkey house. But since Beba considered herself a person for whom nothing human is strange, she stopped at the first roulette table, right by the entrance, to see what something she had only ever seen in films looked like in real life.

Most of the players were laying fifty-euro notes on the table. Although some did put a hundred down. The croupier gathered the money from the table and dropped it into an opening, where the notes disappeared at lightning speed. Then he distributed brightly coloured round plastic chips to each of the players, and the players placed them on various numbers. And then the croupier spun the roulette wheel with the little ball, said something in French and passed his hand over the table as though he were clearing away invisible crumbs. That meant that from that moment no one could place any more chips on the numbers or alter their position. The roulette wheel came slowly to rest and the little ball landed in a metal section with a number on it.

Beba liked the look of it, and thought maybe she should try her luck and incidentally change that wretched five-hundred-euro note. On the opposite side of the table sat that morose Russian jerk with the wild hair, who had mocked her so unpleasantly at the Wellness Centre. He was holding a glass in his hand and shifting a Cuban cigar around between his teeth. Beba, who was standing to one side, felt uncomfortable about drawing attention to herself, so she whispered discreetly to the croupier to buy her chips to a value of fifty euros, and give her the change in cash. And she placed her note on the table. The croupier nodded, took the note, put it into the opening and the note disappeared with the speed of lightning. Unlike the other players, who were given a heap of chips, to her great disappointment Beba was given only one. She put it on number 32. That was the first number that occurred to her, nothing significant, just the number of the entrance to the block of flats where she lived. And just as she was expecting the croupier to give her back the rest of her money, he spun the wheel and waved his hand over the table, saying something in French. The little ball spun and spun, and finally came to rest on number 32. Now, instead of plastic chips, Beba received a sheaf of little plastic cards, also in bright colours. The people who had been watching the game muttered something, but Beba did not hear them properly. The din that broke over Beba made her feel a little dizzy. And, truly, as though something had happened to her hearing, the sounds that reached her ears seemed to be coming through cotton wool. Beba followed the croupier's hands carefully, hoping that he would give her back the rest of her money. She whispered to him again to give her back the rest of her money and the croupier nodded again, and Beba laid her bright plastic cards on number 32 again. In the circumstances she really could not think of a different number, and besides 32 was right in front of her. And again she had no time to think or exchange a word with the croupier; he was already passing his hand over the table as though brushing invisible crumbs and saying something in French. The little ball spun in the roulette wheel, and when it came to a stop the little ball was once again in the opening of number 32. Beba was quite deafened by the clamour and shouting, but again she could not make anything out. Now the croupier handed her a still larger sheaf of bright little plastic cards. Beba gathered them all up, before they could be put back on the table, and now asked the croupier loudly to give her back those four hundred and fifty euros. The croupier told her to collect her money at the cash desk.

'You might have told me straight away,' said Beba and, clutching her little cards in her hand, she tried to find the cash desk through the crush, but halfway there she was met by a gentleman carrying a bottle of champagne on a tray. The gentleman insisted on giving her the champagne, but Beba said she had not ordered anything. They all just want to take your money, she thought, and asked the gentleman where the cash desk was. The gentleman was very kind and took her straight there. The lady at the cash desk asked Beba for her bright little cards, and then in return showed her a pile of notes, but Beba said that she would like her four hundred and fifty euros.

'Would you like us to put the rest into your bank account?' asked the lady at the cash desk.

'But my account's in Zagreb,' said Beba.

'We can transfer your money to your account, if you like,' said the lady.

Beba was afraid that she would be left without change for coffee and fruit juice again, and said that she would prefer to take the money in cash.

'In that case, madam, I would advise you to deposit the money in the hotel safe,' said the woman at the cash desk kindly.

'Do what you like,' said Beba, 'but please let me have my four hundred and fifty euros.'

And then that gentleman, who was still carrying the bottle of champagne on the tray, said something to the lady at the cash desk and she handed Beba a form with numbers on it, which Beba had to sign and attach her passport to. Beba was relieved when the lady finally handed her a bundle of four hundred and fifty euros. The gentleman thrust the bottle of champagne into one of her hands and then shook the other one, which was exceedingly strange.

The whole time, Beba had felt that something was wrong with her. She was slightly deaf, as though she had just got off an aeroplane. And her sense of balance was haywire; she swayed as though she was drunk. Indeed, she kept thinking she was going to fall over. And, just as her eyes began to mist, Arnoš Kozeny materialised beside her and took her by the arm.

'Come and sit down. Over here, in the restaurant ... You're white as a sheet! Is everything all right?

'It's all *white*, don't *hurry*,' said Beba.

Arnoš called the waiter and ordered two French cognacs, which the waiter brought with the speed of lightning.

'Get that down you, you'll feel better,' ordered Arnoš.

And Beba downed the cognac, and she really did feel a bit better. If nothing else, at least her ears had popped.

'Well, warmest congratulations!' said Arnoš, raising his glass and clinking it against Beba's.

'What for?' she asked.

'How do you mean, what for? How much did you bag? Go on, tell me!'

'I don't know what you're talking about.'

'People are saying you cleaned the casino out of half a million euros and that you've ruined that Russian.'

'What Russian?'

'The Russian, they call him Kotik, he's the local con artist and Mafioso.'

Beba felt a wave of exhaustion sweep over her again.

'Are you *yelling* the truth?'

'You're a wealthy woman, my dear,' said Arnoš.

'Me? *Healthy?!*'

'Have a look in your handbag, they must have given you a figure ...'

Beba opened her bag, took out the form and showed it to Arnoš. It had the hotel casino's stamp on it, and some signatures, including Beba's.

'Why yes!' said Arnoš. 'That's what I thought, more than half a million. €612,500 tax free, to be precise.'

'How did that *happen?*' Beba asked as though a great misfortune had occurred.

'I don't know. Ever since I've been hanging around this casino, I've never seen anyone scoop up so much cash so quickly, effectively and in such a stupid way. Didn't you notice that they were all freaked out?'

'Why were they *eked out*?'

'Dear child, you're in a state of shock, you don't know what you're saying,' said Arnoš sympathetically, giving Beba back her piece of paper.

'Put that away. And remember that Latin saying: *Dantur opes nullis nunc nisi divitibus!* Let me see you to your room, I can see that you can barely stand.'

Beba leaned her full weight against Arnoš. She was grateful that he was there. She would think about everything in the morning, *it was best to weep on it.*

Here perhaps it should be said that in addition to her tendency in moments of excitement to pronounce words wrongly, Beba sometimes also reeled off series of numbers. But of course she was not aware of it. So once when she happened to be involved in a short-lived love affair with someone and he had hit her, instead of returning the blow, or bursting into tears, or saying anything, Beba had responded to the shock by listing a series of numbers. The guy was a creep, bone idle, but he did not lack imagination, so he wrote down the numbers, the next day he bought a lottery ticket, and, what do you know, he won a substantial amount of money, which he did not mention to Beba of course. After that the relationship went rapidly downhill, because the guy often hit her, frightened or insulted her, in the hope that she would again spit out some winning combination. Beba soon sent him packing, but the guy did not leave her in peace until she started another love affair, also short-lived, with a policeman.

What about us? We charge ahead at full steam. While life may not know where the rudder and the prow are, the tale cuts through the billows, following its star!

6.

Who knows what factors shape our biographies? Lives can be very different, but Kukla's life was like a bad film. And a very bad film at that. Perhaps Kukla's future life's choices had been determined by an incident that had occurred long ago, when Kukla was a very young girl. And what occurred was something comical, or tragic, or even banal: judgements of this kind generally depend on whether the person is a participant or an observer. In short, in her first sexual contact with a young man, inexperienced as she was herself, Kukla had what the medical profession calls a vaginal spasm. Although later on she found out something about it, she was not consoled by the fact that it was neither as bizarre nor as rare as people think. But in those days psychotherapists and sexual therapists barely existed. Be that as it may, Kukla buried that disagreeable episode deep in her subconscious and simply forgot it. However, the episode did not forget Kukla, and continued to disrupt and interfere with her life. To make matters worse, Kukla married that unfortunate young man, they were connected by the shame of the unpleasant incident, but after their wedding it turned out that the young man had leukaemia and very soon Kukla became a widow. And a very young widow at that.

* * *

Kukla studied English language and literature at university, she got a job teaching in a secondary school and stayed stuck in the same school her entire working life, until she retired. Kukla's second husband was some fifteen years older than her, he was a prominent politician, but almost immediately after the wedding he had a stroke, and Kukla spent the next ten years nursing this man who had turned into a demanding houseplant. And a very demanding one at that.

After her second husband died, Kukla married a third time, this time someone who was already an invalid, a well-known writer, who after an unfortunate fall down some stairs was permanently confined to a wheelchair. The writer was a few years older than her and when she was sixty Kukla became a widow for the third time.

Kukla was a quiet, calm person; she spread serenity around her, she never talked about herself and never complained about anything, so that there was no reason for people not to like her. She had no children. There were children, in fact, of her second and third husbands, from their previous marriages, but the children were grown-up, they lived their own lives and had very little contact with Kukla.

Although she would never have admitted it herself, Kukla's husbands served her as a shield: as a married woman she had tangible cover that there was nothing wrong with her. She had also served her husbands as a shield, although she would have sworn that this was not the case: being married to a woman like her was more than tangible proof that there was nothing wrong with them. Had she wanted, Kukla could have married fifty times, her qualities were highly prized. She was a perfect wife, a wife-cover, wife-prosthesis, wife-mask.

She accepted her role, she made no demands, she did not attract attention in any way. She was feminine, but not provocative, open to a certain point, pleasant, but not overly so. And, what was most important, for all her above average height, Kukla gave the impression of being fragile and so instantly aroused protective impulses in men. And then, perhaps just because of her exceptional height, as well as the fact that she chose invalids as her protectors, those relations quickly changed, and the men perceived Kukla as a protector, nurse, mother, surrogate wife, all in the one package.

As far as Kukla herself was concerned, she had worked things out roughly as follows: the Fates had meted her out a destiny based on a 'bad joke', and she had done all she could to ensure that the 'joke' never saw the light of day. She had buried three husbands and remained a virgin, in virtually the literal sense. She tormented and belittled herself, saw herself as a 'grave-digger'. Under her hand even the flowers on her balcony failed to flourish! She was convinced that her glance was enough to dry out even cactuses on the window-sill. For some reason those dried-out cactuses really got to her . . .

And then one day a young man appeared. He was writing a doctorate on Kukla's third husband, the writer Bojan Kovač. He was interested in everything about this 'enigmatic' man. What intrigued him most was whether there was anything left in the 'great writer's' papers. He was haunted by the idea of understatement, on which, according to him, Kovač's work was based, particularly as it was precisely that – understatement as an integral element of the novel – that was the topic of his doctoral thesis. 'Kovač is the Mona Lisa of Croatian literature,' the young man claimed, 'the enigmatic smile of his prose is the key to reading his whole opus.'

Kovač had left absolutely nothing, as Kukla knew better than anyone. He had written nothing for the last few years, mostly because of his illness. They had lived on her salary and his barely existent royalties. It would have been hard for him to write anything, because with time his disability was capped by diabetes, and then Alzheimer's . . . 'Is it possible that he left nothing at all?' asked the young man. 'What makes you think he left nothing? On the contrary, he left a lot,' said Kukla. 'I can help you organise his archive,' the young man offered pleasantly. There was a great deal of material, over the last years Kovač had not been able to write himself, because of his arthritis, and she had put everything on the computer, she explained. She was Kovač's typist; they had worked for ten hours a day, particularly just before the end, 'because Kovač was determined to finish that novel,' she added. 'What novel? Can I see it?' Of course, but not immediately, she would need time to sort out the manuscript . . . 'Can you at least tell me the title of the novel?' 'Oh yes,' said Kukla, '*Desert Rose*, that's the working title. '*Desert Rose*, hmm, an unusual title, feminine, more suited to cheap romances than Kovač,' observed the young man.

And so Kukla began to write. Later it occurred to her that she might find something else among Kovač's papers: a short romance, for instance, or an unusually interesting essay-novel that he had written earlier, foreseeing events that were yet to happen. Yes, she knew that Kovač's right to a second life was in her hands, that it depended only on her, Kukla.

But then, when the young man appeared, there was only one thing on her mind: to maintain his attention for as long as possible. And she succeeded, only for a time, but that was enough. And the young man was clever, he got his doctorate without waiting to see his favourite writer's last novel, and then he got a scholarship, set off to America and disappeared without trace.

Given that Kukla's life was in any case like a very bad film – at least that is what she thought – let us hope that it will support this one last observation: Kukla never forgot the young man's attention. His attention had been like dew dropping onto a desert rose – and the foreword to Kukla's second life.

What about us? While life stories are muddled and extended, the tale slips along in its rush to be ended.

7.

It is not true that Mevludin knew no English at all. He knew a lot, of course he did. That is why he said to the girl who was standing in front of him, crying bitterly:

'I am sorry, I understand the full extent of your damage.'

Mevlo knew that kind of BBC and CNN English and he was in a position to enunciate eloquently such sentences as: *There has been no let-up in the fighting in Bosnia. Heavy shelling continued throughout the night* . . . Mevludin knew a lot, he knew about *peace negotiations*, about *ceasefires* and *the ceasefire appears to be holding* . . . He also knew about *sporadic gunfire*, *progress towards a settlement*, *wail of ambulance sirens*, *the horror of the early-morning blast*, he knew all about *a pool of blood*, *explosion*, *reminders of horror* and many, many other things.

That is why he said to the girl:

'Stay calm but tense.'

Mevlo remembered the sentence *The atmosphere in the city remains calm but tense as the ceasefire appears to be holding* and he was sure that his words would comfort the girl. The girl glanced at him in horror, as though she had come face to face with smelly socks, and went on sobbing.

Mevlo considered what he could do to console the girl. Then he remembered the cheque that Mr Shaker had given him. He took it out of the little pocket in his jacket, tapped the girl on the shoulder and said:

'Look! Take it . . .'

The girl looked at him with the same expression, as though there were smelly socks in front of her nose, leaned her elbows on the table, laid her head on her folded arms as on a pillow and continued to cry.

'Look!'

Mevludin tore the cheque into little pieces and tossed the pieces into the air like confetti. For a moment the girl watched the little pieces of paper floating through the air, stopped crying, and then remembered that she had been crying, and laid her head back on the table, arranging her folded arms like a pillow, and carried on crying.

Mevludin looked at her lovely round shoulders shaking with sobs. He felt helpless.

'Oh, for God's sake, love, do stop crying, you're going to melt clean away. And then what'll I have left? Tepid water?' Mevludin whispered in his Bosnian, a language Rosie could not understand.

And then Mevludin thought that maybe the girl was hungry, she had probably not eaten anything all day, and he had some food in his bag that he had forgotten about, a boiled egg and a slice of bread. Mevlo placed the boiled egg and slice of bread in front of the girl. For a moment she raised her face out of the tangle of her copper-coloured hair, and then laid her forehead back on the pillow of her folded arms. Her sobs were slightly weaker, or so it seemed to him.

Mevlo took the egg and started to peel it. And, what do you know, as he was peeling the egg, out of the blue, Mevlo was visited by a life-saving recollection. Once, while he was massaging one of his guests, the guest had demanded that they play him his favourite song during the massage, and he had explained the words of the song, so that Mevlo remembered it. When he left, the guest had even presented him with the CD . . .

'You're my thrill . . .' said Mevlo.

The sobs stopped, but the girl still did not move.

'You do something to me . . .'

The girl was as still as a little bug.

'Nothing seems to matter . . .'

The girl was silent.

'Here's my heart on a silver platter . . .' he said, handing the girl the egg.

The girl peeled her forehead off the table, and, without looking at Mevlo, took the egg with her pink, child's fingers. First she nibbled the end indifferently and then went on nibbling the egg, gazing at an imaginary point in front of her. Mevlo crumbled bread with his fingers. He could see, as though through a magnifying glass, a little drop of yolk trembling on the girl's lip. A leftover tear slipped out of her eye and came to rest on the drop of yolk. Mevlo broke off a piece of bread, picked up the drop of yolk and the tear with it and put it into his mouth. The girl watched him with wide-open eyes.

In that instant, Mevlo felt that the tension eight inches below his navel was easing. As though something heavy had broken off him and fallen soundlessly onto the floor. Mevlo knew perfectly well what was happening. Just as that wretched shell had cast a spell on him, so this girl with the egg in her hand had broken it.

'Where is my will, why this strange ceasefire . . .' whispered Mevlo.

The girl smiled. Those copper freckles on her face began to shine with a miraculous glow, and her wide-apart greenish eyes sparkled like two little pools.

Day Four

I.

First thing in the morning, Beba popped into the Wellness Centre to invite Mevludin to a little celebration.

'*Mashallah*! I heard,' said Mevlo warmly. 'So what'll you do now, love?' he added anxiously, as though Beba's win in the casino was a great misfortune.

'I've no idea. But, what's happened to you?' Beba asked, as Mevludin had fervently hoped she would.

'That thing of mine . . . finally drooped!' he said brightly.

And Mevlo told Beba what had happened to him the previous evening, while he was consoling Rosie.

Beba wanted to say something like 'congratulations', but then it seemed inappropriate, so she just said:

'So that's you sorted.'

'I wish I was,' he sighed.

'Come to the pool, and we'll talk,' said Beba.

Dr Topolanek showed exceptional understanding for his three guests' idea, all the more so when Beba rewarded his understanding with a substantial wad of notes. Dr Topolanek ordered a notice to be put up announcing that the pool was closed due to the repair of an unexpected fault, and the three old ladies had the whole place to themselves. The hotel staff carried in vases of flowers, with broad smiles on their faces, as they imagined what fun the three aged nymphs would have in the pool. When Beba thrust a flattering tip into each of their hands, they all became suddenly serious and now they carried the flowers with dignity, as though at a funeral. They brought special sun-loungers for 'the elderly and less agile'. Beba had found a child's one-piece swimming costume for Pupa in the local shop. It had a stupid Teletubbies design on it, but it was better than nothing, she thought, so that problem was solved. Pupa stubbornly insisted on keeping her long white socks on, as she was not allowed to go into the water in her fur boot. The staff placed Pupa carefully on the lounger in the shape of a horizontal 'S', and pushed her off into the waters of the pool. Beba had ordered champagne and a lavish selection of pastries from the hotel confectioner's, which was all arranged on trays on the very edge of the pool. The only other person left in the pool room was a young waiter who opened the bottle of champagne, poured it into the glasses and then silently withdrew.

'Well, cheers!' said Beba with a smile on her face. The three old ladies clinked glasses. The water was agreeably warm, the champagne chilled. Beba took a round chocolate cake from the tray on the edge of the pool and put it into her mouth.

'Girls, this is amazing!'

Then she placed a selection of little cakes on a china plate for Pupa.

'Mmmmm . . .' mumbled Pupa with pleasure, and in a few seconds she had devoured the lot.

Beba and Kukla were astonished by Pupa's sudden enthusiasm for sweet things. If anyone had shown a dedicated delight in food, it was Beba.

For a moment, Beba felt a little downcast. For the first time in her life, she could feel the power of money on her own skin. She had never in her life had money; she had lived from pay-cheque to pay-cheque, not even thinking about money. Money is like a coat made of the most expensive fur, she thought now. People treat a woman in a fur coat entirely differently from a woman in a sports jacket, and no one would be able to convince her otherwise.

'Money is like a magic wand,' said Beba.

'How do you mean?' asked Kukla.

'As soon as you show that you have money, people who had looked at you like scum until then suddenly treat you as though you were Kate Moss!'

'*Ich deck mein schmerz mit mein nerz!*' said Pupa.

'People simply respect you more,' said Beba primly.

'Money is shit. People are like flies. And where do flies land, if not on shit,' said Pupa, resolutely bringing the conversation to an end.

Beba was a little offended at first because Pupa and Kukla did not appear to be particularly pleased about her winnings. She had dreamed up this little celebration for them, as a treat, but they were indifferent, or that is how it seemed to her. But then, thought Beba, she could not take credit for the money; it had come to her by chance. Why should they praise and congratulate her? On her stupid good fortune?

At that moment Mevludin, who had clearly skived off work, because he was wearing his 'uniform', burst into the pool room.

'Well, well, well! What do you mean by starting the party without me, eh?'

'Come on, we're waiting for you,' called Beba brightly.

Mevlo grabbed a glass from the invisible waiter and then, slipping off his clogs, walked slowly into the pool in his wide trousers, little waistcoat and turban.

'Hey, my ladies! Here you are soaking in the pool like gherkins in brine. Well, then, cheers, my lovelies! And I want to toast my granny as well: I sent her some money a few days ago so she could have lovely new teeth made, and stop clicking like castanets all over the place,' Mevlo chattered, and then he stopped in amazement.

Coming face to face with a little old lady on a floating lounger, wearing white socks and a swimming costume from which the Teletubbies gazed out at him, for a moment Mevludin felt as though he were in the presence of some ancient divinity.

'Excuse me for jabbering on like this, madam,' said Mevludin.

With almost youthful sweetness, the lady offered him her little, dry hand. Mevludin was touched by this hand that resembled a bird's claw, and then he was ashamed of his chattering.

'Well, Mevlo, you're right welcome, boy,' said Beba cheerfully.

'Ah, my lovelies, it's all very well for you, drinking champagne and soaking yourselves in the pool,' Mevludin opened his mouth again, but this time he addressed Beba.

'But you're drinking and soaking yourself too.'

'Maybe I am, but I'm not happy.'

'Why not?' asked Pupa.

'She knows,' said Mevludin, pointing to Beba.

‘Shall I tell them?’ asked Beba.

‘Go on, tell them, love. I’ve got nothing to hide. Good things keep mum, while misfortune kicks out, showing its bare bum.’

‘Mevlo’s in love,’ explained Beba.

‘Who with?’ asked Pupa.

‘You know, that little American girl, we told you . . .’

‘So you’ve been blathering to all and sundry!’ said Mevlo crossly.

‘No, I haven’t, honestly, no one knows apart from the three of us!’

‘Kukla knows.’

‘Well, that’s three, presumably.’

The women burst out laughing.

‘Honestly! It’s all very well for you to wet yourselves laughing!’ said Mevlo.

‘That’s right, it’s not nice for us to be cackling, when the girl’s lost her father!’ said Beba.

‘God rest his soul, *rahmetli* Mr Shaker,’ said Mevlo.

‘When did it happen?’ asked Pupa.

‘Yesterday.’

‘How?’

‘The guy kicked the bucket.’

‘How?’

‘He suffocated on a golf ball.’

‘What a lovely way to die!’ said Pupa.

Kukla drank the rest of her champagne in silence, while Mevlo, Beba and Pupa discussed Mr Shaker’s ‘lovely’ death and philosophised on the theme ‘here today, gone tomorrow’. She did not seem particularly interested in their conversation. But she did give a little start when one of Pupa’s observations reached her ear.

'Fine. Now there's nothing in the way of your happiness!' said Pupa, curving her long neck and directing her bright gaze in Mevludin's direction.

How lively she's become, all of a sudden! thought Kukla, who was anxious about Pupa's sudden chattiness. Because on the whole she dozed or said nothing and this unexpected liveliness did not bode well.

'I'm in the way of my happiness, like a log,' Mevlo replied.

'Mevlo thinks he's not good enough for the girl, that he doesn't speak English, which is true, and that he lacks polish,' explained Beba.

Here Pupa raised herself up a little on her lounger and asked in a serious tone:

'Do you pick your nose in the girl's presence?'

'No, I don't, I swear by my granny,' said Mevlo, astonished by the question.

'Are you stingy?' Pupa went on.

'No, I'm not, I swear by my mother.'

'Remember, there's nothing worse than a stingy man!'

'I'm not stingy, I swear by Tito!'

'Do you chatter a lot in the girl's presence?'

'Well, I like talking, I can't say I don't, but I control myself . . . And anyway I can't speak English,' he replied candidly.

'You're as handsome as Apollo, you don't pick your nose, you're not stingy and you don't talk too much. There's nothing at all the matter with you!' announced Pupa in the tone of a doctor who was a hundred per cent sure of her diagnosis.

Beba burst out laughing. Even Kukla laughed, but like someone who was just learning how to do it. Her throat just let out a sound like whinnying.

'Who's this Apollo guy?' Mevlo whispered to Beba.

'She's saying that you look terrific, and she can't see what the problem is.'

'What's the good of it if I don't have even the remotest hint of a brain?' said Mevludin, turning to Pupa.

'You have clever hands!' Beba leapt to Mevlo's defence.

'Beba's right. Do you know how many children I've brought into the world with these hands?' said Pupa, for some reason spreading out the fingers of one hand.

Mevludin stared in awe at the old lady on the lounger, who now reminded him of a holy chicken, because for a moment it seemed to him that instead of her hand she had spread her wing.

'I don't know, madam, perhaps you can tell me how to improve my situation. You're older, wiser, you're educated, so I assume, you can't altogether have forgotten the syllabus,' said Mevlo, evidently enchanted by Pupa.

Beba moved away for a moment and observed the scene. Standing in water up to his waist, a young man in wide trousers, with a little waistcoat pulled over his naked torso and a turban on his head, was gazing in reverence at a little old lady, in the shape of a horizontal letter S, wearing a child's swimming costume with the Teletubbies printed on it, floating on a lounger. The old lady resembled a hen, while the young man looked like a hero out of *A Thousand and One Nights.*

'Shall we order another bottle of champagne?' suggested Beba.

Here it should be added that in reality everything went far more slowly. The reality of a story, however, rarely corresponds to the reality of life. Or, in other words: while in life a cat struggles to catch its prey, in the tale, like a bullet, it strikes home straight away.

Mevlo signalled to the invisible waiter to bring another bottle of champagne. They poured it out, sipped it slowly and then Beba, who had resolved to help Mevlo come what may, made a solemn proposal:

'I've got a suggestion: let each of the three of us choose and describe her ideal man, and then it will be easier for Mevlo to see what he's lacking!'

The women looked at each other. Who knows when they might last have had a conversation along these lines? At school? Beba had evidently drunk too much champagne and it had made her childish. However, what happened next was something quite other than the participants could have anticipated. To start with no one had expected any response at all from Pupa let alone an immediate one, but, nevertheless, it was Pupa who piped up:

'My ideal man is Superman.'

'Why Superman?'

'Because Superman is the best, quickest, cheapest and most comfortable means of transport!' said Pupa and her blue eyes sparkled with a girlish gleam.

'Just because he's mobile?' asked Beba.

'And because he's a handyman.'

'What's that when it's at home?' Mevlo asked Kukla.

'Someone with golden hands who fixes everything round the house.'

'Superman can weld a ton of steel with one glance, so he'd certainly be able to fix a cooker, a blender or a blocked water pipe. He could also be a home diagnostic centre, so you wouldn't have to hang about in hospital queues forever. All he has to do is look at you with those X-ray eyes of his!' prattled Beba.

'There's something else,' said Pupa.

'What?'

'Superman mends the world. He fights evil.'

'Like Tito!' Mevlo burst in.

Here it should be explained that Mevludin was one of those Bosnians who valued the long-dead president of former Yugoslavia, Tito, and who were convinced that had Tito been alive in Yugoslavia, which meant in Bosnia too, there would have been no war, and therefore no shell that had so fundamentally altered Mevlo's life.

Mevlo looked downcast.

'I'm not qualified.'

'Why?' asked Pupa seriously.

'I can fix a leaking pipe for you in a jiffy, I can change a tyre, I can unscrew a bulb and change that, but when it comes to mending the world, I can't do that . . . When that war flared up in our country, what did I do to stop it? Nothing!'

'You've got golden hands, you know that,' said Beba.

'That's what people say.'

'Well, just imagine that Radovan Karadžić and Ratko Mladić, instead of going to The Hague, turn up on your massage table!'

'I'd wring their necks!'

'There you are, clever hands have great power,' said Beba, although she was not too sure of her idea about the clever hands.

'What about you, Beba, who's your choice?' Kukla cut Beba's prattling short.

'Hmm . . . it's difficult.'

'Come on, love, think of something,' said Mevludin.

'You all know who Tarzan was?' said Beba brightly.

'Of course!' said Kukla, Pupa and Mevludin at the same moment.

'But do you know his real name?'

'Tarzan,' Mevlo blurted out.

'Tarzan's real name is John Clayton, Lord Greystoke!' said Beba triumphantly.

'What are you implying?'

'Half-ape, half-lord! That's my ideal man!' Beba burst out.

The three of them started giggling: Pupa asthmatically, Kukla whinnyingly and Beba throatily. Mevlo looked dejected again:

'There you are, I'm not qualified again, love.'

'Why?'

'The monkey bit I can manage, but as for being a lord, there's just no way!' he said.

Once again it should be said that in reality, in this case the watery, poolside one, everything happened far more slowly. But while life will dither and shilly-shally, the tale's seven-league boots leap over hill and valley.

'Now it's your turn, Kukla!' said Beba.

'I don't know . . .'

'Oh, come on; it's not fair to the others!'

They all waited tensely for Kukla's answer. Kukla grew serious, she frowned a bit, sipped a little champagne and then said, slowly:

'The devil.'

'What do you mean, the devil?'

'The devil is my ideal man,' said Kukla calmly.

'Why?' they all asked together, uneasily.

'Throughout history the devil was the most dangerous opponent of ordinary men. Superman cannot be an ideal man. Still less Tarzan. The devil is a man with a long, powerful and convincing history of seduction. The devil is the only opponent of God Himself, who is, as we know, also a man.'

They all fell silent, because it seemed that there was some truth in Kukla's answer.

'Ah well, that counts me out as well!' Mevlo burst out, breaking the silence.

'Why?'

'What do you mean, why, love? My soul is as soft as a Bosnian plum, you can't be a devil with such a wishy-washy heart!'

'But the devil likes women!' said Beba.

'So what?'

'You like women too!'

'I do, my dears, I like you all!' said Mevlo.

'The very fact that you like women qualifies you to be an ideal man!' Beba pronounced her verdict.

It will not be inappropriate to observe once more that in reality everything took a lot longer. For while life always tends to drag its idle feet, the tale dashes on, brisk, swift and fleet.

'Isn't it surprising,' said Beba thoughtfully.

'Isn't what surprising, love?'

'Well, the fact that, actually, very few people actually like us, women.'

'What do you mean?' asked Kukla.

'The only people who like us are transvestites!' said Beba bitterly, then she added: 'And Mevlo!'

All three of them – Beba, who was a bit the worse for wear, Kukla and Mevlo – failed to notice that Pupa's lounger had floated away. And when they did realise that Pupa was not with them, they turned round and spotted her lounger at the other end of the pool. Her head had slumped onto her chest, a little to one side, and now she looked even more like a hen.

'She's nodded off again,' said Beba.

'Why is her hand in the air?' asked Kukla in alarm.

'Why not?'

'She's sleeping with her hand in the air?'

Truly, Pupa was sleeping in an unusual position, with her hand slightly raised, and her fist clenched.

Kukla, Beba and Mevlo put their glasses down on the edge of the pool and hurried towards Pupa. When they got close, they saw that her two fingers were clenched in an unambiguous gesture.

'Maybe she was a bit tipsy and was showing us two fingers,' said Beba.

'Maybe she's kicked the bucket,' Mevlo burst out.

'God, Mevlo, call the doctor!' screamed Beba.

Dr Topolanek came at once. Nurses lifted Pupa out of the pool. Dr Topolanek felt her pulse, pressed her jugular vein, lifted her eyelids . . . No, there was not the slightest doubt, Pupa had finally passed over into the next world.

'Eighty-eight is a ripe old age,' said Dr Topolanek.

He wanted, in truth, to add that it was nothing compared to Emma Faust Tillman, who died aged a hundred and thirteen, but he realised that his enthusiasm with regard to longevity would be inappropriate in these circumstances. So he just added:

'May she rest in peace.'

2.

Who knows what Pupa was thinking about as she drifted away on her lounger towards the far end of the pool? Perhaps at a certain moment she gathered that the warm, cheerful voices that had surrounded her had grown quieter and then disappeared altogether, and she was suddenly immersed in a silence as dense as cotton wool. The brightly coloured blotches – the faces of Kukla, Beba and the young man in the turban – gradually disappeared and she found herself in a world without colour, where it seemed to her that she had already died and that now the nursemaid Death was rocking her in the warm Lethe? Perhaps her memory had suddenly stretched out like that child's toy, that little brightly coloured tongue that straightens out when it is blown, and it had then rolled itself up pliably into a Moebius loop, and, well, well, she clearly recalled that she had already been here, in this very place, before. It was nineteen-seventy something, when she had at last, after a long time, acquired her first passport. Czechoslovakia was at that time one country which vanished into two, just as Yugoslavia was one country, and now there are six. She and Kosta had been invited here to a Gynaecologists' Conference, and stayed in this very hotel, except that then it was called the 'Moscow'.

Pupa slipped along the Moebius loop as though sliding downhill on a toboggan, and, what do you know, she saw everything, it was all lined up, all the events of her life, those that had occurred, and those that were to come, although she would no longer be there. She felt light, all her sense of shame – mostly to do with the fact that fate had ordained that she should live so long – lifted from her. The little bodies of the children she had brought into the world, dozens and dozens of newborn babies, glided past her like stars. Goodness, she thought in wonder as she slipped along her loop, how many there are? Is it possible that she should have brought so many children into the world, and into a world which, to be honest, she liked less and less? And, who knows, perhaps that was the reason why she had clenched her right hand, straightened her bony index and middle fingers and, raising her hand a little, held them up to the world, at once accusing and gleeful.

Or might it have been something quite different? Perhaps after so many years she had gone back to look for some little thing, an earring, which she had lost back in nineteen-seventy something, in this same pool. They were earrings made of onyx and silver, a present from Aaron, which she rarely took out of her ears. A trifle, a knick-knack, but still it bothered her for a long time; what is more she sometimes felt as though her ear lobes were burning because of the loss of that earring. That is why she now sighed deeply and dived – slender, young and elastic as the Moebius loop. She searched the bottom of the pool carefully and, what do you know, she found the earring stuck in the grate-like opening at the bottom of the pool wall. She had to come up three times for air before she could free it. And then she finally managed it. She clutched the earring tightly in her hand, so that it should not escape, and now that she had found what she was looking for, there was no longer any reason to go back up to the surface again.

3.

Pupa's vanishing soul drew away with it that discreet smell of urine, which came with old age and dragged after her like the train of her dress. Pupa's rigid body lay before them, but – as though death were like blotting paper – the smell had disappeared. The 'old witch' was right: death has no smell. Life is crap.

She lay on her back, in the same position in which they had lifted her off the lounger, with her knees bent and slightly parted, like an oven-ready Christmas turkey. Her slightly raised right arm with its hand bent in the unambiguous two-finger gesture, it too remained in the same position in which Pupa, lying on her pool lounger in the shape of a horizontal S, had sent her last goodbye to her friends or to the world, who knows. Unlike her right hand, with its unseemly message, her left lay hanging, as though it were still stroking the edge of the non-existent lounger. A glance at the deceased's legs and feet, now when Pupa's socks were finally off, filled those present with mild horror. The skin on her legs was criss-crossed with broken capillaries and swollen veins which wrapped round the spindly calves like the tentacles of an octopus. From her knees down everything blended into the terrifying colour of rotten meat. Her toenails were so ossified and twisted that they resembled claws. 'God forgive me!' Beba crossed herself, stunned by what she saw.

Two nurses – one small, willowy, red-haired, and the other large, white-skinned and linear as a pillar – were doing their job. After she cut off Pupa's socks with scissors, the willowy one tried to lower Pupa's right hand, exerting particular determination over the fingers. However, neither fingers nor hand would budge, as though they had turned to stone.

'Careful! You'll break them!' Beba protested.

'God forgive me, but I've never seen anything like this in my life, and I've been working for twenty years!' said Willowy, crossing herself for some reason.

The linear one pressed her hands down on Pupa's knees, as though Pupa were a folding umbrella, rather than a human being, a former one admittedly. Her knees offered amazing resistance.

'It's as if she's made of iron,' muttered Linear, rolling up her sleeves and preparing for one last effort.

'Stop! I can't bear to watch you any longer!' cried Beba.

Linear shrugged her shoulders indifferently, ran her tongue round her mouth without opening her lips, just like a camel, and then spat an important question out of her mouth:

'How do you imagine you're going to stuff her into a coffin, with all these bits sticking out?'

'Quite. How?' Willowy joined in, gratuitously belligerent.

'Well, you presumably have coffins?'

'We've got one. A child's. Made by our carpenter, the late Lukas. He made all his coffins too short and too narrow. His corpses were squeezed in like sardines.'

'That was in communist times, when people cut corners everywhere,' said Willowy.

'Lukas skimped on everything apart from drink,' snapped Linear.

'Why don't you turn her onto her side?' asked Beba.

'The foetal position, you mean?' said Linear professionally, measuring Pupa roughly with her hands. 'Hmm, she won't fit,' she shook her head.

'Little body, big problems! I've really never seen anything like it!' Willowy crossed herself.

'Well, it's possible it could be done if you would let her be squashed a little,' added Linear.

'Is there such a thing as an undertaker in this town?' asked Kukla.

'Yes. The undertaker is the carpenter Martin. But he won't

make you a coffin overnight. I had to wait a fortnight for my mother,' said Linear.

'Where did you keep her?'

'Here, in the fridge.'

'We're Wellness Centre staff, we have priority,' explained Willowy.

'What about a crematorium?' asked Beba.

'In Prague. But even there the dead usually go into the oven in coffins. No one's going to burn them in just a sheet.'

'Only Indians are burned in just a sheet,' said Willowy.

'Do you mean no one ever dies here, for God's sake?' asked Beba.

'We're a Wellness Centre!'

'I give up! Lukas, Martin, Indians, I don't understand a thing!' said Beba angrily.

'We don't understand you either. What were you thinking of dragging an old woman about with you, and never thinking that she could snuff it? And in a foreign country as well!'

Willowy probably wanted to say 'shame on you' or something like that, but restrained herself at the last moment, and instead said:

'I'd never drag my mother about, not on my life!'

'You're not very kind, the two of you, you know,' said Beba.

'If I was kind I'd have popped my clogs long ago!' Willowy snapped.

'The conditions we live in, certainly,' said Linear vaguely.

'This is absolutely intolerable! You girls really know how to help a person!' snorted Beba.

'Let's go, we'll think of something,' said Kukla, dragging Beba by the sleeve.

'Think of something, only quickly! Our fridge isn't large. It's Thursday now. We can keep her till Monday morning maximum. Other people die as well, you know,' said Linear, biting her tongue. 'I mean it does happen once in a while, like now for instance,' she added.

'We're a Wellness Centre!' Willowy leapt in, pronouncing *wellness centre* with particular reverence, as though it were a matter of divine law.

'Fuck you and your Wellness Centre!' Beba shrieked, exasperated. She only ever swore in English, and the only English swear words she knew were 'fuck you'.

We should add that we have had to translate this conversation into a language everyone could understand, because in reality it took place in a mixture of Czech and Croatian: that is Linear and Willowy spoke Czech, and Kukla and Beba Croatian. In fact Kukla did try to set her completely forgotten knowledge of Russian in motion, but all that emerged from her mouth was Russified Croatian. Linear and Willowy snorted at it. The Russians, it seems, had got up their noses.

What about us? We'll keep going. Life drags as heavy as lead, while the tale just keeps racing ahead.

4.

A glance at the audience sitting in the lecture hall filled Dr Topolanek with a wave of anger, and, immediately afterwards, a wave of self-pity. He, who endeavoured to give this whole health business its rightful aura of scholarship, could not believe his eyes. The audience consisted not of guests from the hotel, but three local old ladies whom he knew well.

Dr Topolanek, who always carried a little whistle with him, placed the whistle in his mouth and blew it. The old ladies woke up and clapped. Topolanek gave them a little test: he read out loud the shopping list that his wife had thrust into his hand that morning. The old ladies began to snooze at the very beginning of the list, somewhere between 'a loaf of bread' and 'a pint of milk'. Topolanek put the whistle back in his mouth. The old ladies gave a start.

'Mrs Blaha, what are you doing here?'

'Can I be honest, doctor?' the old lady asked.

'Go on,' said Topolanek ironically.

'The children have worn me out with cooking and cleaning, so I've come to have a little rest. Besides, you've got that air-refreshing thing here . . .'

'Air-conditioning!' said Topolanek. 'What about you, Mrs Vesecka, why are you here?'

'I came with her,' said Mrs Vesecka, pointing to Mrs Blaha.

'What about you, Mrs Čunka?'

Mrs Čunka snored.

'Mrs Čunka!'

Mrs Čunka gave a start.

'I'm asking you what you are doing here.'

'Doctor, that list you read us a moment ago . . . When you come to buying the tomatoes . . . Pan Šošovicky has better and cheaper tomatoes today than the ones in the supermarket.'

Topolanek sat down and held his head in his hands. Although his defeat was patently obvious, his nature, fortunately, was not that of a loser. Topolanek may not have been distinguished by a superabundance of backbone, but he was not malicious, and there was only one thing he could not live without – dreams. Topolanek was a child of his transitional times, and no one could blame him for having dreams that were money wise or at least tried to be. Yes: he would fill the hall with local people. The local people ought also to be included in wellness tourism. Once a month every member of the community would have one free session in the Wellness Centre! If they had recently discovered in the south of China old men of a hundred and twenty who were growing a third set of teeth, old women who had begun to menstruate again and whose faces were speckled with adolescent acne, then why should the miracle of the third age not happen here as well, in this Czech spa? He would found, the very next day, a local club for the battle against ageing, which would be called 'Third Teeth'. He was already inventing titles in the leading international newspapers about a newly discovered source of youthfulness in the heart of ancient Europe. And a museum, there would certainly have to be a little local museum, the Museum of the History of Longevity. And he would found an amateur dramatic society. Every year the society would put on a production of Čapek's play *The Makropulos Case*. The play would stimulate public discussion, should Makropulos's recipe for longevity have been burned or not. Yes, thanks to him, Dr Topolanek, the spa town would bloom with ever more beautiful and varied flowers.

As he looked at the three creatures in the audience, Dr Topolanek was overcome with sudden tenderness.

And, what do you know, Mrs Blaha's grey hair began to darken, the lines on Mrs Vesecka's face melted away as though they had never been there and Mrs Čunka's false teeth fell out of her mouth, because new teeth had begun to grow. In the audience sat three young, vigorous women in relaxed poses, snoring loudly.

What about us? While life may land us in a dreadful plight, the tale speeds to be home in daylight.

5.

Towards evening, Kukla and Beba met in the hotel lobby with the intention of walking through the town and clearing their heads. As they left the hotel and Beba was glancing aimlessly around, she bumped into a young man entering the hotel holding his small daughter by the hand. The young man was English and apologised pleasantly to both of them, as though it were his fault. While Kukla, who was in charge of English language requirements, took it on herself to apologise to the young man, Beba involuntarily took in some details. The young man was handsome, tall, elegant, with grey eyes, ash-coloured hair, a disarming smile, while the little girl, the little girl was . . . hm, presumably Chinese. The little girl, who was holding a small puppy in her arms, watched Beba with wide-open eyes, in wonder.

'. . . if you will insist on rushing around like a headless chicken!' Kukla grumbled a little later.

'It's not as if I knocked him over!' Beba defended herself.

'Honestly, you barge about like a tank!'

'So what? I didn't do him any harm!' said Beba, adding caustically, 'besides, at least I choose the people I knock over! They're always handsome young men, and not worn-out seventy-five-year-olds!'

'Oh, sure,' remarked Kukla ironically.

Two unusual figures were ambling through the small town, suffused in a pink sunset. One, tall and thin, cut through the air with a light step as though she were holding an invisible lance. The other, round and heavy, scuttled after her, breathlessly, like her shield-bearer.

'So, what are we going to do, the two of us?' asked Beba anxiously.

'The most important thing is to have papers, the doctor's death certificate and that sort of thing . . .'

'Why?'

'How else will we get a corpse across the border?'

Beba suddenly felt quite unequal to the situation in which she found herself.

'And we have to find out about transport regulations for carrying a dead body,' added Kukla.

'I hadn't even thought about that . . .'

'And what'll we do about the money?'

'What do you mean?'

'Pupa has left her money to her daughter. She would be able quite rightly to accuse us of stealing Pupa's money. And then crossing the border . . . After all, it's all in cash. There are laws about that as well.'

'And I hadn't thought about that either.'

'And what about the money you won gambling? Have you asked about transporting a sum like that?'

Beba was suddenly very angry with Kukla, and then with Pupa as well. What did she mean by dragging them here and dumping them in all of this! Why had she abandoned them to fritter away their time on so many problems? And then she was angry with herself, because she had rushed into the whole thing like a headless chicken!

'Why should we go back at all? We could stay here for a while . . .'

'What would we do with Pupa?'

'We'll go to Prague and have her cremated.'

'It's Pupa's daughter who'll decide about all those things.'

'A lot she cares!'

'All in all, we have a major problem.'

'God, what a fool I am! How did I ever get involved in all of this!' complained Beba, not considering that Kukla had got involved in it as well, through no fault of her own.

As they walked briskly along, the two women did not notice that the whole town had become immersed in a smoky pink colour. The heavy, brocade sunset had turned the little river and lavish façades of the houses pink. The window-panes sent russet reflections to one another. The treetops had sunk into the late-afternoon dusk and were giving off a heavy, intoxicating mist.

Beba and Kukla walked on, deep in conversation, until at a certain moment they stopped as though immobilised. The two women stood with their mouths wide open. In front of them appeared a gigantic – egg! It appeared, just like that, as though the finger of fate itself had rolled it where Beba and Kukla could bump into it. To be more precise, in front of them was a large shop window, and in the window a gigantic wooden egg! They had seen eggs like this, real-life-sized ones of course, they sometimes turned up in the Zagreb markets, where, having travelled from Russia, Ukraine and Poland, they rolled around on the counters, with Russian lacquered boxes, spoons and wooden dolls, the ones that fitted inside each other.

'Good Lord, look at that King Kong of an egg!' exclaimed Beba, almost devoutly.

The egg was painted in shiny, bright colours and muddled patterns of flora and fauna. Beba and Kukla's eyes floated over flowery meadows, with butterflies the size of helicopters flying over them, fields blooming with red poppies, blue cornflowers and golden corn; they plunged their gaze into greenery and creepers, ferns and trees, with monkeys and birds swaying on their branches. Then they lowered their eyes to the undergrowth: there was a rabbit family hiding under one shrub, Adam and Eve under another, does and stags under a third. The egg was girded with bushes of ripe raspberries and blackberries, with mushrooms growing at their feet. Snails slid and ladybirds scuttled over their tops. The boggy areas were particularly striking: there were luxuriant water lilies with frogs swinging on them, large fish wallowing in their depths and wading birds peeping out of the reeds. Finally, Beba and Kukla directed their eyes to a tall palm, with a camel resting in its scant shadow. Somewhere in the air above the camel a small family was sitting in an eggshell, like a little boat: a woman, two children and a man with glasses on his nose and a paintbrush in his hand. All in all, it was a garden of Eden painted by an amateur. The man with the glasses on his nose and brush in his hand was evidently the painter of this grandiose creation. The egg consisted of two parts, and metal rivets and a handsome lock with a hook in the middle suggested that the egg opened like a trunk.

That was not all. All around the gigantic main egg, life-sized eggs were scattered: wooden painted Easter eggs, crystal Swarovsky eggs, more or less successful imitations of the famous Fabergé eggs, a new series of Fabergé eggs. The eggs scattered round the main egg gave off magical reflections of bluish, lilac, golden, golden-greenish, crystal-whitish, milky-silver tones, and the whole thing was a sight that must have left everyone who saw it speechless.

The shop bore the unambiguous name 'The New Russians'. The interior looked more like an art gallery than a shop. The walls were white and almost bare. In two or three places there were art photographs of eggs in glass frames. A young woman was sitting at the elegant white counter, and behind her was a white-painted glass display case full of exhibits.

'How much is that large egg in the window?' asked Beba in English.

'Unfortunately, it's not for sale,' the girl replied politely.

'Why did you put it in the window, then?'

'As an advertisement, to catch people's attention.'

'And what would it cost if it were for sale?'

'We are not an ordinary souvenir shop. We are a specialist gallery,' the girl stalled.

'Specialising in what?'

'Why, eggs . . .'

'And these other eggs, are they for sale?'

'Yes.'

'How much is this "Peter the Great"?'

'Three thousand five hundred.'

'Three thousand what?'

'Dollars. Most of our customers are Russians, you know.'

'Rich Russians?'

'Well . . .' the girl smiled.

'And how much is the "Tsar Alexander Caviar Bowl"?' Beba read from the plaque in the window.

'Six thousand dollars.'

'And a real Fabergé egg?'

'Don't ask!' said the girl with feeling.

'Nevertheless, if you were selling that big egg, what would it cost?'

The girl looked at the two elderly women dumbfounded.

'Are you Russian?'

'No, but we'd really like to buy that Russian egg!'

'In fact, it isn't Russian,' said the girl. 'It was made by our local artist Karel . . .'

'Karel Gott?' Kukla blurted out, half to herself.

'How do you know?'

'I'm not sure. I just said it without thinking. Karel Gott, the golden nightingale . . . That was long ago.'

'*Zlaty slavik!*'* said the pleasant girl. 'But this is our own, local, Karel Gott. I think that he's some relation of the famous singer.'

'So? Give us a price.'

'I'm sorry. It's not for sale,' said the girl apologetically.

Just when it seemed to Beba and Kukla and the girl that the situation was hopeless, and as the two women were preparing to leave, a sullen-looking man with wild hair burst into the gallery. Beba recognised him at once. It was that idiot, the Russian, from the casino. The man went straight from the door into an adjoining room without so much as glancing at the visitors.

For some reason, the girl lowered her voice:

'That is the owner of the gallery. Hold on a minute, I'll ask him,' she whispered in a confidential tone and vanished into the adjoining room.

They heard voices coming from the room, and then the man peered out to take a look at who the potential buyers of the egg might be. Beba and Kukla stood modestly beside the counter, waiting. The man did not recognise Beba at first, but then, when he did, he gave a start. Beba was able to read the traces of an inner struggle on his face. He was evidently wondering whether to show that he recognised her, or pretend that he had never seen her before. The sullen-looking man vanished behind the wall with lightning speed just as he had appeared. The results of his inner struggle remained unclear. However, now his raised voice could be heard

* *'The golden nightingale!'*

speaking Russian interspersed with the girl's indistinct responses in Czech.

'Sell it, no one buys that crap in any case! That idiot of yours, Karel, will make us a new one! Let the old bags pay twenty thousand! For that amount, for twenty thousand, I'd let the old witch rip me off!'

After a while the pleasant young girl appeared out of the adjoining room, now somewhat pinker in the face, and said:

'You're in luck.'

'How much?' asked Beba.

'Twenty thousand,' the girl spoke cautiously.

'Does that include transport?'

'Where to?'

'To the Grand Hotel.'

'Oh, but that's right here! No problem. Are you paying cash or with a credit card?' the girl asked, still disbelieving.

'Cash!' Beba burst out. 'We'll be back in a second. You're not closing yet?'

'No, you've got another full hour yet. I'll wait for you.'

'What's your name?' asked Kukla.

'Marlena,' said the girl.

At that moment the sullen-looking man with wild hair came out of the adjoining room and headed for the door. Despite his evident inner intention of looking neither left nor right, his glance escaped his control and came to rest on Beba. She managed to wave to him.

'*Spassibo, Kotik!*'* she said sweetly.

What about us? Let's keep going! In life there's a lot we can delay, but the tale moves on and cannot stay!

* *'Thank you, pussycat!'*

6.

It was already late when two sulky young men from the 'New Russians' gallery brought the egg and placed it in Pupa's suite.

Beba was sprawled wearily in an armchair, filling it entirely with her body like risen dough in a tin. Kukla was striding up and down, her arms folded on her chest. And then she stopped:

'Well, aren't we going to open it?'

Beba hauled herself out of the chair and waddled over to the egg. They unlocked it together. The room was filled with the pleasant aroma of fresh pine.

'Who would have thought it was so spacious!' said Beba.

'We'll have to make sure we buy enough bags of ice in the local supermarket,' said Kukla drily, closing the egg.

Moths flew in through the open balcony doors into the brightly lit suite.

'And the boot,' added Kukla.

'What boot?'

'We ought to put Pupa's boot in with her as well, don't you think?'

'Sure, put it in.'

'I think Pupa would really like it if the boot was cleaned.'

'We can have it dry-cleaned,' said Beba, waddling over to the telephone to ring room service. 'They'll send someone right up,' she said and made her way to the door. Beba had had enough for the day. She had no strength for any more words.

When she handed the hotel employee the bag containing a large fur boot, he opened his eyes wide and raised his eyebrows, but the question mark that formed for a moment on his forehead vanished at once, proving him a true hotel professional for whom nothing human is strange. Kukla withdrew to her part of the suite, leaving the door carefully ajar, as though Pupa was still in her room. She went out onto the balcony. The night was warm and soft as plush, and the sky was lit up by an enormous full moon. A barely visible mist rose from the trees, at least that is how it seemed to Kukla. The warmth that had accumulated during the day was evaporating from the leaves. Kukla breathed in the warm, fragrant air. Her nostrils caught the sweet smell of elder flowers. And then the door of the next-door balcony burst suddenly and noisily open and a metallic, tart woman's voice rent the silence of the night.

'Why the hell did you close the door? We'll suffocate in here!'

'I didn't close it! Besides, we've got air-conditioning!' replied a male voice calmly.

'Everyone knows who keeps shutting the doors at home!' grumbled the woman.

'So open them!' said the man's voice.

'I have done! Things soon get smelly round you, at home and on holiday!'

Kukla stood with her arms leaning on the balcony railing. The voices scratched roughly over the soft plush of the night. And then she screwed up her eyes, like the first time when she was still unaware of what she was doing, like many times before now – and directed all her thoughts in one direction. The door of the next-door balcony closed with a bang.

A little while later the metallic woman's voice was heard again.

'Why did you open the door?'

'Which door?' asked the man's voice.

'The room door!'

'Why would I open the door into the corridor?

'Because the balcony door banged! Didn't you hear?'

'Heavens, woman, you're crazy . . .'

'The balcony door banged shut, and there's not a breath of wind outside!'

'So?'

'So you must have opened the door onto the corridor on purpose to make a draught, so the balcony door would close by itself!'

'Oh for goodness' sake, give me a break! What's got into you?'

'What's got into you!' sawed the metallic voice.

Kukla stood on the balcony, gazing at the moon. A smile passed over her face. In the park opposite, the trees were lit up by moonlight and the light of lanterns at the base of their trunks. It seemed that the canopies had no weight and that they could at any moment lift off the trees and float away across the sky like luxurious green zeppelins. Large rooks rustled in the treetops. Kukla could not see them, but she knew they were there.

What about us? Unfortunately, we must keep going. While life may lead us on a merry dance, the tale hastens on without a backward glance.

7.

When she got back to her suite, Beba was overcome by indescribable fatigue. She collapsed, fully dressed, onto her bed, managed to catch a glimpse of the full moon in the sky through the balcony door, which was still open, and then sank into a deep sleep.

Beba dreamed that she was entering a sumptuous royal palace. She appeared to be the queen, although she seemed to be dressed in a nightgown and housecoat. She had bare feet, and had not had time to pull on her 'minimiser', which she was immediately aware of, because the weight of her breasts hurt her. That is why she was supporting them with her hands. She held her left breast in her left palm and her right breast in her right palm. She stepped into the hall like a Sumo-wrestler, which must have aroused respect in those present. Her gaze fell on a red carpet stretching away from her and two rows of figures, between which she was evidently supposed to walk. At the end, somewhere in the depths of the hall, stood a podium and a red and gold royal throne. But, amazingly, the rows were not composed of people, courtiers and ladies, but – eggs!

Having seen plenty of films with such 'regal' scenes, Beba decided to treat the eggs as though they were courtiers, to bestow her queenly attention on them and stop for a moment in front of each of them. And, fancy, as Beba stopped, each egg bowed as a mark of profound respect, pronounced its name – Cuckoo Egg, Renaissance Egg, Lily Egg, Tsarevich Egg – and gracefully opened its interior. Beba examined the inside of each egg in amazement, while the egg listed the precious materials of which it was made: gold, platinum, rubies, sapphires, emeralds, pearls, diamonds . . . Heavens, how many splendid eggs there were in each row! And all the eggs had bowed to her, Beba, with the greatest respect, and then charmingly opened up their insides! Some of the eggs stood on little golden legs, others had pedestals made of the finest material, yet others were rocking on little golden saucers, others again stood firmly wedged in silver or gold holders, while others sat on lavish miniature thrones, but when Beba stopped in front of them, they slipped off them and curtsied. Beba was beside herself with pleasure. It seemed to her that her sight had sharpened, because she noticed, amazingly, even the tiniest detail, as though she had strong magnifying lenses built into her eyes.

And then, perhaps on account of those lenses, she was overcome with fatigue. It was tiring to support her heavy breasts in her hands, and the distance between her and the throne did not seem to be getting any less. Nor were the eggs in front of her beautiful now. One of them opened its interior, in which there was a miniature loudspeaker, and said in a metallic voice: *A little house with no windows or doors, when the owner wants to get out he breaks down the walls!* Beba wanted to walk past the ugly egg, but when she tried to take a step, an invisible force prevented her. The sentence the egg had pronounced was, obviously, a riddle, and the invisible force prevented Beba moving until she had solved it. Beba thought for a long time, her breasts had grown so heavy that her elbows and hands were aching as well, and then she finally worked it out and said: 'An Egg!' And, fancy, the invisible force let her move on.

But at the next moment Beba was suddenly attacked by a fresh yellow yolk that splashed in her face. Beba didn't have time to feel offended. She understood that she had to be quick and smart because the eggs had obviously become hostile.

'I have egg on my face,' she said, under the fierce attack of the yolk 'kamikaze'.

'*On ne saurait faire une omelette sans casser des oeufs*,' said Beba quickly, but afraid that eggs didn't speak French, repeated: '*You can't make an omelette without breaking eggs.*' And the eggs backed off.

Yes, the eggs were different now, sort of 'verbal' eggs. Beba found herself in front of a grey one, which bowed down in front of her, said its name, Grandmother's Egg, and opened up its inside. Inside, where there should have been a gleaming white and a golden yolk, there was nothing, as though it had all been sucked out. Beba realised at once that the egg represented that saying about *teaching your grandmother to suck eggs*. Beba had never used that expression. Maybe because she did not like the idea of sucking eggs.

The entire ceremony had become wearisome and pointless, and Beba wondered what would happen if she was to smash all these arrogant high-protein bastards. She was the Queen, wasn't she, and after all this was her dream, wasn't it? 'I am going to make scrambled eggs out of all of you!' grumbled Beba in her thoughts. And, as though they had guessed what Beba was thinking, the eggs suddenly started to run away in all directions and hide. All except one. At the end of the red carpet, a golden egg was waiting for her. When she reached it, the egg made a charming curtsey, like all the previous eggs, and opened up. Beba felt a sharp stab and for a moment the pain took her breath away. In a miniature golden coffin a beautiful, naked youth was lying in the foetal position. She bent down, took the egg in her hands, looked at the little golden body without breathing, and then a painful sob broke from her chest. The egg slipped out of Beba's hands and fell onto the floor and – hop, hop, hop – jumped into Pupa's boot! It was only then that Beba noticed that Pupa's fur boot was standing beside the throne.

The dream had been horrifying and Beba woke up. She shook herself, her cheeks, wet with tears, were trembling and her heart was beating violently. Still sobbing, Beba got out of bed, went to the fridge and took out a bottle of champagne. She sat for a long time on the edge of the bed, calming her heart, drinking the champagne in rapid, small sips like water and – staring at the round moon. Oh, what a nightmare! Beba tried to separate the tangled threads of the dream, but they just kept getting more tangled. Like a glittering medallion, the golden body of her son in the foetal position flickered in front of her eyes. The moon had grown pale and become almost transparent by the time Beba, dazed with champagne and exhausted by successive sobs, finally fell asleep.

Day Five

1.

Beba and Kukla were pleasantly surprised at breakfast the following morning, when they caught sight of the elegant young man whom Beba had almost knocked over the previous day in the hotel doorway. A still greater surprise ensued when the young man got up from his table, came over to theirs and asked them politely whether he could join them. Kukla and Beba's jaws dropped in amazement when it turned out that the young man spoke Croatian, with an English accent, admittedly, but still quite fluently. It turned out that the young man was a lawyer by profession, that he lived in London and that his daughter was at that moment in the pool with the hotel swimming instructor. The young man was evidently not someone inclined to beat about the bush. Kukla and Beba did beat about the bush, however, because if they had not first asked where he lived, what he did for a living and where his daughter was, they would probably have discovered immediately what soon followed. And the discovery that landed in front of them, like a thunderbolt out of the clear blue sky – on the table with its snow-white linen tablecloth and embroidered linen napkins, with its coffee cups and plates of the finest porcelain, with its silver cutlery, with slivers of pink salmon covered in cream and laid on crisp pancakes, with a little basket full of fresh rolls, with butter in a porcelain dish ringed with ice, with a porcelain bowl of raspberries, blackberries and blueberries that looked as though they had just been picked – was that the young man was none other than Pupa's grandson!

'Grandson!?' exclaimed Kukla and Beba in the same instant.

'That's right,' said the young man.

'Can you prove it?' asked Kukla cautiously.

'Oh, yes, I can show you all the necessary documents. We'll get to that in a moment in any case,' said the young man pleasantly.

'So, you're claiming to be Pupa's grandson!' said Beba, presumably to gain some time, although during that time she did not manage to think of anything apart from what she had already said.

'Yes,' said the young man succinctly.

'Thank goodness you've appeared. Your grandmother passed away yesterday,' said Kukla, who evidently coped with surprises better than Beba.

'That's what I thought,' said the young man, not remotely taken aback.

The wind blows, then calms down, but Pupa's trouble lasted her whole life. While life is lived slowly, the tale is told quickly, so we shall now briefly relate what Pupa's grandson told Kukla and Beba.

Pupa Milanović, née Singer, enrolled at the Zagreb Medical Faculty in 1938. In her first year she fell in love with Aaron Pal, a fellow student. Pupa very soon found that she was pregnant, the young couple married and in 1939 Pupa gave birth to a little girl, Asja. In 1940 Aaron's parents could see that things were looking bad everywhere in Europe, so they moved, with the help of family connections, to London, taking advantage of a brief green light offered by the British authorities, and joining Jews from Poland and Germany. Pupa and Aaron decided to stay in Zagreb. Aaron's parents suggested that they take Asja with them, which seemed a sensible solution to Pupa and Aaron at the time.

'How could they agree to be separated from such a small baby?' Beba interrupted the young man. Like Kukla, she was hearing this story for the first time.

'They knew what was coming, and that the doors of European countries were closing to Jews. But they had their studies to complete in Zagreb and they just hoped that the evil would after all not spread there . . . It's hard for me to answer that question. I know that it's because of their decision that I'm sitting with you at this table today,' said the young man, smiling his disarming smile.

In April 1941 Croatia brought in a racial law: 'Legal Provision for the Protection of Aryan Blood and the Honour of the Croatian Nation'. They introduced the obligation to wear a yellow star, soon followed by the persecution of Jews. Pupa's parents and younger brother were deported to the Jasenovac camp, where they were killed, some time in 1943. Pupa and Aaron fled to the woods to join the Partisans at the end of October 1941, after the Jewish Synagogue in Zagreb had been destroyed with the blessing of the new Ustasha authorities.

'There were a lot of Jews in the Partisans, incidentally, from Croatia, Serbia, Bosnia, but you must know that better than me,' said the young man.

'Oh my God, what a story! Why didn't she ever tell us any of it? Did you know?' Beba asked Kukla.

Kukla shook her head without a word. The story had affected her as deeply as it had Beba.

Aaron was killed fighting in 1944, while Pupa, who had meanwhile developed tuberculosis, lived to see the Liberation. Her tuberculosis was cured, she continued her interrupted studies and then, thanks to her Partisan connections, she finally managed to obtain a visa to travel to England. She appeared in London in the spring of 1947, with the intention of taking Asja back with her to Zagreb. Aaron's parents had no intention of returning to Zagreb. The little girl, meanwhile, had such an attack of hysteria that they all agreed it would be better to delay sending her back. Pupa hoped that next time she would manage to procure a longer stay in London, spend time with Asja and manage to persuade her to travel back with her.

'This is terrible . . .' said Beba, choking with tears.

'That's how it was. A lot of women who were in the Partisans left their children in children's homes and orphanages, to be looked after by relatives or families in villages where it was relatively peaceful during the war. I know of several similar cases,' said Kukla.

Pupa returned from London and continued her medical studies. She worked hard, exhausting herself by studying at the same time as volunteering in Zagreb hospitals and provincial medical centres. She qualified, and then came 1948 and the dreadful, dark days of the Cominform. In 1950, Pupa ended up on Goli Otok, or rather in St Grgur, a prison for female political prisoners.* Like all the other inmates, if they

* Goli Otok and St Grgur are islands off the Croatian coast where real or suspected Soviet sympathisers were imprisoned in the clamp-down following Yugoslavia's break with Stalin in 1948.

managed to survive, Pupa never found out why she had been sent to prison or the name of the person who had denounced her. After she was released, it was clear that the frontiers were closed to her and that meant only one thing – she would not be able to see Asja. Pupa married again in 1955, a doctor colleague, and in 1957 she gave birth to her daughter Zorana.

Goodness, you only need a slightly different light, and things we have always known become suddenly different and alien, thought Kukla. The 'doctor colleague' was Kosta, Kukla's brother. That was when she had met Pupa. Over the years they had grown close, but, remarkably, Pupa never mentioned Goli Otok, or Aaron, or Asja. It is true that all the former Goli Otok inmates had one thing in common: they never said a word about it. When they came out of prison, they were strictly forbidden to discuss their experience with anyone, and Goli Otok altogether was a strictly forbidden topic, until, some time in the nineteen-seventies, the taboo was lifted. But time had reinforced the prisoners' own habit of simply saying nothing. Because there, on Goli Otok, every observation, even the most innocent, reached the guards' ears, and the prisoner was made to pay for it. Yes, those were dark days. People landed in prison for no reason, saddled with the crippling accusation of betrayal of the homeland and alleged support of Stalin. Everyone denounced someone. The communists used a Stalinist stick to beat Stalin. Who knows whether Kosta knew? He must have done, only he did not tell her, Kukla. The Goli Otok embargo dragged in wives and husbands and other members of the family. It was simply never mentioned. It is very hard to explain that to anyone else today. And when the ban was finally lifted, few people were interested in hearing those old Goli Otok stories. Kukla tried to summon up a picture of the young Pupa, but despite her best efforts she could not do it. She thought about the fact that Pupa's grandson – the child of a different culture and different age – had succeeded in solving a puzzle, which they, both Kukla, who was closer to Pupa, and Beba, had been unable to solve, and indeed had made no effort to do so. The invisibility in which we live next to one another is appalling, thought Kukla.

Aaron's father died in 1952, the same year that Pupa came out of prison, and his mother died in 1960. A little later the same year, Asja Pal married Michael Thompson and four years later she gave birth to a little boy, David, and then to a little girl, Miriam. Asja had never been to Yugoslavia, nor had she ever wanted to go. For her Pupa was a monster, a woman who had abandoned her own child in order to join the communists. Pupa's second husband, Kosta, died in 1981. Their daughter Zorana studied medicine and got a job in a Zagreb hospital.

'In the Vinogradska Hospital! Where I spent my working life as well!' In her thoughts Beba whispered to David. It was through Zorana that Beba had met Pupa and somehow it happened that they had become friends. Zorana could occasionally be a bit jealous. 'How come you get on so well with my mother,' she would say, 'when I'm forever quarrelling with her . . . ?' Who knows, perhaps the whole secret is that daughters always make excessive demands on their mothers. The mothers feel guilty, and then protest at both their guilt and the demands made on them. The daughters feel the same mixture of guilt and anger. And round it all goes in a closed circle. Oh, life is so confused! And then stories like this one come like a bolt of lightning out of the blue and turn the picture we have of others on its head. Perhaps that is why people hang on so desperately to their stubborn little truths, because who knows, if everything was put together, as in this case, people would fall apart. It is the brutal truth that what we know about other people could be contained in an insultingly small package.

Pupa tried to get in touch with Asja, without success. When she was finally able to travel, she went to London again. Asja had been so reluctant to meet her that Pupa went home in complete despair. That was why David had appeared like balm for a wound that had never healed. He learned Croatian and came to see Pupa whenever he could. The two of them, Pupa and he, became secret allies. Pupa adored him. When he opened his own legal office and began to earn a decent salary, David set about trying to trace the property of both his Jewish families, the Singers and the Pals. And by some miracle he succeeded in getting back the Singers' family home in Opatija. It did not mean much to Pupa and she immediately offered to leave the house to him. He refused. Then, with his help, she sold it. The major part of the proceeds from the sale was invested in the bank in Pupa's name. Quite recently, Pupa had called him and asked him to alter her will.

'I presume that she didn't tell you . . . That is, Pupa left a significant sum from the sale of the house to each of you,' said David.

Beba, filled with a vague sense of guilt, started to count the things she had recently spent money on, some on massage, some on make-up and some on clothes, and then she had gone to change that five-hundred-euro note, but no one in this town was prepared to, and that was how she wound up in the hotel casino, because she thought that they would be able to change it there, because, in fact, she only needed fifty . . .

'Pupa has left you a sum that will guarantee you a secure and peaceful old age,' David repeated, because he could not work out what Beba was prattling on about so frantically.

'I don't need money. I've got my pension,' said Kukla quietly.

'So have I!' said Beba, blushing, because she still could not take in the fact that the money in the hotel safe was hers.

'I've brought all the papers with me. Pupa signed everything before you came here,' said David.

'So, you knew everything! Where we were going, and everything! She tricked us all, the old witch!' cried Beba.

'That's what we used to call her . . . the old witch,' said Kukla, apologising in her own and Beba's name.

'It's only old witches who lay golden eggs!' said David.

Kukla thought that the young man's Croatian was not as good as it had seemed to her at first. Who knows where he came across that clumsy sentence?

'What do you mean by that?'

'It's an old Polynesian proverb. It means that old women do good deeds.'

Let us pause here for a moment to say that life is a field where the wind always blows, while the tale may expand and contract as it goes.

At that moment Mevlo came into the restaurant, holding the little Chinese girl's hand. The child was hopping from foot to foot and carrying a puppy in her arms, while a smile was spread over Mevlo's face. When they came up to the table, Beba, wiping her tears away, remarked:

'And since when have you been a swimming instructor?'

'Oh, love, when they tell me "swim", I swim! When they say "massage", I massage!'

Mevlo sat down at the table, set the little girl down beside him, spooned raspberries, blackberries and blueberries into a bowl, poured cream over them and placed the bowl in front of her.

'Here you are, sweetie-pie, try that!' said Mevlo, as naturally as though the little girl were his daughter.

'What's the child's name?' Beba asked David.

'Wawa.'

'Wawa?'

'And another thing,' said David cautiously. 'She's not my daughter – she's your granddaughter.'

There are all kinds of people in the world, good and bad. Beba had a heart as big as a frying pan and a mind that those around her did not consider worthy of mention. Between her heart and her mind there was a sudden short circuit. Beba was simply not in a position to take in the quantity of new information that had splashed over her like a bucket of cold water. That was why her eyes narrowed, she swayed on her chair, cried out something that sounded like 'Awaw!' and, dragging the tablecloth with her, crashed to the floor. There was general consternation in the restaurant: the waiters flocked round like seagulls, picked up the cutlery, wiped up the spilt milk, ran after a bun that was rolling over the floor. In a few seconds two male nurses appeared. They put Beba on a stretcher. The stretcher was followed by Kukla, after Kukla came David, after David Mevlo and after Mevlo skipped the little girl with the puppy in her arms. In the whole scurrying procession, it was only the little girl whose face showed no trace of anxiety.

'Honestly! Why are you giggling, my pet?' grumbled Mevlo.

'Old ladies are funny!' said the little girl.

'My special friend has fainted, and you think it's funny. What's funny about it, eh?'

'Awaw! Awaw!' the child chirped, hopping from foot to foot.

'Aw! Aw!' the puppy joined in for the first time.

From his pocket Mevlo took a little wooden ladle decorated with Czech folk patterns that he had picked up on some local souvenir stall:

'Here, see if this will help you calm down.'

'Why?'

'Vai, vai, vai! So you can make me soup when you grow up, that's vai.'

The little girl burst into peals of silvery laughter.

Here it should be said that Mevlo found nothing strange about the fact that the little girl was speaking English and he Bosnian, but they understood each other very well. The only thing Mevlo could not understand was why the little girl kept repeating 'Awaw! Awaw!' But the little girl was only saying her name – Wawa – backwards, which was after all what Beba had done as she passed out. It was one of Beba's little quirks, that at moments when things started going awry she would pronounce words backwards.

What about us? We keep going. While life finds humps and bumps to stumble on, the tale keeps hurrying and scurrying along.

2.

Mr Shaker, Pupa, Pupa's grandson, that *nepos ex machina*! Goodness, how much had happened, and at what breakneck speed! Kukla had not yet managed to take any of it in properly, nor give it due consideration, and, what do you know, here she was dragging a completely strange little girl around after her and having to find some way of entertaining her until Beba came to and was able to get her bearings. And then the news that Beba's son had died of Aids, that his partner had refused to take over care of the child and that Beba would have to take legal charge of her, because there was no one else to do it . . . It was all too much, too much even for a very bad novel, thought Kukla. But, then again, things happened, and, besides, life had never claimed to have refined taste. Each of them, Pupa, Beba and Kukla, had her own life, each of them had accumulated baggage on her way and each of them dragged her own burden after her. And now, all that luggage, piled up in one great heap, had collapsed under its own weight – the suitcases had burst at the seams and all their old junk was out in the open.

As soon as Kukla opened the suite door, the child's gaze was drawn to Pupa's fur boot, as though to a magnet. The boot had stood there since the hotel staff brought it back from dry cleaning. To start with the little girl just looked at the boot in wonder, then she went cautiously up to it and peered in. Slowly she raised one foot, then the other, and stepped into the boot. At first she stood in the boot, looking all around her, and then she slipped deftly into it and sat down, without letting her puppy out of her embrace.

'Are you hungry?' asked Kukla.

The child shook her head.

'Thirsty?'

'Umm . . .' replied the child non-committally.

'You're not thirsty?'

The child shook her head again.

Kukla was a little embarrassed. Looking after small children was evidently not her greatest talent. The child peeped out of the boot, tensely following Kukla's every move. Kukla sat down wearily on the edge of the bed and gazed at the little girl.

'What am I going to do with you?' she asked.

The child raised her shoulders and let them fall.

'Do you like the boot?'

'Aha . . .'

'My friend used that boot to keep her feet warm,' said Kukla, because she didn't know what else to say.

The child stared at Kukla without stirring.

'Her name was Pupa.'

'Apup saw eman reh,' said the child.

Kukla gaped at the little girl: that was not Chinese, for sure. The child watched her blithely, knowing that she had attracted Kukla's attention.

'Pu-pa,' repeated Kukla.

'Apup!' said the little girl.

'Kukla.'

'Alkuk,' said the child.

No, it's not possible! thought Kukla. The little girl is far too bright for her years, no adult is capable of playing with words like that at such speed. Kukla shuddered. What if reversing words was the symptom of some serious illness?

'Mum makes lunch, Dad reads the paper,' said Kukla, knowing that what she was saying was stupid, but it was the first thing that occurred to her.

'Mumdad makes lunch and reads the paper!' said the little girl.

'Who's Mumdad?' asked Kukla surprised.

'Filip,' said the little girl and drew herself into the boot.

* * *

There was a silence. Again, Kukla did not know what to say.

'What are you doing in that boot?' she asked after a while.

The little girl said nothing.

'Where are you? I can't see you.'

'I can see you,' said the little girl.

'You're like a mouse . . . Like a mouse in a slab of cheese doing just what you please.'

'I'm a little girl.'

'Come on, then, get out of that boot.'

'I can't.'

'What are you doing in there?'

'I'm flying,' said the little girl.

'Floating, more like,' Kukla corrected her.

'Flying, more like,' said the child.

Good heavens, thought Kukla in surprise. She had no experience whatever of children, admittedly, but it seemed to her that little girls of four did not talk quite like this.

'Hey, come out of there a minute, I want to ask you something.'

'What?' asked the little girl, but she did not poke her head out.

'Do you know what two plus two makes?'

Out of the boot poked the little girl's hand, showing four fingers.

'And how old are you?'

The little girl showed four fingers again.

'What about you?' came a little voice from the boot.

Kukla stood up, found a piece of paper and a pencil, wrote a large figure 80 on the paper and turned it towards the child.

'Come out and I'll show you!' said Kukla.

The child peered out.

'Eighty!' she said.

'Not quite, actually, I'll be eighty in December.'

'You're twenty times older than me,' said the little girl.

'Which makes you twenty times younger than me,' said Kukla.

Kukla was alarmed again. She wondered whether the little girl was not too clever for her years. She would have to talk to Beba. Poor Beba, she must be lying in her room in despair. David was inaccessible. You couldn't ask him anything. He was rushing about sorting out Pupa's affairs.

'Listen, little one, what would you say to the two of us ordering something sweet from the cake shop?'

The little girl poked her head out of the boot and nodded.

'Ice cream or cakes?'

'The first,' said the little girl.

Kukla felt better. She was a child after all. A dear, sweet little girl . . .

'What about Toto?'

'Who's Toto?' asked Kukla in surprise.

Wawa pointed at the puppy.

'Hmm . . . OK, let's go for a walk; we'll buy some dog biscuits for Toto, and the two of us will find somewhere to sit and have an ice cream. How about that?'

The little girl clambered out of the boot and cheerfully held her hand out to Kukla. Kukla noticed that the little girl had dark eyebrows, almost touching in the middle. On her round face they looked like a child's drawing of a bird in flight.

3.

Everything had fallen apart, as though the cupboard in her little office in the medical faculty had burst open. The office was where she had spent her whole life drawing sketches that no one needed any more, and now those sketches, rolled up in dusty bundles, had tumbled out of the cupboard and unfurled like little rugs. Fragments scampered in front of Beba's eyes: bones, muscles, nerves, the nervous system, cells, reproductive organs, the urinary tract, the cardiovascular system, the heart, veins, arteries, the liver, ears, the auricular canal, the spleen, stomach, intestines, large and small, the rectum, anus, lungs, windpipe, oesophagus, the eye . . . That was Beba's field, Beba's *Guernica*. And in that paper snowstorm a lost child wandered, Beba's son.

Yes, Beba had a son, Filip. He had inherited her talent for drawing, and as soon as he graduated from the Academy, he had gone abroad: Italy, France and London. That was where he met his partner ('partner?' What a clumsy word!). According to David, at a certain moment Filip had wanted a child; he had gone rushing about, investing all his time and energy in the business of adopting one. Finally, he got lucky, and they, Filip and his partner, succeeded in adopting a little girl who was just a few months old. But then Filip began to obsess about what would become of the child if anything happened to him. And he would not rest until he had drawn up a will with David's help, according to which, in the event of his death, Beba would take over care of the child. When Filip died of Aids, exactly what he had foreseen occurred. His partner left the little girl to David, collected all Filip's paintings and disappeared. That was all Beba managed to glean from David. But she would ask, she would try to find out. Because ever since he left home, Filip had rarely been in touch. The occasional letter, more often a postcard, just to let her know he was alive. He had never given any address. He had never contacted his father. In truth, he had no reason to. His biological father had never shown any interest in him, and if he had done, there would have been a scene as soon as he learned of Filip's inclinations.

It was all her fault, of course, and it would not have been right to blame his father. Because she was the one who had pushed the unfortunate father to one side, proclaiming him 'biological', and then 'hypothetical', in order to have Filip to herself. Yes, her passion had drawn misfortune in its wake. God, now that she thought about it, she had bought him clothes as though she was his lover, rather than his mother. When he was little, she had dressed him like a doll, and then, when he grew up, like the lover she had never managed to acquire. When he was not at home, she sometimes went to his little room and stood for a long time in the doorway, breathing in his smell. It was her fault. And when he left, she had spent days dreaming of his return. Yes, she had wanted him all to herself, and had only pretended that that was not the case. She concealed her feelings, she acted, she did all she could not to suffocate him. She went out with men, pretending to have her own life, to be an independent woman who lived life to the full and did not care about anything else. But still, love seeped out of her and, like the foam putty used to fit window-panes, it filled all her cracks, pores and openings. She could not deceive him, it was impossible to breathe: the air in their apartment was just too dense. She followed him like a dog, arousing first his pity, and then his revulsion.

And then one day, returning early from work, she went into his room and found him in bed with a young man. She stopped, dumbfounded, in the doorway, he shouted something, but she did not understand the content of his words. She stood there without breathing, without thoughts, without interest, without curiosity, without censure. He got up and banged the door in her face. And the very next day he packed and left, forever. At first she agonised about it; she could not understand why he had been so angry. Because she was innocent, if that is the right word, she had wronged him only for a second, for heaven's sake, for just one single second. She had been entranced by what she saw, the image of a male body, to which she had given birth, that was her blood, her flesh. She had forgotten herself, astounded, she had disregarded human decency, and she had been justly punished. She could have shut the door, been ashamed, apologised, but she had not done that. She was to blame, she had driven him from the house. Oh, God, how come she had not thought of that then? That win at the casino was only an intimation of imminent loss.

There was a soft tapping at the door. She did not respond; she did not have the energy to get up.

Mevludin came into the room. Beba did not stir. Her lips were dry, her eye make-up had run and now it streaked her face in thin streams.

Without a word, Mevludin went to the bathroom, wet a face cloth under the cold tap and began to wipe Beba's cheeks.

'Poor you . . . you look like a chimney sweep . . .'

Beba burst into tears again.

'Drink this. And stop crying, love, you'll run out of tears,' said Mevlo, offering Beba a glass of water. Beba drained it and felt able to breathe more deeply.

‘Here, have a smoke, you’ll feel better,’ said Mevlo, handing her a lit cigarette.

Beba and Mevludin smoked in silence.

‘Don’t be cross with me,’ said Mevludin after a while.

‘What about?’

‘For acting the fool. But then, I kept thinking it’d be more fun . . .’

‘And it was.’

‘It’s right for me to say it, though.’

‘I know.’

‘Then you must also know that I think you’re great. And I won’t forget you.’

‘I know.’

‘Well then, now that we’ve said all there is to say, I’m off.’

Mevlo got up and set off towards the door.

‘Wait,’ said Beba.

Beba got out of bed and took an envelope out of the safe.

‘Just in case . . .’ she said, handing him the envelope.

The envelope contained a bundle of notes.

‘I can’t take this.’

‘It’s a present from me. You’ll need something to get you started, to buy a ticket to America and to keep you going while you find your feet . . .’

‘I can’t . . .’

‘Which of the two of us is older and stupider?’

‘You,’ Mevlo smiled.

‘Well, then, your place is to do as I say. You’ll find my address inside. So one day, when you’re passing through Zagreb . . .’

‘I’ll look you up.’

Mevlo and the stout old woman hugged. Beba burst into tears again. Mevlo patted her shoulder and grumbled:

'You women are all made of water. The quantity of tears you have in you is unbelievable. You should all be packed off to the desert and used for irrigation.'

Mevlo took a cigarette out of his packet and stuck it behind Beba's ear:

'Just in case,' he said and left the room.

4.

When he was making his new spa, Dr Topolanek had thought about his grandmother, to whose place they had always gone for lunch on Sundays. Afraid that she would not get everything ready in time, his grandmother always started cooking so early that by the time they, the Topolanek family, arrived everything on the table was cold. Every Sunday his grandmother got upset, and every Sunday his father consoled her:

'Come on, Agneza, calm down, you know yourself that there is nothing in the world tastier than cold meatballs and – warm beer!'

Topolanek called his new spa 'Granny Agneza'. It sounded local, but still a little mysterious, because people would wonder who Agneza was, why Agneza, which Agneza . . . ? As well as this private justification, Topolanek had an objective one for his choice of his grandmother's name: Agneza lived ninety-one years, which was a pretty decent age.

The previous evening, Linear had made a heap of meatballs, which were piled in a round dish on the edge of the swimming pool, while Willowy had brought gherkins and mustard. The girls moved Topolanek to tears with this gourmet detail. Now the three of them were sitting, naked, immersed in the hotel jacuzzi, which had been transformed into a vast tankard.

Topolanek had had the jacuzzi filled with beer, and reduced the churning to a minimum, to ensure that, heaven forbid, they did not suffocate in froth. As it was, the froth was flying about in all directions.

It was a scene worthy of Lucas Cranach Senior, and, were he alive, he would have been able to paint *Fountain of Youth* 'Part Two'. Except that, on the table, in the top right-hand corner of the painting, instead of a fish on a platter, there would have been Granny Agneza's meatballs.

The girls were having the time of their lives. Willowy had made herself a beard of beer froth, while Linear had made a wig. Topolanek himself had gone beerily berserk. He was chasing Linear and Willowy round the little circular pool, repeating:

'Little seals, come to daddy, little seals . . .'

And then the little seals came closer, slurped some beer from the pool and started rubbing their bodies against Topolanek's. They were both smooth, slippery and agile, just like the seals in the zoo pool. Exclaiming, 'Here!' Topolanek tossed one meatball with his right hand into one mouth and another with his left into the other. The little seals fed from his hands. Willowy dunked her meatball in the beer froth, claiming it was nicer with froth than mustard. Then they dived under the surface, gambolled, played tag, clapped their hands in the foam, threw balls of beer froth at each other, touched each other, petted and kissed each other, from time to time chanting a little song that Linear had made up:

> Merrily we swim, like little bugs in beer,
> Beer is our element: clear, dear and here!

Topolanek felt magnificent, like a great reformer, like a scientist after a revolutionary discovery. If he had not actually discovered the formula of longevity, then with 'Granny Agneza' he had at least composed an ode in praise of vitamin B, and discovered yet another of the ways life could be merrier and more relaxed, and that, in our anxious and dismal age, could be regarded as a capital contribution, could it not?

And us? While life is often gloomy and cheerless, the tale runs on, bright and fearless!

5.

'I can't. I simply can't,' Beba kept repeating, as though in delirium.

Beba and Arnoš Kozeny were sitting in the half-empty hotel bar, sipping French cognac.

'I entirely understand,' said Arnoš Kozeny, puffing smoke from his cigar.

'My granddaughter!? Why, I don't know her at all!' said Beba.

'And how could you, for goodness' sake! You only discovered a few hours ago that you're a grandmother.'

'And the murderer of my own son,' said Beba bitterly.

'Come now, don't exaggerate, we're all murderers. First we murder our own parents, and then our own children.'

'I don't know. All I know is that whoever wrote the screenplay of my life was completely incompetent.'

'They're all incompetent.'

Arnoš was right, they're all incompetent. Few can boast that their screenplay writer really suits them. Who knows, perhaps the bureaucratic offices of Destiny are like Hollywood or

Bollywood, perhaps instead of millions of diligent bureaucrats, there are millions of bunglers copying, rewriting, smudging the paper and scribbling. Maybe there are even different departments, and some do the dialogue, others the storyline, still others the characters, and maybe that is why our lives are such an indescribable mess. As soon as we are born, an invisible bundle is thrust into our hands and we all scatter off into our lives like Boy Scouts, each of us clutching our invisible coordinates in our hands. And perhaps that anxious race is the reason for our monstrous ignorance of other people's lives, the lives of those who are closest to us.

'So why don't you intervene?' asked Arnoš.

'How could I intervene?'

'Well, for instance, you could go back to your hotel room and confront the new circumstance in your life, your little granddaughter! And then endeavour to make the very best you can of the situation.'

'How?!'

'You'll know, when it comes to it.'

Perhaps Arnoš was right about this as well. Perhaps intervening in the screenplay is all that is left to us? To offer our shoulder at the right moment for someone to cry on, to hand someone a handkerchief, show them the way. Because people often do not know the most basic things. Once Beba was waiting in a queue at the bank when a man asked her: 'Excuse me, which is the right-hand side here?' Everyone who heard him burst out laughing. It was only Beba who felt sympathy for the confused man. Showing someone which is right and which left, that is perhaps the intervention Arnoš means. We cannot do more than that, even if we wanted to. Take Pupa. Ever since she had known her, Pupa had always been reticent and restrained. If she ever said anything it was usually a comment on what others were saying. Beba had always thought that tiny little woman was as strong as an oak. Now she recalled a distant scene which she had forgotten. She had once gone to see Pupa, her door was open, and she had gone in and found Pupa kneeling on the floor, sobbing. It was a chilling scene, and Beba had wanted to tiptoe out again, to simply run away from the place of someone else's misery. That was when she realised for the first time that we are capable of swallowing all sorts of things. After all, she had herself had her fill in hospital – of stomachs split open and guts falling out – and all that could be borne; there was only one thing that it was very hard to accept: the sight of someone else's pain, a glimpse of a soul seeping unstoppably out of a body like a stream of urine. In the face of such a sight, we are hypnotised, like a rabbit confronting a boa constrictor. Beba sat down on the floor, without a word, spread her legs, placed Pupa in her lap, clasping her with both her arms and legs, pressing her to herself like a cushion, and who knows how long the two of them sat there like that in silence, fitted one into the other like two spoons. They never mentioned it afterwards, Beba did not ask, and Pupa never told her what it was about. Perhaps it had not been anything special. Perhaps some inner sorrow had risen up in her and stuck in her throat like a fish bone. Beba had helped her cough it out. And that was all. As we grow older, we weep less and less. It takes energy to weep. In old age neither the lungs, nor the heart, nor the tear ducts, nor the muscles have the strength for great misery. Age is a kind of natural sedative, perhaps because age itself is a misfortune.

'How will I know? I was a lousy mother. I've wasted my own life pointlessly. I'm not qualified to be a grandmother,' said Beba.

'Just take a look around you, see how many people have placed their stakes on you!'

'How do you mean?'

'Your son, for example, he placed his stake on you! And the dice went in your favour! And your late friend, she too gave you a chance. And I, talking to you now, I am placing my stake on you. Admittedly it's only a small coin, but I've placed it on you, and not on anyone else.'

'You're a good man, Arnoš.'

'Perhaps, but I was a bad husband, father and grandfather. All I cared about in my life were women. I'm nothing but a scatterbrain, my dear. But still I'm lucky. There are few people my age who can afford such luxury.'

'I don't know. I'm seventy years old; I haven't learned anything sensible in my life. Sometimes I think it would be best to kill myself . . .' mused Beba thoughtfully.

Arnoš looked at her and said cheerfully:

If you want to end it all, do it with good taste:
You would not wish to leave a pall or a bitter taste.
Choose with care, as though it were a matter of fine wine:
Leave those who stay here with a sense of touching the divine.

If you want to end it all, do it with good taste:
Let others know you had a ball, your life was not a waste.
Choose a plaited rope of silk, in the hour before dawn,
When the air is smooth as milk and dew bejewels the lawn.

If you want to end it all, do it with good taste:
Find a sparkling waterfall, its spray spun and laced,
Scatter it with flowers whose fragrance lasts for hours,
Take something sweet to sustain you through the moment's heat,
Breathe in and dive arrow-like, in your most graceful style
Straight as a die through the narrow gate, wearing a blissful smile.

'Who wrote that?'

'I did. I've written quite a pile of worthless verses. And so as not to fall into the temptation of reciting any more, let's clink our glasses and drink to a good night and a forthcoming bright, sunny morning!' said Arnoš Kozeny in high spirits.

And us? While life stumbles through thickets and briars, the tale is one of the constant high-fliers.

6.

The young man and the girl were sitting on a bench in the local park under a large chestnut tree whose luxuriant branches shrouded them like a green crown. The grass around them was moist and soft. It looked like a field prepared for an unusual ritual whose pagan signs no one was capable of deciphering. The local birds were changing their plumage and leaving their feathers everywhere. From a distance, it looked as though the young couple on the bench were protected by a feathery net, a large Indian 'castle of dreams'. The birds hidden in the thick branches of the chestnut hushed their song to listen to the human chirruping.

'You're my pudding, my fruit pudding . . .'

The girl listened breathlessly, but her gaze was directed somewhere towards her feet, where from time to time she scratched one foot with the other.

'You're my peach melba, my cream alpine, my blueberry anglaise, my floating island, my chocolate éclair, my choux chantilly, my kirsch bûchette . . . you're my kirsch puff.'

'What?' the girl laughed delightedly.

'You're my croque-en-bouche, my brioche, my brioche au sucre, my almond cookie, my rum baba, my biscuit, my biscuit de savoie, my profiterole,' whispered Mevlo into the girl's ear, which was pink as orange rind.

'Ah, Mellow . . .' whispered the girl, trembling from the intoxicating shivers running through her round body.

'Mevlo . . .' Mevlo corrected her.

'Mellow . . .' repeated the girl, looking at Mevlo with wide-open eyes.

'My name is Mevlo . . .' repeated Mevlo, plunging into those two green pools.

'Mellow . . .' said the girl sweetly.

'*OK, mala moja, vidim da mi to nećeš naučit . . .*'* Mevlo sighed resignedly.

Mevlo had taken a menu from the hotel confectioner's and spent the whole night learning the names of cakes and sweets. That was the cleverest piece of advice that anyone could have given him. And it was advice given him by Arnoš Kozeny.

'My dear young man,' Arnoš Kozeny had said, when Mevlo complained in despair that he could not speak English and that he did not know how he could explain to the girl that he cared about her, 'the fact that you don't speak English is to your advantage. Because if you could, you might make a

* *'OK, little one, I see that you're never going to learn.'*

mistake. Whereas this way it's quite immaterial what you say, chemical formulae or car parts. In any case in the first phase of being in love couples don't talk. They chirrup . . .'

'Like birds?'

'Like birds, my boy . . .' said Arnoš Kozeny, adding enigmatically: 'Not only do they chirrup, but feathers fly in all directions.'

'You're my truffle, you're my black forest gateau, you're my gateau basque, my guadeloupe, my nian gao with one hundred fruits, my vassilopitta efkoli, my tremolat, my black devil, my gianduja ganache, my sachertorte, my caramel, my marzipan, my marquise, my mousse au chocolat, my passion fruit cream, my passion fruit, my fruit, my passion . . .'

'Ah, Mellow . . .'

'You're my little strudel, my truffle, my fudge . . .'

'I'm feeling mellow . . .'

'Oh, Rosie, Ružice, my little rose, my rosebud . . .'

The young man and the girl were so deeply engrossed in their twitterings of love that they did not notice that a slight breeze had got up and lifted the feathers from the grass around them. The branches of the old chestnut rustled and feathers flew through the air.

Day Six, Epilogue

Even on this Saturday morning, the receptionist Pavel Zuna did not neglect his exercises in the warm hotel pool. Particularly as he was assisted by Jana, a young student at the Physiotherapy training school, who, thanks to her daddy's connections, was doing her month's placement in the best possible place, the Grand Hotel.

Under the command of the lovely Jana, Pavel Zuna was doing his exercises obediently. One-two-two-two-two-three . . . Zuna's condition had markedly improved over the previous few days, and that nerve, taut as a bowstring until a little while ago, had relaxed. Immersed in warm water in the small pool, like an experienced hotel professional recognising a future professional, Pavel Zuna kept repeating:

*'Vy jeste velice talentovana, Jano, velice talentovana . . .'**

On Saturday morning, at his usual time, Arnoš Kozeny was sitting sprawled in an armchair in the hotel lobby, sipping a cappuccino, puffing smoke from his cigar and running his eye over the newspaper. His attention was drawn to the news that two days earlier on the two farms near Norin, where the H5N1 virus had been identified, successful decontamination

* *'You are very talented, Jana, very talented . . .'*

measures had been put in place and 70,000 chickens had been destroyed. The H5N1 virus had been found at the end of June in Germany and France, and the governments of those countries had taken the necessary measures. The spokesman of the Czech Veterinary Service, Josef Duben, had announced that a further 72,000 chickens had been destroyed, although there had been no trace on those farms of the H5N1 virus, which had so far killed some two hundred of the three hundred or so people infected, mostly Asians. Although there had not been a single European among the victims, and therefore no Czech, the Czech Veterinary Service had taken the decision to cull the additional 72,000 chickens as an exclusively preventative measure. The European Union compensation for the culled birds amounted to 1.5 million euros . . .

With an expression of boredom on his face, Arnoš Kozeny folded his newspaper and thought about his first wife Jarmila, who lived in Norin, where she had a small house with a garden. They had not been in touch for more than a year, and this would be an opportunity to give her a call. 'You'll phone me when you hear the footsteps of the Grim Reaper. And you'll come to me, you bastard, to be buried, because there won't be anyone else to do it!' Jarmila had been inclined to complain. Who knows, perhaps she was right, because after all she was never wrong. But it would be a while yet before the bell tolled, thought Arnoš Kozeny, particularly as he had noticed a middle-aged woman strolling into the hotel lobby leading three miniature poodles. Like an old warrior, Arnoš Kozeny automatically straightened his shoulders and drew in his stomach, pulled onto his face the mask reserved for such strategic situations – the mask of a moderately interested veteran in the field of sexual supply and demand – and drew on his cigar with relish.

* * *

That Saturday morning Mevludin was awoken by bright sunlight splashing into his room. His glance fell on Rosie's shoulder, sprinkled with tiny freckles, flashing like a tiger's eye. Rosie was lying on her side, sleeping peacefully as she sucked her thumb. Mevludin tenderly pulled her thumb out of her mouth. The girl wriggled and pursed her lips.

'*Lijepa si mi ko jaje od prepelice,*'* whispered Mevludin, looking at the young woman in wonder. And then he got up and closed the curtains. He climbed back into bed, sighed deeply and plunged into her luxuriant copper-coloured hair . . .

'Ah, Mellow . . .' whispered the young woman sleepily.

On Saturday morning the Grand Hotel was bathed in luxurious sunlight. From room number 313 came a hoarse male voice – which betrayed the fact that its owner had given his vocal chords a thorough soaking in alcohol the previous night – berating a person whose name was Marlena: '*Marlena, yesli ty menya pokinesh, ya tebya ubyu, chestno, ty ne smeysya, ya tebya, suka, ubyu, ty tolko smotri, slyshysh,* . . .'†

On Saturday morning Willowy, Linear and Dr Janek Topolanek were lying in a symmetrical arrangement on the large king-sized bed in the suite to which Topolanek, as a hotel employee, had permanent access. Little fruit flies were swarming round their heads. At one moment Dr Topolanek felt an irresistible urge to empty his bladder, but when he sat up to go to the bathroom, he was doubled up by a terrible pain in his lower back. The doctor cried out and

* *'You're as lovely as a quail's egg.'*

† *'Marlena, if you leave me, I'll kill you, honestly, don't laugh, I'll kill you, you bitch, just watch me, I'm telling you . . .'*

fell back on the bed as though felled. Willowy and Linear woke up.

'What is it?'

'My back hurts!'

'*Heksenschuss!*' said Linear calmly.

'A witch's blow!' said Willowy.

'What do we do now?' wailed Topolanek, although he knew quite well what was coming.

'Rest!' said Linear, yawning.

'Maybe a Voltaren injection,' said Willowy, yawning as well.

The girls wrapped themselves round Dr Topolanek and fell asleep again.

Dr Topolanek did not have a chance to be indignant at their lack of care, because he was wondering obsessively about just one thing – how was he going to pee. And, when there was nothing else for it, he yelled:

'I neeeeed a botttttle!'

On Saturday morning, when David's car left the famous spa town, the sky was blue, the grass green, the trees with their dense branches were casting sharp shadows, and between the shadows, as though jumping over invisible strings, large black crows were scampering. David was thinking over the whole tangle of unusual circumstances, about people's lives, Asja's, Pupa's, Kukla's and Beba's, about the chance chain of events that had led him to Filip, Beba's son, then a bit about his own life. They had all been drawn towards each other for a moment like magnets. He thought about Pupa. Lives could turn out one way or another, most of us live our lives shoddily, but at least then that famous metaphorical descent from the train ought somehow to be calculated in time and an effort made to ensure that the descent itself is not shoddy.

We are not responsible for our arrival in the world, but perhaps we can be for our departure. At the last moment, Pupa had thrown the ball that had been placed in front of her (in which David too had played his part), and the little ball had first of all flown in the expected direction – towards her grandchildren, Zorana's and Asja's children – but then in the end it had rolled away where no one had anticipated, and, what was most important, where its fall would cause it to spin in a livelier and more useful way: towards Kukla, Beba and Wawa.

What a young man! What a wonderful young man! thought Kukla, sitting comfortably sprawled on the back seat of the car. David had not only arranged everything, but now he was even driving them home, to Zagreb. Pupa was at this moment flying in her egg from Prague to Zagreb, and she would be met at the airport by a funeral service that would take her to the morgue. David had thought of that as well. And he had managed to organise Pupa's funeral: that would take place in two days' time. He had found the requisite addresses on the Internet and got everything done with a few phone calls. The money that Pupa had left in her will to Kukla and Beba had already been transferred to a newly opened joint account in both their names. Beba's money, the sum she had won gambling, had also been transferred to the joint account, at Beba's insistence. All the papers had been signed, not a single detail had been overlooked. A special account had also been opened with money intended exclusively for Wawa's future education. All the rest had been left up to Beba and Kukla, although David had promised that he would be available to help at any time.

Through the car window Kukla watched the clouds, white and weightless as beaten egg white. She let her thoughts run once again over the list of things she had to do. She had to buy a new computer and would have to start looking round schools. That would be a challenging task, to find out which were the best schools. And then, maybe Wawa would want to go to ballet school, and music school, and skating, oh, there were so many things! Kukla decided that she would sell her flat and put all the money in one place, and then she and Beba could talk everything over, how, what and when. Because who knows how much longer she would be on hand for Wawa. If she had inherited lucky genes, and it seemed as though she had, she would be in this world for a while yet, absorbed in a new, wonderful and unique task – Wawa! She would be Wawa's auntie, Wawa's auntie Kukla. But if she thought about it all, perhaps it wasn't so important that she and Beba should plan things in advance. Perhaps they ought to instill something different into Wawa, some learning that would make her wise, something that no school in the world could give her.

Beba too was composing a list in her head. First of all she would have to take herself in hand and put her neglected body in motion. She would need her body because of – Wawa. There, things were suddenly crystal clear. She would have to renew her driving licence, she'd neglected that as well, and buy a new car. Otherwise, who would drive Wawa to kindergarten, to school, to ballet, if she wanted, and music school, if she wanted, and to foreign language classes, if she wanted that as well? Perhaps she, Beba, would be able to enrol in a Chinese class? Admittedly Wawa did not know a word of Chinese, but what if she wanted one day to see her Chinese homeland? Then she, Beba, would have to accompany her, and knowing Chinese would come in handy. As soon as they got back, she would sell her small flat, put all the money in one heap, and talk things over with Kukla.

They'd sit down and talk it through. They'd certainly need to buy a shared house, a wonderful house, with a large garden with fruit trees in it. And one big walnut tree, for shade. That would be Pupa's tree, in her memory; after all, it was she, the old witch, who had stirred this all up. And they'd plant a raspberry patch, so that she could make Wawa raspberry jam. There'd be a little kennel in the garden for a dog, for a rabbit, a tortoise, a hedgehog, whatever Wawa wanted. And a little studio in the garden, so that Wawa and her future friends could learn to draw, and perhaps, who knows, she herself would return to the dreams of her youth and finally start painting real pictures. In her mind Beba touched wood: just let her stay well, and let her see Wawa start secondary school. Wawa would study, they would have to help her choose the best university. But on the other hand, when she came to think of it, she had a degree and it had never done her much good. Perhaps Wawa ought to learn other, more important things. Life was an endless garden filled with hidden Easter eggs. Some people collected basketfuls, others did not find a single one. Perhaps that was what they ought to teach Wawa: how to be a hunter, a hunter of wonders. Not to miss anything, to enjoy every second, for life is the only thing we are given free of charge. Beba suddenly felt immense gratitude to her son. She felt that all those drawers in her that she had kept closed for years were opening and she was now breathing freely. At this moment nothing else mattered, all that mattered was this enchanting creature. Ah, those little cheeks, those thick, calm eyelashes, those eyebrows like wings and that breath, oh God, that sweet child's breath . . .

'Don't you think she looks a bit like Filip?' whispered Beba.

'Of course, of course she does . . .' said Kukla, who had never seen Filip, not even in a photograph.

* * *

Through the car window Kukla looked at the landscapes that were slowly moving past them. The sky was blue, the grass green, the trees with their dense branches were casting sharp shadows, and between the shadows, as though jumping over invisible strings, large black crows were scampering. And the clouds, the clouds were gushing over the sky like the foam of beaten egg whites.

Wawa was curled up inside Pupa's boot with her puppy in her arms, sleeping. Out of the boot poked her little hand, in which she was firmly clutching Mevlo's wooden ladle. And then, just as though she could feel Beba and Kukla's thoughts swarming over her, she wriggled, scratched her little nose with her free hand and – went back to sleep. Beba and Kukla, each for herself, stroked the side of the fur boot protectively and daydreamed . . .

What about us? Our work is done, a bitter-sweet feat, but a treat-filled one: roast chickens fell out of the blue, drumsticks for us and bones for you! We were there to drink wine fresh from the vine: with Pupa from a mug, with Kukla from a jug, with Beba from a flask – a toast to our task. We must leave them here and wish them good cheer! If you want any more, don't knock at our door!

PART THREE

If You Know Too Much, You Grow Old Too Soon

Slavic Folklore Studies
Joensuu Yliopisto, University of Joensuu
PO Box 111
FI-80101 Joensuu
Finland

Dear Editor,

I must admit how surprised I was to get your letter. I do not know how you came to choose me out of all the excellent scholars in Folklore Studies. I only joined this university recently and haven't yet gained the sort of reputation here or in international academic circles for my name to mean anything to you. Of course I am pleased that you turned to me, but I must warn you before we go any further that, although I do indeed specialise in Slavic folklore, myths and ritual traditions, this does not make me an expert on your topic by any means. Secondly, I am under a good deal of pressure trying to finish a book about 'Bulgarian popular beliefs related to childbirth', and unfortunately I won't be able to give as much time as I would like to answering your questions. Be this as it may, flattered by your trust in my ability, as also by a wish to maintain this contact (which, who knows, may be more than coincidence!), I have read the manuscript you sent me with pleasure. I confess that the brevity of the text contributed not a little to my enjoyment.

* * *

As far as I gather from your accompanying letter, your author undertook to provide a text based on the myth of Baba Yaga. By the way, I was touched by your admission that you 'don't have a clue' about Baba Yaga yourself. Nevertheless, you only have to surf the Net a bit to see that, while Baba Yaga may not be Oprah Winfrey or Princess Diana, she isn't a completely obscure mythical nonentity either. A shamanist group in northern Holland is named after her; likewise a table-lamp shop somewhere in Poland, a Polish–American magazine (*Baba Yaga's Corner*), a home for the elderly and infirm, a family hotel and a language school in Germany. Restaurants, patisseries and health-food shops seem to be drawn to the name Baba Yaga, a circumstance which, bearing in mind Baba Yaga's own culinary preferences, is not without its amusing side. A number of fitness centres also bear her name, maybe because their owners think Baba Yaga must have some connection with – yoga?! There is a German dressmaking business called 'Baba Yaga', a Dutch 'spiritual website' (where interested parties can purchase crystal balls and teapots) and a women's choral society, likewise Dutch. The character of Baba Yaga has also served as an artistic stimulus to theatre companies and pop groups, art projects, film directors, comic strips and animators, the authors of graphic and non-graphic books, horror and porno websites, blogs and adverts. For example, there is a Serbian advertising slogan for the Porsche Carrera GT: 'the Baba Roga of the roads' – Baba Roga being the Serbian equivalent of the Russian Baba Yaga.

Along with these broad uses and abuses of her name, I suppose the average non-Slavic reader does not know much about Baba Yaga. Even for most Slavic readers, she is just a hideous old hag who steals little children. Which brings me precisely to the problem that we share. You modestly admit that you don't have a clue, and are asking me to explicate the correspondences between your author's text and the myth of Baba Yaga. In these circumstances you will surely agree that the task you set me is by no means an easy one.

To make my reply as clear and simple as possible, I have compiled a 'Baba Yaga For Beginners' – a short glossary of themes, motifs and mythemes linked to Slavic mythology, and therefore also to 'babayagology'. At this point I should remind you of the notorious fact that Slavic mythology is only conditionally 'Slavic'. Myths, legends and oral traditions are like viruses. Similar 'stories' exist everywhere – in Slavic forests, on African deserts, the foothills of the Himalayas, in Eskimo igloos – and they seep through to our own time and our own mass culture, to TV soaps, sci-fi series, Internet forums and videogames, to Lara Croft, Buffy the Vampire Slayer, and Harry Potter.

Perhaps there is no need to mention that my 'Baba Yaga for Beginners' is more or less a compilatory work, for compilation is what we scholars do. The following works were invaluable in preparing my glossary: the *Encyclopaedic Dictionary of Slavic Mythology* (*Slavjanskaja mifologija, Enciklopedicheskij slovar*), the Russian two-volume encyclopaedia of world myths (*Mify narodov mira*), Vladimir Propp's well-known study *The Historical Roots of the Wondertale* (*Istoricheskie korni volshebnoj skazki*), various scholarly studies and reviews (e.g. the excellent *Codes of Slavic Culture / Kodovi slavenskih kultura*), the most recent and comprehensive study of Baba Yaga – *Baba Yaga: the Ambiguous Mother and Witch of the Russian Folktale*, by Andreas Johns, and the ever-inspiring books of Marina Warner. I won't burden you with scholarly references, but

I can supply a more extensive bibliography should you need it.

Here, then, is how things stand. First: your author is a writer, and any interpretation in literature is 'legitimate'. There are no better and worse literary interpretations, there are only good and bad books. Secondly: myths are memes, 'units of cultural transmission' or 'units of imitation', as defined by evolutionary biologist Richard Dawkins. Myths take themselves to pieces, add bits on, mutate, get transformed, adapt and readapt. Myths travel; in travelling, they retell and 'translate' themselves. They never reach their destination, they are locked forever in a transitional–translational state. There is usually no single, clear-cut mythic story: there are only numerous variants. It is like this with the story of Baba Yaga. Thirdly: the lack of explicit references to Baba Yaga in your author's text stems in part from the muddle around the figure of Baba Yaga herself, around her ambiguous character and authority, and partly from popular superstition. For the Slavs, as for many other peoples, the utterance of names is swathed in taboos. As such, the source of your author's 'discreet' handling of Baba Yaga's name may lie in folklore taboos related to witches and witchcraft.

The Montenegrins, for example, believe that punishment awaits anyone who looks for a witch. They spread the legend of how Jesus when he fled from persecution found shelter with an old witch, whom he blessed with these words: 'Whoever would seek you out is doomed to fail.' It follows that witches cannot be identified because *Jesus blessed them when his persecutors tried to capture him in Judaea, and he hid with a witch, and how she did not betray him, and he blessed her so that her activities would remain secret from everybody.*

(This, according to Tihomir R. Đorđević in his *Witches and Fairies in our Popular Tradition and Belief / Veštica i vila u našem narodnom predanju i verovanju.*)

In short, Baba Yaga plays a supporting role, but her interventions in a fairytale are crucial, and it is difficult to say anything about her without mentioning her part in the tale and her relationship to the other characters. Baba Yaga's roles in fairytales are changeable: sometimes she helps the principal hero or heroine to reach their goal, and at other times she puts obstacles in their way. Overall, I shall do my best to steer you towards the basic 'facts' about the mythical figure of Baba Yaga: who she is, where she comes from, where she lives, what she looks like, what she does and so forth. Then we will go over some of the details that may seem unnecessary to you – too comprehensive, and in fact boring. I assure you, however, that every detail has its place in our Baba Yaga puzzle. As we go along, I shall try to draw your attention to the significant links between Baba Yaga and your author's fictional diptych. The purpose of my commentary will not be interpretative or evaluative, and it will emerge within the separate entries as 'Remarks'. These 'remarks' of mine should be taken as personal interventions which put you under no kind of obligation whatever. For that matter, nothing here puts you under any obligation.

I would wish you to understand the following text as one path through the forest of meanings, in other words a path through a fairytale turned inside out. I shall try to make the path as easy as possible (because it is my job to roam around the forest and peer under every shrub, while it is yours to pass through it). All I ask is that you should be a little patient. Why? Because only patient and steadfast heroes – those who are ready to cross seven mountains and seven seas and wear out three pairs of iron shoes – can expect a reward at the end of the tale. Whether this is what's waiting for you, I cannot say; that is for you to find out.

Yours very cordially,

Dr Aba Bagay

BABA YAGA FOR BEGINNERS

BABA

Baba[1] comes from the Indo-European, whence it spread into many languages. In Slavic languages, the principal meaning of baba is an old woman, grandmother, lady. In colloquial Russian, a baba can be any woman (e.g. *horoshaya baba,* a good-looking woman), likewise in other Slavic languages. Baba can be a married woman (e.g. *moja baba*, my wife). Baba can also be a female with bad traits: a fishwife, a gossip, a quarrelsome nag, a shrew. Baba is also a colloquial expression for a cowardly, fearful man. *Babica* means a midwife, whence the word *babinje*, which means the postnatal period.

[1] I should warn you at the outset about the difficulties of transliterating Russian and other Slavic languages into English. There is no consensus on the best mode of transliteration, and the scope for confusion is broadest in texts – such as this – which cite from languages that are written in the Cyrillic alphabet (Russian, Bulgarian, etc.), as well as from those written in the Roman or Latin script (Croatian, Czech, Polish, etc.). As this is a private letter, meant 'for your eyes only', I have not tried to take a consistent approach. Russian and Belorusian names and words have for the most part been transliterated. The other Slavic languages are easier to pronounce than you suppose, if you follow these simple rules: š = sh (Mokoš = Mokosh); č, ć = ch (domaći = domachi); ž = zh (život = zhivot); j = y (Jaga = Yaga), đ = dj (prođe = prodje), etc.

Slavs also use the word baba to refer to female mythic characters, particular days, atmospheric effects, astronomical events, illnesses and so on.

Female demons are often called babas. Mother Wednesday (*baba Sereda*) watches over the weavers at their looms and stops women from using them on Wednesdays (or it might be any other day). White Lady (*Belaja baba*) is a watery demon, while *Bannaja baba* (*banniha*, *bajnica*, *baennaja matushka*, *obderiha*) is a spirit that lives in the traditional Russian steam bath (*banya*). In Ukraine, the Wheaten Lady (*Žitna baba)* is the spirit of the fields; and the Wild Lady (*Dika baba*) is the female demon that leads young men astray. Witches, fortune-tellers and healers are all called – baba.

Baba also turns up in the names of **illnesses** (*babice*, *bapke*, *babushki*, *babuha*, *babile*, etc.). In Bulgaria, Baba Šarka is a folk name for measles. Baba Šarka is homeless, footloose and gluttonous. When she turns up in someone's home, nobody is allowed to prepare any food for nine days. Then Baba Šarka abandons the inhospitable house to look for somewhere more generous. Baba Drusla and Baba Pisanka also bring sickness into the house.

Baba is also connected with the **popular concept of time**. Baba Marta personifies the third month of the year, especially in Bulgaria, but also in Serbian and Macedonian folklore. In Croatia and Serbia, Baba Korizma (Lent) walks with seven sticks, and she throws away a stick for every week of fasting. In Serbia, snowy days in March are called 'baba's days', 'baba's billy-goats' or 'baba's kids'. In Romania and Ukraine, Baba Jaudocha (also Jeudocha or Dokia) is accountable for all wintery precipitations. Snow falls when she shakes her fur coat. Many regions have a carnival custom of 'burning the baba'. In Croatia, people mark New Year's Eve symbolically by burning a doll, called Baba Krnjuša, so that the new year can take her place.

In Slavic folklore, **astronomical and meteorological phenomena** are also named after baba. Moonlight is called 'Mother Moonshine', and the moon itself is 'Baba Gale'. 'Baba's belt' is a metaphor for rainbow, and 'baba's millet' for hail. Bad weather usually comes out of 'baba's smock' in the sky. In Poland, when there are dark spots on the moon, people say 'Baba is churning butter' or 'Baba's baking bread'. When it is rainy and sunny at the same time, Polish children chant 'Rain is falling, sun is shining, Baba Yaga's butter's churning'. When the first snow falls, the Casubians say 'The old woman has gone to the dance'. Carpathian farmers use the expression 'the old woman is freezing cold' to describe the high mountains dusted with the first snow. In time of drought, Polish peasants believe that an old witch is squatting in an oak tree (meaning, in a nest), keeping eggs warm and that the drought will go on until the chicks hatch. In Bulgarian folklore, baba is a picturesque synonym for day and also for night.[2]

So, **lots of things** are called baba. In Slavic harvest festivals, the last sheaf is called the baba, and the peasants celebrate the end of harvest by dressing this sheaf in women's clothes. One kind of mushroom is called a baba, in Slavic languages, as is a butterfly, two kinds of fruit (a pear and a cherry), a cake or pastry (called *babka* in Polish) and a fish. Baba

[2] 'They approached the hearth where they found two old grannies with two balls of wool: one was winding the wool, the other unwound it. The one who was winding was day, and the other was night.'

crops up in the names of mountains, towns and villages (Velika Baba, Mala Baba, Stara Baba, Babina Greda, etc.). 'Baba's summer' is a colloquial expression for a long mild autumn, an Indian summer.

Many Bulgarian **sayings** are linked with the word *baba*. The expression 'There's one thing baba knows, and she never stops saying it' is used for someone who is forever telling you the same thing. 'Baba's fiddle-faddle', 'baba's babbling': these are synonyms for nonsense, silliness. There are similar sayings in the language of the Croats, Bosnians and Serbs. 'There went the old woman with the cakes' is a saying that refers to a missed opportunity. 'Baba wants what baba dreams' is a saying with unambiguous sexual connotations, but it means that when somebody mentions something, that's what they're hoping for, which is, in fact, a popular equivalent of Freud's theory of parapraxis. 'The old woman's busy fiddling and faddling' (*Trla baba lan da joj prođe dan*) is what people say when somebody fritters away their time, loafing around or being pointlessly active. Mixing 'old women and frogs' (*babe i žabe*) means mixing things that would otherwise have no connection with each other. 'Any old woman can do that', or 'even my old woman can do that', means that anybody can do whatever it is, even the most incompetent person. 'Whatever grannie says, she only talks about cakes' is another way of referring to somebody who won't stop talking about the same thing. 'Too many midwives, crippled child' means that too many cooks spoil the broth. 'If grandma had balls, she'd be grandpa' is another saying. At the same time, *babo* or *baba* means father in some languages (Farsi, Arabic, Turkish, Italian), but it can also refer to an older male member of the family, any old man or a holy man.

* * *

All things considered, the Slavic world is positively teeming with babas! On the other hand, let us not forget that all these ugly, sexist notions, proverbs, sayings and beliefs involving 'grandmas' were thought up by 'grandpas'. Who, naturally, reserved the more heroic parts for themselves.

BABA YAGA

Baba Yaga, along with her innumerable variants in Russian, Ukrainian, Belarusian (Igaya, Iga, Yega, Yagaba, Yagabova, Egabova, Egibitsa, Yegiboba, Yaganishna, Yagivovna, Yagichina-Babichina, Yaga-bura, Egibishna, Yagishna, Yega, Lyaga, Oga, Aga Gnishna, Yagabaka), and in other Slavic languages (Indži-baba, Ježibaba, Jedibaba, Jedubaba, Babaroga), is a female anthropomorphic being, an old hag-cum-sorceress, a witch. There have been many interpretations of her name. Some authors hold that Jagok, Egga, Iga, Yuga, Yazya, Yaza, Yeza, Yagishna, Ajshi-baba, and other similar designations all have a single Old Slavonic stem: **ega** or **esa**, which is close to the Lithuanian **engti** and the Latvian **igt**, and which mean, approximately, evil, horror, nightmare, sickness.

Baba Yaga lives in a forest, or on the edge of a forest, in a cramped little hut that stands on hen's legs and turns around on the spot. She has one skeleton-leg ('Baba Yaga, bony leg!'), dangling breasts that she dumps on the stove or hangs over a pole, a long sharp nose that knocks against the ceiling (*nos v potolok ros*), and she flies around in a mortar, rowing herself through the air with a pestle, wiping away her traces with a broom.

* * *

Baba Yaga is a unique oral–textual 'patchwork' of folklore and mythico-ritual traditions (shamanism, totemism, animism, matriarchy), and her status, function and authority change from tale to tale, from one zone of folklore to another, from male story-tellers to female. Baba Yaga is a **text** that is read, studied, told, adapted, interpreted and reinterpreted differently at different times.

Baba Yaga's origins are not all that clear. One theory has it that she was the Great Goddess, the Earth Mother herself. Another, that she was the great Slavic goddess of death (*Yaga zmeya bura*); a third, that she was the mistress of all the birds (hence the hut on hen's legs and the long nose like a beak); a fourth theory has it that she was a rival of the Slavic goddess Mokosh, and that she evolved over time from a great goddess into an androgyne, then into the goddess of birds and snakes, and then into an anthropomorphic being, until she finally acquired female attributes. Some associate her with the Golden Baba, an archaic goddess from the age of matriarchy, and they see the hen's legs beneath her hut as the vestige of a fertility cult.

Baba Yaga appears as a spinner and weaver, roles which always symbolise power over human destiny (Baba Yaga gives the heroes a ball of thread that will lead them to their goal), but also as a warrior who sleeps with a sword over her head and fights against knights (sometimes she appears as a mother of dragons). In some tales, Baba Yaga has power to turn people to stone (like the Medusa); in others, power to command the forces of nature: winds, tempests and thunder (which is why she is sometimes associated with the Slavic god Perun). Vladimir Propp, whose influence in this field of research has been immense, holds that Baba Yaga is the mistress of all the forest fauna, of the world of the dead, and also the priestess of initiations.

The elusive and capricious Baba Yaga sometimes appears as a helper, a donor, sometimes as an avenger, a villain, sometimes as a sentry between two worlds, sometimes as an intermediary between worlds, but also as a mediator between the heroes in a story. Most interpreters locate Baba Yaga in the ample mythological family of old and ugly women with specific kinds of power, in a taxonomy that is common to mythologies the world over.

Along with many points of contact with other 'babas', Baba Yaga has earned her own name and individuality. Although Baba Yaga is widespread around the Slavic world, 'the problems of Baba Yaga's genesis, mythological nature, function and semantics in fairytales are highly complex and provoke continual debate.'[3] Some authors even maintain that the name Baba Yaga is unknown in Slavic mythology, and that she belongs exclusively to the world of fairytales. What's beyond dispute is that Baba Yaga sprouted in mythological soil, but also that, as a character, she took shape in Russian folktales between the 18th and 20th centuries, when hundreds and hundreds of versions of these tales were written down. Baba Yaga grew out of the complex and long-lasting interaction between folklore and mythico-ritual traditions, the tellers of folktales, folklorists and commentators; out of the blending of Indo-European and pre-Indo-European mythologies. Maria Gimbutas includes Baba Yaga among the 'goddesses inherited from Old Europe, such as Greek Athena, Hera, Artemis, Hecate; Roman Minerva and Diana; Irish Morrígan

[3] K.V. Chistov, *Zametki po slavjanskoj demonologii, Baba Jaga.* Moskva: Zhivaja starina 1997.

and Brigit; Baltic Laima and Ragana; Russian Baba Yaga, Basque Mari, and others, are not "Venuses" bringing fertility and prosperity [. . .]. These life-givers and death-wielders are "queens" or "ladies" and as such they remained in individual creeds for a very long time in spite of their official dethronement, militarisation, and hybridisation with the Indo-European heavenly brides and wives.'[4]

BABA YAGA / WITCH

Baba Yaga has a fanciful character, and researchers are cautious when it comes to defining her status. Some maintain that Baba Yaga is simply a (Slavic) witch, while others are ready to grant her a much more complex and individualised role in the system of Slavic demonology.

Let us look first at **ordinary** witches: who they are, what they look like and what they do. According to Tihomir R. Đorđević, witches are mainly old women with 'devilish souls'. 'A woman is called a witch if she possesses a sort of devilish soul,' according to Vuk Karadžić, 'which emerges while she sleeps at night and turns into a butterfly, a hen or a turkey which flies from house to house, eating people up, especially little children: when she finds someone asleep, she hits them with a rod of some kind on the left breast, their chest splits open, she plucks out their heart and eats it, then she closes up the hole again. Some of the victims die straight away, others live on for a while longer, according to her whim as she eats their heart; and then they die, just as she intended.'[5]

* * *

[4] Maria Gimbutas, *The Language of the Goddess*. London: Thames & Hudson 2001.

[5] Tihomir R. Đorđević, *Veštica i vila u našem narodnom predanju i verovanju*. Beograd: Srpski etnografski zbornik 1953.

Slavic languages have many names for witches: *ved'ma*, *vid'ma*, *vedz'ma*, *veštica*, *veštičina*, *czarownica*, *wiedzma*, *jedza*, *cipernica*, *coprnica*, *štrigna*, *štriga*, *morna*, *brina*, *brkača*, *konjobarka*, *srkača*, *potkovanica*, *rogulja*, *krstača*, *kamenica*, *čarovnica*, *mag'josnica*, and others besides. Synonyms have a protective function, and the protection they offer is mostly used to protect children. People often refer to a witch as **she over there**, for fear of uttering her name.

Like many other mythical beings, witches have a talent for metamorphosis. (In contemporary popular culture they are 'morphs'.) A witch can turn herself into a bird, a serpent, a fly, a butterfly, a frog or a cat.[6] Most often they turn into **a black bird** (raven, crow, black hen and magpie). There is also a popular belief that moths are really witches, so it is best to throw them on the fire or scorch their wings. The next day, you need to find out which 'baba' in the village 'got burned in the fire', 'roasted right through like a roasted devil' or simply passed away. That baba is – was – a witch. 'A hen with scorched feathers, or any other bird that a witch turns into, can also give the witch away.' There is a sort of moth that is actually called a *witch*. People believe that any woman who is touched by the wings of this 'witch' will be barren.

It was believed that when a witch falls asleep, a butterfly or bird flies out of her mouth, 'and if she turns over, the butterfly

[6] In the classic film *Cat People* (1942), directed by Jacques Tourneur, New York fashion designer Irena Dubrovna is a Serb by extraction. When they are smitten with jealousy or rage, women from the land of her ancestors turn into bloodthirsty wildcats, or in this case panthers, that kill their mates. In the scene that takes place in a New York restaurant, called The Belgrade, an unknown woman recognises Irena Dubrovna and her secret feline self. This woman comes up and says something in Serbian (with a strong American accent, naturally): *Ti si moja sestra*, meaning 'You are my sister.'

or bird cannot return whence it came, so it will die, and so will the woman. It can happen that the bird or hen flies away, the sleeping woman's husband turns his wife around so that her head is where her feet were, the hen cannot go back into the woman's mouth and the woman dies. When the grieving husband puts his wife back in the position she had when she fell asleep, the hen can go back into the woman again, and the woman comes back to life.'[7]

Witches can be recognised by 'the wart of some kind that every one of them has on her head, the same as the long cockscomb on a strutting cockerel'. Witches are cross-eyed, they are prone to vomiting (hence the saying 'He threw up his guts like a witch') and they don't sink in water. A witch has the ability to change her physical size, 'she can make herself absolutely small, so that she can pass through the narrowest crack, through a keyhole, and emerge on the other side.' (T. R. Đorđević)

In Herzegovina, a witch is a woman with a moustache 'like a young man's first whiskers'. Baba, a character in P.P. Njegoš's epic poem *The Mountain Wreath* says: 'It is an easy thing to recognise a witch: grey hair and a cross under her nose.'[8] Hence, a witch has 'big whiskers and hairy thighs'; a witch is 'plethoric, with a foul temper and a cross under her nose'; witches are always ill-humoured, they always wear an evil expression and they have 'shaggy legs'. A witch is 'whiskery, with bushy eyebrows, bent-backed, her eyes sunk deep in her

[7] Tihomir R. Đorđević, op. cit.

[8] Petar Petrović Njegoš (1813–1851), the *Vladika* (Prince-Bishop) of Montenegro, was a great poet as well as a ruler and warrior. His verse drama *Gorski Vijenac* (*The Mountain Wreath*), about a massacre of 'renegade', i.e. pro-Turkish, Montenegrins, is a classic of South Slavic literature.

head'. A witch has 'thin little moustaches, bloodshot eyes and sharp teeth, but the moustache is the surest sign'. Hairiness is not such an issue in Bosnia. On the contrary, the Bosnians maintain that a witch is 'a woman with no hair in her armpits or her lower body'.[9]

Mythical beings are distinguished from humans by their **physical size**: they are significantly smaller or larger than people. In Istria,[10] they believe that the *plague* is a gigantic woman. According to Serbian beliefs, the witch called *karakondžula* is a large fat creature. In Montenegro, they used to believe that *Mother Wednesday* was an enormous female, 'wide as a haystack', with great bosoms, grey hair and steel teeth.

Like other mythical beings, witches have some kind of **physical defect**, which may be expressed as a surplus, a deficiency or an imbalance. It is sometimes believed of witches that they have a rudimentary tail, or even rudimentary wings. Slovenian folklore mentions *preglavica*, a headless woman in white who only appears at midday. Her Russian counterpart is called *poludnitsa*. The Croats believed in faceless female demons: dead mothers coming back to give suck to their babies. Great dangling dugs are not reserved to Baba Yaga alone. The Serbs used to believe in the existence of the *giant mother* (*divska majka*) who would knead dough with her breasts. The *kuga* in Konavle[11] and the *koljara* in Montenegro have great

[9] This lack of hair even features in Roald Dahl's popular children's story *The Witches*, where baldness is one of the clues that a woman is a witch. ('That is why they have claws and bald heads and queer noses and peculiar eyes . . .') Which is why witches all wear wigs to hide their real identity.

[10] Istria is a triangular peninsula on the northern coast of Croatia.

[11] Konavle is a valley at the southern end of Croatia.

dangling dugs that they can sling over their shoulders. The goddess *Kshumai* (worshipped by the Kaffirs of the Hindu Kush), the mythical *peri* (Farsi: *pari*) and the Arabic *salauva* – they all have the same traits. *Alavardi* (also *Alabasti*) is an immemorial mythical being familiar to many Asiatic peoples. She is a tall woman with pendulous breasts that she tosses over her shoulders.

Witches may have only one eye and no nostrils, or only one nostril. One of Baba Yaga's legs is made of bone (or iron). Blindness or monocular vision is typical of mythical beings. Baba Yaga is blind (or grumbles that her eyes hurt). She identifies her 'guests' – random passing travellers – by their human scent, because, as far as we know, she cannot see them.

Mythical beings give themselves away by the **noises** they make (they whistle, laugh, clap their hands, etc.). If a human catches their attention, certain mythical creatures will repeat the human's words over and over, like an echo. Baba Yaga uses repetitious phrases and can be recognised by her remarkable wheezing breath: 'Oof . . . oof . . . oof.' Many of those attributes – specifically 'noisiness', hand-clapping, whistling, repeating words (echolalia) – could be put down to autism, while simple infirmity, difficulties with walking, blindness and dementia were due to sheer old age. In folklore, however, such longevity has been crowned with a mythic halo. This is why it is believed that witches live 'for a very long time indeed', longer than mere mortals, and 'give up the ghost' only with great difficulty. Baba Yaga herself is about a hundred years old. There is a folk belief that witches continue to do evil after they are dead. Therefore, when a witch dies, 'it is worth slitting the tendons at their ankles and under their knees with a black-handled knife so that she will not return home from the grave and do people harm'.[12]

In some areas of Slavic folklore, Baba Yaga is considered to be the 'aunt of all witches'; elsewhere she is seen as the 'mistress of all witches', or even as 'the devil's sister', while in Belarus, she has a difficult role to play: death delivers the souls of the deceased to Baba Yaga, and she and her underling witches have to feed these souls until they gain the requisite feathery lightness.

[12] The following observation may strike you as trite, but isn't it interesting that commonplaces related to genocide are so rapidly forgotten? If nothing else, this is a reason why we need to keep reiterating that universal male misogyny, down the centuries, has produced cultural and symbolic genocide against women. One of the worst eruptions of this misogyny was the European inquisitorial witch-hunt that lasted practically for four centuries. The Inquisition began around the end of the 12th century and the beginning of the 13th, when Pope Gregory IX sent his inquisitors to the territories contaminated by heresy, and then officially entrusted the conduct of inquisitions to the Dominican order (1235). The congregation of cardinals was established fully in 1542, with legal authority over the inquisition. An estimated 100,000 witches were burned in Europe between 1560 and 1660, though the actual numbers are not known. The first trial of witches took place in Toulouse in 1335. After that, witch-hunting spread across Europe like a prairie fire, and 1486 brought the publication of the remarkable book by Kraemer and Sprenger, the *Malleus Maleficarum.* The inquisitors now had ideological underpinning: the first textbook which put their labours on 'a solid scholarly foundation'. There are documents about the victims of inquisitorial torture: incomplete, to be sure, but they do exist. Moreover, many more women suffered outside the inquisitorial system. Their inquisitors were their neighbours, from the same village, motivated not so much by Christian obedience as by local beliefs and superstitions. Village women suspected of being witches were dunked in water. If they sank and drowned, it proved they were not witches. If they kept afloat, they were fished out of the water and beaten to death. Women believed to be witches were even defiled after death. Their bodies were penetrated with wooden poles and pierced with needles, or iron nails were driven into their mouths, and their graves were sown with poppy seeds (the dead woman would have to count each and every seed). The graves of suicides were treated in the same way.

Now we come to the first, and completely random, correspondences between your author's manuscript and Baba Yaga. It is not without significance that the author gave one of her heroines, Pupa, a medical vocation: gynaecology. Midwives, sorceresses, healers, 'witches' all had an important and irreplaceable role in childbirth.

Although the physical appearance of your author's heroines has no link with the aforementioned signs for recognising witches – otherwise every older woman could be a witch – let us mention some details anyway. The author's mother wears a wig and often lets out a sort of groaning noise – uh-hu-uh-hu! Baba Yaga is well known for her puffing: Oof, oof, oof! Pupa has a beak-like nose, she is uncommonly thin, half-blind and highly sensitive to smells. Kukla has big feet. Beba has conspicuously large breasts and the little girl Wawa has eyebrows that meet in the middle.

By the way, in not-so-far-off times, all middle-aged women were bound to look like 'witches'. Our own time is characterised by panic over ageing, obsessive efforts to delay and disguise the onset of old age. Fear of ageing is one of the strongest phobias among contemporary women, and increasingly among men as well. This very fear gives powerful impetus to the cosmetics industry. Naturally, the 'anti-Baba Yaga' industry feeds this fear and lives off and by it.

Hair removers help to keep our skin smooth: they lift the hairs from joined-up eyebrows, moustaches, whiskers from our chins, armpits and legs (no more *shaggy* thighs!), and the latest fashion is not only for removing the shameful hair but for styling it. Wigs, hair restoration and transplants have practically done away with female baldness. Dental implants have put a stop to toothlessness, and if they had been invented in the times when artists' canvas overflowed with portraits of lovely ladies, their faces would have stretched in beaming grins; instead, they all had pursed lips or wore an enigmatic smile like the Mona Lisa. The cosmetics industry, the growth of plastic surgery, along with its increasing affordability: all this is changing the physical appearance of the inhabitants of the richer portions of the globe. The recent achievement of the first face transplant may stimulate a new appetite: for a total makeover, the transformation of mortal 'frogs' into deathless 'princesses'. The age-old belief that witches drink blood has turned, today, into the real and highly profitable practice of blood transfusion or replacement, a therapy that is widely believed to rejuvenate the organism and prolong life. Only rich people can indulge in such treatments, which they do in exclusive private clinics. The Astana cycling team from Kazakhstan and its star Aleksandr Vinokurov were asked to withdraw from the Tour de France in 2007 after Vinokurov tested positive for using blood transfusions as doping.

To end with, let us just add – as solace for witches! – that a negligible minority of humankind (let's call them 'vampires') still drinks the blood of the majority of humankind (let's call them 'donors'), and does it so 'innocently', through a clear plastic tube, just as if they were sucking juice through a humble straw.

THE HUT

'The fence around the hut is made of human bones, skulls with eyes intact are stuck on the posts: instead of bolts on the gate – human legs; instead of a latch on the door – a hand; instead of a lock – a mouth full of sharp teeth.'

* * *

Baba Yaga's hut terrifies the passing traveller. The first things the hero or heroine sees are the skulls; beyond the hut itself there is most often nothing at all. ('There stands the hut, the path no further runs. Only the darkling dark, nothing else to see.') The hut looks highly unwelcoming. Often there isn't so much as a window or a door; the hut stands on hen's legs and turns eerily around on the spot.

If he wants to enter, the passing traveller has to know how. Heroes like Prince Ivan (Ivan Tsarevich) usually blow into the hut and call out: 'Little hut! O little hut! Stay still, little hut, as you once did, with your front to me and your back to the forest.' Or: 'Little hut, o little hut! Turn your eyes to the forest and your door to me. I shan't stop here long, just a single night. Let the lone traveller in.'

Girls, by contrast, are warned in advance what they must do to humour the dangerous hut: 'There, my girl, a birch tree will whip your eyes, so tie it down with a ribbon; there the door will creak and thump, so oil the hinges well; the dogs will attack you, so throw them some bread; the cat will scratch your eyes, so give it some ham.'

Vladimir Propp argues that the myths of many tribal cultures contain two worlds: the world of the living and the world of the dead. A wild beast stands on the boundary (wild animals guard the entrance to Hades), or perhaps a hut with zoomorphic traits. In many tribal cultures a hut like Baba Yaga's is involved in the initiation rites for young males when they enter the adult world. First they have to be devoured (by the hut itself, whose door puts us in mind of jaws) in order to be born again and join the adult world.

* * *

Thus the hero stands before Baba Yaga's hut and says: 'Little hut, o little hut, turn your front to me and your back to the forest.' The young man is afraid, many have died on this spot, which is proven by the skulls on the fence, but even so, he pleads to be let inside ('Let me come in, to eat salted bread!'). Meanwhile Baba Yaga in her hut murmurs, satisfied: 'All alone you came to me, like a lamb to the slaughter.'

When they gain entry to the hut, the heroes come face to face with a new terrifying sight: 'On the stove, on the ninth brick, lies Baba Yaga with her bone leg, her nose touching the ceiling, her slobber seeping over the doorstep, her dugs dangling over the *lug*,[13] sharpening her teeth.' The descriptions of Baba Yaga vary: stretching from one corner of the hovel to the other, in some accounts, she rests one leg on a shelf and the other on the stove; sometimes she tosses her breasts onto the stove or hangs them 'over a pole', or even 'shuts the oven door with her breasts', while snot trails out of her nose, and she 'scoops up soot with her tongue'. Very occasionally the descriptions are unambiguously sexual: Baba Yaga leaps out of the hut with 'sinewy rump' and 'polished cunt'. Baba Yaga has become so much a part of her hut, growing into it, that the hut dances up and down instead of her, or spins on its axis like a child's top.

How do the heroes cope with their fear? Before their first meeting with Baba Yaga, they appear very impudent: 'Come on, old girl, what's all the fuss about? What's all the racket for? I want food and drink, get the steam-bath ready, then I'll tell you all the news.' We recognise a stereotype in the

[13] In traditional Russian huts, the lug (in Russian: *grjadka*) was a staff or pole where the peasants hung their washing or babies' cradles.

tone and substance of these words: this is how men in patriarchal societies address their women. One does not expect such behaviour from a young man when he meets an old woman for the first time, but curiously enough, the magic formula does the trick. Hearing the tone and substance of his retort, Baba Yaga is tamed in a trice, and she does everything he asks straightaway. The young traveller's uncouth familiarity is the key that unlocks her door.[14]

The hero comes face to face with *vagina dentata*, and behold! He lives to tell the tale.

Let me add at once that, while the obscenity of old women is nothing rare in the mythico-ritual world, it is rarely sexual. Obscenity has its ritual nature and its obvious purpose. Baubo is the famous old girl who pulled up her skirts and exposed her genitals to Demeter. By mocking the absurd role of wise consolatrix (which everybody expected her to play), Baubo managed to make Demeter laugh.[15] The Japanese goddess Ame-no-Uzume tempts the sun goddess Amaterasu out of her cave with an obscene dance, to drive away the darkness that had fallen on the earth. In some parts of Serbia and Bulgaria, there was a custom that the old women would lift their skirts and show their vulvas as a way of defending their village from hail, and thereby save the harvest. Old women in southern Serbia would even strip naked and run round the house to drive away the hail, imploring as they went:

[14] 'Here are your answers!' said the beautiful princess. 'The little wooden box – that's me, and the little golden key – that's my husband.' (From *The Enchanted Princess*)

[15] Baubo appears as a figure with a hypertrophied vulva, or more often with a vulva-face. Sometimes she is shown as a *dea impudica*, a shameless goddess, riding a hog with her legs spread wide.

Don't you, dragon,
fight my monster,
it's devoured lots like you!

or,

Flee, you monster, from my monster!
Flee, you monster, from my monster!
They can't both be master here.

The vulva – the 'dragon' or 'monster' – had a magical strength that could dispel clouds. People believed that the clouds were led by dragons, so the lines 'Don't you, dragon, fight my monster' pitted the vulva against the clouds. Let's not forget that Baba Yaga rules over the powers of nature: she often appears in the role of mistress of the winds.[16]

Baba Yaga has an initiatory meaning for male and female heroes alike. Female initiation rarely has a sexual character, while the male equivalent is explicitly so: on the psychoanalytic level, the meeting with Baba Yaga is a confrontation with *vagina dentata*, the mother, the granny, the ugly old crone who is a grotesque inversion of his future bride.[17] Certain native North

[16] 'The old woman came onto the porch, shouted in a voice like thunder, whistled vigorously, and at once strong winds blew up all around her and whirled about, making the hut shake.' (From *The Enchanted Princess*)

[17] In a Serbian fairytale, *The Bird Girl* (*Tica devojka*), a baba sits on top of a mountain with a bird in her lap, luring young men and turning them to stone. Only if he approaches from behind and roughly overcomes her can a young man avoid being turned to stone (i.e. symbolically made impotent) and obtain what he yearns for, i.e. 'the baba's bird'(!). When he kisses and fondles the bird(!), it turns into a maiden, the young man's bride-to-be: 'She yields, giving him the bird from her skirt, and emits a sort of sky-blue wind from her mouth which wreathes around all the petrified people and brings them back to life. The King's son catches hold of the bird and begins kissing it sweetly, and his kisses turn it into the most beautiful maiden of all.'

American tribes have a myth of the Terrible Mother, who has a fish concealed in her vagina that gobbles men up. The hero's task is to vanquish the Terrible Mother, more exactly to break the teeth of the fish that lives in her vagina.

Remarks

The hut, *vagina dentata*, is a male castration fantasy. Your author's text proposes a remarkable inversion by means of the character of Kukla. Kukla is a victim of her own *vagina dentata*. The incident that occurred at the outset of her sexual life decides her entire later life. Kukla's problem is two-fold: her sexuality and her creativity are both petrified. She is like the Medusa, who was not made to look in the mirror by others; she did it by herself. She has no children, and only begins to write when her husband dies. And she does so, naturally, hidden behind his name.

Only when Pupa leaves home, her 'hut', can she die. Leaving home is the emancipatory deed that leads Pupa where she wants to go – to death.

Returning home, your author returns to the maternal 'hut' and repeats the initiation rite for the nth time. She must respect the law of Baba Yaga's hut, otherwise Baba Yaga will eat her up. The quip about good girls going to heaven while bad girls go everywhere contains the whole female history (as seen by men), where women's fate has been determined by two opposed poles: home (cleanliness, order, security, family) and the space outside the home (dirt, disorder, danger, chaos, loneliness). The outer space was traditionally reserved to men, and inner space, the home, to women.

Finally, something interesting which can be read as a metaphor realised by contemporary society. The *vagina dentata* has fled from the field of sexual fantasy into reality. A female condom, the 'Rapex', has been invented by a South African woman, who wants to help African women defend themselves against rapists. Just like the Terrible Mother of native North American myths, the female condom has fish teeth in it that can wound the penetrating penis. Apparently the inventor was inspired by meeting a rape victim who said: 'If only I had teeth down there.'

THE MORTAR

The mortar, a common object in everyday peasant life, plays a strongly symbolic role in European and Asian mythologies. It symbolises the womb, while its partner the pestle is – what else? – the penis. In Belarus, for example, there is a funny explanation, meant for children, of how children come into the world: 'I fell from the sky, and landed in a mortar, I climbed out of the mortar and look! How big I've grown!'

Slavs used to involve a mortar in comical wedding customs. They would fill the mortar with water, and the bride-to-be had to pummel away with the pestle until all the water was gone. There was a wedding ritual of dressing up the mortar as a female and the pestle as a male, and then this symbolic bride and groom were placed on the wedding table.

The Russians and Ukrainians used the mortar in healing rituals. It was believed that sickness could be *beaten away* in a mortar, sick animals could be *beaten back* to health with a pestle and mortar and even a fever could be *beaten to death* in a mortar.[18]

* * *

[18] In India and South Africa today, men infected with Aids sometimes believe that intercourse with a virgin will cure them. There are specialised brothels where girls aged five to ten are bought from their parents and made available for 'medicinal purposes'. The girls almost always catch Aids themselves.

The Indian Vedas, too, celebrate the mortar and soma (the drink of the gods, like nectar, though it is quite possibly really sperm), but here the sexual symbolism is raised to a cosmic level. For the mortar is a cosmic womb in which life itself is renewed, while the pestle is a cosmic phallus.

An iron mortar is mentioned in a Russian spell from the 17th century: 'There is an iron mortar, on that iron mortar stands an iron stool, on that iron stool sits an iron woman.' (*Stoit stupa zheleznaja, na toj stupe zheleznoj stoit stul zheleznyj, na tom stule zheleznom sidit baba zheleznaja . . .*)

A mortar is Baba Yaga's means of transport, and in the mythical world she has exclusive permission to fly in it. 'Ordinary' witches travel by broomstick, flying up the chimney and out of the house. Baba in *The Mountain Wreath*, by Petar Petrović Njegoš, says: 'We move around with silver oars, our vessel is an eggshell.' This verse draws on the folk belief that witches ride in eggshells. That is why people would break eggshells into little bits before they threw them away, so that witches could not use them. And on the Croatian island of Krk they believe that witches and sorceresses can only cross the sea in eggshells.

The mortar, Baba Yaga's transport of choice,[19] is symbolically closer to an eggshell than a broomstick. Baba Yaga rides in her own symbolic womb (which is so hypertrophied that it can even hold her standing up) and paddles through the air with a pestle-penis. Liberated from human laws that

[19] 'Soon a frightful noise is heard from the woods: the trees tremble, the dry leaves rattle; Baba Yaga bursts from the woods, riding in a mortar, waving a pestle, brandishing a broom and rubbing out her traces as she goes.' (From *Vassilissa the Beautiful*)

determine what we can and cannot do, the unrelenting laws of the sexes, Baba Yaga makes use of both organs, male and female, and she flies, which is a very strong mythic representation of human sexuality. This sexuality is, it goes without saying, grotesque and carnivalised. As she is an old woman (supposedly a centenarian), Baba Yaga does not only travesty human sexuality: she *transvesties* it.

Of course, other interpretations are also possible: as a female, Baba Yaga's 'wings' were 'clipped' in advance, so she was compelled to 'fly' in a mortar, an everyday object, like flying in a stewpot or a kneading-trough. There is also the interpretation that Baba Yaga is actually a hermaphrodite, hence a perfect human being, a Slavic folklore version of Tiresias, who – thanks to the gods – switched gender more than once (and decided in the end that being female is much better!). In Slavic carnival travesties, in Croatia for example, they carry a doll around the village; they call it 'grandma carries grandpa' (*baba dida nosi*), and it is formed of woven parts of male and female bodies.

A popular Russian woodcut (*lubok*) from the early 18th century depicts an unusual scene: Baba Yaga going into battle with a crocodile. Supposedly the crocodile is Peter the Great (because that was what the Old Believers called Peter the Great: 'the crocodile'), and Baba Yaga is his wife. Baba Yaga rides on a swine, holding the reins in one hand and a pestle in the other. Her belt is a tangle of a hatchet and a distaff, one 'male' object and the other typically 'female', although they both have a phallic shape. Hence Baba Yaga, in the imagination of the anonymous woodcut-artist, possesses both symbols of power.

Pupa's foot warmer is a modern equivalent of Baba Yaga's mortar. This connection becomes even more obvious when the girl Wawa claims Pupa's boot and uses it as a mother's womb in which she falls asleep and dreams her dreams.

Kukla, the *vagina dentata*, longs for a penis so that she can start up her 'flying machine' and become an independent flier. But in order to come by the requisite part, its owner has to die. Perhaps this is why Kukla's men all die, or are invalids: in other words, Kukla does not need a complete man, she only needs a bit of him – the 'pestle'. A current, a faint and gentle breeze, can be felt enveloping Kukla, who would in ancient times have been the mistress of the four winds.

CANNIBALISM

Baba Yaga is dogged by evil rumours that she 'ate people like chickens'. Her hut or hovel, surrounded by heaps of human bones, plainly signals to the passing traveller that he has stumbled upon a cannibal's lair.

Baba Yaga's cannibalism, from a folkloristic point of view, is linked to a ritual with a frightful name: 'baking the child properly' (*perepekanie rebenka*). This ritual was performed on children suffering from rickets (the folk name for which, in Russia and Ukraine, was 'dog's old age': *sobachya starost'*).[20]

[20] In Ukraine, for example, a witch-doctor would bring water from three wells early in the morning, mix the dough, bake bread in the oven, take it out and then pretend to push the sick child into the oven instead. Meanwhile the child's mother had to go around the room three times, stopping each time in front of the window to shout: 'Old woman, what are you doing?' The witch-doctor would call back: 'I'm kneading the dough!'

The actual witchcraft consists of 'burning' the sickness. This ritual was accompanied with chanting a spell: 'Just as we bake the bread, so, dog's old age, you'll bake too!' (*Kak hleb pechetsja, tak i sobachja starost pekis!*) During the ritual, led by the village witch-doctor, they would pretend to push the sick child into the bread oven. In other words, the bread was symbolically identified with the child, and the oven with the mother's womb. Returning the child to the oven, meaning the womb, signified rebirth. The ailing, rickety child was not 'fully baked' in its mother's womb, so it has to be 'baked properly' in the oven. At the same time, the oven symbolises life after death, the provisional descent into it, and provisional death.

In most fairytales, Baba Yaga appears as an old woman living by herself. Sometimes she turns up as a mother with a single daughter, and sometimes as a mother with forty-one daughters. From a psychoanalytic point of view, of course, the most interesting thing is the motif of devouring her own daughter. Baba Yaga (like the Greek Thyestes, who is tricked by his brother Atreus into eating his own sons) gobbles up her own daughter by mistake, or even accidentally kills all her forty-one daughters.[21]

The South Slavs hold that a witch can *only* injure her own family and friends. 'We cannot do any harm to those who are hateful to us, but those who are dear to us, or our own kin, they have no escape,' says the Baba in *The Mountain Wreath.* There is even a South Slavic saying: 'Where else will

[21] 'Chuviliha ran to the hut, ate and drank her fill, then she went outside. She rolled on the ground, and said: "I'm rolling around because I ate Teryoshka's flesh." High in an oak tree, Teryoshka shouted down: "Roll, witch, it is your own daughter's flesh that you ate."' (From *Vassilisa the Beautiful*)

a witch go but to her own kin?' In a Serbian folksong, a shepherd describes his dream like this:

> Witches devoured me:
> my mother plucked out my heart,
> while my aunt held a torch to light her work.

The people on some Croatian islands believe that 'witches like best to pluck out the hearts of their own kin, a bit less to pluck out their friends' hearts, and if a witch is not satisfied with her husband, she plucks out his heart as soon as she can.' In Herzegovina and Montenegro, they believe that witches only eat children that are 'dear and kindred to them, even if they are not their own'(!). The common folk suppose that a woman cannot become a witch until she eats her own child. In Konavle, they think a witch 'has no strength at all until she kills her own child'. And the Montenegrins think that 'a woman who wants to be a witch must eat up her own child first, only then can she eat other children too.' (T. R. Đorđević)

Slavs think that what witches like best is drinking the blood of children and others with sweet blood. A witch 'sups the blood with a little spoon and very soon the child withers and dies'. It is believed that witches sometimes kill older people too: 'they drink a young boy's or girl's heart dry, and whosoever they drink up, is no more: they fade away and die in the flower of their youth.'

Blood is very rarely found on Baba Yaga's menu. There is a rare motif in a Siberian fairytale, of Baba Yaga drinking blood from the breast of Princess Marfita. The principal hero cuts off Baba Yaga's head, but the head uses Marfita's legs to run away.

* * *

It can happen that human fingers are found floating in Baba Yaga's soup, but her basic diet is ordinary enough. What is not ordinary is Baba Yaga's phenomenal appetite.[22]

The scale of Baba Yaga's cannibalism is modest by comparison with ordinary witches, or with the Maenads, the Bacchae, who in their trance rend the flesh of living creatures with their bare teeth, and once (according to Euripides) led by Agave, mother of Pentheus, tore Pentheus himself to pieces.

Remarks

Allow me to draw your attention to the camouflaged details in your author's fiction which could be linked with Baba Yaga. In the first part, the author's mother barely allows her daughter to have access to her space. The mother identifies herself with her house, or more precisely she *is* the house, and she experiences her daughter's presence, like the things that she brings into the house, as a territorial violation. Although it is trivial at first glance, the incident with the little cupboard has a symbolic value: the cupboard becomes acceptable to the mother precisely when it has been painted, when it has undergone this transformation, when it is symbolically 'chewed up' and 'devoured'. Although these relationships are only hinted at, Pupa and Beba have traumatic relations with their own children, something which can easily be explained as symbolic cannibalism. In one place, Beba admits that she is her own son's 'killer'.

[22] 'Vassilisa lights the kindling in the skulls along the fence-posts, goes to the stove and takes out the food and sets it before Baba Yaga, and there is enough for ten. She fetches kvass, honey, beer and wine from the cellar. The old woman eats it all up, drinks everything to the last drop, and leaves Vassilisa only a little broth, a breadcrust and a morsel of pork.' (From *Vassilisa the Beautiful*)

MOTHER, SISTER, WIFE

Baba Yaga's family status is contradictory. She is a woman without a husband – a spinster. In the Czech version, Ježibaba has a husband, Ježibabel, and his mere name says everything about the power relations between that couple. It is Baba Yaga's status as mother that causes the most confusion: sometimes a daughter, Marinushka, is mentioned, and occasionally the number of daughters grows to forty-one. Sometimes Baba Yaga appears as a mother of dragons. In one fairytale, tricked into gobbling salt and flour, Baba Yaga drinks seawater to slake her thirst, until she bursts and gives violent birth to frogs, mice, snakes, worms and spiders. Some tales mention Baba Yaga's sisters (they are identical except in age; they are even called Baba Yaga). 'Blue-eye', *Sineglazka*, a young warrior woman from Russian fairytales, is Baba Yaga's niece. Even so, the predominant version has Baba Yaga as an old woman who lives alone.

Baba Yaga represents the dark side of motherhood. She appears as the wicked stepmother, the fateful midwife and false mother (in one tale, she even mimics the voice of the hero's mother in order to lure him closer and gobble him up). Motifs of perversity crop up here and there, though rarely; in one place, she sucks the young heroine's breasts, in another she asks her to sing her a lullaby and rock her to sleep. Baba Yaga is surrounded by (potential) symbols of female sexuality: her oven is a womb, the hut on hen's legs is a woman's belly, Baba Yaga's mortar also symbolises her womb, though at the same time it could be her mother, Baba Yagishna's womb. Baba Yaga sometimes chatters away to her mortar and calls it her little mortar-mother (*stupushka-matushka*).

* * *

Baba Yaga's reactions to women are misogynistic, and she is prone to excessive rivalry with young heroines. Generally she treats the heroines as her servants, finding barely possible tasks for them to perform around the hut.[23] Yet, more often, she appears as a helpmeet and liberator of maidens in misfortune. Even when by mishap she loses her own daughter (or daughters), Baba Yaga seems preoccupied less by despair over her loss than by anger and desire for revenge. She is evil to boys, she'll eat them up, but she is kind to young men, virtually submissive: she'll give them food and drink, chat with them, give them magic objects that save them from misfortune and help them in their relationships with beloved maidens. And if the heroes are nice and polite, Baba Yaga and her sisters turn into loveable, generous grannies.[24]

Although she is surrounded by hypertrophied female symbols (big breasts, the mortar, the hut, the oven), Baba Yaga has certain male characteristics as well. She speaks in a *basso profundo* voice, she has a long nose, a bone or iron leg, long iron teeth and – she can't cook! She often serves inedible stuff to her guests: iron bread, salty cakes, soup with children's fingers or spittle swimming around in it. And Baba Yaga often talks 'like a man'. In the tale *Go there – I know not where – and bring me back a thing I lack*, Baba Yaga says: 'He

[23] Baba Yaga drives away Vassilisa, who, on completing Baba Yaga's tasks, helps the mother's spirit that is embodied in a doll: 'You know what, blessed daughter, be off with you! I don't need blessed ones!' (From *Vassilisa the Beautiful*)
[24] – 'And you, granny, rest your old head on my strong shoulder, and tell me what to do.'
– 'Many's the young man that has passed this way, but very few that spared a kind word for me. Take my horse, child. It is faster than your own, it will carry you to my middle sister, she will advise you what you should do next.' (From *About the Apples that Restore Youth and the Living Water*)

is an ordinary fellow; we could deal with him easily – like taking snuff.' In other words, Baba Yaga knows about taking snuff.

Baba Yaga's one and only rival among men is Koshchey the Deathless. While she respects him, Baba Yaga won't hesitate to give away the secret of his strength to the young hero. Koshchey the Deathless expresses the same kind of respect for and rivalry with Baba Yaga.[25]

By combining such (potentially) female and male symbols, Baba Yaga is, psychoanalytically speaking, what's called a phallic mother. Some interpreters (such as Geza Roheim) see Baba Yaga's hut as an image of heterosexual coitus. The image of Baba Yaga – sprawling in her hut with legs spread wide, breasts dangling over a pole, nose poking the ceiling – is really (from a child's point of view) a matter of the child confronting its parents' coitus. Other details can be explained in a similar way, for example Baba Yaga's cannibalism may be a projection of a child's aggressive hunger. A hungry child wants to eat its mother. Conversely, the mother is a cannibal who wants to eat her own child.

* * *

[25] 'I know it very well!' says Baba Yaga. 'She is with Koshchey the Deathless. It will be difficult to reach her; it is no simple matter to deal with Koshchey the Deathless: his death rests on the point of a needle, that needle lies inside an egg, the egg is inside a duck, the duck is inside a rabbit, the rabbit is inside a trunk, the trunk is at the top of a tall oak tree and Koshchey guards that tree as if it were his own eye.' (From *The Emperor's Frog Daughter*)

– 'Beyond thirty lands, even the thirtieth kingdom, beyond the fiery river, lives Baba Yaga. She has a mare that can circle the earth every day. She has many other fine mares besides. I was her shepherd for three days together, I did not lose a single mare, and afterwards Baba Yaga gave me a foal for my pains.' (From *Marja Morevna*)

Vladimir Propp explains Baba Yaga's masculine attributes as a travesty (disguising a man as an old woman) of tribal rituals for the transition from matriarchy to patriarchy. The tribal mother acts the part of a man dressed as a woman, hence a man with a phallus and women's breasts. There is an interesting detail in Andreas Johns's book about Baba Yaga. One of the folktales describes how the hero strikes Baba Yaga with a magical wand, and she turns into a woman(!). If Baba Yaga has the ability to turn into different things, to become an intermediary between worlds, the non-human (fantastical, forested, subterranean or unconscious) and the human, then her androgynous nature – or her role of mediating between genders – becomes understandable.[26]

Remarks

Your author's heroes are mostly women. The female characters chop and change their roles around, or, more precisely, they assimilate and overlap each other. The daughter in the first part of the diptych takes over the role of the mother: she is not only her nurse but at one moment she becomes her surrogate, her *bedel*. Kukla has no children. In the web of psychoanalytic

[26] The most interesting tale from the transsexual point of view comes from Bulgaria: *The Old Woman's Maiden* (*Babinoto devojče*). Several times, the old woman's maiden puts on a man's clothes and saves the emperor's daughter. The emperor offers her his daughter's hand in marriage, but the false young man thrice refuses to become the emperor's son-in-law. In truth, the maiden is more interested in the dragon, whose prisoner she was for some time, but the dragon is angry with her because she accidentally burned him with candle wax (castrated him?), and the wound won't heal. She tries to return to the dragon several times, but the dragon harshly spurns her, sending her to one of the lower kingdoms. These kingdoms are, amazingly, arranged like the floors in a high-rise building: three above, six below. In the end, the maiden is forced to change gender when she is turned, magically and forever, into a young man, who then marries the emperor's daughter.

meanings, Kukla could be a man, as for that matter all the heroines could be. Beba has a homosexual son, but he is more mature than she, taking over the role of the mother which she herself, allegedly, has not been able to fulfil, and leaving her his adopted daughter. Overall, your author's diptych could be an interesting field for reading-in and reading-out gender meanings.

THE BATH

'The archer returned from the stable; that same moment, the servants grabbed him and shoved him in the cauldron. He roused himself, jumped out of the cauldron – and turned into such a handsome fellow that he cannot be described by mouth or pen.' (From *The Firebird and the Empress Vassilisa*.)

In all cosmogonic myths, including the Slavic ones, water means primeval chaos, the original principle and creation of the world. In Slavic beliefs, water flows through the earth's veins like blood through the human body. Many Slavic beliefs, customs, rituals, demons (*vodjanoj*, *vodjanika*, *vodnik*, *vodjanik*, *vodovik*, *rusalka*) and saints (the pre-Christian goddess Mokosh and her Christian descendant St Paraskeva, also known as St Petka) are linked with water. For water is an ambivalent principle: it brings evil (*Gde voda tam beda* / Where there's water, there's misery), but also cleansing and renewal.

The *banya* (bath, spa, sauna) has a special place in Slavic folklore, for the Russians above all. The bath is in principle a dirty place, but also a site of purification: you soak in the hot water, letting it chase away illnesses, spells, the thoughts of evil people and so forth. The spirit called *Bannik* lives there (also known as *Bajnik*, *Bajennik*, *Bajnushko*, *Laz'nik*). He is either invisible or takes the appearance of a naked, dirty, long-haired old man whose body is caked with mud and leaves. A female spirit lives in the baths as well: *Obderiha* is a frightful hairy old woman who appears naked or in the shape of a cat, and lives under a little wooden bench. *Shishiga* is a female demon that takes the shape of a relative or acquaintance, luring people into the baths where they suffocate in the steam.

A proportion of nuptial, birth and funerary rites belong to the bath. Pre-nuptial rituals involving the bride are very similar to those for funerals, for the bride's departure from the home where she grew up marks her ritual death to her family.

Sensing that a passing traveller is before her, Baba Yaga furiously threatens to eat him up. The hero, as we have already mentioned, tames Baba Yaga with his insolence, and asks her to heat his bath, to begin with, and to prepare him something to eat, and only then will he tell her where he is going and what he seeks.

I.P. Davidov argues that the steam-bath in Baba Yaga's household is equivalent to the funerary rite that is linked to the site of the bath.[27] The bath is a place of transformation, of ritual 'deadening'. The principal hero gets ready to travel to the world of the dead, and the ritual steam-bath and the meal are necessary preparations for this journey. The half-blind Baba Yaga recognises the hero by his scent: he smells

[27] I.P. Davidov, *Banja u Baby Jagi*. Vestnik Moskovskogo Universiteta, Serija 7. Filosofija 2001.

of 'living human' (*russkim duhom pahnet, russkoj koskoj*), and as a living man he cannot survive in the world of the dead. Baba Yaga herself lives on the frontier between the worlds of the living and the dead. She is the 'customs officer', and her hut is the 'customs house'. It follows that Baba Yaga is 'bilingual', fluent in the language of the dead and that of the living. This is why she alone can give the hero his symbolic visa to enter the world of the dead. The ritual steaming is intended to 'deaden' the hero (so they won't recognise him by smell in the world of the dead), to modify or adapt him (so that he can see and talk in the kingdom of the dead). Vladimir Propp argues that ritual food serves the purpose of releasing a dead man's mouth in the other world. If he is to descend into the kingdom of the dead, the principal hero of the tale must learn a number of other tricks as well: how not to fall asleep there, how not to laugh, how to talk and see like a dead man. Baba Yaga will give the hero a horse for the road to the kingdom of the dead and a ball of thread that will lead him where he wants to go. Baba Yaga herself only rarely leaves her (sentry) post.

The hero's return to the world of the living is accompanied by new rituals in which water once again plays a key part: dead and alive. Dead water heals wounds and amputated parts of the body, while living water restores the soul to the body.

Remarks

I think your author's choice of a spa as the setting for the second part of her fictional diptych is unusually successful. Spas are an important literary topos: a significant portion of Russian literature originated in spas (to mention just one: famous Baden Baden), or take place in or around spas, or even – like Mikhail

Zoshchenko's classic, *Scenes from the Bathhouse* – take as their theme the comic-absurd communist customs linked to the popular Russian *banya*. Milan Kundera chose a Czech spa for the settings of his novel *The Farewell Party* and his story *Dr Havel After 20 Years*. The topos of the spa succeeds in folkloristic terms, for merely by choosing it as her setting, the author brings together a whole series of ancient legends connected with healing springs, legends about water that heals and apples that restore youth, about living and dead water, and water that gives strength and takes it away (*voda sil'naja i bezsil'naja*). Baba Yaga's steam-bath, where the hero ritually steams himself before setting off on his long journey, and the heroines bathe (because Baba Yaga treats them as so many potential tasty morsels), belongs to this series. ('Go and heat the bath to bathe my niece, and be sure to bathe her well: I want to eat her for breakfast!')

FEET, LEGS

Demonic beings have feet that give away their demonic nature: they might be hooves, or birds', ducks', geese or hen's legs, or they might have too many toes on their feet (six instead of five), or even have a single solitary foot.

In old China, as also in the Buddhist, Islamic and Christian worlds, it was believed that erosion marks on rocks were the footprints of gods, heroes, prophets and saints. The mother of the founder of the Chou dynasty, for example, became pregnant when she stood in a god's footprint. The beliefs about footprints in stone – which were left by gods, saints and prophets, but also by beings such as fairies, witches, giants and devils – are scattered all over the place. They have survived down to the present day, with the pavement in front of Grauman's Chinese Theater in Hollywood, where movie stars – our modern gods and goddesses – leave their foot and hand prints.

Some psychoanalysts prefer the interpretation that men see the female foot as a 'missing penis', whence, allegedly, stems the male fetish for women's feet and shoes. And this, we could say, is where the traditional Chinese practice of binding women's feet (to keep them smaller and 'more beautiful') belongs, along with the belief that witches and other female demons have big feet or birds' feet.

Baba Yaga is perceived as one-legged, even though she isn't: 'Ah, you, Baba Yaga, peg-leg!' (*Ah, ty, Babushka Jaga, odna ty noga!*). In the fairytale *Ivan the Fool*, Baba Yaga appears before three brothers and hops around them on one leg.

Baba Yaga's most frequently mentioned feature is her skeleton leg (*Baba Yaga, bony leg!*). This leg most often turns up in the singular, and in different guises: made of wood, gold and (most often) bone. Although it is easiest to suppose that the reason for this lack of precision lies in errors that crept into the retelling of the story, some commentators have latched onto this detail, seeking a deeper reason.

In one tale, Baba Yaga turns into a snake before she dies, leading some commentators (such as K.D. Laušin) to find evolutionary characteristics in the figure of Baba Yaga. In other words, first she was a snake (embodying death), then she evolved into the one-legged goddess of death and then she migrated from myth into fairytale, becoming a *character*: Baba Yaga, bony leg. Her mortar also has its evolutionary aspect: originally, Baba Yaga jumps into the mortar – 'the mortar runs along the road, and Baba Yaga sitting inside' (*bezhit stupa po doroge, a v nej sidit Baba-Jaga*) – but later she flies in it, too. One of the supporting arguments for this 'evolutionary' interpretation lies in Baba Yaga's name: Yaga supposedly derives from the Sanskrit word ahi, meaning 'dragon'.

(In Serbia, by the way, Baba Yaga appears as an old woman with a hen's leg – *Baba Jaga, kokošja noga!*)

Vladimir Propp explains this by reference to certain archaic forms of the Russian tale, where a billy-goat, bear or magpie lies in the hut instead of Baba Yaga. The frontier between animal and human is a person with an animal leg. In the case of Baba Yaga, who according to Propp guards the entrance to the world of the dead, this leg is replaced with the skeleton leg. The Empusa, who guards the anteroom of Hades, has one leg of iron and the other of donkey excrement.

Remarks

The wheelchair that Pupa uses or the walker, a metal walking-frame that the author's mother uses, are modern technical equivalents of Baba Yaga's bony (golden, wooden or hen's) leg. The description of the dead Pupa's leg, which has the ghastly colour of rotten meat, might be an allusion to Empusa. And Kukla's big feet too associate her discreetly with all those female mythical creatures with animal legs.

CLAWS

Baba Yaga's hut stands on either one or two hen's legs. These legs have prominent claws. The three-digit hands that can be seen on European vases of the early Neolithic are really birds' feet. The mythic importance of birds' claws dates from the

Palaeolithic, when prints of birds' feet were put on cave walls in northern Spain. Later the same three-toed prints appeared on vases, urns and figurines with female shapes. According to Maria Gimbutas, the bird-claw prints testify to the existence of the Great Goddess, half-woman and half-bird. Let's remind ourselves once again that, in some Slavic versions, Baba Yaga herself, not only her hut, is described as an old woman with a hen's leg.

Remarks

Women's fingernails are seemingly the only strong connection with the great goddesses from the era of matriarchy that has lasted down to our own time. Women's nails take various forms: there are fashions for trimming them, false nails with different shapes and lengths that can be glued onto the real ones underneath, then there are different coloured varnishes for nails and – most recently – a fashion for decorating fingernails with miniature designs. Men still feel that long, pampered nails have an erotic appeal. Only *femmes* with long, painted nails can be *fatales*. Long (usually scarlet) nails and shoes with ostentatiously high, tapering heels (which are nothing more than exaggerated substitutes for those dangerous toenails) belong to the stubbornly imperishable attributes of seductive women.

Mevludin experiences Pupa's outstretched hand as a claw (and her raised hand as a hen's wing). It is interesting that even in the swimming pool Pupa insists on covering her legs, so they dress her in knee-socks!

NOSE

A long pointed nose is one of Baba Yaga's most striking features. Her nose was once a bird's beak which did not manage to turn itself into a regular nose. In other words, all the evidence suggests that Baba Yaga used to be a bird (the Great Goddess) before she turned herself into a humanoid of the female gender and a caricature of her former divinity.

Besides, the nose is a symbol of intelligence. Many tribes, in their ritual invocations of spirits, ancestors and other invisible forces, make use of dust mixed with ground-up, dried animal snouts. The peoples of Siberia – Yakuts, Tungus and others – preserve the snouts of foxes and reindeer, believing as they do that an animal's spirit dwells in its snout, while the Chukchi utilise the snouts of wild animals as household spirits, guardians of their homes. The Lapps use the snout of the polar bear so that its perfect sense of smell will pass into them.

Psychoanalytically minded researchers will say that Baba Yaga's nose is a phallic symbol, which fits with the thesis that she herself is a phallic mother.

Remarks

By assenting to plastic surgery on their noses – and rhinoplasty was the first massively popular cosmetic procedure – women consciously disown their (own) symbolic power and submit to a male concept of beauty. The folk saying 'My nose – my pride' expresses the judgement that someone's nose is an inalienable part of their human identity, one that may not be changed, no matter what it is like. In other words, by disowning their noses, women disown their pride and power. If we adopt this point of view, the whole of women's history can be read as the history of female self-castration, the deliberate disowning of power. This process of self-castration accelerated with the development of plastic surgery, of its 'populist' element, meaning the encouraging of women to kowtow to a particular (male) stereotype of beauty. In women's history, which proceeds from *ugly* Baba Yaga towards the *beautiful* Virgin Mary (or 'from Beast to Blonde', as Marina Warner would put it), the Virgin has achieved total victory. Thanks to this victory, many women today look like the cheap plastic Virgins in village churches, or in other words like Paris Hilton!

GUYS

The guys in Russian fairytales are mostly called Ivan: Prince Ivan, Ivan the Knight, Ivan the Peasant's Son, Ivan the Soldier's Son, Ivan the Robber, Ivan the Bean, Ivan the White Shirt (*Ivashka-belaja rubashka*) and so on. If the mother or father conceived the child with an animal, then the Ivans have a 'bestial' surname: Ivan the Bull's Calf, Ivan the Cow's Son (*Ivan Korovij' syn*), Ivan the Mare's Son (*Ivan Kobylij' syn*), Ivan the Bear (*Ivashko medvedko*) and suchlike. Ivan is usually the youngest of three brothers, and he is in a more difficult position than the other two. The parents punish Ivan, throwing him out of the house, or he gets punished for his own misdeeds. This initial affliction is the motor that drives the plot. Ivan has to solve the problem, defeating the foe and surmounting obstacles, if he is to be rewarded at the end with the throne and the beautiful princess's hand in marriage.

The most popular Ivan of them all is Ivan the Fool (*Ivan-Durak, Ivanushka-Durachek*), a passive hero, a fool who whiles away the time stretched out on the stove (*Ivan Zapechnyj, Zapechnik*), catching flies and spitting at the ceiling. Ivan the Fool is nondescript and grubby, because he spends his days digging around in the ashes (*Ivan Popjalov*), and his nose is always runny. The two older brothers, busy with practical matters, ignore Ivan the Fool, they play jokes and tricks on him, they often beat him, they try to drown him in the river and so on. When their mother sends him to his older brothers with dumplings for their lunch, Ivan the Fool feeds the dumplings to his own shadow, thinking that it's a living man. When they leave him tending the sheep, Ivan the Fool blinds them all so that they won't run away. When they send him to town to buy things for the house, he puts the new table on the road to make its own way home, seeing as how it has four legs like a horse. When he sees scorched tree stumps along the roadside, he thinks they will freeze and he puts cauldrons over them to keep them warm. When the horse reaches the river and refuses to drink, Ivan the Fool pours a whole sack of salt into the water. When the horse still refuses to drink, he kills it.

Emelya the Simpleton is cut from the same cloth, except that he has a powerful helper: a pike-fish that has been given its freedom. It is enough simply to say 'By the pike's command . . .' – and his wishes are granted straightaway. One day he has had enough of being stupid and ugly, and he orders the pike-fish to turn him into a very handsome young man who is gifted with great intelligence. He duly marries the king's daughter. Ivan the Bear – human above the waist, bear below it – being tasked by his stepfather to guard the barn door, lifts the door off its hinges, carries it into the house and guards it, while thieves steal all the grain. To get rid of him, the stepfather sends him to the lake with the task of making a rope out of sand on the shore. He is hoping that fiends will catch Ivan and drag him down to the bottom of the lake. But Ivan uses his cunning to trick the fiends, and he returns home with a wagon full of gold.

* * *

Ivan the Fool's most senseless and stupid actions turn out later to have been sensible and clever. For example, he accepts a bag of sand instead of money from a gentleman that he has worked for, but later he meets a beautiful girl who is trapped in a fire, and saves her by pouring his bag of sand over her. The girl is, of course, none other than the emperor's daughter, and she becomes his wife.

In overcoming his obstacles, Ivan gets help from many quarters: animals (horses, pike-fish, birds, cats and dogs, bears, snakes, frogs, etc.), people, Baba Yaga, magical objects (a ring, a magic flute, etc.). Ivans are 'chosen ones' who, thanks to their own wrong choices, magical objects or unusual relatives (sisters that marry powerful bird-emperors), overcome all hardships and finally become heroes: they vanquish their foes, marry the emperor's daughter, secure great wealth and eventually become emperors themselves.

In their *Slavic Mythology*, V.V. Ivanov and V.N. Toporov distinguish between two kinds of hero: Ivan the Fool and Ivan the Prince. While Ivan the Fool belongs to the ranks of 'holy fools' (*yurodivi),* who are deeply rooted in the Russian spiritual tradition, Ivan the Prince is a true mythic hero, for he passes the ultimate test, the most difficult of all: the encounter with death. By following the rules, Ivan the Prince finds the way out of the world of the dead and returns to life transformed, which we connect with the ancient mythical motifs of death and resurrection.

Remarks

The character of Mevludin is undoubtedly analogous to the character of Ivan the Fool. (*I'm a fool, love. And once a fool, always a fool* – says Mevludin). Pupa, Kukla and Beba – like the three Baba Yagas in the fairytales – indirectly help to make Mevludin's dream come true, and it is precisely here that the correspondence between your author's literary exercise and the myth of Baba Yaga is strongest. The character of Mr Shaker can be identified with the character of the capricious emperor in Russian fairytales, whose rival is Ivan (the Fool or the Prince) and who will try to destroy Ivan before giving him his daughter's hand. The sexual dimension is more explicit in your author's text, because Mr Shaker is the king of protein-enriched beverages, with added hormones that turn out to cause impotence. Mr Shaker will end up dead, just like emperors in the Russian tales. One of the 'Baba Yagas', namely Kukla, will bring about his death. Dr Topolanek and David, Pupa's grandson, are minor characters and do not show any particular connection with the Russian fairytale, yet they too are 'fabulous' in their own way: David as a *deus ex machina* (or, as Kukla says, a *nepos ex machina*), and Dr Topolanek as some kind of contemporary wizard or trickster. Arnoš Kozeny has, of course, the potential to become like Koshchey the Deathless, Baba Yaga's one and only true rival (and the relationship between Beba and Arnoš Kozeny could be revealing in this context), but even so, this motif remains undeveloped in your author's text.

Allow me to mention here that a stupid girl, one who spends the whole day picking her nose and lazing on the stove, and eventually becomes a princess or a queen, is completely unthinkable in fairytales! The imagination of folktale-tellers created an equivalent of male heroism in the characters of Slavic Amazons (the Russian *Sineglazka*, or the 'Giant Girls', *Div-devojke*, in Serbian folksongs), but grubby, idle, stupid girls are usually punished with death. Wealth, a throne and love are only conceivable as rewards for grubby, idle, stupid guys!

DOLLS

There is an interesting motif in the fairytale *Vassilisa the Beautiful.* As the mother lies dying, she calls for her daughter and gives her a doll that will help her in life. The doll can only be asked for advice after it has been given food and drink.[28] Vassilisa keeps the doll in her pocket as long as she lives. A doll as the abode of ancestral spirits (the mother's, in this case) is something that features among the most ancient tribal beliefs of many peoples around the world.

The doll symbolically replaces the dead member of the family, it is the tomb of that person's soul. Some African tribes have a custom that a widower who remarries makes a little statuette of his dead wife and keeps it in his hut in a place of honour. Respect is shown to the statue, to prevent the deceased from being jealous of the new wife. In New Guinea, after a death, members of the family make a little doll that protects the soul of the deceased. The dead person who is incarnated in the doll only offers to help if the rest of the household looks after it, feeds it, tucks it up in bed and so forth.[29]

* * *

[28] 'Vassilisa went to her larder, fetched supper for the doll and set it down before her, saying: "Here you are, dolly, taste it and hear about my misfortunes: they are sending me to Baba Yaga, by torchlight, and she will eat me up!" The little doll ate her supper, and her eyes lit up like two candles: "Fear not, Vassílisa!" she said. "Go where they send you, and take me with you. As long as I am with you, Baba Yaga can do you no harm!"' (From *Vassilissa the Beautiful*)

[29] The Japanese electronic invention, the so-called 'digital pet' called tamagotchi, needs taking care of in just the same way as the wooden dolls in folk beliefs. The toy's owner has to monitor its 'happiness level' every day (tamagotchi has to be fed and bathed, and the owner has to play with it a bit), otherwise the digital pet 'dies'.

Among the tribes of northern Siberia, dolls' heads are made from birds' beaks. The doll is a pledge of fertility, so newly-weds take it into the bedroom on their wedding night. The evil spirit *Kikimora* can also pass into the doll. Then it has to be burned. In Kursk, for example, the doll's face is left blank, without eyes, mouth or nose, for fear that an evil spirit will pass into the doll and harm the child that plays with it. Dolls which possess protective power are hereditary: mothers bequeath them to their daughters.

The Hantis, Mansis, Nenets and other peoples of north-eastern Siberia made a special doll, called the *itarm*. They dressed it up and put it in a deceased person's bed. At meal-times, they would bring it morsels of food and make a show of deferring to it, for the doll served as the dead person's double. This ritual passed into Russian fairytales. In the tale *Teryoshechka*, an old childless couple dress a little log in babies' clouts and put it in a cradle. The log turns into a boy – a motif that endured long enough to reach Carlo Collodi and his famous Pinocchio. The well-known Russian wooden dolls, the *matryoshka*, emerged from the same typology of mythico-ritual thought.

Hunters in the forests of north-eastern Siberia build little wooden cabins that they call *labaz* or *chamja*. A *labaz* is erected on top of high wooden stilts (like the hen's legs under Baba Yaga's hut!) and it serves as a hunters' storehouse, to keep dried food and other supplies safe. The back of the *labaz* is turned towards the woods, and the front towards the passing traveller. On ritual sites called *urah*, similar cult cabins were built, without windows or doors. *Itarm* dolls were placed in these cabins, dressed in furs. The *itarm* dolls occupied the whole interior – whence the description of Baba

Yaga's body filling her hut. For that matter, *yaga* or *yagushka* is the name of the furry 'dressing gown', a garment worn by women in north-eastern Siberia. Arkadij Zelenin insists on this interpretation, and very convincingly; he develops a theory that the *Golden Baba* or *Sorni-nai* was a shamanistic divinity of the northern Siberian peoples, who were resisting conversion to Christianity. Later, the legend of the Golden Baba spread – thanks to soldiers, travellers and missionaries – and was revived in fairytales as Baba Yaga.

Remarks

Although Beba, Pupa and Kukla are female nicknames, it is difficult to believe that the choice of these particular monikers is just coincidence. Beba is a common female nickname in urban Croatia, Serbia and Bosnia, while Pupa is found in northern Croatia, where it derived from the German, and in Dalmatia, where it derived from the Italian. Beba (a doll, but also a newborn baby!), Pupa (Latin: *pupa*; German: *die Puppe*; Italian: *pupa*; French: *poupée*; English: puppet; Dutch: *pop*),[30] Kukla (Russian, Bulgarian, Macedonian, Turkish, etc.) and finally Wawa (Chinese): they are all polyglot synonyms for 'doll'.

There are several possible explanations of why your author uses nicknames. The first is connected with the author's principle, which is to say the simple idea that the heroines are just dolls that come to life in the author's hands. Perhaps the nicknames serve a ritual–protective function, insofar as your author has respected the taboo against mentioning any witches' names. One of the reasons could be linked to Baba Yaga, who has sisters, also called Baba Yaga (like the Irish girl Brigid, whose two sisters are

[30] The people of the Mansa tribe, in Siberia, say *pupig* or *pupi* for guardian spirits or the spirits of their ancestors, dwelling in little totemic wooden dolls.

both called Brigid). The reason could also lie in the culture of male domination, where women's names do not matter much anyhow (for a name is a symbol of individuation and identity), in other words where *one* woman is *all* women.

In the language of our contemporary culture, a discriminatory gender linkage between women and dolls is stubbornly persistent. People often coo over little girls: 'My little doll!' or 'You're as sweet as a doll!' Young girls are 'as pretty as a doll'; they are 'Barbies', 'babes' or even 'dolly birds'. People don't see anything odd when grown-ups carry their childish nicknames around.

As for Pupa, Beba and Kukla, that trio has its roots in old Indo-European mythology, where goddesses appear in threesomes: as three different goddesses (like the Greek *Moirai*, the Roman *Parcae* and the Nordic *Norns*), then as a single goddess with three functions, or a triad that represents the life cycle: maiden–mother–crone.

Slavic mythology, too, is familiar with the Fates, the goddesses that ordain human fate. In Bulgaria, for example, they are called *orisnici* (or *narachnici*), or *sudički* in the Czech language, or *rođenice*, *suđenice* or *suđeje* in Serbia, Croatia and Bosnia. *Rođenice* are invisible; they turn up when a child is born; they can only be seen by the mother of a newborn child or by a beggar if one happens to come along. What *rođenice* assign to people is called good luck or destiny, and it cannot be changed. In one short fragment, the author's mother remembers the story that her own mother told her about her own birth, about seeing three women, two arrayed in white and the third in black.

I would draw your attention to one further detail. The author's mother, in the little flat that is 'tidy as a box', with a wig on her head and a lipsticked mouth, is reminiscent of a doll in a *labaz*.

In one place, the author compares her mother, not without a certain cruelty, to 'a traffic warden'. The *labaz* were also used to mark out the forest. The mother, too, stubbornly keeps a souvenir doll in Bulgarian national costume in a prominent place, completely unaware of its deeper meaning. 'It's to remind me of Bulgaria,' she says simply.

COMB AND TOWEL

A comb and a towel are magical objects that often appear in fairytales. A comb can be turned into a dense forest, a towel can be turned into a river or a sea and either can thus defend the hero or heroine from their pursuer. This pursuer is most often Baba Yaga herself.[31]

The **comb** is an important object in all mythologies. It occurs in Slavic mythologies as a deadly object, a female symbol, a means of healing and a magical means of liberation. Precisely because of the magical properties that have been given to it, the comb is associated with rules and taboos. For example, a comb must not be exposed to the gaze of the household, left out on the table or other such places, otherwise 'the angel won't come' (*angel ne sjadet*). Combs have medicinal and protective effects: if somebody was losing his hair, people would comb his scalp with a comb for carding yarn. The comb (and bobbin) were kept in cradles so that the infants

[31] '"Here are your comb and towel," the cat said. "Take them and flee; Baba Yaga will set off in pursuit of you, and you keep your ear to the ground, and the moment you hear that she is drawing close, throw down the towel – it will turn into a great, broad river. If Baba Yaga crosses the river and sets after you again, put your ear to the ground once more, and as soon as you hear her drawing near, throw down the comb – a thick, thick forest will spring up, and she won't be able to make her way through."' (From *Baba Yaga*)

would sleep soundly. The South Slavs had a habit of wedging one comb into another, which – in an era without antibiotics! – served as a defence against sickness.

In ceremonies linked with childbirth, a comb served as a symbol of women's destiny. A newborn boy's umbilical cord was cut with an axe, but with girls, it was cut with a comb. At christenings, the midwife would hand a male infant to its godfather across the threshold, and a girl across a comb.

Combs were used for prophesying. Girls would place a comb under their pillow when they went to bed with the words 'Destined one, come here and comb my hair!' (*Suzhenyi, ryazhenyi, prihodi golovu chesat!*). If the maiden then dreamed of a young man, it was believed that he would be her chosen one. This is why young girls were given the gift of a comb at weddings.

A comb that was used to comb the hair of a deceased person was held to be 'unclean'; it would be thrown away in a river, so that death disappeared from the house as soon as possible (*chtoby, poskorej uplyla smert*), or it would be put in the coffin with the deceased, along with whatever remained of his or her hair.

The **towel**, linen, kerchief, napkin, shirt, embroidery – all these things are of the highest importance. Vassilisa the Wise, for example, has three crucial possessions which make her strong: a napkin, a comb and a brush.

Sometimes we come across Baba Yaga in fairytales with a bobbin in her hand, and she often gives the heroine of the tale a weaver's task to do.[32] What is more, if Baba Yaga is well disposed, she will give the heroines gifts beyond price: a golden ring, bobbin and embroidery frame.[33] The bobbins, the hanks of yarn and the yarn itself connect Baba Yaga with ancient Ananka, who rules the world and every single destiny in it. The yarn also connects Baba Yaga with the *Moirai*, who spin human destiny: black thread for black destinies and white or gold thread for the lucky ones. Baba Yaga's balls of thread, which help the heroes to reach their goal, are like the ball that Ariadne gave to Theseus so that he could find his way out of the labyrinth when he had killed the Minotaur. Those weaver's threads connect Baba Yaga with all those powerful old women who oversee the weaving work that women do.

The weaving, spinning, embroidering and sewing that women do have a ritual-magical significance in many cultures. A specially woven piece of linen has protective powers. During plague or cholera epidemics, old women and widows wove linen and sewed towels from the linen. The towels would be placed in the church, hung up on icons or laid in a ring

[32] 'The little girl came and arrived, came and arrived. The little hut stands still, and Baba Yaga bone leg sits in it, weaving. – "Hello, auntie!" – "Hello, dearie." – "Mother sent me to borrow a needle and thread to sew up my shirt." – "Very well, sit yourself down without ado, and weave." ' (From *Baba Yaga*)

[33] In the fairytale called *Palunko the Fisherman and his Wife*, by the Croatian writer Ivana Brlić-Mažuranić, the goddess Dawn-Maiden gives 'embroidered linen and a pin' to a faithful wife, and these things save her from misfortune. 'A white sail arose from the linen, and the pin turned into a ship's wheel. The wind filled the sail until it bulged like a bonny apple, and the wife grasped the wheel with her horny hand. The wreath around the shuttle broke, the shuttle flashed across the vast sea like a star across the blue heavens! Wonder of wonders, the boat flies from the dreadful pursuer, and the fiercer the hunt, the more it helps: the stronger the gale, the faster the boat runs before it, and the faster the sea, the faster the boat across the sea.'

around the house. The aim of these rituals was to protect the place from sickness.

In Serbia and Romania, old women – usually nine of them – would gather at midnight and weave linen in total silence. They would stitch the linen into a shirt, which the young men would take turns to wear before they went off to war. Donning the shirt was meant to protect them from death. There is a magic shirt in Russian fairytales that makes the hero invulnerable.

Weaving and embroidering are the most important skills in the heroine's repertoire of accomplishments. Linen, embroidery and embroidered kerchiefs serve as a young girl's fingerprint, her identity card. Vassilisa the Beautiful weaves linen so fine that it can pass through the eye of a needle. She turns it into shirts for the emperor, who is so delighted by her skill that he has the unknown seamstress brought to him. Then he falls in love with her and marries her.

Weaving is a metaphor for the human lifespan: each of us has as much thread and yarn as has been given to us. In the Russian fairytale called *The Witch and the Sun's Sister*, Prince Ivan encounters two old seamstresses on his path, with two wooden chests, and they say: 'Prince Ivan, we don't have much time left in this world. When we break all the needles in this chest and use up all the yarn in that chest, death will come for us.'

Remarks

There is an interesting detail about combs and combing in the first part of your author's diptych, where the daughter is worried about the mother's wig and 'ritually' washes it while her mother is in hospital. I don't suppose this detail has much to do with ritualistic thinking, but let me mention in passing that care over hair has great ritual importance among primitive tribes. The Eskimo goddess Nerrivik is an old hag who lives under the sea and guards the spirits of the dead. She refuses to defend the walrus hunters until the shaman has ritually combed her hair!

As for the towel, there is an affecting moment in your author's text: the image of the mother's father, going into the house with a towel folded under his arm. Who knows, maybe the mother's subconscious added this image – which had stirred feelings of guilt in her for years – this little salutary detail: the towel that will, as in a fairytale, protect her aged father from adversity.

And one more detail: the author's mother keeps old embroidery, made by her relatives, in a cupboard. Although her memory is playing up, she knows exactly whose hand made which bit of embroidery. The character of the mother merges on a symbolic level into unarticulated, 'female', pre-feminist and pre-literate history. The mother, in short, can 'read' embroidery like Braille.

BROOM AND RUBBISH

The broom was witchery's helpmate: witches fly on broomsticks, they steal milk with their brooms and lay waste crops by dragging their brooms across a field. Baba Yaga covers her tracks with a broom.

Many beliefs and superstitions in the Slavic world are connected to the broom. For example, a house may not be swept when one of the household dies, in order not to chase wealth out of the house, or to offend the soul of the deceased. When they move house, Russians take an old broom with them, for the *domovye* (brownies) live under the broom. Because it was believed that brooms provoke quarrels, sickness and misfortune, a broom would be tossed down next to the house (or over the roof) of people that you wanted to harm. Envious people hid a broom in the newlyweds' wagon in order to bring them hurt. Stepping over a broom brought bad luck.

House-cleaning is a sort of test that a maiden must pass when she finds herself in Baba Yaga's power.[34] Baba Yaga has magical servants in the form of three pairs of hands that perform all her tasks, so she does not need any real help, but she enjoys testing the maidens' maturity, diligence and character. Clarissa Pinkola Estes, in her book *Women Who Run with Wolves*, falls back on psychoanalysis to explain this detail as cleansing the soul, purging it, bringing it to order, an educational process of separating the essential from the inessential. Baba Yaga uses the word *rubbish* figuratively, too, and she thanks the maiden for not showing any undue curiosity.[35]

In Mexico, they have broom festivals to honour the earth goddess Teteo-Innan, with the aim of clearing away all illnesses and troubles. In Christian iconography, a broom is associated with St Martha and St Petronila, who protect all housewives and everyone employed in the household. There is an interesting tale involving a familiar figure from Italian folklore, La Befana, the best and tidiest housewife in the city, who was so absorbed in her domestic duties that she not only failed to recognise the Three Kings among her guests, she even missed joining in their search for Jesus. La Befana appears with a broom, enters the house down the chimney and leaves

[34] 'When I go out tomorrow, take care to sweep the yard and the hut, prepare some food, do the laundry, go to the barn and take four ells of wheat and sort it from the cockles. If you don't do as I say, I'll eat you up.'

[35] 'I don't like my rubbish being taken out of my hut, and nosy-parkers get eaten up!' says Baba Yaga. (From *Vassilissa the Beautiful*)

presents for the children. Even today she survives as a sort of female Father Christmas (she appears at the Epiphany, twelve days after Christmas), yet she also incorporates some elements of the ancient tradition of burning the old year so that the new year can come forward and take its place.

Many beliefs in the Slavic world are linked to 'rubbish' and 'cleansing'. Particular attention was paid to rubbish in the funeral rites. In Moravia, the room where the deceased had lain would be swept clean and the sweepings thrown in the fire. In Serbia and Russia it was forbidden to sweep the house as long as the deceased was there, so as to be sure not to sweep away the living at the same time.

Rubbish was even used for prophesying. In Bohemia and Moravia, the girls would take the rubbish to the crossroads or the midden, and predict who would be their beloved. They would say: 'Out with the rubbish, young men, widows, whoever wants can come, from east, from west, ahead, behind, through the orchard and into the barn.' In Siberia, before Christmas, girls used to put the rubbish in the corner of the house, to 'spend the night' there, and in the morning they would take it to the crossroads and ask the name of the first man they met. They believed that their future husband would have the same name.

The house could not be swept during certain holidays (Christmas, weddings, Ivan Kupala and so forth),[36] because

[36] Ivan Kupala is a traditional holiday in Russia, Ukraine and Belarus. Celebrated in late June or early July, Ivan Kupala began as a pre-Christian fertility festival to mark the country people's connection with *Dažbbog*, the Slavic god of the sun. Rituals involved water (for healing and purification) as well as fire (for light energy).

the souls of ancestors would appear on those days. In Belarus, the householder brandished a little broom around the house after a holiday, saying: 'Shoo, shoo, little spirits! The older, bigger ones – out through the door, and the smaller ones – use the window.' (*Kish, kish, dushechki! Ktora starsha, i bol'sha, ta dver'mi, a ktora mensha oknami.*) The holiday rubbish was burned along with the straw in the courtyard or the orchard, and this custom was called 'warming the dead' (*gret pokojnikov*, or *diduha paliti*). The ashes were thrown in the river; it was believed this would protect the fields from weeds and wolves. On occasion, they simply 'swept' the Christmas holidays. The Bulgarians forbade children to go near the midden, and housewives were not allowed to throw away rubbish when they were facing east. (It was believed that this would make the cattle barren.) The Belarusians and Slovaks used rubbish as a specific against bewitchment. They would secretly collect rubbish from three adjoining houses, burn it and fumigate the suspected victim with the smoke.

Remarks

It is hard to say if the author's mother's manic obsession with cleaning has anything to do with the heritage of Slavic folklore. Yet, it won't do any harm if I bring this aspect to your attention. The description of the author's mother asleep in her armchair, with a duster in her hand, could be connected to the Italian legend of La Befana, that devoted housewife, whose sense of domestic duty leads her to neglect what matters so much more in a 'historic' perspective: the quest for Jesus. Cleaning is, it would seem, the mother's strategy for forgetting. She cleans the house of 'the ancestors' souls', and the whole text is a sort of anamnesis of amnesia.

* * *

The most inspiring interpretation of the clean–dirty antithesis is Mary Douglas's classic study *Purity and Danger: An Analysis of the Concepts of Pollution and Taboo*. The coordinate system of 'clean–dirty' structures practically every primitive social community, where thinking about the world, behaviour and customs has been organised via an elaborate system of taboos. Purity, however, which is not a symbol but rather a part of our emotional make-up, can be a way to petrification. Purity is the pledge of our security, it is the enemy of change, ambiguity and compromise.

Interestingly, then, our de-tabooed age, an age of 'leaving home' for a space of chaos, is obsessed with cleanliness. Most television adverts, for example, advertise cleaning materials (for our homes, bodies or clothes) and are forever warning us with the formula 'clean: positive, dirty: negative'. Even the 'dirty' has become the 'cleansed'. Thanks to the media (the Internet and television), in fact, we can indirectly take part in 'dirty' things (pornography, sex, war, misery, natural disasters, murders, collective misery, poverty and so forth) while staying clean!

EGG

According to the *Encyclopaedic Dictionary of Slavic Mythology*, the egg is the beginning of all beginnings, the symbol of fertility, vitality, the renewal of life and resurrection. In the cosmogonic myths of the South Slavs, the egg is a proto-image of the cosmos. In South Slavic children's riddles, 'God's egg' is the sun and 'a sieve full of eggs' is a starry sky. Slavs believed that the whole world was a gigantic egg: the heavens were the shell, the water was the white, the clouds were the membrane and the earth was the yolk. There is a riddle: 'The living gives birth to the dead, and the dead gives birth to the living', which contains the old scholastic inquiry: 'Which came first, the chicken or the egg?' – and the answer that Silesius gave: 'The egg is in the chicken, and the chicken is in the egg.'[37]

Symbolising as it did the renewal of life and resurrection, the egg played an important part in funeral rites. An egg would be placed in the dead person's hands, or in the coffin, or it would be dropped into the grave and buried with the coffin, so that the deceased could come back to life one day. Earthenware eggs have been discovered in Russian and Swedish crypts; statues of Dionysus with eggs in his hand have been found in Beotian graves. The same semantics of the renewal of life define Slavic and other rituals at Easter: painting eggs, decorating trees with eggs, hunting for Easter eggs and so forth. Slavs would place an egg in the first furrow ploughed in a field, and scatter bits of eggshell around the field to make the harvest a good one. Because of their multiple symbolic value, eggs could be used in many situations. People believed that eggs could stop a fire from spreading. If a fire broke out at home, the members of the household would surround the house with eggs in their hands. According to some folklore beliefs, if a man carries a rooster's egg in his armpit for forty days, a guardian spirit will emerge from the egg and bring the man great wealth.

The egg is a universal symbol. The mythopoetic image of the world emerging from a cosmic egg is common to many peoples: the Celts, the Greeks, the Egyptians, the Phoenicians, the Tibetans, the Indians, the Chinese, the Japanese, the Finns,

[37] It suffices at this point to remind you of the couplet, quoted above: 'We move around with silver oars, our vessel is an eggshell' – meaning Baba Yaga's mortar or womb, which is the daughter's and the mother's at the same time (*stupushka–matushka*)!

and others besides. The world was born from an egg, and in some traditions the first human being likewise (Prajapati, Pan Gu). Heroes, too, came out of eggs (if the mother ate the egg). Castor and Pollux, the sons of Leda and Zeus, were born from eggs.

The notion of the world being born from an egg, and of splitting the egg in half, has many variants. The Egyptians imagined that the egg appeared on top of a hill that emerged from the waters of the primordial ocean, Nuna. The god Khnum came out of the egg and created the variety of beings. According to the traditions of Canaan, in the beginning was the ether from which Ulomos (Boundlessness) was born. Ulomos gives birth to the cosmic egg and to Shansora, the creator. The creator breaks the cosmic egg in two and makes heaven out of one half and earth out of the other. According to Indian cosmogonic beliefs, Being springs out of non-Being, and Being gives rise to the egg that cracked in two: a silver half and a golden half. The silver shell became the earth and the gold, the heavens. The outer membrane gave rise to the mountains, and the inner, to the clouds. The tiny veins in the egg became rivers, and the bubble of water in the egg became the ocean. In Peruvian myths, the Creator begs the Sun to make people and populate the world with them. The Sun throws three eggs down to the earth: the higher estates are born from the golden egg, their wives come out of the silver one and the ordinary folk emerge from the copper egg. For some African tribes, the egg is absolute perfection, for the yolk represents the ovum and the white, the sperm. Everyone should aim for perfection – in other words, to become an egg.

Simply lying on eggs has a symbolic significance. Certain Buddhist sects revere hens, for a hen sitting on a clutch of eggs symbolises spiritual centredness and fertilisation of the spirit.

Remarks

The egg symbolism in your author's text is plain to see. Apart from the title, *Baba Yaga Laid an Egg*, and the spectacular egg-coffin, let me remind you of the obscure episode where the author *spits out a tiny breathing body, all wet from tears and saliva,* into the palm of her hand, which is already damp with tears and snot. In this ooze (or egg), she makes out a deformed miniature likeness of her mother, just as Beba dreams of an egg in which she can see her own son, in miniature, curled in the foetal position. An egg is simultaneously tomb and womb. In the Russian tale, the emperor's daughter's love is hidden in an egg, the very same that Mevludin offers Rosie as his 'heart on a silver platter'.

THE HEN'S GOD

In Russian folk traditions, the hen's god is a ritual object, or amulet, that watches over hens. A stone with a hole in the middle, a clay pot, a dish with no bottom, old worn-out slippers: anything like this can serve as the hen's god. Usually it would be hung up in the henhouse or the yard in front of the henhouse. The hen's god guaranteed that the hens could lay eggs continually and it drove away spirits, mostly nasty brownies (*domovye, doma i*) and *Kikimora.* An old cracked pot stuck on top of a pole or tree could catch the eye of a passer-by and so avert his bewitching gaze from the household. A hole in the pot, a dish without a bottom, a cracked jug: these were all symbols of mature female sexuality and fertility. A pebble with a hole in the middle had an additional purpose: to protect its owner from toothache.

Remarks

I would draw your attention to one detail: Beba, representing mature female sexuality, carries an unusual amulet or charm around her neck – a flat stone with a hole in the middle.

BIRDS

Birds appear in all mythopoetic systems and traditions as demiurges, deities and demons; a means of transport for the gods, demigods and heroes; celestial messengers, wizards, immortals, prophets and totemic symbols. Although the symbolism associated with birds is rich and multilayered, birds are above all symbolic postmen, intermediaries between heaven and earth.

The bird plays a key part in all cosmogonic myths, including Slavic myths. The creator sends a bird (a grebe, a dove or suchlike) to bring clay, sand or sea-foam from the bed of the primordial ocean. The creator makes the earth out of this sand or sea-foam, and in the centre of this earth he plants the tree of the world. It has its roots in the earth, its crown in the heavens and its trunk connects heaven and hearth. The crown, or upper world, is an abode for birds (two birds for every side of the treetop, symbols of the sun and moon, day and night).

There is a hierarchy of birds. The eagle usually has the highest, most powerful position. In Bulgarian folklore, the eagle has access to *the end of the world*, where heaven and earth meet. Fairies, dragons and other mythical beings live at the end of the world. A magpie drops in. The fairies call the magpie every year to harvest the immortelle, which is why they let her bathe in the fairy lake. There she changes her feathers and returns to earth. This is why the magpie is believed to possess healing powers. When a Bulgarian child loses a milk tooth, it throws the tooth onto the roof of the house and says: 'A bony tooth for you, magpie, so you can bring me an iron one instead!' The Czechs and Slovaks have an identical custom, except that the children appeal to Baba Yaga instead of a magpie (*Ježibaba, stara baba, ty maš zub kosteny, daj mi zub železny!*).

In Bulgarian folklore, God came down to earth before the great Flood. Seeing a poor widow-woman with many children and a single hen with chicks, he decided to save her. He told the woman to gather up her children, hen and chicks, and flee from the house, but – he warned her – she should not look back. The inquisitive woman, even so, turned around and she and her children were turned to stone. God succeeded in saving the hen and chicks, and turned them into a constellation that people call *Kvochka* (the brooding hen) – meaning the Pleiades.

Bulgarian – and other – cosmogonic beliefs include the notion that the earth is a flat board supported on a cockerel. Earthquakes happen if the cockerel moves or flaps its wings.

Avian typology in myths encompasses not only actual birds, but also feathered mythical creatures such as Anzuda (Mesopotamia), Garuda (India), Simurg, Varagani (Persia), Tanifi (Maori), Ruha (Arab), Straha-Raha, the Stratim Bird, the Nogot Bird, Voron Voronvich, Siren and the Firebird (Russia). There are also hybrid beings with birds' wings that are able to fly (sphinxes, chimeras, gryphons, sirens, gorgons, etc.). Many gods and divinities turn into birds (e.g. Zeus into a swan), they have bird-like features or birds are included in their attributes (Apollo with a swan and crow, Aphrodite with swans and sparrows, Athena with an owl, Juno with a goose, Brahma with a goose, Saraswati with a swan or peacock, Krishna with a peacock's feather headgear and so on).

A bird is a symbol of the spirit and the soul. Birds recur most often as the souls of the departed, but according to the beliefs of some Siberian tribes a bird can also be the symbol of someone's other 'sleepy soul', the one that only appears in dreams. The 'dream-bird' takes the form of a female grouse, and its likeness can be seen carved on Siberian cradles as a talisman.

The Australian tribe of the Kurnai cherishes gender totemism linked to birds, hence one kind of bird embodies the male sex organ and another, the female. A bird is a metaphor for the sex organ among many peoples. Here are two examples from Croatian folk poetry:

> Oh precious soul, my maiden true
> Your nightgown is so precious too;
> Beneath that gown the quail sits,
> It wants no wheaten bread to eat
> Nor wine to drink from purple vines
> Its one desire – meat, no bones!

The quail in this instance is a substitute for the vagina, while in the next example the rooster is a substitute for the penis:

> The Turk rolls the old woman
> Across the flat field
> Pushing her as far as the fence
> Then he puts in his rooster

In the folklore mythology of many peoples, birds are messengers. They presage death (cuckoos, owls, crows), misfortune, unhappiness, as well as big disasters such as epidemics and wars, but they also herald the birth of a child or a future wedding. As well as portending weather conditions, the life of a bird also serves as a natural calendar (announcing spring and winter).

In popular creeds, birds possess healing powers. Hens are used as a 'medicine' against fever, epilepsy, night-blindness and insomnia: 'Let the hens take away insomnia and bring back sleep' (*Pust kury zaberut besonnicu i dadut son*). It is believed that birds can beat illness away with their wings, dig sickness out of the body with their beaks and sew up wounds. Birds can break spells, as many folklore enchantments and oaths testify.[38]

The link between woman and bird brings us to the Palaeolithic era. Unusual combinations of female and avian traits appear in Palaeolithic cave drawings (Lascaux, Pech Merle, El Pindal): a beak instead of a mouth, a wing instead of a hand, a bird's expression on a human face. In the well-known 'narrative' drawing of the dying man and a wounded bison, and the bird with a woman's face watching it all, some see the bird as a symbol of the soul leaving the man. The statuettes

[38] 'The white bird flew over the white field; it carried white milk in its beak, which it let drip as it flew. The white milk fell onto white stone. This left a trail which bewitched our . . . [the name of the person who is under a spell should be inserted here]'; 'Be gone, spell, to the yellow sands, where there are big birds with yellow beaks and grey wings. With their beaks they will tear off, with their wings they will sweep away, and will help . . . [the name of the person]'; 'On the white birch-tree, the Nagaj-bird is sewing up the wounded chest with its beak'; 'Three brazen-birds, don't bore holes in the oak, bore out the spells instead.'

of the woman-bird, a woman with a bird's head, date from the same era. The notion of a half-woman, half-bird (Siren) and a bird-soul belong to humankind's primal imagery, more ancient than the cosmogonic mythologeme of binary birds and bird-demiurges. In the Neolithic era, according to renowned archaeologist Maria Gimbutas, a figurine of a woman-bird with breasts and bulging rump turns up among different representations of the Great Goddess (statuettes of a naked woman, pregnant or giving birth, symbolising fertility).

Birds – ravens, black hens, crows, magpies, swans, geese, etc. – are linked to witches, female demons and ancient goddesses, Baba Yaga among them. Mythical female creatures often have birds' features (claws, legs, wings or head), the ability to turn into birds or to fly like them. According to one legend, Ivan the Terrible gathers all Russia's witches together in Moscow so he can burn them, but they turn into magpies and escape. According to another, Metropolitan Aleksey was so convinced that magpies were witches that he banned them from flying over Moscow(!). Peasants often hang dead magpies from the roof to frighten off witches.

In Bulgarian folklore, an ordinary woman can become a witch if she carries a black hen's egg in her armpit until a black chick hatches. If she slits its little throat and smears the blood on her joints, that ordinary woman will gain a witch's power – including the ability to turn herself into a black hen.

Peasant farmers in southern Bulgaria believe that freakish creatures called *mamnici* can steal their crops. *Mamnici* have no feathers, but they have two heads, and as they hatch from witches' eggs, they are witches' offspring. The souls of un-christened children turn into small, chicken-like, evil, demonic beings that are called *navi.* Croats and Serbs believe the souls of unchristened children have birds' bodies and human heads. In Ukraine and Poland, such a creature is called *potrečuk* or *latawiec.*

In Bulgarian folklore, chickens are 'unclean', 'dark' animals, related to demons. A chicken is a bird that cannot fly. It pecks the ground with its beak, hence it connects people with chthonic powers. Thus the chicken encompasses contradictions: as a kind of livestock, it belongs to people, but equally it belongs to the heavens (being a bird), and at the same time to the underworld (being unable to fly). Notions of Baba (Yaga) sitting on eggs in a nest made in a treetop, of her hut on hen's legs, of her ability to give birth to forty-one daughters (a quantity that could only have hatched from eggs!):[39]

[39] I assume that your author's title, *Baba Yaga Laid an Egg*, derives from this archetypal image. However, a parallel reading of the title is possible, one that would see the egg as, to put it bluntly, a symbol of (female) creativity. If we pursue the reading in this key, then the picture of female creativity looks rather grim. Female artists are Baba Yagas, isolated, stigmatised, separated from their social surroundings (they live in the woods or on its edge), wholly reliant on their own powers. Their role, just like the role of Baba Yaga in the fairytales, is marginal and constricted. On the other hand, the same title can be read as a cheerful apology for women's creativity.

Linguistic analysis could lead to a comically grotesque inversion of the phenomenon of female creativity. For every child in Croatia, Serbia and Bosnia knows the nursery rhyme:

Okoš-mokoš
Prdne kokoš
Pita baja
Kol'ko tebi treba jaja?

(Okosh-Mokosh-marting
The black hen is farting
The basket is full, full is the dish
How many eggs do you wish?)

these all build up a picture of a black-feathered demon that is linked with all three spheres of the world.

Birds have always fascinated the human imagination, because they are connected with people's deepest dreams of flight. Mere mortals are chained to the earth, whereas wings were the endowment of demons, angels, fairies and other mythical creatures. Birds are the gods' transport of choice (Garuda carried the Indian god Vishnu, and Brahma flew on a goose).

In one of the most beautiful Russian fairytales, *The Feather of Finist the Grey Falcon*, a maiden begs her father to buy her a feather from Finist, a falcon. After three attempts, her father finally gets a feather and gives it to his daughter in a box. When she opens the box, the feather flies out, lands on the ground and turns into a handsome prince before the girl's very eyes. The maiden and the prince love each other every night, until the maiden's sisters find out about the unusual sweetheart from the box and wound him badly. The falcon flies away, and the girl, if she is to find him again, must pass through thirty lands in thirty realms, wearing out three pairs of iron shoes and wearing down three iron staffs. On the way, three good Baba Yagas give her useful gifts: a silver distaff and golden spindle, a silver dish with a golden egg and a

---

Mokosh, as we know, is the pagan Slavic goddess of fertility (*Mokoš, Makoš, Mat syraja zemlja*). Over time, Mokosh became the guardian of pregnant women and women in childbirth, and under Christianity she gained the name of St Paraskeva or St Petka (meaning 'Friday').

In American showbiz jargon, the expression *to lay an egg* means to fail in a performance – more bluntly, to 'corpse' or 'die'. Presumably your author did not mean to invoke that remote connotation; even so, given that our theme is Baba Yaga in all her ambivalence, it invokes itself.

golden embroidery frame and needle. In the end, the maiden finds her sweetheart, her feather, and marries him.

The most feathery and aerodynamic Russian fairytale is the tale of Elena the Wise.[40] Everyone flies in this tale: the 'dark

[40] I have adapted and abbreviated this tale for you. The portions in italics belong to the original.

Once upon a time, a young soldier guarded a demon which, taking pity on it, he released. The demon put the soldier on its wings and carried him off to its castle, where the soldier's only task was to guard the three beautiful daughters. It was not a difficult service, the young man could have carried on forever, but he noticed that the maidens disappeared somewhere every night. One night he crept into their room and saw the girls stamp their feet on the floor, turn into doves and fly out of the window. The soldier followed suit, turned into a robin redbreast and flew after them, until the doves flew down and alighted in a grove of green trees.

The doves in that place were beyond number; they covered the whole grove. There was a golden throne in the middle of the grove. Time passed, and then heaven and earth flashed, a golden carriage flew through the air pulled by six dragons in harness, with Queen Elena the Wise, whose beauty was beyond imagining, let alone describing.

The youth fell in love with Elena the Wise, mistress of the doves, and he decided to follow her by stealth to her castle. By hiding in a tree, he could keep her chamber in view as he warbled so sweetly and sadly that the queen did not sleep a wink all night. In the morning the queen caught the robin and set him in a golden cage, which she carried into her room. As soon as the queen fell asleep, the robin turned into a fly, flew out of the cage, landed on the floor and turned back into the fine young man. He approached the bed and could not help himself kissing the queen on her honey lips. Then he turned straight back into a fly, went back into the cage and became the robin again. Elena the Wise awoke, looked around, saw no one. She was awoken several times again that night, and in the morning she used her magic book to see everything as plainly as if it was written on her hand.

'Ah, so it was you, impudent fellow!' shrieked Elena the Wise. 'Out of that cage with you! You shall pay for your impudence with your head.' What else could the little robin redbreast do but fly out of the golden cage, land on the floor and turn back into the good-natured young man? He knelt before the queen and begged her forgiveness. 'Not for you, knave,' screamed Elena the Wise, then called for the executioner to cut off the soldier's head.

forces', the ordinary soldier (turned into a robin redbreast), the three sisters (turned into doves) and Elena the Wise herself.

The age-old human fantasy of flight has persisted down to our own aero-age, into mass culture and its genres (sci-fi, cartoon strips, films), and has bred two of the mythical mega-icons of our time: Superman and Batman. Interestingly, among the mass media myth-icons of our time, there aren't any strong female counterparts. Wonder Woman stays in the margins. Even in the lowlier zones of human imagination, the pilots' seats are reserved for men.

Only in ancient mythical zones is women's power of flight unlimited. There they fly on equal terms with men. In the oldest times of all, aerial traffic was unusually dense: the heroes flew on huge birds and magic carpets; along with

---

At this, the soldier wept and wailed so mournfully that the queen took pity on him: 'I shall give you ten hours to hide yourself so well that if I cannot find you, you shall have my hand in marriage, but if you don't succeed, I shall have your head!'

The soldier ran out of the castle and into a thick forest, sat under a bush and despaired. At that moment, the demon appeared before him, stamped on the ground and turned into a grey eagle. The soldier climbed onto the eagle's back and was borne up to the highest heaven. But Elena the Wise saw all this in her magic book: 'You fly in vain, eagle, for I see you, and you know full well that you cannot hide from me. Come back to earth!' What could the eagle do but return to earth? So that is what he does, then he rounds on the young man, strikes him on the face and turns him into a needle, and then himself into a mouse. He picks up the needle in his teeth, slips into the queen's castle, finds the magic book and thrusts the needle into the book. Elena the Wise searched for the soldier in her book, and she saw him, yes she saw him indeed, but she could not find him. When ten hours had passed, the queen threw the book into the fire in a rage. The needle flew out of the book, hit the floor and turned into the good young man. And that is how they got married.

anthropomorphised winds, flashes of lightning and thunderbolts, dragons and witches, flying daggers, brooms, mortars, dark forces, demons and demonic creatures, gods, deities and brave heroes went in search of their sweethearts – pea-hens, doves, swans and graceful ducks – falcons, eagles and hawks. In these zones, Baba Yaga herself could fly freely. She flew in her mortar, in her mortar-womb, to be sure, but the thing is, she flew.

Remarks

Your author's narrative has a striking ornithological framework: the story in the first part, for example, is set in a three-year temporal framework which limits the invasion of the starlings to one of Zagreb's neighbourhoods, and their departure likewise. In the second part, right on the first day we learn from the newspaper that Arnoš Kozeny is reading that the H5 strain of bird 'flu has been discovered, while on the last day, we learn – again from Arnoš Kozeny's newspaper – that thousands of hens were slaughtered on Czech farms because of suspicions that they were infected with the H5N1 virus. All in all, there are feathery motifs to spare. I shan't offer a more detailed analysis here, rather I shall leave you to brood a while on the symbolical eggs in your author's text.

OLD AGE

In one of the old Bulgarian legends, the Archangel Michael meets a woman and asks where she comes from and who she is. 'I'm a witch, and I slither into the house like a snake,' the woman replies. The archangel ties her up and starts to hit her with an iron rod. 'I shall beat you until you tell me all your names,' he says. The witch reels off her names, until she reaches the nineteenth. The legend is hard to translate because the multiple oral traditions have produced a 'Chinese whispers' effect, creating a delightful alloy of Hebrew, classical Greek, Bulgarian and who knows what else, so that many words can hardly be deciphered with any certainty. This is how it happens that – in the text that has come down to us – the witch did not reveal all her names or all her faces.

Likewise with Baba Yaga. The story about her circulated for hundreds of years by word of mouth, from ear to ear. Although the storytellers (and later the interpreters) set about her with their interpretive rods, they still could not bring all her 'names' to the surface. Only partly misogynistic herself, Baba Yaga was (and remains) the object of frightful misogyny: they beat her, dunked her, threw her in the fire, shoed her like a horse, banged nails into her, cut off her head, pierced her with swords, forged her tongue on an anvil, roasted her in the oven, monstrously insulted her in fairytales, children's jokes and epic poems.[41]

Let us say it once again: Baba Yaga is a witch, but she does not belong to the coven of witches; she can be both good and evil; she is a mother, but she is her own daughter's killer; she is a woman, but she has no man, nor ever had one; she is a helper, but she also plots and schemes; she has been excommunicated from the human community, but she does communicate with humans; she is a warrior, but a housewife too; she is 'dead', but also a living being; she roasts a little child in the oven, but the

[41] 'And this is what Ilja says: / "Eh, you, Dobrynja Mitkevich / there's no honour or fame / if two heroes fight the old woman / you should beat the woman in the proper manner / on her tits and arse." / And he remembered the old ways, / he starts to beat her on the tits and arse, / and he kills the whore Baba Yaga.' (As cited by Andreas Johns)

outcome has her being roasted herself; she flies, but at the same time she is riveted to the ground; she only has a 'supporting role', but she is the hero's mainstay as he (or she) makes his (or her) way to fame and fortune.

Baba Yaga's character emerged from oral traditions, innumerable nameless storytellers, male and female, who built it up and added to it over many decades. She is a collective work, and a collective mirror. Her biography begins in better times, when she was the Golden Baba, the Great Goddess, Earth Mother, Mokosh. With the transition to patriarchy, she lost her power and became an outlawed horror who still manages to prevail through sheer cunning. Today Baba Yaga ekes a life in her hut like a foetus in the womb or a corpse in a tomb.

In modern terms, Baba Yaga is a 'dissident', beyond the pale, isolated, a spinster, an old fright, a loser. She never married, and apparently has no friends. If she had any lovers, their names are not known. She does not care for children, she is no devoted mother, nor – despite her advanced years – has she become a granny surrounded by beloved grandchildren. She is not even a good cook. Her function is at once crucial and marginal: 'courteous' or 'rude' heroes stop when they reach her hut, they eat, they drink, they steam in her bath, take her advice, accept magical gifts that help them to reach their goals and then disappear. They never come back with a bunch of flowers and a box of chocolates.

The chief reason for Baba Yaga's heresy is her great age. Her dissidence only takes place within the system of life-values that we ourselves have made; in other words, we forced her into heresy. Baba Yaga does not *live* her life; she *undergoes* it. She is an old maid or virgin, who serves as a screen for the projection of (castrating) male and (self-punishing) female fantasies. We have stripped away the mere possibility of accomplishment on any level and left her nothing but a few tricks to scare little children with. We have pushed her to the very edge, in the forest, deep in our own subconscious; we have made a symbolical doll and assigned her a symbolical *lapot*.[42] Baba Yaga is a surrogate-woman, she is here to get old instead of us, to be old instead of us, to be punished instead of us. Hers is the drama of old age, hers the story of excommunication, forced expulsion, invisibility, brutal marginalisation. On this point, our own fear acts like acid, which dissolves actual human drama into grotesque clownishness. Clownishness, it is true, does not necessarily have a negative overtone: on the contrary, in principle it affirms human vitality and the momentary victory over death![43]

Remarks

It is interesting that your author chose to foreground old age as the most relevant theme, although in truth she gave clear warning of this in her introduction ('At first you don't see them . . .').

[42] *Lapot* was an ancient custom, supposedly practised in Serbia and Macedonia, whereby old women who were no longer able to earn their bread were killed with an axe or stoned to death. In Montenegro, this custom was called *pustenovanje*, from the world *pust*, 'felt'. They would cover the old people's heads with a piece of felt, then press a heavy stone on their heads. Supposedly the Montenegrins also stoned unfaithful wives.

[43] The Russian Baba Yaga is currently being revived in cyberspace, where nameless Russian authors launch their stories into orbit. These stories are comic, often brutal and pornographic, in keeping with these new times, but Baba Yaga's treatment is in no way worse than the treatment meted out to other popular heroes of Russian folktales: *Ivan the Fool*, *Vassilisa the Beautiful*, *Elena the Wise*, *Koshchey the Deathless*. The lively decanonisation of the heroes of Russian folktales carries on apace in Internet forums – along with their recanonisation.

Precisely because the author promotes this theme above the others, she achieves an interesting re-semantisation of all the elements linked to the character of Baba Yaga. I shan't analyse this more deeply, because that's not my job, but I will mention one example. The title of the first part, 'Go there – I know not where – and bring me back a thing I lack', is the slightly changed title of a Russian fairytale (Go there, I know not where, bring back I know not what / *Pojdi tuda – ne znaju kuda – prinesi to – ne znaju chto*) and one of Baba Yaga's most popular riddles. And the title of the second part – 'Ask me no questions and I'll tell you no lies' – belongs to one of Baba Yaga's sayings in a folktale *Vassilisa the Beautiful*, although it differs a bit in its meaning from the original (*Sprashivaj; tol'ko ne vsjakij vopros k dobru vedet* /, Ask, but not every question leads to something good). For some reason your author left out the next bit of Baba Yaga's reply, which goes: 'If you know too much, you grow old too soon!'(*Mnogo budesh znat', skoro sostareesh'sja!*) All in all, the riddle is meant to prove Baba Yaga's wisdom and manipulative powers. In your author's text, Baba Yaga's riddle suggests the opposite: deeply moving senility. There are other such details. Rereading your author's text through the prism of Baba Yaga, and vice versa, once again reading Baba Yaga through the thematic prism of old age that your author provides, is a refreshing experience. Don't let's forget that epochs of history, cultures and whole civilisations are the result of a struggle for meaning. Once, long ago, Baba Yaga was the Great Goddess, the Golden Baba. Living through the long and burdensome history of her own degradation, Baba Yaga has come down to our own day as, unfortunately, her own caricature.

BABA YAGAS OF THE WORLD, UNITE!

Baba Yaga is a 'dissident', excommunicated, reclusive, an eyesore, a failure, but she is neither alone nor lonely. In many mythic and ritual folklore traditions besides the Slavic ones, she has innumerable sisters.

The Slovak **Ježibaba** (also Jenžibaba, or in Czech, Jahababa or Jahodababa) has a nose like a pot and a wide, fat mouth. She uses different stratagems to get her way: she turns princesses into frogs, and can turn herself into a frog or snake. Ježibaba is polycephalic: she can have seven, nine or twelve heads. Polycephaly, cannibalism, metamorphosis and great wickedness are the chief traits of this dangerous Czecho-Slovak Ježibaba. She possesses magical objects: shoes for walking on water, a skull that can bring rain, a golden apple, a golden purse, a stick that turns anything living into stone. Ježibaba often comes into contact with hunters who are hunting the forest animals in her vicinity.

There is an ancient female terror in the folklore of the Serbs, Croats, Bosnians, Slovenes, Macedonians and Montenegrins. She is called **Baba Roga**, **Baba Jega**, **Gvozdenzuba** (Irontooth). These peoples are much more afraid of their local witches and sprites than of Baba Yaga. *Baba Roga* is a bugbear that very few people take seriously, and in that sense it is hard to compare her with the Russian Baba Yaga. Serbian folklore, to be fair, has the **Forest Mother** (*Šumska majka*), who combines the characteristics of witch, water-nymph, mountain fairy and Baba Yaga. The Forest Mother is described as a young woman, full-breasted, with long, black, wanton hair and long nails (though she can also be old, ugly and toothless). She shows herself to people naked or dressed in white. The Forest Mother has the power to turn herself into a haystack, a turkey, a cow, a pig, a dog or a horse. She most often appears at midnight. She is skittish, she attacks the newborn babes and infants, but she defends them too. She knows how to cure barren women with preparations of forest herbs. The Forest Mother supposedly has a beautiful voice and is unusually sensual: she often waylays men, leading them deep into the woods, where she has sexual intercourse with them.

Instead of Baba Yaga, the Bulgarians have the **Mountain Mother** (*Gorska maika*), who causes insomnia among little children, as well as 'the witch *Mag'osnica*', the *Samodiva* (a sort of Bulgarian *Rusalka*) and the *Lamia*, a female monster, who is a Slavic derivation from the ancient Greek creature of the same name.

The Romanian **Mamapadurei** lives in the woods in a hut with hen's legs. The hut is surrounded by a palisade fence with human skulls stuck on the posts. She steals little children and turns them into trees. **Baba Cloanta** (Jaws) is a tall, ugly old hag with teeth like rakes. She guards a barrel of human souls. **Baba Coaja** is a child-killer with a long glass nose, one leg made of iron, and nails of brass. **Baba Harca** lives in the oven and steals stars out of the sky. The Romanian equivalent of Serbian St. Petka (Friday) or St. Paraskeva is **Sfinta Vineri**, who oversees women's weaving work. She looks human, but her hen's foot gives her away.

Vasorru baba is an old woman with an iron nose almost reaching her knees, who lives in Hungarian folktales. Vasorru baba tests young heroes and heroines, and if they aren't kind to her, she turns them into animals or stones.

The **Ragana** is a mythical Lithuanian evil-doer (*regeti* is Lithuanian for to know, to see, to predict; *ragas* means horn or crescent moon). The Ragana has a mortar that she sleeps in or flies in, propelling herself with a broom and pestle. In winter, the Raganas swim in the open air, amid the ice, and sit high in the birch-trees combing their long hair. Their evil nature is more obvious in summer, when they destroy the crops, curdle the milk, kill newborn babes and make trouble at weddings, where they have been known to turn the groom into a wolf. The Ragana is connected with death and resurrection, or rather regeneration.

The Polish **Jendžibaba**, or **Jedsi baba**, is a woman who trots along on hen's feet (*pani na kurzej stopce*), and she shares all the general characteristics of the Russian Baba Yaga.

The Lusatian Sorbs[44] believe in the **wurlawy** (or *worawy*), women of the forest who emerge from the trees at precisely ten o'clock in the evening. They set about ploughing the fields, and as they plough, they make a great hubbub. **Wjera** or **Wjerobaba** is the Lusatian Sorb version of Baba Yaga.

An old woman with an iron nose (**Zhaliznonosa baba**) ambles through Ukrainian fairytales, legends and creeds. She is followed by thirty babas with iron tongues and an iron baba (**Zhalizna baba**) whose house stands on duck's feet.

The Norwegian variant of Baba Yaga could have been assembled from three women who appear in Norwegian fairytales. One is an old woman, the 'old mother' (**gamlemor**), whose long nose gets wedged into a tree stump and stays wedged there for a hundred years or so. The hero Espen Askeladd (a Norwegian version of the Russian Ivan the Fool or Ivan Popjalov) helps the old woman to free her nose, and in return he is given a magic flute. The second is the **trollkjerring** or **haugkjerring**, an old witch, while the third is the **kjerringa**

[44] Lusatia is part of Saxony, near the German–Polish border; the Sorbs are a Slavic group.

mot strommen (roughly, 'the woman who goes against the stream'), a stubborn woman, a contrary character, even a shrew.

Finno-Karelian folklore has the **Syoyatar**. Sparrows fly out of her eyes, crows fly out of her toes, vipers slither from under her fingernails, ravens flap out of her mouth and magpies out of her hair. The Syoyatar embodies evil and never helps anybody, but it is a comfort to know that she is no cannibal. **Akka**, another Finno-Karelian evil-doer, is much closer to Baba Yaga. She lives in the woods or near the seashore, she threatens to eat passing travellers, she has breasts the size of buckets and she can wrap her legs three times around the hut. Like Baba Yaga, Akka wants the hero or heroine to accomplish different tasks (heating the bath, feeding the animals, caring for the horses), and she rewards good service with useful advice.

Baba Yaga has numerous relatives in Western Europe. Let's just mention that in France – the land of foie gras – there are legendary females with goose feet. **Arie**, or Aunt Arie (**Tante Arie**, **Tantarie**) has iron teeth and goose feet. Tantarie punishes lazy weavers and rewards hard-working ones. During the Christmas holiday, she appears on a donkey and hands out presents. Tantarie lives in the cave where she guards her chest with its jewels, and she only takes off her golden crown, studded with diamonds, when she bathes. In Germany, **Perchta** is an old woman with big goose feet, who carries her broom around with her, as well as a needle and scissors. She cuts open the stomachs of lazy girls and sloppy housewives with her scissors and fills them up with rubbish. The famous **Frau Holle** – a tall, grey-haired woman with long teeth, who frightens little children and tests the kindness and patience of young maidens – has features in common with Baba Yaga.

* * *

Turks, Tartars, Bashkirs, Uzbeks, Chuvash, Turkmen, Kirghiz, Azerbaijanis, Kumyks, Nogais and many other peoples believe in the **Alabasti**. The Alabasti is demonically evil, a hideous woman with dangling breasts, chaotic hair and a talent for metamorphosis. She has bird's legs (or so they believe in Azerbaijan), or even hooves (according to the Kazakhs). The Tartars of Kazan believe that Alabasti has a single eye in the middle of her forehead, and a stone nose. She has no flesh or skin on her back, so her internal organs are exposed for all to see, and she has sharp talons instead of fingers and toes. In Kirghizia, they believe in two Alabastis: the very evil black one (*kara*) and the less dangerous blonde one (*sari*). Alabasti is never without her magic book, comb and money. In the picturesque legends of the Chuvash, Alabasti is a voluptuary who keeps company with hunters, brings them luck, gives them her own milk to drink and feeds them with her own flesh that she slices from her ribs. Alabasti can be tamed by stealing a hair from her head or her precious possessions: the comb, book and money. The Turks believed that Alabasti becomes good and docile if you pass a needle through her clothes. Alabasti brings illness and nightmares, she drinks her victims' blood and she is especially dangerous to women in childbed and to newborn babes. Alabasti loves horses, and she rides them by night. Her origins are by no means clear. Some suppose that she is Turkish, and others, Iranian. *Al* may be the name of an ancient deity, close to *ilu* (among Semitic tribes), while the Indo-European *basti* means spirit or deity. Alabasti's kith and kin are scattered among many peoples, and their names are **al pab, ali, ol, ala zhen, hal, alk, ali, almazi, almas, kara-kura, shurale, su anasi, vutash**. Baba Yaga is her Slavic sister.

All in all, it is not hard to conclude from this quick survey that Baba Yaga straddles the globe: the 'baba genus' is international, and Baba Yaga's kinsfolk can be found in Asia, South America and Africa; 'Baba Yaga's International' is making trouble here, there and everywhere, as it has always done.[45]

* * *

[45] It won't do any harm to list the most notorious female scourges of the ancient world. The **Empusa** is a female demon with one leg of iron and the other made of donkey excrement, vampirical and voluptuous, who can turn herself into a beautiful girl, seducing young men and drinking their blood. **Lamia** eats little children, is punished with perennial insomnia, but finds comfort in the gift of being able to take out her own eyes at will. **Hecate** is a three-headed goddess, a beast, a witch, a seducer of young men. **Eos (Aurora)** and her sister **Selena (Luna)** are voluptuaries, **Erida** is envious and jealous and **Ino** is an evil schemer. **Medusa**, one of the **Gorgons**, is a female monster with snakes instead of hair and a petrifying gaze. The **Graeae** were born old; they share one tooth and one eye between them. The **Keres** bring death, decay, fever, blindness, impotence and old age. They have staring eyes, lolling tongues, black wings, bird's claws and clothes reeking of blood (for they drink from the veins of dying warriors). The **Erinyes** (or **Eumenides**) are old hags with vipers twisting in their hair, they avenge crimes of parricide, matricide and perjury. The **Harpies** are birds with women's heads, which steal little children, pollute food and bring sickness and hunger. The **Stymphalides**, birds (or even women with birds' heads), eat human flesh and pollute the fields with their excrement. The **Mormo** is a deadly seductress. The **Sphinx** has the head of a woman, the body of a lion, bird's wings and she likes to dine on dimwits. The Roman **Larvae** are ugly, skinny as sabres and embody dead souls. The **Strige**, like the Harpies, are voracious birds with croaking voices, large heads, a fixed stare and a crooked beak; they steal little children, and also take human form, as witches. The **Manias** punish whoever offends the gods by driving them mad (when Orestes saw the Manias, he symbolically castrated himself by biting his own thumb!). **Echidna** is a monster that gives birth to more monsters: she is the mother of Cerberus, Hydra, Chimera and Orthrus. The dangerous **Moirai** – Clotho (the Spinner), Lachesis (Destiny) and Atropos (the Merciless) – sit on their thrones, all garbed in white, turning their mother's (Ananke, Necessitas) bobbin and ruling all the spheres of the world. Their Roman sisters, the **Parcae**, are harsh, gloomy and inquisitive old hags, three sisters, spinners who spin out human destiny so that one picks out the thread, the second spins it and the third cuts it. Let us add here that the **Norns** are their nordic sisters (Urt is responsible for the past, Verthandi for the present and Skuld for the future).

This impressive, grandiose mythic transmission has been going on for centuries. The 'old crones' International' – all those monstrosities, malefactors, frights, freaks and demons, those 'scum of the earth', those 'prisoners of want' – is united by the fact of female gender. Ancient (and other) myths diffused around the world, getting contaminated by Christianity and Christian myths, as well as local pre-Christian, folkloric and mythico-ritual creeds. And all that long-lived, labyrinthine, fertile, profoundly misogynistic but also cathartic work of the imagination gave birth to Baba Yaga.

AND HERE, MY FRIEND, COMES THE STORY'S END

It seems, dear editor, that the moment has come for us to part. I hope the sudden change of tone won't confuse you: we have sped through several thousand signs together; we have pecked at grains of language side by side; they say that reading should be interactive, just like making love, so the assumption is that we have not remained total strangers to each other. Human rituals require that we stay together for a little longer and share a prohibited postcoital cigarette.

I'm sure you won't mind admitting that there was too much of everything. In fact, you were afraid at one point that I would never stop. In some places you sighed with boredom, in others you yawned, in others again your forehead creased in a frown. You had fiendish folklore coming out of your ears. You were given an overdose, I know. At first you felt as if somebody had shut you in a box. It was cosy enough – mummy's tummy, an improvised cottage, a bit of unthreatening darkness: they all stir the childish imagination. And then you felt cramped, and more cramped, until you almost couldn't breathe. In a well-made text, the reader should feel like a mouse in cheese. And that's not how you felt at all, is it?

I realise that this attack of textual claustrophobia was brought on by repetitious rituals from the world of folklore. Don't touch *this*, do touch *that*; don't *cross* the threshold – *step over* it. Throw that tooth over the roof, no no, good grief, over the fence. Spit over your right shoulder, wait, stop! Over the left! You only have to go home to the next village and the signal code changes. In the fucking village of Small Baba, the locals spit over their left shoulder, against spells, while in fucking Big Baba, they do it over their right shoulder. And how lucky you are, you're thinking, to live in a de-ritualised and de-mythologised world where a person can relax, kick off his shoes, put his feet on the table and twiddle his thumbs without fear of baleful consequences. But perhaps there's something else on your mind? Fear of the existence of parallel worlds, for example?

In the Serbian fairytale called *The Speechless Language*, a shepherd goes into a wood, on his way to his sheep. All at once the woods catch fire, and a snake is trapped by the blaze. The shepherd takes pity on the snake and saves it. The snake winds itself around the shepherd's neck and orders him to take him to his father, the snake-emperor. He warns him that the snake-emperor will offer him immense riches, but he says no, all he'd want from the snake-emperor is to know the animal language. So that is what he asks for. At first the snake-emperor refuses, but the shepherd is stubborn and eventually the snake-emperor gives in.

'Stop! Come closer, if that is what you want. Open your mouth!'

The shepherd opens his mouth, and the snake-emperor spits in his mouth and says: 'Now you spit in my mouth!' The shepherd spits in his mouth.

They spit in each other's mouths three times, and then the snake-emperor says: 'Now you possess the animal language. Go, and tell no one what you know, for if you tell a living soul, you will die that same moment.'

And this shepherd with the newly acquired skill – of understanding speechless language, the language of animals and plants – became a wise man.

Language serves the process of mutual understanding. We enter effortfully, we gesticulate, we wring our hands, we explain, we translate our thoughts, we interpret, we break into a sweat, we furrow our brows, we act as if we have understood, we are convinced that we have understood, we are convinced that we know what we are talking about, we are convinced that they understand us, we translate other languages into our own. And all our endeavours boil down to this: we miss the meaning. For if we were truly to understand one another, speaker and listener, writer and reader, you and I, we would have had to spit into each other's mouths, entwining our tongues and mixing our spittle. You and I, editor, we speak different languages: yours is only human, whereas mine is both human and serpentine.

Are you frowning now? Thanks a lot, you're thinking, it's too much already. Don't forget that what you have found out, struggling through to reach the end of my text, is only a smattering, a trivial fraction of the whole 'babayagology'. And what were you thinking of? That the entire history of Baba Yagas (*sic!*) can fit into a few dozen pages? And that you have solved the problem with a bit of help from Aba Bagay, an obscure Slavic scholar from eastern Europe who is only too pleased to shed a bit of light on these matters?

I opened the door just a crack, and let you scratch the tip of this enormous iceberg. And the iceberg is formed of the millions and millions of women who have always kept the world going and still keep it going. (I'm speaking your language now, that's enough of the picturesque stuff.) I am sure that in reading my 'Baba Yaga For Beginners' you did not notice one particular detail: in many tales, Baba Yaga sleeps with a sword beneath her head. We have found all manner of things in your author's fictional dyptich, but not a single mention of a **sword**!

Let me make myself quite clear: I am not like your author. I know about that sword under Baba Yaga's head, and I believe in its deep significance. I'm convinced that accounts are kept somewhere, that everything is entered on the record somewhere, a painfully huge book of complaints exists somewhere, and the bill will have to be paid. Sooner or later, the time will come. So let us imagine women (that hardly negligible half of humankind, after all), those Baba Yagas, plucking the swords from beneath their heads and sallying forth to settle the accounts?! For every smack in the face, every rape, every affront, every hurt, every drop of spittle on their faces. Can we imagine all those Indian brides and widows rising from the ashes where they were burned alive and going forth into the world with drawn swords in their hands?! Let's try to imagine all those invisible women peering out between their woven bars, from their dark bunker-burkas, and the ones who keep their mouths hidden behind the burka's miniature curtains even when they are speaking, eating and kissing. Let's imagine a million-strong army of 'madwomen', homeless women, beggar women; women with faces scorched by acid, because self-styled righteous men took offence at the expression on a bare female face; women whose lives are completely in the power of their husbands, fathers and brothers; women who were stoned and survived, and others who perished at the hands of male mobs. Let's now imagine all those women lifting their robes and drawing their swords. Let's imagine millions of prostitutes around the world reaching for their swords; white, black and yellow slaves who were trafficked, sold and resold at meat markets; slaves who were raped, beaten, stripped of their rights, and whose masters cannot be stopped by anybody. The hundreds of thousands of girls destroyed by Aids, victims of insane men, paedophiles, but also of their lawful husbands and fathers. The African women who are shackled with metal rings; the circumcised women with their vaginas sewn up; the women with silicone breasts and lips, botoxed faces and cloned smiles; the millions of famished women who give birth to famished children. The millions of women who pray to male gods and their representatives on earth, those shameless old men with purple, white, gold and black caps on their heads, tiaras, berets, keffiyehs, fezzes and turbans, those symbolic substitutes for penises – all those 'antennae' that help them to commune with their gods. That all these millions of women, instead of going to the church, the mosque, the temple or the shrine, which anyway were never really theirs, go in quest of a temple of their own, the temple of the Golden Baba, if they really have to have temples at all. That they would finally stop bowing down to men with bloodshot eyes, men who are guilty of killing millions of people, and who still have not had enough. For they are the ones who leave a trail of human skulls behind them, yet people's torpid imaginations stick those skulls on the fence of a solitary old woman who lives on the edge of the forest.

* * *

I, Aba Bagay, belong to the 'proletarians', to the hags' International, for I am **she over there**! Don't tell me you're surprised. You might have expected it; you know yourself that women are 'masters' of transformation, a talent that has been dinned into them by many centuries of living underground, where they 'mastered' all the skills of survival. After all, weren't they told right at the start that they were born of Adam's rib and only had a place in this world so they could give birth to Adam's children.

Farewell, dear editor! Soon I shall change my human language for a bird's. Only a few more human moments remain to me, then my mouth will stretch into a beak, my fingers will morph into claws, my skin will sprout a covering of glossy black feathers. As a sign of goodwill, I am leaving you a single feather. Take care of it. Not to remind you of me, but of that sword under Baba Yaga's sleeping head.